RED SOCKETS

A 1950'S LOS ANGELES MYSTERY

SAM SEEGMILLER

Red Sockets by Sam Seegmiller

Published by Raw Noir Press LLC

For information contact:
Raw Noir Press LLC
rawnoirpress.com
editor@rawnoirpress.com

Cover design by Stefanie Fontecha
Book design by Rachel Bostwick

ISBN: 979-8-9911765-0-7
ISBN: 979-8-9911765-1-4 (e-book)

Library of Congress Control Number: 2024915036
First Edition: September 2024
10 9 8 7 6 5 4 3 2 1

Dedicated to the Memory of Sam Ross

Screenwriter, novelist, teacher, friend. Sam, I hardly 'ran all the way' in finishing my first novel, but I would never have been able to write it at all without your help and belief in me. You are missed.

"There are thirty-two ways to write a story, and I've used every one, but there is only one plot – things are not as they seem." – *Jim Thompson*

ONE

Desilu Studios, Los Angeles - November 15th, 1956

Gordon Kraus thought Superman's cape looked as thin as a flophouse bedsheet. It didn't float behind him the way you'd expect a cape to behave. It clung to his back like a sock stuck to a blanket with static electricity. Superman moved what had to be an eight-hundred-pound piano from the wall like it was a folding card table. His cape hung so low, Kraus thought his legs might get tangled up in the thin fabric. *"What was the purpose of that thing?"* he wondered.

"Cut!" a director yelled. An assistant cameraman slapped a very oversized clapperboard. The studio audience began to murmur while makeup artists rushed onto the set to touch up the actors. The director and stage manager talked over camera angles and blocking. A production assistant fussed with the blocking tape on the stage floor. Desi Arnaz traded jibes with a stagehand on the scaffold above the living room stage set. The clapperboard's episode title read "Lucy and Superman". The storyline looked to be Superman showing up for Little Ricky's birthday party.

"Holy shit, Reeves has a great haircut," a voice remarked over Kraus' shoulder. Kraus looked around to see a tall, heavyset man wearing a shapeless fedora atop a ruddy face and not-so-great haircut. He had on a dingy, lightweight gabardine sports jacket which was tight around the middle. His dress shirt was once white. A tie so wide it had to have been pre-war. The man's fat neck stretched his collar button tight. It took a second for Kraus to register that it was Oliver McBride. His old friend had aged beyond the sixteen years Kraus had known him.

"Hey, Ollie, I didn't see you there," Kraus said. He raised his voice to keep the buzz of three hundred studio audience members from drowning him out. "Yeah, he's been going to Sydney Guilaroff at MGM for his haircuts since 'Gone with the Wind'".

"How the hell does a barber cut Superman's hair? Isn't it as indestructible as the rest of him?"

Kraus laughed. They had been LAPD squad car partners. That was exactly the kind of offbeat riddle Ollie would puzzle over during their shifts. "He'd better be indestructible. He's still running around with Eddie Mannix's wife. If he's not careful they're going to find him slumped over a steering wheel with a slug in his head."

"No kidding?" Ollie whistled through his teeth. Kraus picked up fumes of Old Crow. "Eddie Mannix as in Metro's hatchet man? Mannix's wife? I'd heard once that Reeves was a little light in the loafers."

"Are you joking?" Kraus said. "He's one of the biggest hounds in Hollywood. Lately he's pretty much chained to Toni Mannix, but he used to get more tail than a Tijuana whoremaster. That whole homo rep got started when he was with the Pasadena Playhouse. He was Gilmor Brown's secretary." Brown's homosexuality was well-known in the industry. People presumed any man in the Playhouse founder's inner circle shared his sexual proclivities.

"Wow ... you're a regular Hedda Hopper with all this inside stuff, aren't you?"

"I do a lot of work for the studios. It helps to know who's who," Kraus said.

"You know, when I was on Parker's G-2 squad, we rolled up Brown a couple of times in fairy nest raids. I don't remember Reeves' name ever coming up on the busts or when we sweated Brown," Ollie said.

"I'm not surprised. Reeves only worked the Brown angle to get choice Playhouse roles. From what I heard, he kept stringing Brown along. Always a month away from being a month away."

"Yeah, I've run after some women like that," Ollie said.

"It's the same game whether you're putting your legs into pants or stockings."

"Jesus, speaking of legs, who is the dame over there who pranced in?" Ollie pointed his chin at a stunning redhead who had appeared in the studio.

Kraus looked that way. The shapely young woman was in her thirties. She stood with an almost regal posture, wearing a carmine halter top tucked into the snug waistline of a wiggle skirt. She had incandescent green eyes. Her hair was a dense riot of soft, henna curls reaching to her bare shoulders. Her skin was so creamy it made you want to eat her up with a spoon. She was so beautiful that it was difficult for either man to take their eyes off her. She stood near the edge of the studio audience section with one hand resting on the plumber's pipe stair railing as she scanned the stage set.

Ollie wiped his forehead with a thin pocket handkerchief, "Man, she's a real high stepper, and look at that rack! It's like two pigs in a gunny sack."

"That's Rhonda Fleming. She must be here to see Reeves. They know each other from a Hope movie they were both in." The actress finally caught Reeves' attention. He left the stage, cape flapping behind him, making his way to where Fleming stood at the edge of the audience bleachers. Fleming teased Reeves by making a show of squeezing his bicep. They both laughed and edged further back into the shadows beyond the audience section.

"Christ, Gordy. The broad in the movie where she played a girl pirate? I *loved* that picture and she was hot stuff in her pirate wench outfits. Shit, there was one scene when I thought she'd spill right out of her blouse! Reeves! Some guys, huh?"

"She's scheduled to shoot an MGM oater up in Humboldt next week. Filling her pockets with male adoration before heading out. She'll be out of commission for a couple of weeks up there."

"So, Gordy, what are you doin' here?" Ollie asked.

"On a case for Desilu. They think the craft services caterer is stiffing them big time."

"Lordy, it would be more of a shock to find out they weren't. What contractors *don't* hustle the studios?"

"I know. But they've gotten greedy. Lucy squeezes nickels until the buffalo squeals and she wants it to stop. This is my last day. I can tell you Desilu has nine soundstages and they're skimming to the tune of ten dollars per soundstage per day."

"Two grand a month?" Ollie said. That quick. Kraus smiled. Ollie looked in decline, but he was still razor sharp when figuring the take on a skim. "Jeeze, that's a nice head of cabbage," he said, almost dreamily.

"Yeah, well it's going to come to a grinding halt after today. What are you doing here?"

"Followin' up with a guy I've been workin' for. Someone's been leaning on him and he wants clear of the squeeze."

"You get him loose?"

"Probably ..." Ollie lowered his voice, switching gears. "Gordy, I've glommed onto something. Somethin' that'll get me off the *schneid* for years if I play this right."

Ollie looked away towards the far end of the stage where a young man stood looking around. He wore a gray cardigan sweater vest, pencil behind his ear, holding a clipboard. To Kraus he looked like a third-string studio gopher. The young man spotted Ollie and gave him a nod.

"Look, I gotta go, Gordy. Great seein' you again, it's been too long." He took a step away, then made a sudden about-face, "Hey, why don't you come over to my place for Thanksgiving? Violet will love to see you. She's tearing herself away from her women's club golf and bowling outings to cook the bird and all the trimmings. I'll tell you all about how this big play is going to pay off," Ollie said with the easy, presumptive confidence of all luckless gamblers.

"Same place and number over on Denker?" Kraus asked, observing the ritual of every barroom promise.

"Yeah, I mean it. Come on over."

"I just might," Kraus said, both knowing it would never happen. "If my mother doesn't give me too much grief over not coming to the house. I'll call you if I can." Ollie smiled, flashing the bright gold cap of his left incisor. He turned on his heel and rushed to catch up with the retreating errand boy.

Kraus walked over to the craft services table set up near the rear of the soundstage. He rummaged through a tray of candy bars, spotting one he was looking for. He turned next to a wooden crate of Coca Cola bottles. The crate was full and looked like a ring toss carnival game. He ran his eyes over the labels of several bottles until finding one he was looking for. He placed his selection on its side next to the Charleston Chew bar and flattened down a copy of that day's shooting schedule next to both.

The labels on both the bottle and candy bar had been marked by Kraus with a small notation of Monday's date. He pulled a Nikon camera, his most expensive piece of equipment, from his jacket pocket. He adjusted the shutter speed and lens settings before snapping off three photos of his still life objects.

He tucked the camera back into his pocket and gathered up the bottle, candy bar and schedule sheet. The whole process took less than thirty seconds. No one seemed to notice him as he exited the soundstage out onto the studio lot.

Kraus stepped out of the soundstage door into the bright midday sun. It was still in the mid-seventies, but the air felt cool compared to the hot soundstage. Kraus took a deep breath to savor the fresh air. Three hundred people seated on a small studio bleacher can get pretty ripe as the day wears on. Studio lights can sometimes ratchet up soundstage temperatures to almost eighty degrees. Today the soundstage smelled like a vat of cheap perfume, dime store cologne and lanolin hair tonic simmering on a radiator.

He picked his way through the busy backlot and crossed Lilian Way to the adjacent parking area. Kraus opened the driver's side door to his car to let the interior cool down. He used the time to jot down some notes in his notepad.

Kraus loved his car, a 1954 Lincoln Capri hardtop coupe. It was a two-tone beauty. White top over a smart hunter red body. The original owner was a small-time Glitter Gulch producer. Last year he decided to sell it to raise the cash for a film project he was trying to get off the ground.

Kraus had heard on the grapevine that the car was up for sale. He made the producer a cash offer of twenty-nine hundred dollars. The Capri only had three thousand miles on it and went for four thousand dollars new off the lot. The producer jumped at the cash offer. In turn, Kraus was able to give up his old 1940 standard Ford black coupe in favor of this snappy set of wheels. The Capri sported snowy white sidewall tires. A snazzy chrome hood ornament was the shape of a sleek rocket ship in flight. The two-hundred horsepower V-8 under the hood made it seem as if the car could indeed blast off into the sky.

The Lincoln rumbled out of the Desilu parking lot. Kraus steered up Lilian Way to Santa Monica Boulevard. He turned left and made an immediate right onto Cahuenga. He headed for the Owl Drug Store at the next intersection, parked and went in. Kraus could have used a studio payphone, but clients depended on his discretion. A call from the studio lot stood too big of a risk of being overheard. The payphones were down the aisle leading to the rear of the store. Kraus dodged bustling salesclerks assembling Christmas display placards. The shelf goods were already packaged in bright holiday colors. All the music piped into the store was Christmas songs. Bing Crosby crooned *"Rudolph the Red Nosed Reindeer"* as he settled into a phone booth. He smiled to himself while shimmying the booth's sticky wooden bi-fold door closed. Kraus' younger brother, Rudi, hated the song. His name made him the target of unmerciful teasing every Christmas.

Kraus thumbed a nickel into the phone slot and dialed the office number. He amused himself by reading the graffiti on the small shelf while the call rang through. Kraus rented a small space in a Mid-Wilshire office suite from Stanley Hodges, a CPA.

Before finding Hodges, Kraus shared office space further down Wilshire with a young attorney. The set up seemed ideal at first. Kraus figured he would get a lot of investigation jobs from the attorney. That part was true, but there was a downside to renting an office from a busy personal injury attorney.

The arrangement resulted in doing even more work on the arm. It was too easy for the attorney to ask Kraus to find a last-known or an outstanding warrant every now and then. Quick work that would have seemed petty to ask a fee for. The office rent was way below average, but Kraus began to realize that was intentional. The crafty lawyer figured that by renting to an experienced investigator, he'd get a lot of freebies. Turning down these requests would have been awkward. If he did, it wouldn't be long before his rent would start going up and the secretary he shared would start doing a poor job.

His current deal with Hodges had turned out to be much better. Hodges had only recently set up shop and wouldn't need the spare office until he built his practice up. The auxiliary office was small, but it was perfect for Kraus' needs. He paid extra to share the services of Melinda, Hodge's Girl Friday. Melinda was taking night school accounting classes. Her day job was as a receptionist and secretary for both Hodges and him.

Melinda answered on the second ring. "Hodges Accounting. How can I help you?"

"You've got to quit feeding me those straight lines."

"Well, if it isn't our own 'Boston Blackie'. You didn't call in on your own line. What's up, shamus?"

"I don't want to tie my own phone up. I'm checking in. I need you to call Jess Oppenheimer's office over at Desliu. Tell them I got the pictures and hard proof. The studio's definitely getting overcharged on a daily basis. The same sodas, chips and candy bars are on the 'December Bride' set on Monday, show up at the 'Adventures of Jim Bowie' set on Tuesday. On Wednesday they're on the 'I Love Lucy' set. So on and so on. They're charging Desilu multiple times for the same snacks."

"Is that really such a big deal?"

"Figure ten dollars each day for every one of the nine soundstages. It adds up." Kraus could hear Melinda working her Underwood adding machine. The crank sounded like a Las Vegas one-armed bandit.

"Two thousand dollars a month. Wow. Will they get fired?"

"I doubt it. They'll get called out on the scam, then the studio will demand they keep catering at a thirty percent discount. Otherwise, every studio and production outfit in town will know they're not on the square. I bet Desi will ask them to cater their private parties for free also. Tell them I'll drop off the pictures and other proof on Monday."

"Will do. So, 'Adventures of Jim Bowie', huh? Did you see Scott Forbes? He's a dreamboat!"

Kraus chuckled. Melinda was in her mid-twenties and as starstruck as a tourist gawking out the window of a Hollywood tour bus. "I wouldn't know Scott Forbes if I tripped over him."

"Oh, that's right," Melinda teased with a mocking tone, "you don't have a television set."

"No, I don't. I'll be sure to mention your disapproval to my fellow prehistoric friends bobbing around in the tar pit down La Brea. I did see 'Superman' today." An attempt at consolation.

"Oh," Melinda continued with teasing sarcasm, "that would be exciting if I were a ten-year-old boy."

"I saw that picture of you with your girlfriends in bathing suits on the beach in San Diego. Looked like you were giving those ten-year-old boys a run for their money." Melinda snorted. She was a very attractive girl. Honey blonde hair and a knock-out figure, and she knew it. She didn't let Kraus' teasing faze her.

"Oh, is that so? Well, I'm so devastated by that remark I may be too emotional to give you the message Clancy left for you."

"Okay. Now you're talking. What did he have?"

"One of his cabbies spotted that Studebaker."

"Great! Where?"

"Parked on Lorraine just north of Wilshire." She read off the street number.

"Damn. That's five minutes from here, but the keys are in my desk's middle drawer. By the time I pick up the keys and get back, the car is apt to be gone."

"You want me to call Manhattan Beach Motors and tell them where to pick it up. They're sure to have a set of keys."

"No," Kraus said, "if I start having Max and the other lot owners doing half the work, they're going to start wanting lower fees, or wonder why they need me at all. I'll go to the car first. I've got a backup plan for this sort of thing."

"I'm all ears," Melinda said.

"Listen. I'm starving. Do me a favor. Put the keys in an envelope and take them across to the Melody. Priscilla is bound to be working at one of the counters. Leave the keys for me and ask her to have a grilled cheese sandwich with caramelized onions and bacon ready for me. I'll want a Coke too. I should be there in less than an hour."

T W O

Kraus rushed out of Owl Drugs and hopped into his Lincoln. He gunned it onto Cahuenga and sped south towards Hancock Park. He compared Melinda and her adding machine to Ollie's instant mental tabulation of the Desilu catering cheat. His old partner had more than a little bit of larceny in his blood. Kraus threaded his way through midday traffic towards Wilshire.

His thoughts drifted back to when he first met Ollie McBride.

———◆———

LAPD Newton Division Station, Los Angeles - 1940

Kraus came out of the LAPD Academy in 1940, only its fifth graduating class. He drew a patrol officer assignment to the Newton Division in southeast Los Angeles. In those days, Newton was home to the majority of the city's negro population. It was a tough neighborhood, particularly after dark. When the sun set, the streets transformed into a lively bazaar of gambling, drugs and prostitution. Rough-edged pimps roamed the streets with impunity. Every dark corner sold women, drugs, guns and countless other illicit commodities. Policemen and citizens alike referred to the district as "Shootin' Newton".

Unlike every other LAPD division in 1940, Newton had two separate morning watches. Earlier in the year, Sergeant Rocky Washington was promoted to Lieutenant Watch Commander. Washington was a veteran LAPD police officer. He was popular with a vast amount of experience. He was also a negro. Washington was the department's first colored lieutenant. There was a lot of concern about a negro having authority over both colored and white subordinates. The department brass solved this dilemma by creating an early-morning segregated roll call for Washington and Newton's negro officers.

Kraus didn't know about this fragmented command structure. He discovered it the hard way by arriving at the station in the middle of the early first roll call. The room had the burned-husk smell of scorched coffee and fried donut grease. He ended up standing around waiting for the first watch meeting to finish up. The watch room walls were an institutional green. The Sergeant and patrolmen were all colored.

Sergeant Shearing, the white watch commander of Newton's second morning roll call, was a seasoned LAPD veteran. He was the first to enter the watch room after the early shift filed out amidst the clanking and scraping of chairs.

Kraus looked at every white policeman trickling into the station. He saw several spit-and-polish types and found himself hoping to get paired with one of them.

"Kraus," Shearing called out. He moved in closer to his new plebe, "welcome to Newton Division." He sized up his division's new trainee in seconds.

"Thank you, sir," Kraus answered, shaking his new commander's outstretched hand with an air of confidence he didn't completely possess.

"Look, I've read through your records. You did well at the Academy. I bet you learned a few things some of the older guys could stand to pick up on."

"Thank you, sir. I think it's me who will be doing all the learning."

"Good attitude, Kraus," Shearing said as he pointed across the room. "I've decided to team you up with McBride over there."

Kraus looked in the direction his new commander indicated. He saw a tall, beefy patrolman busy holding court over three other old-timers. His new mentor sported a dusty cap with greasy fingerprint smudges on the bill. A day's beard growth was below the cap. A cracked Sam Browne belt that hadn't seen a drop of mink oil since the Great Crash strained across the start of a beer belly. Dirty rubber soled brogans completed the picture. Kraus returned his gaze to the knot of recruitment poster types standing near the first row seats. Teacher's pets waiting for the first period bell to ring.

"I know McBride isn't the picture of an ideal officer," Shearing explained to a crestfallen Kraus. "Hell, he *isn't* an ideal officer," the watch commander admitted. "But Kraus, you already know how to follow the book and turn up with pressed pants and a shiny belt buckle.

Those types in the front can't teach you a thing. McBride isn't a great police officer, but he will be an outstanding partner to teach you how to be a cop."

Shearing walked over to Ollie and whispered a few words in McBride's ear. McBride nodded and took a long look at Kraus. A racetrack punter sizing up a questionable nag in the next race. He smiled and approached Kraus with long strides.

"Kraus? Oliver McBride! Everyone calls me 'Ollie'."

Kraus shook the hand of his first partner. "Good to meet you, Ollie. I'm Gordon, but everyone calls me 'Gordy'."

"'Ollie and Gordy'. Ha! Sounds like a vaudeville act. You couldn't have drawn a better partner. We're going to have fun."

After roll call, both men made their way out to their squad car. "Kraus, I'm going to drive for the first few shifts. Don't worry. You'll get behind the wheel before long."

The new partners started their patrol and went through the introduction rites. Kraus told Ollie about college and joining the force.

"College boy, huh? Good. You're our report writer from now on. I won't miss the commander ridin' my back about misspellings and grammar."

Ollie had the Irish gift of gab. He settled into a lengthy life story. Grew up in San Pedro. His size made him a formidable inside lineman on the high school football team. Grades kept him out of any kind of college. Father was a foreman of a stevedore team at the nearby Port of Los Angeles. McBride spent a couple of years on the docks himself after high school. He realized he didn't want to follow in his father's footsteps as a longshoreman. "Too much like work," Ollie declared.

A job as a turnkey at the new Lincoln Heights jail was much more to his liking.

"It was like a vacation after being at the port for two years. Great chow. Easy duty."

"It wasn't all about knockin' the chumps around, either," Ollie continued. "Lots of chances to pick up some spare change. Don't get me wrong, a longshoreman gets a lot of stuff that falls out of broken crates on the docks, but sometimes it isn't stuff you want and can't be turned into ready cash very easily. Inmates will pay cash money for all sorts of simple things. Sending mail. Giving out extra smokes. Light work assignments. Sick bay passes. You've still got to let these mokes know who's boss, but it was a carrot and stick kind of deal. That job gave me some real insights into the minds of these birds, which gives me a little bit of an edge out here on the streets."It was Ollie's skill at intimidation and force at the jail that caught the attention of the department. The department recruited him in '36 for an auxiliary LAPD squad. Chief James "Two-Gun" Davis dispatched one hundred thirty-six officers to sixteen major points of entry into California from Arizona and Nevada. The squad's nickname became the "Bum Blockade". They worked with local county authorities in clearing out migrant ditch-bank camps and turning away incoming Okies and Arkies at the borders.

The blockade work used intimidation and sometimes physical violence - two of Ollie's specialties - to stop the stream of Dust Bowl refugees into California's rich agricultural regions. It was a tough, pitiless job. The "Bum Blockade" was controversial and ultimately disbanded. Ollie's flair for the work earned him a full-time LAPD patrolman position. Ollie always found himself assigned to the seamier Los Angeles division beats. He'd been at the Newton Division for over a year.

"Okay, Gordy. I'm going to reveal to you my pearls of wisdom." Kraus flipped open his notepad.

"Don't write these down, you knucklehead. These are the natural principles of a cop's life. You need to know these like the Catechism. One: People on the street will always lie even when the truth would serve them better. A classic is the 'my dog doesn't bite' claim. Ranks right up there with 'the check's in the mail' and 'I only want to get the shiny part in'. Always a lie."

"Sounds like the voice of experience."

"Oh, you can bet on it. Two: If a moke is swiveling his head around while you're talkin' to him, he's looking for the best path to run. Furthermore, if some hump, particularly a *cholo*, is clenching his fists and leaning their body towards you, they're about to fight."

"Good to know," Kraus said.

"Three: Never volunteer for anything."

"I'll keep that one in mind," Kraus said.

"I never doubted it for a minute. You look like a smart lad. Four: Never try to get revenge on anyone in the department who has pulled one on you."

"Won't that make you a pushover?" Kraus asked.

"You must have been the oldest brother," Ollie laughed.

"Yeah," Kraus said.

"I thought so. If someone in the department shits on you, it's because they know they can. If you try to get back at them, they'll know you're a spiteful little bastard and see you as someone who isn't trustworthy. It's the whispered reputation that bottlenecks your career."

"But some people deal out shit to others for the fun of it," Kraus posited.

"Big brother stuff," Ollie chuckled. "Yeah, but those types deal it out to everyone." McBride honked his horn at a car that tried an unsafe lane change in front of them. "Idjit. We're in his blind spot but the asshole can't be bothered to turn his head to look back. Where was I?"

"You were about to tell me about people in the department who harass everyone for the fun of it," Kraus answered.

"Oh, yeah. They're the ones who end up with a reputation that hamstrings them. You just have to persevere."

Ollie glanced over at this new partner, gauging his reaction. "Listen, Gordy," he continued, "my old man used to say, 'Ollie, my lad, if you're patient and wait long enough, you'll look out the pub window and ultimately you'll see every one of your enemies in the back of an ox-driven tumbril on its way to the gallows.'"

"What's a tumbril?"

"I don't know. You're the college man," Ollie said. "It's what my da' said when he was in his cups. I think it's some sort of prison wagon. But you're missing the point. What he meant was to be patient and keep your head down when someone is doing you dirt. Let them shoot themselves in the foot."

"Okay. I think I have all that."

"Good. Those four rules will get you further on the force than all the Academy classes put together. Bonus rule: Take advantage of a quiet radio to grab a smoke and get some chow. Ever gotten anything from that taco stand at Atlantic and Live Oak? They make corn tortillas fresh every day. I swear, it's like eating cake! I love that Mexican stuff."

"Live Oak and Atlantic? Isn't that south of Newton's boundary?"

"You Lowell Thomas all of a sudden? If we can see Florence from where we're eating, we're in the division."

"Another rule?"

"You're catching on. Call 13-Adam-Five in for a Code 7. Don't say 'Fiver'. The dispatchers hate that. They think we sound like a guy who calls out bingo numbers at the Legion Hall."

Los Angeles - November 15th, 1956

Kraus' thoughts returned to his driving. The traffic was beginning to bunch up as Cahuenga neared its end at the Wilshire Country Club. Kraus was in a hurry to get to the Studebaker and turned left on Clinton to avoid the inevitable jam.

A lot of auto repossession business came Kraus' way. He had a working relationship with several independent car lots scattered around the Los Angeles basin. It was lucrative work. These lots carried their own paper. When a car buyer fell behind on payments, the lots would sometimes order a skip trace. More often than not, a repossession assignment followed the skip trace.This particular job concerned a female buyer. She bought a car off of the Manhattan Beach Motors lot. Plunked down some earnest money, drove off and never even made the first payment. This was two months ago.

The dealership gave Kraus a skip trace job on the recalcitrant borrower a week earlier. Kraus came up empty after a two-day search. He got a call to come down to the lot. The owner, Max Snyder, wanted to discuss a repo assignment. He bought the lot in '46 after returning from the Pacific. He had been at the same location on Manhattan Beach Boulevard for ten years. He was a good customer.

The small dealership had come a long way in ten years. Civilian car manufacturing had all but ceased during the war. Car lot inventories dried up. In 1946 the lot featured a run-down sales office and an unused storage building at the rear of the lot. The dealership's inventory consisted of an unpromising quartet of four dilapidated Prohibition-era heaps. They languished on bald, sun-bleached tires, adding to the forlorn look of the cracked, weed-choked asphalt. The owner saw nothing but hopelessness and put the lot up for sale. Max saw an opportunity and scooped it up at a bargain basement price.

Before Max took ownership, the sales office was a weather-beaten shanty. It had a leaky roof and faulty wiring. A studio location scout would have earmarked it as a long-abandoned mining shack. Max was a Navy Sea Bee during the war. He spent four years building airfields and bivouacs in a span of days while under enemy fire. He whipped the sales building and lot into a modern showcase in less than a month.

Now the sales office always had a fresh coat of exterior paint. Its spotless terracotta roof tiles gleamed in the sun. The inside walls sported vivid, bright colors. Merigold, red, blue - colors that promoted warmth, excitement and trust. Promotional posters hung on every wall. Happy families piling into a new station wagon. Beach-going couples driving spiffy convertibles along the shore. Single women in bathing suits waving to a group as they drove up to a lakeside picnic area. Postcards from the American Dream.

It turns out that the Sea Bee's "can-do" attitude made for an easy transition to a civilian sales persona. Max still had the dark tan from years under the remorseless South Pacific sun. The tan no longer had the chapped, leathery texture of a pack mule's harness.Regular facial treatments with salt scrubs and emollients transformed it to a country club tan. He lost his Navy buzz cut in favor of twice monthly, ten-dollar trims at an exclusive Beverly Hills men's salon. His barked knuckles and calloused palms changed into smooth, cuticle-pushed hands. Businessman hands. Oil-stained dungarees made way for tasseled cordovan loafers and Sy Devore suits. The look worked. Max was very successful.

The front of the sales building held a table with sales brochures, a few cushioned chairs and a secretary's desk. Kraus sat in Max's private rear office. He glanced out the window. A yard boy in a stained guinea tee and frayed cut-off shorts that once were dress pants was washing a car. The boy applied himself with a gusto only seen in a worker who knows the boss could be watching.

"Gordy, that broad put a hundred down and drove that Studebaker Commander right off the lot. I've been doing this a long time and never felt more solid about a finance deal."

"Those are the ones that usually go south," Kraus said.

"I know. But this gal seemed rock solid. The Commander wasn't even two years old. Perfect condition. Not even fifteen thousand miles. Azore Green." Max waved a Studebaker sales brochure in front of him. Sizzle instead of the steak. "A color the public's screaming for." Max smacked the brochure on the palm of his manicured hand.

Kraus thought the color looked like a regular green. But he'd never been to Portugal, so he kept his mouth shut.

"I could put that Studebaker out front, and every passing car would slow down to look. The cops would give me a citation for blocking the flow of traffic. Kraus, if you bring it back with less than twenty thousand on the dial, it'll mean another fifty for you. That peach sold for twenty-two hundred new and I know I can get sixteen hundred for it without breaking a sweat. But not if it's been driven all to shit."

So, Kraus enlisted his network of Los Angeles cabbies to look out for the car. Every dispatcher got a ten-spot for putting out the word. The cabbie who spotted the car got a fiver if Kraus was able to recover the vehicle. Cabbies covered a lot of turf taking fares all over Los Angeles and beyond every day. It was a pretty effective system.

There was something about this repo that bothered Kraus. The woman who bought the car must have been slick. Max wasn't an easy touch. Kraus felt as though this wasn't her first scam. Not even her tenth. Repossessions always have a slight element of danger. This one felt dodgier than most. Kraus had a feeling in his gut that this was much more than a simple case of a deadbeat trying to get one over.

Private detective work could be like that. Like tuna fish salad in the fridge. It smells fishy by definition. Hard to sniff out if it's going bad. All you have is a hunch and wonder if it's your imagination. With little warning it can decay into something capable of doing serious harm. This job had that feel.

He turned south onto Larchmont, heading for Third so he could make his way over to Lorraine. Kraus reached under the seat and removed his back-up weapon from a custom pocket he'd installed. It was a Remington 51 .380 ACP automatic tucked into a clip-on belt holster. Kraus checked the magazine, racked the slide, pushed the automatic back into the holster and clipped it to his belt.

"You never know," he said out loud.

THREE

Third Street and Lorraine was a very wealthy and fashionable part of Hancock Park. The average person would call the houses "mansions". The homes were stately. Driveways often featured ornate entry gates flanked by stone columns. Lawns looked like country club greens.

Kraus slowed as he made his way down Lorraine. The sun was still bright but starting its post-noon descent. Long shadows of the palms lining the street already laced the roadway. Visibility was challenging while moving through the light-then-dark laddered pattern of the shadows.

He switched off the radio. Christmas tunes were already dominating the airwaves. It wasn't even Thanksgiving yet and Kraus wasn't in the mood. He knew Nat King Cole's home was a few blocks to the right. Did he let *"The Christmas Song"* be played under his roof? Cole had to be as sick of it as Kraus was.

Kraus' father was a skilled finish carpenter and over the years had worked on many of these houses. His father had done some work at the home of a famous silent star a block or two east of Lorraine. He couldn't remember if it was Lon Chaney or William Haines. He did remember the actor had a Boston bull pup. The dog gnawed at the exquisite, scrolled door and floor moldings. His father had an artist's sensibility. The sight of the splintered chew marks inflicted on fine craftsmanship outraged him. "Americans and their pets," his father would grumble.

It occurred to Kraus that this was an unusual neighborhood for a deadbeat to park their car. Automobile theft of any kind in Los Angeles could make for a dangerous situation.

Vehicles were a statement, a status symbol - and as such - a valuable commodity. A commodity worth stealing. The right car could be a no-questions-asked passport to the pinnacle of the Los Angeles social stratum.

Between 1910 and 1920, the population of Los Angeles doubled to one and half million. The city fanned out rather than building up. The non-stop sprawl spurred the evolution of the L.A. car culture. The criminal element noticed the early, rapid increase of car ownership almost immediately.

By 1910, car theft specialists targeted Los Angeles vehicles. By 1914, independent thieves gave way to a major car theft ring. Dozens of stolen car reports were filed every day. Stripped parts from stolen vehicles were shipped across the country and sold as factory replacements. Delivery trucks and custom roadsters were built using the remaining frames and chassis. Roadsters made from the carcasses of stolen cars became known as "hot rods".The Automobile Club of Southern California created their Auto Theft Squad in 1915. The squad worked with the LAPD and the Los Angeles County Sheriff's Department to track and catch these sophisticated auto thieves. Many of the LAPD's best detectives joined the Auto Theft Squad.

The Sheriff Department's auto theft division ultimately replaced the Automobile Club's civilian task force. Car theft in Los Angeles remained one of the largest categories of reported crimes to this day.

Repossessions usually involved seizing cars from everyday citizens. Far removed from the world of violent organized car boosting gangs. Still, a normal repo would occasionally turn into a run-in with a gang. It wasn't unheard of for criminals to use a straw man to buy a popular car with a small down-payment. The straw man drives away, and the car disappears into the maw of an organized gang. Four hours later the car is being taped off in a Tijuana spray paint tent. What begins as a common repossession can turn into a dangerous confrontation in the blink of an eye.

Kraus sensed something off about this situation. He managed to spot the Studebaker parked across the street about one hundred feet from where he was. The model, color and license number were a match. Bingo. Kraus pulled over to the curb, switched off the engine and waited. He took stock of the entire area, looking up and down both sides of the street and at the homes set off from the sidewalks. He used his side view and rear-view mirrors to do the same without turning his head. The neighborhood was quiet. Lorraine was not an arterial road. Western Avenue a few blocks to the east was the main north-south thoroughfare in the area.

The coast looked clear. Kraus climbed out of his car, walked to the rear and opened the trunk. He removed a long, slender object in a felt sheath. He stuck it in his waistband and covered it with the side flap of his sports jacket. Next, he grabbed a small canvas gym bag. Kraus moved towards his target as though he owned it. He glanced around as he approached the Studebaker. There didn't appear to be movements on the street or in the windows of the surrounding homes.

Kraus positioned himself in front of the driver's side door. He placed the canvas bag on the pavement. He withdrew a thin flat blade of spring steel from the felt sheath under his coat. The blade's nickname was "Slim Jim". There were notches at one end. Kraus wedged the notched-end flat between the car window and door. He lined the blade up with the lock cylinder and pushed down a few inches. Kraus felt the blade make contact with what locksmiths call the "lazy pawl" - a tailpiece on the lock assembly. He hooked the tailpiece with the notch and pulled it up. The Studebaker's door unlocked with a soft click. No damage to the lock or the car.

This tool had become the favorite automobile entry method of car thieves. Kraus had developed a facile touch with the "Slim Jim". He could open a car door with it faster than many car owners could using their actual keys. Kraus swung the door open. The interior gave off a faint aroma of expensive, French milled soap and spearmint gum. He pulled a length of carbon steel chain and a burly, machined brass, five-tumbler padlock from the canvas bag. Kraus worked with a smooth, practiced dexterity.

He threaded the chain onto the Studebaker's steering wheel. The pattern he used resembled a cow's hitch knot one would make with a rope. The half-hitches straddled one of the steering wheel spokes. Kraus then stretched both chain lengths down to one of the car seat posts. He looped one around the post and padlocked both lengths together. Now the steering wheel wouldn't turn more than a few inches. Even sitting in the driver's seat would be difficult.

This was a technique he had used during the war. Kraus signed for his jeep on D-Day plus three, offloaded from an LST at Omaha Beach. He drove it through France, across Belgium all the way to the Wurm River in Western Germany. He never left his jeep unattended without following this ritual. Probably the 2nd Armored Division's Military Police Platoon record for longest sole possession of a jeep.

The glove box held a woman's hairbrush, a stick of spearmint gum torn in half and a couple of receipt books. Kraus flipped both receipt books open. Both books had the carbons of several receipts hand-printed in neat block letters. They looked like rent receipts. Kraus jotted down the names and addresses in his notepad. Almost done, he tugged on the chain to test it. A tinny rattle came from the car's floorboard.

He reached back under the seat. An aluminum case, about the size of a hip flask, was fastened with a rubber band to the same post the chain was wrapped around. The case and rubber band were black, the same color as the post. A casual glance would have missed it.

Kraus unhooked the case and unsnapped its lid. He tipped the contents out onto the car seat. Another receipt. This one was from a different receipt book. Square rather than rectangular. A name, "Margaret Woodward", in a quivery cursive hand on the "from" line. An October date. Same name as the woman who bought the car from Max.

There were also five twenty-dollar bills and three California operator's license photostats in the cache. One for "Brenda Reed", one for "Connie Cooper" and another for "Anna Karolina Bjorkquist". All three cited the same stats and characteristics. Black hair. Green eyes. Five-foot four. Hundred-eighteen pounds. 1925 birth year. Photostats were tricky, but the thumbprints all looked to be identical. He copied down all the information from the licenses in his notepad.

There was one other item in the case. He shook out an old Brownie snapshot carefully preserved in a cellophane sleeve. Pictured was a little blonde girl. About two or three years old. A look of shy uncertainty on her face. Dressed in a traditional Swedish folk costume. He was very familiar with the costume style. His parents dragged Kraus and his brother to Vasa Park at the foot of the Santa Monica mountains almost every June for a Midsummer Festival. An annual event put on by the Swedish community in Southern California.

The little girl wore an embroidered linen headscarf called a *Halskläden*. Light-colored curls poked out from the edges. She sported a traditional *förkläde*, an apron with dark vertical stripes - probably red - over a simple, solid-colored dress. Her feet were in wooden clogs called *Trätofflor*. He'd picked up the terms from listening to his mother chatting with costumed festival attendees. She would ask, in her imperious High German, which Swedish parish was linked with their costumes. Kraus was always too eager for the first strawberries of the season, served up with rich cream, to pay complete attention to the conversations. He couldn't remember all the details.

Kraus presumed this was a childhood picture of his car thief. The words, "Juni *1928*", were written on the back. Not helpful for identification purposes, but she was adorable with her pudgy hands clasped nervously at her chest. She wasn't looking at the camera. Probably at her mother. It may have been the first time she'd been photographed. A treasured memory. He wasn't surprised she went to great lengths to protect it.

He pushed the photo, licenses and money back into the tube, then reached back under the seat to refasten it to the floor post. Kraus was still thinking about the fun times at those Swedish festivals.

The crunch of a dry leaf from behind that brought Kraus back to the present. He heard the familiar snick of a revolver's hammer being thumbed back.

FOUR

Kraus spun around as he raised himself from a crouch. He drew the Remington as he turned. The noise had come from a spot across the road. Right behind him. He extended the handgun out in a point shooting stance, his arm steadied on the top of the door frame. Being caught by surprise, this was as perfect a position as he could have hoped for. He was still exposed but pressed against the car door. This offered some protection, and he could track his assailant right or left with the swing of the door.

A man wearing khaki work clothes held a pistol grip aimed roughly in Kraus' direction. He was on the lawn of the home across from the Studebaker. Fifteen feet tops. He was in Kraus' gun sites. An easy target.

One problem. It was the pistol grip of a Bakelite grass seed broadcast spreader. Kraus had the same tool in his garage. The snick sound must have been the volume control selector clicking in place. Mexican gardener. Clearly harmless. Skin sunbaked to a tawny tobacco hue. Eyes were wide with shock. A dingy long-billed fisherman's cap shaded his high forehead. A canvas tool belt held up his work pants. A leather holster at his hip carried a worn set of pruning shears. The underarms of his short-sleeved work shirt were dark with sweat rings as big as dinner plates.

"*Hijole!*" The gardener held both hands out from his waist. Surrendering. The lawn spreader tilted in his hand. Grass seed spilled from the hopper with a dry, rasping sound. A small mound of husks formed on the lawn near his worn work shoes.

"*Lo siento, amigo.*" Kraus offered the gardener a weak, apologetic smile while he holstered his automatic. He added a "what can you do" shrug of the shoulders. The gardener turned and retreated to the rear of the house without another word.

"Jesus," Kraus muttered. What was spooking him about this job? That was too damn close to being a complete disaster. His armpits were putting his shirt in competition with the gardener's sweat stains. He figured most Mexican gardeners were of the see-no-evil variety, but he wasn't going to hang around to find out. He may have gone to tell the homeowners who were certain to call the cops. Time to leave. He closed the Studebaker door, grabbed the gym bag and trotted back to his Lincoln.

Kraus was a mile down Wilshire before his nerve endings stopped sparking. He scolded himself for being so jumpy. He'd been a pound of trigger pressure short of a ticket to Miseryville.

Traffic was light for mid-afternoon. He made good time as he sped towards the Melody. Several vacant lots along Wilshire had vee-shaped, ground-level billboards. No wasted opportunities in the land of plenty. A life-size cutout of Santa's sleigh and reindeer sat on top of a bomb shelter display. Only $795. Easy payments. Kraus liked the optimism of the timepayment offer. The Big One must not be that imminent if bomb shelter outfits are offering installment plans.

The Melody Lane Cafe was a favorite of Kraus'. In his mind it had a true Hollywood look. A place young casting directors would eat. A place young actress hopefuls would go to be spotted by young casting directors. Crisp neon lights spelled out "Cafe" in Art Deco lettering above the entrance. Most of the Wilshire frontage was a squat, windowed turret. The top of the turret offered outdoor seating. Resort-style umbrellas protected diners from the California sun.

He intended on running in and out to grab the Studebaker keys and his food. Time was of the essence. Kraus glided up to the curb in front of the lesser used street entrance. The door had a large, windowed keyhole shape cut into it. It always reminded him of "Alice in Wonderland" for some reason. His park job was sloppy but this was a quick stop and go. Kraus jumped out and pushed open the cafe's door.

The counter surface ran in a wavy line. Two or three waitresses worked the counter. Several others roamed about waiting on tables. The lunch rush was over and it was too early for the dinner trade. Priscilla was standing behind the counter at a spot near the door. She was swapping out saltshakers and fluted glass sugar dispensers. A paper bag and manila envelope sat on the counter near her elbow.

"Hey, handsome! I've got your lunch right here." Priscilla snapped her gum after her greeting. Kraus was never sure if her gum chewing was legitimate or an obligation to hold up her end of the stereotype. She tugged her scalloped apron down tighter against her bosom and threw her shoulders back to show her figure off to a better advantage. Tip building tactic. "Your Girl Friday left this for you."

"Thanks, Priscilla."

Kraus lifted the flap to make sure it held the right keys. It did.

It also contained a large nickel postcard. It looked like the ones in the revolving display rack near the front cash register. It was a picture of a sunny Southern California beach. A tanned, buxom young woman sunbathed on a beach chair in the foreground. She wore a tight, bare shouldered one piece, cut low at the neckline and high at the thighs. In the background, a few children frolicked in the sand. Melinda had drawn an arrow pointing at the young woman. She had written "Twenty-year-old woman" in her sharp Zaner-Bloser cursive. Another arrow pointed at a young boy in swim trunks in the background. "Ten-year-old boy" was its label. She wrote, "Stay tuned for next week's lesson" on the postcard's bottom margin.

"I needed that today," Kraus laughed, showing the postcard to Priscilla.

"I think every man needs that. She has a crush on you, you know."

"She's not buying what I'm selling. Besides, I'm saving myself for you. I've got to get going." Kraus slapped three dollars down on the counter. "Hey, ask Hector to make a batch of his sausage chestnut dressing for me next week. I'll pick it up Wednesday evening."

"Still telling your mother you make it yourself for Thanksgiving?"

"I tell her I *prepared* it. I add pepper to it after I move it into a bowl. I could make it myself, but never have the time this time of year."

"My goodness. Pretty slippery. Sounds like the kind of con my husband would pull."

"They say married men make the worst husbands. Gotta run." He rushed out while tucking the envelope under his arm and gripping his lunch bag.

"See you later, alligator," Priscilla trilled in a fusillade of gum snaps.

Traffic was slow going east on Wilshire, giving Kraus a chance to wolf down his sandwich. It had an ideal amount of crispy bacon and the cheese - a perfect blend of cheddar and Gruyere - was still warm. He polished off his soda just before reaching Lorraine. He'd have to grab the Studebaker and drive it over to Manhattan Motors. Max or one of the car lot staff would drive him back to his car.

Dusk was coming fast and the shadows of the tall palms added to the developing darkness on the boulevard. Lights were already on in many of the homes along Lorraine. Several side windows were dimly lit by the eerie bluish glow cast by a television set.

Kraus hoped there wouldn't be a squad car parked on the street. Patrolmen looking for a gun-toting car booster. He looked down the avenue for any sign of the police. No cops. No terrified gardener. No Studebaker. Could the cops have towed it away?

He parked his car near the spot where the Studebaker had been and looked up and down the road as he climbed out. Nothing. Almost nothing. In the gutter, near where the Studebaker was, his chain was neatly coiled into the shape of a metallic nest. The opened padlock was resting in the center of the coiled links like a bizarre bird's egg.

"Well, shit," Kraus grumbled.

FIVE

Kraus arrived at his office early the next morning. Although the Studebaker got away the day before, he had some solid leads. But there were bills to pay. He needed to finish up his Desilu report and get it all back to the studio that morning.

He'd taken Olympic up to Masselin on his way in. Dropped into Van de Kamp's on Wilshire to pick up a couple of fresh bear claws. Kraus loved them. Dense ribbons of cinnamon snaked through the almond paste filling. Sweet white frosting was piped over the warm crust. He brewed coffee in the office drip pot and munched on the bear claws at his desk while he did his paperwork.

Melinda came in at nine. "Smells like someone's made coffee."

Kraus finished putting the report and evidence into a box. He left his small office and approached her lobby desk.

"Melinda, any messages for me?"

"Only that alert from Clancy. How did the tip pan out for you?"

"An ongoing investigation."

"In other words, she got away." The phone rang. She signaled a pause with her forefinger while lifting the receiver. Finished, she hung up and made a note in her phone log. "Jess Oppenheimer's office said you could come by anytime this morning. He'd make five minutes for you. Do you want me to type up an invoice or was seeing Superman enough compensation for you?" She plucked an almond sliver off Kraus' shirt front and placed it on his palm.

"I'll need the invoice," he scribbled a few numbers on his pocket notepad, ripped the page out of the booklet and placed it on her desk. "Superman was just the icing on the bear claw." He winked and popped the almond sliver in his mouth.

It was almost eleven by the time Kraus left Desilu. Time to follow up on the missing Studebaker. The best lead he had was the address on the rental receipt squirreled away under the Studebaker's seat. He checked his notepad. A Hawthorne address. He made his way onto Western and headed south hoping to beat the noon traffic.

The address turned out to be a six-unit bungalow courtyard north of El Segundo Boulevard. These setups were still scattered around Southern California. Kraus had rented one in the Melrose Hill district east of Western before buying his present home. During the twenties and thirties, bungalows like these were part of a studio contract package for promising talent. Rent free. Convenient love nests for studio brass and new starlets.

The best ones felt like a link to the glory days of Hollywood. Large post-war apartment buildings were rapidly elbowing them aside. Multi-stories. Denser tenancy. Higher revenue per square foot. California charm exchanged for a better profit statement.

It would have been charitable to call this bungalow courtyard a link to anything glorious. Any charm it once possessed had evaporated long ago. Two rows of identical bungalows faced each other across an overgrown center court. Mirror images. The units looked embarrassed by what they saw in the mirror.

Wire mesh was visible in many places through a chipped stucco exterior. The terracotta Spanish roof tiles were dirty. Many tiles were misaligned and cracked. Edges broken off from years of battering by the Santa Ana winds. Tufts of pine needles stuck out from under the tiles like straw ticking from an old mattress.

The windows were all double-hung Arts and Crafts period originals. A row of three vertical glass grilles topped each one. A few windows had deep cracks in one or more of the small panes. All the glass was missing from one grille. Patched with a cardboard piece jammed into the empty grille frame. Dusty black electrical tape held it limply in place.

Kraus spotted the "manager" placard on the front left bungalow. A cement pathway led to the front door. The single front step was a worn concrete slab. Windows with closed blinds flanked the door. The left one had a faded, dog-eared pasteboard sign wedged between the glass and the grubby blinds. It was an Adlai Stevenson campaign poster. Cobwebs clustered on the edges like bunting. No reference to the election year. It could have been from fifty-two. It could have been from this year's election. A caption below Stevenson's picture read, "Our Next President". The candidate looked tired and defeated. Kraus knew how he felt.

Pressing the doorbell button produced no audible buzz. Kraus rapped a knuckle on the cheap aluminum screen door frame. It sounded more like a slug rattling in a beggar's tin cup than an actual knock. He opened the screen door enough to get his fist between it and the door. Kraus knocked on the door with a wrist snap motion. Feet scuffed on the other side. The door opened a few inches, drawing the security chain taught.

"Yeah?" An older woman gripping the soup-stained lapels of a patterned housecoat. She peered through a cigarette smoke haze to look Kraus up and down. "I ain't buyin' anything and I don't rent to men." She tried to close the door, but Kraus had wedged the toe of his shoe against it.

"You're in luck. I'm not selling anything. Just a few questions."

"Hey," she tried to close the door with more shoulder pressure. "I ain't takin' no survey either."

"I'm not a canvasser." Kraus pulled a five-dollar bill from the inside pocket of his sports coat. He held it discreetly, like bribing a head waiter for a better table. "I have two or three questions and would like to compensate you for your time."

The courtyard manager eyed the currency and pushed the cigarette back into her mouth. One hand free now to grab the loot. "Okay, what's on your mind?" A mélange of gray and mousy brown hair held fast with an impressive lacework of metal curler clips.

"Do you have a tenant named 'Margaret Woodward'?"

"Did have. Moved out four days ago. Dead of night. No notice."

"Owe you money?"

"Nope. Moved in November one. She was paid up through the end of the month. Left the place Dutch clean, too."

"Any trouble with her?"

"Not while she was here. She on the run?"

"Why do you ask that?"

"Two types of gals rent my units. Those wantin' to be found and those not wantin' to be found."

"And you think she didn't want to be found?"

"Asked for the unit furthest from the street. Kept all her clothes in one of them fancy wardrobe trunks. The ones open up with hangers and little drawers. Like a carny worker. Close the trunk and you're ready to lam it as quick as it takes to fasten two latches."

"How's that different from a gal who wants to be found?"

"Mister, most of my gals are out here from Hicktown, USA. They want to make it in pictures. Everything stuffed into two pieces of Puerto Rican luggage. They move in. Ten minutes later, a couple pillowcases worth of clothes and warpaint get strung all over Hell's half-acre. Take an hour to gather it all back up. They're just dying for some Hollywood bigshot to catch sight of them at Schwab's. You know. I was one of them gals."

"You don't say?" Kraus asked. Keeping her talking.

The landlady primped a lock of battened-down hair near her temple. The metal edge of a hair clip scuffed across a dry chickenpox scar, making her wince.

"Oh yeah!" She unfastened the chain lock and held the door open a little more. Warming up to her story. "I'm from New York City originally. Worked as a cigarette girl at Minsky's. This was back in Prohibition. I was a looker."

"You're holding up pretty well," Kraus lied.

She flashed him a row of corn yellow, mail-order dentures. Her grip on the lapels loosened to open the housecoat an inch. The skin below her collar bones was a nest of spider veins. "Abe Minsky himself told me I should go to Hollywood. I'd be a cinch. The next Norma Talmadge. And he had connections, don't you know."

"Did he?"

"Oh, yeah," she exclaimed with an ironic chortle. Her laugh had a waterlogged quality. Like a scoop of pancake batter had been ladled into her lungs. "He gave me the name of what he called a big-time agent. So off I go. Eight days on a train. Damn near got shanghaied by a white slaver on the transfer in Chicago. But I made it."

"What happened?"

"Oh, he was a big-time agent all right. He handled animal acts." Kraus laughed.

"I know, ain't that the goddamned limit? Only animals! Said he could see I had something, but he had his hands full managing 'Waddles the Duck' and couldn't take on a new client."

"What did you do then?"

"I was so upset. My dreams shattered, you know. His office was near the Bradbury building. I walked two blocks and jumped on the Red Car headed back to the rooming house I was staying at in West Hollywood. I started crying. The conductor saw me. He finished his route at my stop and walked me back to the rooming house. Got married four months later. Carl was a good man. I slung hash and he worked for Pacific Electric right up to retirement. We bought this place as an investment. When he passed in forty-four, I sold our place and moved in here. Been here ever since."

"Sounds like you got lucky."

"Yeah," another swampy laugh. "Saved by 'Waddles the Duck'."

"So, ma'am," Kraus changed topics.

"Call me Delores."

"So, Delores. Margaret Woodward. You seem a good judge of horseflesh. What did you make of her?"

"I don't ask a lot of questions, you understand. But she was beautifully put together. Glossy black hair down to her shoulders. Bangs like that pin-up girl, Bettie what's it. Classy, though. Porcelain skin. Smart clothes. Pricey makeup. Professional manicure."

"Working girl?"

"Nah. Didn't keep the right hours for that game. Smooth. Really sure of herself. Didn't talk a lot yet came off real smart."

"What do you think her story was?"

"Rich girl hiding from her parents. Office girl who dipped into the till. Gangster moll who'd had enough. Coulda been one of a dozen things."

"Okay. Delores, you've been a big help. Could I take a look at her unit?"

"Sure. Last one back on the other side. I left it unlocked this morning 'cause I've got a kid from the market does handyman work around here comin' to fix the commode. On the fritz."

"Delores," Kraus handed her the fiver folded over his business card. "If you think of anything else, please call me. The right info will get you another one of those."

"Will do," she peered at the card, "Mr. Kraus. You was real nice. I liked talkin' to you. Not like that other guy. I didn't tell him shit."

"Other guy?"

"Yeah. Two days ago. Big guy. Taller than you. About six-two, six-three. Cheap suit. Walnut shells for knuckles. Oily hair. Looked like a dago goon to me. Put me in mind of a bouncer that worked the El Fey in New York during Prohibition. I didn't like him either."

"Think he was in the rackets?"

"Maybe. Nowadays, who knows. Didn't ask about her by name. Had a picture. Asked me if she lived here or if I'd seen her around. I played dumb for that bastard."

"Been around since? Did he leave a number to call in case you saw her?"

"Nah. Didn't lay down any palm oil, either." She wiggled the folded five in her hand.

"Okay. Delores, thank you for your help. I'm going to take a look at the unit."

"Leave the door unlocked when you go. 'Backstage Wife' comes on the radio in a minute. I don't wanna have to get up and unlock the door for that kid if he shows up during my program."

"Got it," Kraus said.

He crossed the center court at a diagonal, watching for dog turds in the tousled grass. There were only six units, but a metal number nine dangled on the panel above the door. It started life as a six before the tack holding it upright rusted away. The blinds were up on both windows. Sheer curtains pulled closed. Kraus twisted the knob and walked through the door. He closed the door behind him. No surprises like yesterday, although this place could have used a Mexican gardener.

Delores was right. The place was spanking clean. Some sad thrift store pieces in the living room. A sway-backed single bed and scarred chest of drawers in the small bedroom. Empty trash bin.

A claw-foot tub with a shower pole running up from the faucet squatted in the bathroom. The shower curtain was held up by a wobbly oval curtain rod. It had been cleaned recently. No musty smell but a belt sander couldn't have gotten the hard water scales off of it. A faint scent of French milled soap around the tub, but no shampoo or soap bars left behind. No trash in the bathroom bin either. The toilet tank hissed in commiseration.The small galley kitchen was clean and neat. Salt and pepper shakers stood guard over a ceramic spoon rest. An apple and some grapes in the fridge. Empty freezer compartment. The garbage can behind the curtain under the sink was lined with a fresh shopping bag from Ralph's. The top folded over in a neat cuff. Half of a Wrigley's gum wrapper was caught in the bottom seam of the paper bag liner. Kraus extracted the gum wrapper and was looking it over for notes when a shadow passed by the window.

The shadow had a feminine form and gait. Margaret Woodward coming back? The movement was too spry to be the landlady. Kraus scooted beside the front door as the knob was turning. The door would open up with him between it and the wall. He rested his right hand on the butt of his holstered automatic.

SIX

The door pushed open. A tall woman breezed in. Too tall to be the Studebaker deadbeat. Too pretty and fragrant to be a Mexican gardener. Kraus stepped out from behind the door.

The woman started, but smiled as she ran her eyes over him. The smile dimmed when she saw his right hand resting on the gun butt.

"Whoa, hold on there, Billy the Kid. Just checking out the action here. Saw you go in and thought that old biddy was finally letting the place go co-ed." Honey blonde hair in a long bob. It fell an inch or two below her shoulders. Thick waves looked so natural, they could only have been done in an expensive shop.

She lifted her arms from her sides in a theatrical gesture. Ready for a pat down. Unarmed. Not with a gun at least. She was wearing a tight, long-sleeved sweater. Its narrow horizontal stripes hugged the bullet bra underneath. Her large breasts jutted out in a way that looked lethal.

"Sorry. I was looking for your neighbor. It looks like she moved out."

"Yeah. A few nights ago. I heard her dragging her trunk out the door. Figured she was leaving. You're lookin' for her packing a pistol? She have a body in that trunk?"

"Not that I know of. Did you know her?"

"Not very much." She looked around the bungalow. "This unit has nicer paint than mine. I'd switch but I'd probably break a heel once a week on those catawampus pavers out there. My name's Patricia. Patty Fulhorst. But I'm going by my stage name now. 'Penelope Westgate'. You can call me 'Penny'." She extended her hand.

"Penny, nice meeting you. About the girl?" Nudging her back on track.

"Oh, Margaret. Right. She moved in at the beginning of the month. I went down here to meet her the next day. You never know. Make friends with the right sized gal and you've automatically doubled your wardrobe." She tugged her sweater down a little tighter over her breasts. "Too bad she wasn't the right size. She had some style."

"It looks like your wardrobe is pretty stylish already."

"You like this?" She lifted her skirt up a few inches and made a couple of quarter-turns on the toes of her Baby Doll pumps.

"It's not baggy."

Penelope giggled and moved closer. She planted a palm on Kraus' lapel. "I just got back from an audition for a United picture. 'The Young Lovers'." She drew out the last word, making it sound like a growl. "The star is that kid from 'The Boy with the Green Hair'. I read for the role of an older sister. The scene was me warning her younger sister about the dangers of heavy petting."

"You look pretty qualified on the subject."

"Big sister or backseat make out artist?"

"I'd have to do my own research on the second one," Kraus said.

"You're cute." She flashed him a suggestive smile. "That's the idea, silly. I'm playing the older sister conflicted. She's a little racy herself but doesn't want her sister to be that way. See? My agent's had me taking acting lessons. I've had walk-ons in a couple of B's. One-liners in a 'Bomba the Jungle Boy' and another in 'The Bowery Boys Meet the Monsters'. I'm ready for bigger things."

Kraus didn't take the bait on the obvious straight line. "So, what did you and Margaret chat about?"

"I could see right off that she wasn't the right size for borrowing clothes. I told her about my acting career. Said she was a traveling drummer for an East Coast boutique cosmetics line. Very top shelf. I asked her if she had any samples she could throw my way. She didn't. Said she'd get them in soon. I thought that was funny, 'cause she left every day as though she was going to work. All dressed up, you know. How do you sell cosmetics without a sample case?"

"Good point," Kraus conceded. "Maybe you should be the detective. What did you think she was up to?"

"Well," she looked up at the ceiling as though her thoughts formed in the water stains. "She was real chic, you know. My acting coach calls it 'poised'. You would have thought she was someone's mistress hiding out, waiting for an appointment with one of those Beverly Hills 'Doctor Kill-Cares'. In trouble, if you take my meaning. She was way too swanky for one of those tee-jay scrape-apes. Don't matter. She wasn't in the Pudding Club. No way. Didn't have the look. Girls always look guilty and nervous while they're waiting their turn, you know?"

"Okay. We've got a good idea of what she isn't," Kraus flicked the gum wrapper stub with his forefinger, "I wonder what exactly she is."

Penny pointed at the gum wrapper. "Oh yeah. Half-sticks. When we met, I offered her a stick of Spearmint. Said she'd only take half a stick. I told her if she wasn't woman enough to put the whole stick in her mouth, I'd keep my gum." She leaned into Kraus a little more, shifting her leg against his knee. Her body heat flared even higher. She crooked her forefinger over the edge of his coat lapel and moved it up and down against his chest. Wet her lips with a moist tongue and whispered, "I always put the *whole* stick in my mouth. Goes in stiff and long. Comes out shriveled up, wet and sticky."

"Sounds about right," Kraus said. He wondered if she was vamping for him or practicing for a callback audition.

"You think the other guy looking for Margaret knew more about her? What did she do, anyway? Is she in trouble?"

"Someone else was looking for her? Maybe more trouble than I know."

"Well, now that I'm talking to you, I'm guessing he was looking for Margaret. I was leaving for work Monday and a big bruiser was lumbering up and down the sidewalks. He was looking at all the apartments. Cheap sports coat and worse tie." She made a face. "Like the ones they put on actors at Ciro's when they show up without them."

"Did he speak to you?"

"Are you kidding? I didn't make eye contact with the brute. Looked like a boxer who lost every match in the ring but won every back-alley fight. Saw him stalking away as I walked to the bus stop, so he must not have seen her or her car."

"Car?"

"Yeah, a real snazzy number. Nice green. She didn't park it around here. But I was going to a cattle call on Gower last week and there she was, stopped at the light on Lexington. It was her for certain. I waved but she didn't see me."

"Okay, Penny." Kraus handed her one of his business cards. Her body was still draped against him. He wasn't going to complain. "Would you give me a call if you think of anything else? If that guy shows up again?"

"Investigator. How exciting! I will, Gordon. Hey, when you wrap this up, give me a call here and fill me in, would you?" She brushed her crooked finger across the place where his shirt covered his nipple. "I would love getting filled in."

"*Jesus*," Kraus thought. He wondered if he had time for a cold shower after he left.

"These units aren't set up for phones. Delores has a separate phone in her mud room the renters can use." She drew a card from her skirt's stash pocket and handed it to Kraus. The front displayed a single name. Penelope Westgate. He turned it over. A number with a Hawthorne exchange was written on the back. "It'll ring eight or nine times before she can tear herself from the radio and shuffle over to get it."

"You and Delores must have a lot of Hollywood tales to share with each other."

"Oh, that harpy told you her Hollywood story, did she? Yeah. I've heard it a dozen times. I'm surprised the agent didn't just sign her on. She looks like a damned toothless schnauzer."

Kraus peeled himself away from her. "Now, now. Be nice. You're both in the Hollywood Sisterhood."

She stuck out her tongue at him, then kissed his earlobe. "Phone me, Gordon. I bet we have some things to share with each other."

"It's Gordy, and I will. But I've got to leave before this goes any further. The handyman from the market might catch us in the middle of some heavy petting. What would *your* big sister say?"

She laughed and walked out the door with Kraus. He closed it, careful to leave it unlocked. "You're alright. Easy to look at, too. Make that call, Gordy. We could have some laughs." She wiggled down the walkway and gave him a long farewell look before stepping into her apartment.

"*I'll bet we could*," Kraus thought. He tucked the card into his jacket pocket. Kraus drove north up to Florence. He was hungry for a medium rare cheeseburger with onion rings. He headed for the Yellow Basket, his favorite burger joint. He loved the way they made their onion rings. Thin slices with a light, crusty batter. The onions were crunchy and flakes of fried batter clung to the rings. He dipped them in catsup. They tasted sweet and salty all at the same time.

He left the booth carrying the rest of his milkshake. Two payphones hung on the wall near the restroom doors. Kraus dropped a nickel into the one furthest from the dining area. He dialed Manhattan Beach Motors.

"Manhattan Beach Motors," was the answer. It was Jill, Max's office girl. She was about thirty, blonde and dressed like she had come from a Vogue fashion shoot. Always perfectly made up. The Vanity Fair and Elle magazines on the office coffee table were hers. Kraus figured Max wanted her out front to symbolize the kind of gal you'd win over with a swell new car.

"Hi, Jill. Gordy. Have you heard from the gal who drove off with the Studebaker?"

"I haven't and I'm sure Max would have said something if he had. Why?"

"I almost had her yesterday. She slipped out of the net. Sometimes a close call makes a deadbeat get a conscience. They try to put things right."

"Not this time, I guess. You know, she took me in just like she did Max. She was such a solid gal. Nothing on the cheap. Elegant, you know? I'd have killed for her eyebrows. Marvelous hair style, perfect manicure. Her polish was a pale pink that Elizabeth Arden just put out. I asked her. So chic. Only a couple of the top salons are carrying it right now."

"Okay, Jill. Let me know if you guys hear from her," Kraus said. He started to hang up, then jammed the receiver back to his cheek. "Jill. Wait a second. Tell me some more about this nail polish and these salons."

SEVEN

The next call Kraus made was to Eugenio "Gino" Laveroni. Gino was a few years older than Kraus, but they'd been in the same LAPD Academy Class of '40. Kraus' rookie assignment sent him to "Shootin' Newton". Gino's was in the tamer Hollenbeck division. His old classmate's career continued that way. Easier assignments. Regular promotions.

Most cops guessed Gino had a sponsor of some sort in the top brass. A rabbi. Gino never let on. Few people cared because he worked hard and was a good cop. Kraus liked him and considered him a friend. Laveroni was a Detective Lieutenant now. He worked all Central divisions out of the new Police Administration Building.

Gino was at his desk and agreed to what Kraus asked. Kraus said he'd drop into the PAB later in the afternoon. The detective division would be close to emptied out after four. Gino always felt more comfortable giving Kraus a hand without an audience.

Kraus made one more call, then drove to his office. He thought about his next moves while he downed the rest of his milkshake. Melinda was at her desk, busy entering figures into a ledger book.

"Hey, Mel. Anything come in for me?"

"Nothing new and I've asked you not to call me that. 'Mel' sounds like the name of a bowling alley manager who swabs his ears out with a matchstick."

"Fine way to talk to the guy who's paying for your next beauty shop visit."

"Why would you do that? A Christmas fruitcake will be just fine. Heck, the cut-rate place I go to is probably cheaper than a fruitcake. I'd be that much ahead."

"You'll be going to a first-class shop and Manhattan Beach Motors will be paying for it." Kraus plopped his haunch on the edge of her desk. "I'll still get you the fruitcake."

"What gives?" She leaned forward. Interested.

"I've been tracking down this Studebaker gal. I'm getting a real feel for her."

Melinda squinted at Kraus. She opened a desk drawer and removed a tissue, then reached up and swabbed his earlobe with it. "You've gotten a feel of something, it looks like." She opened the tissue to show Kraus the smear of lipstick she'd wiped off.

"Enthusiastic witness. Had to let her do that to keep her talking."

"Uh, huh," Melinda muttered. Kraus thought she was like Jiminy Cricket, only not as nice. She threw the tissue in her waste bin like it had been used to mop up bird droppings from a windshield. "Tell me more about this beauty shop trip. Is it a stakeout?"

"More like a reconnaissance mission." Kraus told her what he'd learned from Jill at the car lot.

"Okay, you want me to keep going to get my hair and nails done until I spot her? That might take a while. You could probably buy Max a replacement car for what you'll spend."

"With all the grease I've been spreading around so far, I might already be in the red on this job. It's a matter of principle at this point." He didn't tell Melinda about the thug also looking for their quarry. Kraus hadn't even laid eyes on this gal, yet he had an irrational sense of concern for her. "No, handled right, you'll only need one visit."

"So, what's your plan?"

"Two salons in town carry the Elizabeth Arden line. Elizabeth Arden on Sunset, of course. Also, the May Company Beauty Salon right here on Wilshire."

"Oh, I've always wanted to get made up at Elizabeth Arden. Can I bring a girlfriend along?"

"You can do anything you want on your own dime. You won't be going to Elizabeth Arden. That joint's the longshot. I called Clancy and asked him to have his cabbie scouts watch that part of Sunset for the Studebaker."

"Why do you think May Company has better odds?"

"It's a crowded department store. She's slippery. Cagey. If something went south at Elizabeth Arden, she wouldn't have a lot of options for a clean getaway. At May Company, she could go up or down floors. Melt into any number of crowded departments. Blend in with the shoppers. Half a dozen ways to leave the building unseen. She'd feel more comfortable there."

"Makes sense. What am I supposed to do when I go in?"

"You're going to have to improvise a little. Hopefully there won't be a gigantic coincidence and she's there when you go in. We wouldn't be ready for her. She told Jill she had a manicure on September fifteenth. That was a Saturday. Busy day. Odds are she wasn't a walk-in. She's too organized for that. She had an appointment."

"Okay. How does that help?"

"You tell a story about shopping that day. Passing through the mezzanine level, you thought you saw an old sorority sister, neighbor, shared a locker with her in high school, whatever, in there getting a manicure. You were meeting a friend. Couldn't stop. Blah, blah."

"I get it. Ask her to page back to that day and see if it was my friend."

"Right. If it was our gal, it should be easy for you to find out if she has another appointment on the books. But here's where it gets tricky. This gal uses a lot of aliases. I have no clue which one she may have used to book the appointment. Brenda Reed, Connie Cooper, Margaret Woodward, Anna Bjorkquist. Could have been one of those or another I don't even know about."

"Sounds like I could paint myself in a corner really quick."

"If you're not careful. Don't even use a name at first. Describe her. Everyone I've talked to seems to feel she's unforgettable. Glossy raven hair down to her shoulders. Bangs. Creamy pale skin. Eyebrows a woman would kill for, evidently."

"You want to catch her or ask her out?"

"See what I mean? Those were descriptions I got. Every person is floored by her."

"When do I go?" Melinda asked. Excited.

"I'm going to the PAB right now. I may have more for us to go on. I think tomorrow is best. Call and make the reservation. Saturday before Thanksgiving. They may be busy but give it a try."

Kraus set out east on Wilshire. Traffic started to slow at MacArthur Park, but he knew the alternate Sixth Street route would be worse. He parked at the PAB at four-thirty. It was getting dark. Kraus doubted many detectives would be hanging around.

The building was new. A block or so from the old First Street location. Eight floors of glass windows. He thought it looked like the headquarters of an insurance company. Kraus looked around as he made his way to the third floor. Everything made the old building look medieval by comparison.

The Central detective's bullpen was all but empty. Laveroni was seated at his desk. He was thumbing through a stack of police bulletins.

His bald head was nut brown from the Los Angeles sunshine. Laveroni never wore a hat. One of the few men Kraus knew who looked better bald than he did with a full head of hair. He was shorter than average, but his broad shoulders and muscular torso made him look taller. Laveroni always had his sleeves rolled halfway up his forearms. His muscles strained the sleeve plackets to the point of splitting. Laveroni saw Kraus out of the corner of his eye.

"Gordy, how's tricks?"

"Same as always. Chasing down cheating spouses and deadbeats. Reminds me. Tell your wife she's late with my retainer."

"She told me once she wished I'd start cheating on her. Figured the guilt would make me do more work around the house."

"She's always been practical," Kraus laughed. "Business isn't bad. Crossed paths with Ollie yesterday."

"Yeah? God, the department isn't the same without that pirate," Laveroni guffawed. "How's he doing?"

"Didn't look at the top of his game. Still full of piss and vinegar, though. How's it going running the detectives in Central?"

"Got a two-story jail right behind that auditorium on the first floor. Never any room at the inn."

"Looks ritzy, though. Your repeaters probably don't gripe as much when you run them in."

"Those cells are better than my first apartment. Better grub, too." Laveroni riffled a thumb across the edge of the bulletin stack he was holding. "These just came up from the second floor. The records division here is greased lightning." He handed them to Kraus. "For a young gal, she's collected a lot of paper. I put them in chronological order for you."

"All bulletins?"

"Yeah. She's managed to keep out of the slam. At least under those names." Kraus looked at the first document. A one-page list of 1940 truancy reports in St. Paul, Minnesota. "Anna Karolina Bjorkquist" listed as a long-term truant. Hardly a surprise. Kraus had worked enough missing person cases to know that up until the war as many as two million kids were listed as incorrigible truants at any given time.

"I figured this was her real name. No one uses a tongue-twister like that as an alias. Too memorable." Kraus turned the paper over. Nothing. "No record of any Truancy Court appearances?"

"No," Laveroni said. "And what's more interesting, no missing person reports for her. None. Keep reading through 'em. Your gal may have been a truant, but she's been gettin' an education."

Kraus paged to the first of the police bulletins. A 1942 Tampa beef. Suspected as a steer and a stall for a pickpocket team. No charges filed.

The next was later in 1942. This one under the name of "Connie Cooper". Card bending in a Biloxi carpet joint. Released for lack of evidence.

He was jolted by the following one. A 1943 bulletin from Tulsa included a picture of her along with details on "Connie Cooper" working as the in-and-out in a small con. She definitely looked eighteen or so but was showing her form early. Confident eyes looked straight at the camera. Chin up. No shame. Charming rather than surly. Every hair in place. The bangs combed to perfection. The booking desk clerk probably fell in love with her.

Kraus turned to the next sheet. This one was from 1948. "Brenda Reed" this time. Newport, Kentucky. Dealing poker at a sawdust dive. Accused of chopping payouts. Released when the player who claimed she'd been palming chips withdrew his complaint. Politely asked to leave town.

The last sheet was for "Olivia Reed". Shill for a lonely hearts scam out of Phoenix in 1951. Dismissed for insufficient evidence. This bulletin also had a picture of her. She looked a little more mature, but no real signs of wear. Some felons were that way. The life agreed with them.

"Ran the application records for the operator's licenses, too." Laveroni handed over a sheet of paper.

Kraus looked it over. "All the aliases reference a South Dakota birthplace. Smart." South Dakota had only started requiring operator's licenses the previous year. The last state to mandate it. It was easier to buffalo your way through an application process in California if all you had to show for proof of identity was a South Dakota library card or utility bill receipt.

"No hooking beefs? Narcotics?" Kraus asked.

"None against the aliases you have. I wasn't surprised. She doesn't read like the type. Gets in with a gang and shows she's an earner as an accomplice. A near equal. Stays onboard until she sees she can't control 'em anymore. Dangerous game."

"Yeah. That's my take, too. She should have taken a trip out to Chino last year. Had lunch with Barbara Graham. Babs could have explained how well that worked out for her."

"Like hand-feeding rattlesnakes," Laveroni agreed.

"Yeah. I think it's backfiring on her right now. There's a mug looking for her. Everywhere I've been looking, he's been there ahead of me."

"Know why?"

"No. She's been running a phony landlord scheme lately. Rents a house, then plays like she's a rental agent for it. She had six or seven deposit receipts for three different properties. Some included first and last. I put the total at three thousand bucks and change. That's just from the receipts I saw."

"Busy girl," Laveroni said.

"Yeah. Too many moving parts to work solo. Probably started with a crew. But it looks like she's been cut from the herd. Maybe got cross-threaded with them somehow."

"Want me to ask Bunco about it?"

"Not just yet. I've got a good line on her. If I work this right, I can recover the car and deliver her to you. You can deal her over to Bunco. Build some credit in the favor bank."

"I like the way you think."

"You get. You give. I don't expect you to do me favors for nothing."

"Alright then," Laveroni said. "Gordy, we've got dupes on all those bulletins. You want the two with the photos?"

"Just the earliest one," Kraus showed Laveroni the two bulletins side-by-side. "See how she sucked in her cheeks when the later one was snapped. Made her face look thinner just as the shutter clicked."

"She's been learning, for sure."

"You bet. Learned enough to beat a stainless-steel Yale padlock with a five-tumbler brass plug."

"No shit? Your chain-up trick? She picked it?"

"In less than twenty minutes. Probably less than five. Didn't use a rake. The plug face was smooth as a bowling ball. Must have picked it one tumbler pin at a time. Turned the cylinder with a coated tension wrench."

"Must have a nice touch. High end tools. Real pro."

"Yeah. Well, she's got a real pro after her now. I'll keep you up to date."

"Hey, Gordy," Laveroni lowered his voice. "I've got solid dope that Sullivan on the DA's investigator team is pulling the pin early next year. Good job. City benefits. My contact thinks with your department and military record, you'd be their guy. Your patrolman years would count towards your retirement. Seventeen in and you're out with a full pension. Pretty sweet. Think about it."

Kraus smiled to himself. So, Gino's rabbi was in the District Attorney's office. Maybe the DA himself. The job was worth considering. "I will, Gino. Thanks for that. After I wrap this up I'll talk to you about it some more."

Laveroni smiled and slapped Kraus on the shoulder. "Good. Good. I'll remind you."

"I'll be in touch. Thanks, again, Gino." Kraus tucked the police bulletin with Anna Bjorkquist's photo into his jacket pocket. He hoped it would help him find her before anyone else did.

EIGHT

Morozov lifted the tumbler to his mouth and took another gulp of the fine vodka. The head of the Los Angeles Russian consulate could always count on Kuznetsov to have the best liquor.

Splendid vodka did not seem out of place in such an opulent mansion. It was built in the twenties on the grandest of scales. The Russians leased the property to house their new consulate in 1935. Twenty years later it was still mistaken for the estate of a film star.

The previous vice-counsel looked and dressed like the film star, Adolphe Menjou. Word got around that the consulate was Menjou's home. His name and the Glendower Avenue address often appeared in smeared ink on one of those cheap "Home of the Stars" broadsheets flogged to tourists on Sunset Boulevard. Once or twice a week, the consulate's security men had to run off a camera-wielding tourist straining for a glimpse of the screen star.

"So, Kuznetsov, tell me more about the goat herders, Pavel and Viktor. You say the tale is an allegory of Moscow politics?"

"Absolutely. As I was saying," Kuznetsov refilled his superior's glass with a heavy pour. "Pavel and Viktor were two village goat herders. About the same age. Same sized plots of land."

"Yes, I understand," Morozov said. He looked out Kuznetsov's office window as he took another pull from his glass. The Hollywood sign was visible to the northwest. The Hollywood Bowl was directly west of the office windows. Concerts could be heard some nights. Kuznetsov invited him to the office one evening a few years ago. Otto Klemperer was conducting Beethoven at the amphitheater. The sound was so clear, he felt as though he was front row center. A common consular agent would never rate such an office. The vice-counsel knew Kuznetsov was much more than a common foreign service worker.

"That's where their similarities ceased," Kuznetsov laughed, leaning into the story. "Viktor works hard. Tends to his goats. Keeps them sheltered and fed. Continually improves his holding with better fences, a deeper well and so on. His goat herd size increases over the years. Before long, Viktor had over one hundred goats. He does very well selling excess goat kids, meat, cheese and milk. Greater volume every year."

"An enterprising kulak," Morozov exclaimed.

"Oh, to be sure," Kuznetsov agreed. He fake-sipped his vodka. "Meanwhile, the other village goat herder, Pavel, proves to be the worst kind of wastrel."

"How so?" Morozov slugged down another mouthful of the fine elixir from Mariinsk. He held the highball glass up to the light. Exquisite vodka.

"Pavel is lazy, you see. Spends most of his time drinking in the village pothouse, playing dice, whoring, you name it."

"The worst kind of Western decadence," Morozov declared. Toeing the Party line even for a fable. "The very thing Premier Khrushchev warns against."

"Oh, the very worst," Kuznetsov said. "Pavel often sees Viktor in the village, selling his products, buying supplies, chatting and joking with the villagers. Respected."

"He earned his respect like any true Soviet," Morozov added.

Kuznetsov could see the vodka amplified the vice-counsel's political zeal.

"Yes, indeed. But Pavel was the very opposite of the 'Soviet Man'," Kuznetsov said. "Pavel's land is in a state of neglect. Parched and fallow. What goats remaining in the herd are skinny and barren."

"Disgraceful," Morozov said.

"One day, Pavel is on his land, drunk, looking at his hovel of a home with the greatest disdain. He sees an old bottle that must have settled at the edge of a creek bordering his holding. He kicks it in a fit of bitter rage. The bottle breaks. A plume of smoke rises from the glass shards."

"A genie," Morozov gasps.

"Yes, a genie," Kuznetsov confirms. "The genie says, 'Pavel, you've freed me from the bottle! It is your lucky day! In return for my freedom, I'll grant you your fondest wish! What is your greatest desire?'"

"Yes, what did he ask for," Morozov queried.

"Just let me tell you, comrade. Pavel looks around his bedraggled farm. His one room shack with the leaking roof. His pathetic livestock. He thinks for a minute, then says, 'Please kill all Viktor's goats!'"

Morozov was quiet for a beat, letting the punchline register through the alcohol. He released a constrained laugh, unsure how finding humor in the parable would be looked upon in the Kremlin. The vice-consul slapped his host on the shoulder. "Moscow politics, Kuznetsov? In this tale, are you Viktor or his goats?"

"Does it matter?" Kuznetsov asked. "Look around us," Kuznetsov swept his hand in an expansive arc to indicate the entire building and grounds of the Los Feliz hills compound. "Czars never had such lavish mansions. Sixteen-thousand square feet of opulence. Garden hedges rivaling those at Versailles. Mahogany and walnut wainscoting gleaming like teak. Swimming pool. Two theaters. Wine cellar. Gymnasium. Comrade Morozov, *you* live in separate quarters. A dacha fit for a senior Politburo!"

Morozov looked a little uncomfortable with the assessment. "Yes," he admitted. "We are foreign diplomats and live where we're billeted." His voice took on a raw, wary quality. An accused man pleading his innocence before a tribunal of hardliners.

"A reasonable defense for a loyal Party Man climbing the diplomatic ladder," Kuznetsov pointed his finger at the vice-counsel. "First Hollywood. Then London. Every posting more lavish than the last. Moscow surely understands. When in Rome. All that. Rising higher and higher. Retiring from the foreign service to a professorship at the Diplomatic Academy."

Morozov smiled at the rosy future Kuznetsov described. A future he himself had mapped out in his imagination more than once.

"That is," Kuznetsov continued, "unless you rise too high, too fast." The consular agent raised his hand, like a hot air balloon floating to the clouds. "Others - those like the jealous Pavel - may see you as having acquired a taste for the Western lifestyle. Then, an Icarus fate, perhaps." Kuznetsov let his hand descend below the level of the tabletop. Fingers fluttering like a wounded dove.

Kuznetsov took advantage of the misdirection. He dumped the vodka unnoticed into the magician's reservoir hidden under the desk. It was important that Morozov believed he was drinking too much. Inebriated.

Morozov became alarmed by the thought of such a fate. He tried not to let it show. "But little chance of that with a diplomat of your caliber, Comrade Morozov," Kuznetsov reassured.

"I appreciate your kind words and confidence, Comrade Kuznetsov."

"Not at all," Kuznetsov slurred his words a little. "But a low-level factotum such as myself? Now that is a different story." He reached into his desk drawer, withdrew a vodka bottle and poured himself another glass. Morozov placed the flat of his palm over his glass as Kuznetsov knew he would. No more for him.

"How so," Morozov asked. Relieved to have the subject matter shift away from him.

"I have been ordered back to Moscow," Kuznetsov waved a buff-colored envelope. "Yes. The directive came from the Washington embassy itself."

This news caught Morozov by surprise. Although he was in charge of the Los Angeles consulate, Kuznetsov reported directly to the KGB. He was merely posted out of the consulate. Morozov wasn't read-in on anything to do with Kuznetsov.

Rumor had it he was an engineer of some sort and carried out industrial espionage within the American industrial sectors. He came and went as he pleased. A car completely at this disposal. His entitlement was the source of more than a little envy and resentment in the consulate. Morozov included. The vice-counsel was shocked to learn Kuznetsov had fallen out of favor in Moscow. The Kremlin's mysterious, capricious nature could be unsettling.

"Morozov, in Moscow's eyes, I am tainted. Corrupted by the very culture I am sworn to vanquish. Only two possible fates await me in Moscow. Best case: banishment to one of the Siberian Sharashka outposts. I may have some value for the research activities conducted out there. Enough to warrant eighteen hour shifts and a thousand calories per day. I could live a year or more under those conditions."

Kuznetsov took a deep swallow from his glass. A glass that now held water. He remained silent for a moment, letting the bleakness of his prediction fully sink in with his guest. "Worst case: spirited off to Lubyanka Square. Granted a six-grain amnesty." He pointed a finger at his head, mimicking a gun. "Unmarked peasant's grave." He poured another glass of faux vodka.

"Well," Morozov said, rising from his chair. "I am sure you are mistaken, comrade," he lied. "Other matters require my attention.

Thank you for your hospitality." He left Kuznetsov's office with a feeling he'd escaped.

Kuznetsov removed another document from the desk drawer. He sipped some genuine vodka while reading it over a second time. Detailed material requisitions from Minsk. Great amounts of material.

The Minsk Radio Plant was the largest producer of civilian radio and television sets in the Soviet Union. Five thousand workers. Nested in the compound like a Russian doll was a smaller, secret military research and technology department. A small cluster of buildings sat on the northeast section of the property. A factory in a factory.

These buildings produced prototypes and small production runs. Radar equipment. Military-grade radios and cameras. Radar-jamming devices. The department had a bottomless need for all the electrical and electronic components required for this apparatus. But Russia did not have the technology or infrastructure to produce them.

That was Kuznetsov's job. His assignment was to quietly and anonymously procure American electronics for Russia's nascent technology industry in Minsk. A full-time job. Kuznetsov had a generous budget at his disposal. A budget undoubtedly much less than what RCA spent on office supplies in a year. But Russia didn't have RCA's overhead. It only had to buy the components like any other electronics manufacturer, then assemble finished products using stolen blueprints and schematic diagrams. Secrecy was of the utmost importance.

Kuznetsov had developed an effective supply chain network for this purpose. He often used guile and intimidation to pay for these products. He kept much of the hard currency for himself. Working alone made that easy. But does any Russian operative *really* work alone? Actions undetected? Had Moscow learned of his embezzlement? Probably not. Not yet.

He was just another functionary who had outlived his purpose. There were rumors the KGB had established another supply line in the San Francisco region. He had not exaggerated the dire fate awaiting him upon his return.

But Kuznetsov did not intend to return.

Feet up on the desk, he looked west out his office window. The Los Angeles landscape sprawled out below him. Forty years ago, Houdini had lived in a small bungalow only six miles away. Kuznetsov often imagined he could see the roof of the house. The showman practiced underwater stunts in the swimming pool of a mansion two doors away from the cottage.

He thought of Houdini's 1903 escape from a Siberian Transport Carette in Moscow. According to his family legend, Kuznetsov's grandfather, Igor Timofeyevich, managed Houdini's Moscow and St. Petersburg performances that year. It was this connection that inspired Kuznetsov to take up magic as a hobby.

Kuznetsov now needed to manage his own escape from a Russian death trap set for him. Not merely to disappear. He planned to orchestrate his own death. He looked at the summons from the embassy. Less than a month to complete the arrangements.

Now Kuznetsov had this meddling American to contend with. How had his activities been discovered by an American and not his KGB masters? Balabanov was searching for this extortionist. Not that the KGB strongman knew exactly why. All he knew was the American was a danger to a vital Soviet mission. If Balabanov came back empty-handed tomorrow, Kuznetsov would deal directly with the matter. He would kill the profiteer himself.

NINE

Kraus felt both relieved and anxious about the success of Melinda's May Company mission.

Melinda told Kraus she was taking along a girlfriend, Perrin, to May Company. Their appointment was on Saturday. A cold wave and manicure. She reasoned it would appear more natural. Two young women out for a Girl's Day pampering. More casual. An easier sell.

"Perrin," Kraus said. "What kind of name is that? Sounds like a co-ed at an East Coast girl's finishing school. Art history major who plays field hockey."

"You're not too far off," Melinda giggled. "Her parents are loaded. Her father has patents for some sort of quick-disconnect hardware used on movie sets. Cuts the time to strike a set in half. Every studio and stage set in the world uses them. The money has been rolling in for years and they're very nouveau riche. Even their children's names must be stylish. Perrin means 'rock' in French. Very posh. She's on the women's fencing team at USC. Gorgeous and dangerous."

"Sounds like a secretary I know."

"I wish. Half the boys in high school were madly in love with her, the other half scared to death of her. She's going to make a perfect teammate on this job."

Her instinct turned out to be right on target. Melinda was almost breathless with excitement over the phone. She described how it went to Kraus.

She and her friend, Perrin, walked into the May Company salon. The receptionist greeted them with a high-wattage smile. Their ruse began during the check-in process.

"Melinda," her friend said, "remember, you were going to ask about who you saw here in September."

"Oh, Perrin, thank you for reminding me." Melinda turned to the receptionist checking them in. "I walked by the salon on September fifteenth. I could have sworn I saw our best friend from high school getting a manicure right over there." Melinda waved a hand at the manicure stations. "I couldn't stop and say hello. My mother was waiting downstairs in women's shoes. She's impossible."

"Oh, I'm sorry you missed her," the receptionist gave her a knowing nod and protruded her lower lip in sympathy.

"You'd remember her for sure. Five-five. Beautiful brunette with perfect bangs. Sage green eyes. Porcelain skin like *crème fraîche.*" The French did the trick for the receptionist. Guaranteed legitimacy in every tony Miracle Mile salon and boutique.

Perrin broke in with an improvisation, "Oh, does she still have that dreamy complexion?" Enjoying her part. Making the role her own.

"Yes," Melinda flashed a mock envious scowl. "I hate her." All three girls joined in a conspiratorial chortle.

The receptionist bought the act. She knew exactly who Melinda was talking about. "That black hair is so lustrous," the receptionist gushed. "All the girls here are insanely jealous of how thick and glossy it is."

She flipped back to the appointment book's September section. Finding what she was looking for, she spun it around with a triumphant flourish. She pointed out the square for the fifteenth. Melinda saw that "Margaret Woodward" had indeed been there that day. The receptionist returned to the November pages. She showed the girls Margaret's upcoming one o'clock appointment on Wednesday, the twenty-eighth.

Now it was Thanksgiving Day. The appointment was in less than a week. Kraus was both encouraged and impatient. Every passing day meant more possible miles on the car. His bonus fading with every click of the odometer dial. Additionally, he believed Anna Bjorkquist was in greater danger every day she was in the wind. Six days is a long time when you're hiding out. He still had cab drivers scouting for her. Kraus would have to be patient. Hope for a break.

He made the drive into Redondo Beach following Western then west on Artesia. More and more childhood memories bubbled up the closer he got to the little beach town. He and Rudi built a home on a North Redondo lot they purchased three years before. They moved their mother into the new home the year before. This home was smaller, modern and more manageable for their widowed mother. It was three blocks from his childhood home. His mother could still visit all her friends and shop at all the same stores.

Herman, a cook at the Melody, made him a foil pan of roasted sausage-chestnut stuffing the day before. Kraus took it home and transferred it into one of his own bakeware bowls. He added some pepper and French's poultry seasoning. He could now make an honest claim he had prepared the dish. A feeble charade, but implying he knew his way around a kitchen was a survival tactic. Otherwise, his mother and sister would smother him with domestic tips and help.

The ceramic lid on the bowl rattled an indictment each time he drove over railroad tracks and potholes. He ignored the denouncements. Bachelors take desperate measures to preserve their independence. He turned north onto his mom's street and saw the first signs of Christmas in Redondo Beach. The community's lampposts were concrete and topped with acorn shaped glass tops. Some of Kraus' earliest Christmas memories centered on those streetlights. City workers had already clamped masts to the lamp poles. Fake holly wreaths hung from the masts. The wreaths had a festive look with red bows knotted into fat Regency Victorian Ascot ties. A scattering of dark red berries peeked out from the holly leaves.

To Kraus, the decorated lampposts always signaled Christmas was around the corner. Instant excitement. Novembers in California were always warm. Sometimes sunny. Despite all that, it felt like Christmas in Old London Town to Kraus. He pulled up in front of the house. His old Ford sat at the curb. Kraus had given it to his sister, Astrid, when he bought the Lincoln.

Astrid ran out to greet her oldest brother. Everyone called her "Austie". She still lived at home. Nineteen. Very cute and vivacious. "Hey, stranger!"

"Hey, yourself." Kraus handed her the bowl of stuffing. "Here, make yourself useful and take this in." Kraus made a show of examining his old Ford. "Austie, why don't you get your boyfriend to wash and polish your car? You're giving the neighborhood a bad name."

"It's cleaner than when you gave it to me. And he isn't my boyfriend anymore."

"He finally get glasses?"

"Ha, ha! You're so funny. No. He got another girl."

"More fish in the sea, little sister."

"Says the man coming to Thanksgiving alone."

"Too many girls to choose from," Kraus said. He continued inside the house. Even though his mother's house was new, it held the same aromas his childhood home always held.

His brother Rudi and his wife, Louise, were already there. They were sitting around the living room. Rudi was drinking a beer, and his mother was darting all over the house, doing this and that. Fussing over everything. She saw Austie bring the bakeware bowl into the kitchen.

"Gordon, there aren't any oysters in that stuffing, are there? All seafood is out for Louise." Louise was close to being full-term. His mother smothered her daughter-in-law and future first grandchild with fierce protectiveness.

"No, Ma. Just snips and snails and puppy dog tails."

"Oh, you are quite the *Witzbold*, aren't you?" His mother slapped him with a damp dish towel she was carrying. Sit down and talk to your brother and his wife. Austie and I have more work to do." Kraus looked around as he settled into one of the living room chairs. His mother's house was only a year or so old. The savory holiday aromas were the same, but the decor had changed. His parents' furniture at the old house was clunky, Weimar-era furniture. Imposing walnut chests and heavy chandeliers. In the new house, the decor was influenced by his sister's taste. Modern textured fabric in muted primary colors covered the low-slung sofa and chairs. The coffee table was a bi-level kidney-shaped affair. Two slabs of Formica, offset from one another, sitting atop spindly legs.

Several of his parent's artwork made the cut. Signed lithos by Bauhaus artists Joost Schmidt and Georg Muche mingled with his sister's acquisitions. A good copy of a Gunta Stolz weaving sandwiched between Plexiglas sheets. A Blaire Fields original watercolor of an L.A. River bridge. The combined effect was warm and tasteful. Kraus was impressed with his sister's sense of style. He had enlisted her help in decorating his place.

Both brothers inherited their father's company upon his passing. Kraus acted as a silent partner in the construction company. Rudi was the operating partner. He bought vacant lots all over the Los Angeles area and built homes on them. Some were kept as rentals. Others were sold. Kraus invested a sizable amount of capital into the firm. Rudi's wife was their receptionist and kept the company books. That would have to change once the baby was born.

The brothers chatted. Some lots they were considering buying, new equipment, troubles with subcontractors. The conversation drifted to a variety of subjects. Movies. News. Sports. Everyday topics.

Dinner was soon on the table. Everyone was having a great time. These family get-togethers were fun, but Kraus felt an unease he couldn't quite get into focus.

"I saw Lucy and Desi the other day," Kraus said matter-of-factly.

"You didn't," his mother cried out. She was a die-hard Lucy devotee. "What did her hair look like?"

"The color of a fresh-picked apricot at the Hollywood Ranch Market. Ollie was there, too," Kraus added.

"Oh, Ollie," his mother issued a wistful sigh. "I miss seeing that man. I wish he would visit more often. I still keep that Crosley radio in my bedroom. It works better than the Grundig we bought last year." She pointed to the table in the living room that the handsome radio box sat upon. "I'll never forget what that man did for us."

———— ◆ ————

Los Angeles - December 1941

It had been right before Christmas in 1941. Pearl Harbor had thrown the country into a world war. A decree came down from the government. All Los Angeles residents of Japanese, Italian and German heritage were to surrender their radios and cameras at the L.A. Central Jail. Kraus and Ollie had been discussing what their plans were for their day off the next day.

"I'm taking Culverson's spot on the bowling team tonight. He sprained his arm running down a purse-grabber yesterday. What're you up to?"

"My folks have to go to Central Jail tomorrow morning." He told Ollie about the decree requiring German, Japanese and Italian immigrants to surrender their radios and cameras. "They have to give up their Crosley tabletop and a Kodak folding camera my pops bought just before the Depression. One of those bellows type. My mom is really going to miss her shows. Rudi is going to manage things at Pop's building site and I'm taking them over to Central."

"Wops, too, you say? Jesus, good thing they're not callin' for stolen hubcaps. They'd have to put an addition on Central's property room," Ollie laughed. "Gordy, this whole thing will blow over quick." He tried to sound reassuring, but Kraus said little more during their shift.

He took his parents to the Central Jail the next morning. They joined a long line of Japanese, Italian and other German Angelenos. Boxes and bags of radios and cameras. The Japanese looked cowed. Embarrassed and ashamed by the horrible sneak attack their mother country launched a few weeks before. Apprehensive about what might be in store for them later.

The Italians were behaving as though it was some sort of party. Sharing some bizarre inside joke. They passed around calzones wrapped in newspaper and questionable beverages in dubious ceramic jugs.

Most Germans maintained a look of stoic acceptance. Resigned indignation simmering below the surface. The line inched along.

His parents were particularly insulted. They were very proud to be Americans. Loyal. Patriotic. He hated what his country was doing to them. They reached the counter of the property room and handed over their radio and camera in silence. The property clerk handed them a scribbled receipt. Simple as that. Very little was said on the way back. Kraus went directly to his apartment after dropping them at home. His emotions were a witch's brew of anger, resentment and helplessness.

A few hours later, Kraus' parents saw Ollie's new, dark plum DeSoto pull up to the curb in front of their home. He hopped out of the car, went around to the back and popped open the trunk. Ollie hoisted out their Crosley radio and carried it up the walkway. Kraus' parents watched from the front stoop.

"Officer McBride, *was ist los*," his father called. Refusing to erase all German from his vocabulary.

"Mr. Kraus, I liberated your radio and camera from Central. Go down and grab the Kodak."

Kraus' mother trotted down to the DeSoto and brought their camera out of the open trunk. She gave Ollie an incredulous look. "Won't this make trouble for you?"

"Nah," Ollie said as he walked through the front door Kraus' father held open for him. "Where does this go?" Kraus' father was almost speechless. He pointed at a living room side table. Ollie stepped cautiously to the table to avoid bowling over Kraus' little sister. She was jumping around his legs like an excited puppy.

"Those pogues downtown don't have the sand to say anything to me," Ollie continued. Kraus' mother came through the door. Husband and wife stood before Ollie. Kraus' mother held her little daughter against her legs. "Now, listen. Anyone comes here asking about you or your stuff, call me. Anyone. LAPD. Sheriff's Department. FBI. Anyone.

Call me anytime of the day or night. I'll be here in fifteen minutes, and they'll be gone five minutes later." Ollie said this with an air of finality.

The following day Ollie and Kraus were back on duty. Ollie was driving and telling Kraus about his bowling team debut. "I marked every frame, partner. Especially the seventh frame." The beer frame. Kraus laughed.

"I want to see you in one of those bowling shirts. A whole colony of silkworms would have to sacrifice their lives to fit you out with one."

"They're satin, not silk. I have one on order already."

Kraus switched to a serious tone, "My mom told me what you did yesterday."

"Oh, yeah," Ollie said. He kept his eyes straight ahead.

"Yeah, they wanted you to know how much they appreciated it."

"Yeah, they said so," Ollie said. "No big deal. I figured you didn't need the whole family piling into your living room every Wednesday listenin' to Dinah Shore on your sorry-ass Philco. Cramping what little action you have. Besides, we're partners, Gordy. That's how we do."

———◆———

"Gordy," Kraus' sister broke into his thoughts about that long ago day. "Do you want to take the rest of your stuffing home?" his sister asked.

"No, Austie. You guys keep it. It'll be good with leftover sandwiches and casseroles. Go ahead and put it in that Azore Green Kelvinator we got Mom for a housewarming gift."

"The *what* Kelvinator?" Austie asked.

"Azore Green. It's all the rage."

"If you say so. You're a nut. I'll transfer this into one of our bowls." His sister went into the kitchen. "I'm putting together a platter of leftovers for you to take home, Buster Brown. No telling what horrors are lying in wait in your own fridge," she called out.

"Hey, you guys, I'm going to sit out on the front porch for a while. I'll be back in a little while," Kraus said.

Kraus took a fresh bottle of beer from the fridge and went out to the front of the house. He plopped into one of the metal patio chairs on the front stoop. A teen girl was shaking out a tablecloth on the porch of the house across the street. Kraus watched her as she snapped and shook the fabric.

He thought of another teen girl from years ago. Her parents moving back to Germany. Eager to go back to the Fatherland. Leave the hardships of the Depression behind. Reap the rewards of economic vitality Germany's False Prophet was promising. Taking their teenage daughter with them.

Kraus remembers himself, a teen boy with a hopeless crush on the girl. He offered her a *bon voyage* gift before a taxi whisked them away to the train station. A book of poems. She looked at the book, then at Kraus. A love that hadn't even begun was melting away. "I'll never forget you," a forlorn Kraus whispered. The girl hugged Kraus and kissed his cheek. "I'll see you again," Kraus promised. A promise he kept.

"Goodness, the house can get so loud with all of you," his mother said. She'd slipped out onto the porch. She sat down in the chair next to her oldest son. "I see you've spotted the new family across the street."

"Sure did." Kraus motioned towards the house across the street. "When did they move in?"

"Late summer. They're from New Jersey. He came out for a job with Mattel. He's a toy designer. Promised me a lot of toy samples for the new grandbaby."

"No kidding? Where was he when I was eight?"

Kraus' mother tittered. He always liked her easy laugh. She nodded at the young girl folding the tablecloth across the street. "She looks a lot like Charlotte, doesn't she?" More serious now, "It's nice to be reminded of old friends while we make our way through life." She didn't pursue the subject, letting the silence finish making her point. Satisfied, she shifted gears.

"Gordon, don't you think you'd be better off going into business with Rudi full-time? I don't think all this *Sam Spaten* foolishness is making you happy."

"*Spaten?* Ma, it's 'Sam Spade'."

"Oh, God," his mother placed a palm against her cheek. "This language. All this time here and I'm still making those mistakes."

"I knew what you meant."

"You know," ignoring the reassurance, "in Germany, when I was a young girl at gymnasium, I chose English as my Modern Language subject."

Kraus smiled. Gymnasium. He remembered how he and his siblings would always giggle at that word. The concept of their mother attending all her classes in a school gym.

"I was so frustrated with that damn language," she continued. One day, I asked my teacher what the past tense for 'cut' was. He said, 'cut'. I screamed and threw that damned book across the room. I wanted to cut his throat - past or present tense - no matter. I said that I didn't care if I ever heard another word in English." She laughed. "And here I am," she patted her lap with the palms of her hands. "In America almost forty years. There is a lesson in there somewhere, Gordon."

"There is, huh? Am I supposed to figure it out, or are you simply going to tell me?"

"You're the 'Sam Spaten'," she said.

TEN

Union Station porters will tell you the time between New Year's Day and Valentine's Day is the high season for The Reno Cure. Disenchanted wives heading to the Divorce Capital of the World. The holiday season paves the way for this exodus.

The demands of family intensify during the holidays. Wayward husbands find it difficult to carve out time for both their girlfriends and family. Excuses and subterfuge that work in April don't hold water in December. Suspicions flare. Limits reached.

That's when Kraus gets a call. He had two jobs over the long weekend. Divorce work. Two serious attorneys with decent retainers. He took photos of a husband enjoying an intimate shopping spree with his secretary. Other snapshots of another husband with his girlfriend enjoying brunch at her parents' house. Great family photos. Wrong family.

Kraus sprinkled some chopped green onions and shredded cheese into the sausage scramble frying on the stove. He thought about the week ahead while whisking the onions into the egg mixture. The divorce work brought in some solid fees. Anna Bjorkquist would be at the May Company salon on Wednesday. He was confident he'd recover the Studebaker while she was getting her nails done. Should be a pretty good payday. It was going to be a good week.

The radio was on while he fixed his breakfast. He chuckled at the new KNX morning host's antics. Kraus liked listening to this new guy, Bob Crane. He was funny as hell and interviewed interesting celebrities. It was a fun show. Sound effects like slide whistles and squealing brakes dropped in with spot-on timing.

This morning Crane was clowning with Soupy Sales. A cash register sound effect played each time Soupy plugged his radio or television show. It got to the point that Soupy couldn't help laughing out loud as Crane razzed him.

Soupy began talking about his Detroit nighttime radio show. How it focused on the city's jazz scene. Crane confessed he was a decent jazz drummer. Said he often sat in with bands playing local Los Angeles jazz venues like the Tiffany Club. Soupy sounded impressed and they went on to swap stories about Buddy Rich.

Kraus kept his eye on the toaster. It was a pre-war model. It either produced lukewarm bread or something resembling slates of burnt charcoal. This time the slices sprang out with a very light tan. Good enough. He was slathering butter across the toast when the phone rang.

"Yeah," Kraus answered, wiping butter grease from his hands.

"Gordy, sorry to ring you so early." It was Laveroni.

"I was up. I've got a full day."

"Yeah, well, it might get fuller."

"What's up?"

"I'm over in the Arts District. A junk salvage guy called in a DB about four this morning. I drew the squawk."

"Okay. How do I fit in?"

"I'm calling from a bodega down the road. Told the guys I needed some smokes." Laveroni lowered his voice, "Gordy, you and I were just talkin' about the vic."

A pint of ice cold adrenaline washed across Kraus' stomach lining. Did someone find Anna Bjorkquist before he could reel her in? "Who is it?"

"Not on the phone. I could get my ass in a sling just for makin' this call. Just get down here while I still have control of the crime scene."

"Where exactly are you?" Laveroni gave Kraus his location. An alley off Mateo west of the Sixth Street Viaduct Bridge. "I'll be there in about twenty." He piled some scrambled eggs between his toast slices, wrapped the mess in a napkin and ran out the door.

Kraus suspected the advance work on the new Santa Monica freeway would slow traffic on Venice Boulevard. He took Pico east and followed a series of back streets until he dropped into the Arts District off Seventh, parking in the lot of a tavern at Industrial and Mateo. Walked the rest of the way. Best his car wasn't spotted near the scene for Laveroni's sake.

The Arts District consisted of fifty square city blocks jammed between Skid Row and the LA River. The name came from the dozens of little artist studios that popped up there at the turn of the century. Citrus groves thrived nearby in those days. The fruit went to market from the Santa Fe Freight Depot on Third Street. Artists in the district designed the artwork for the labels pasted on the packing crates.

The nickname stuck. But the Bohemian quaintness surrendered to the invasion of small factory buildings in the late 1930's. By the war, both the citrus groves and art studios had disappeared. Then, post-war industrial consolidation gobbled up the independent manufacturers. The likes of Lockheed, Hughes and Northrop raided the Arts District industrial base. The neighborhood lifeblood siphoned away. Empty buildings, deserted storefronts and closed cafes bobbed around in the wake.

The desolate side streets and alleyways were now home to bums and dope pushers. The area became a popular dumping ground. Discarded furniture, broken appliances and stolen cars stripped to the wheel drums. The occasional corpse.

Kraus took the sidewalk north towards Jesse Street. It was fifteen minutes or so from sunrise. Most of the streetlights in the district were out. He made his way through the gloom. The windows of the factory building to his right were soaped with fat, grayish swirls. A sewer rat scrabbled out of a doorway recess and hugged the brick wall to evade Kraus' footsteps.

Graffiti adorned a building wall across the street. A crude drawing of a cartoonish bulldog. The past label artists had nothing to worry about. The mutt wore a spiked collar and stood on its hind legs. Fangs bared. A spray-painted caption read: "Dog Town". The Dog Town gang ran out of Main Street at the LA River. Several miles to the north. The first Los Angeles County dog pound was built there. Hence the gang's name. They were a rob and rape crew. This was Little Avenues gang territory. Latino car theft teams. Some home burglary. A territory dispute? Did Anna Bjorkquist stumble into a dustup while trying to unload the Studebaker? Kraus sped up his pace.

He saw a faint nimbus of light playing out of the alley mouth up ahead. The alley ran the block from Mateo to Imperial. Rear access lane for the buildings it bisected. Kraus turned into the alley. A narrow service road branched off at a right angle from the alley. He could see the little bypath bent back towards Imperial. The light spilling out at the curve was much stronger. He jogged the last few yards to the bend.

There was a squad car and a detective's plain wrap sedan parked side by side. Headlights on. The road was narrow. A tight squeeze. A uniform leaned against the front quarter panel of the patrol car. Laveroni stood a few feet in front of vehicles. His bald head reflected the headlight beams. Kraus approached, arms raised at chest level, showing empty palms. The patrolman and Laveroni heard the crunch of his steps as he got closer. The uniform started to reach for his service weapon. Laveroni waved his hand. "It's okay, Dunbar. I know him."

The cop shrugged and leaned back against his prowl car. "Gordy, you made good time," Laveroni checked his watch.

"Monday after Thanksgiving weekend. Still early. What've you got?" Kraus had to shuffle sideways to get by Laveroni's city car. He cleared the side and faced forward.

The headlights threw shafts of yellowish light across a blanket contoured into a vague human shape. A body. Kraus couldn't tell who or even what gender. A covered DB was deceptive. Difficult to guess size or gender. The low trajectory of four light beams threw crazy shadow patterns across the blanket surface. Kraus looked at Laveroni.

"Gordy, that's Ollie."

Kraus could feel the blood drain from his face. Only his police training and combat experience kept him from throwing up. He looked at the covered body, then back at Laveroni.

"Go ahead. We've been here since four-thirty. Got all the preliminaries."

Kraus kneeled beside the covered body of his best friend. The shape beneath looked too small to be Ollie McBride. Dying does that to a person, Kraus thought. Shrinks them. People's spirits gave them the size. Ollie was a bigger than life character. A lot for Death to deflate.

He drew back the blanket, completely uncovering the body. Ollie was facedown. Body curled a little. Arms down at his sides. Bareheaded. Dark gray suit with scuffed up black rubber soled Oxfords. A neat bullet hole into the left occipital bone behind his jaw. Clean contact shot. Thin powder burn ring encircled the entry wound. Kraus gently turned his head. Ollie's face was frozen in an expression of disdain. He recognized the set of the jaw. Ollie's "*oh yeah, you're going to be sorry*" look. He looked back up at Laveroni, who was lighting a cigarette. "No exit wound."

"Right. You can see from the powder mark it was small caliber. Looks to be a .32. We'll know more after the post. The blowback knocked his hat over there." Laveroni pointed the tip of his cigarette in the direction of the dark shadows a few feet beyond the body.

Kraus heaved Ollie's body up onto his side. Laveroni stepped up closer. "Looks like you pulled out his shirt here." Kraus pointed to a place where Ollie's shirt hung out over his belt. The first of many indignities for any victim's corpse. "Any color?"

"Not then. I pulled that up when I got to the scene. Gave it the once-over with my flashlight. No signs of lividity. I make time of death around two this morning. We'll find out more later today."

"Look. Didn't even have his holster strap unsnapped," Kraus said.

"Saw that. I figure he knew who he was meeting," Laveroni said. "Didn't expect any trouble. Angle of entry tells me the shooter was a head shorter than Ollie. Otherwise, getting the muzzle under like that would have been awkward. I'm thinkin' a right-handed shooter."

The sky was lighter to the east. Scattered gray clouds hung overhead. The thin dawn turned their easternmost edges into ribbons of whites, pinks, and yellows. Wispy tendrils of the clouds clutched at the retreating indigo night sky. Dark clouds trying to escape the false promise of the new day.

Kraus looked around the alleyway. No apartments. One weak gooseneck barn lamp ten yards away. "Cloudy last night. Hardly any moon. Dark place to meet."

"Yeah. Not much chance it was a random thing," Laveroni said. "His billfold ended up over there." Laveroni pointed towards the squad car. "No ID. Eleven bucks. See that DeSoto of his anywhere when you drove in?"

"No. I wasn't looking for it, but there weren't many cars around and that bull-headed tank stands out," Kraus said.

"Yeah. I've got Dunbar's partner walkin' around lookin' for it. If he drove his own car here, it's a good bet the shooter drove away in it. Might still have it."

"No keys. Still has his Waltham Premier on," Kraus lifted Ollie's left arm and pointed at Ollie's wristwatch. Rectangular shape. Pre-war Art Deco style. Pricey timepiece. Kraus' father had given it to Ollie for Christmas in '41. Appreciation for his help after Pearl Harbor. "Wedding band, too."

"Yeah. Gun, watch, ring and cash all left behind. No mugging. But if not, why look at the wallet?"

Kraus reached inside Ollie's left pants leg and pulled out a slim leather bifold case. The kind white-shoe lawyers use to hold their embossed calling cards. "He kept his operator's license and some cash stashed here when he worked a case. Didn't want to get made if he was undercover."

"Thanks. We would have found it later, but that confirms a key element."

"I know. Whoever shot Ollie didn't know who he was. At least who he really was. "Why did it matter who Ollie was once he was dead?" Kraus wondered. Ollie's words came back to him. "*Gordy, I've glommed onto something. It'll get me off the schneid.*" He looked down at Ollie's lifeless body.

"*You're off the schneid for good now, buddy.*" Kraus thought. He decided to hold back some of his questions for the time being.

Kraus still had Ollie's body propped up on his side. A loop of rope swung from under Ollie's suit coat. About ten inches and knotted at one end in a complicated Gordian's Knot. The knotted end thunked on the pavement.

"Hell's Bells, I thought that was a rat for a second," Laveroni said. "He still carried that bosun's cosh?"

Kraus unhooked it from the special loop Ollie had sewn on the inner flap of all his jackets. "It's called a Monkey Fist. Ollie learned to tie these when he was a kid working on the docks. The knot is filled with lead shot."

"I've never seen this up close," Laveroni bent at the knees and hefted the end of the knotted rope. "Heavy as sin."

"Yeah. Ollie hated using a sap. Said it forced you to work in too close. He was good with this. Always carried it. Don't think it means he expected trouble."

Kraus thought back to the first time he saw the Monkey Fist.

ELEVEN

Los Angeles - July 1941

It was July in 1941. Kraus and Ollie were on the night rotation. Ollie was riding shotgun on this shift. A hot night. The kind that drove Newton residents onto their front stoops until the early morning hours. No breeze. The car was stifling even with windows rolled down and short-sleeve uniform blouses. It was about eleven and they were making their second pass through the north part of their beat.

"Gordy, swing up Naomi for a few blocks. The skipper's taking heat from downtown about girls on the stroll drifting too close to Venice Boulevard. The mayor's office doesn't like the tourists eyeballing that shit."

"Gotcha." Kraus turned north on Naomi heading for 20th. A lot of the girls had taken to working near a cluster of retail stores there. At night the alleys and deep-set rear loading doors were like a rabbit warren for them and their johns.

There was a lamppost and mailbox near the corner. In the dim light they saw a negro male and white woman standing nose-to-nose, shouting at each other. The negro lashed a sharp backhand across the woman's right cheek. She screeched like a banshee.

"Ollie, put your spot on those clowns over there."

Ollie was already twisting the interior handle that controlled the spotlight. He focused the bright beam on the duo.

"Gordy, slow down. It's fuckin' Butterbeans. Goddamned coons. Why do they have to pull these monkeyshines out on the street?"

They would have driven on by if it had been a colored hooker. But this was a negro pimp slapping a white woman. Even though she was clearly one of his whores, that scene might result in a concerned citizen calling the station. If there was such a person in Newton. "Ollie, lower the spot a little. Just behind the mailbox," Kraus said.

"Great," Ollie spat out. The light fell on a middle-aged man sprawled at the foot of the mailbox. His arms wrapped around his head. "Hump a nun. That's a citizen! Now we *have* to stop. Let's go, partner. We're going to be drowning in paperwork tonight."

Kraus and Ollie clambered out of their prowl car and approached the scuffle. The hooker had a hand pressed against the cheek the pimp slapped. Blood dripped from her nose. The pimp looked both cops up and down. He wore a wide-lapel gray suit coat and pants with carrot orange pinstripes. A matching felt Homburg hat sat on his head. The brim was trimmed with carrot orange colored ribbon. An orange feather peeked out from the black silk hat band ribbon. Dapper look.

Butterbeans' long-forgotten given name was Daryl. Newton denizens christened him with the "Butterbeans" moniker because he sounded like the funny man in the "Butterbeans and Susie" comedy team. Any of his whores who called him Butterbeans risked a fierce whipping from the fan belt he kept hanging next to his bed. He saw it as a term of disrespect from his stable. Thought it made him sound like a field nigger. He allowed them to call him "BB". That sounded respectable. Like a bank president.

The pimp squared around to face Ollie and Kraus as they approached. His hackles were up. Nostrils flared as his chest heaved with ragged breaths.

"This ain't none of yo' business. You harness bulls just push on by," Butterbeans demanded. "My girl here," he drove an elbow back to nudge his whore, "was gettin' sassy. I was tellin' her what time it was, when this white bread muthafucka comes 'round the corner. Tries to take her away without payin'."

"So, you knocked him senseless, Bean?" Ollie said as he and Kraus slowed their approach. They fanned out a little. Easier to flank Butterbeans if he bolted.

"Damn fuckin' straight, I did," Butterbeans said. "Do it again, too. Bitch is my property."

Ollie squatted down next to the fallen man. "You okay, pal?"

The man looked up at Ollie from under the forearm hooked around his head. "Uh, yeah, officer," he stammered. "Can I get up now?"

"Sure. Let's take a look at you," Ollie said.

The man wobbled to his feet and held his face up to Ollie. A little boy submitting to a mother's scrutiny before bed. A purple mouse had already puffed to life under the man's right eye. A minor split had opened at the bottom of his right earlobe.

Butterbeans bounced up and down on the balls of his feet. A boy needing to go to the bathroom. "Little prick's okay. Shee-it. Man has a little bump? That coulda come from anything."

Ollie ignored the pimp. "Sir, do you want to press charges?"

"No, no," the man's eyes widened. "I don't want this gentleman to get in trouble. I should have minded my own business."

"Gentleman," Ollie said in an amused tone. He looked at Kraus. They both raised their eyebrows and rolled their eyes.

"That's okay, sir. We understand," Ollie said. "Ol' Butterbeans here is still in trouble, though. My partner and I saw him assault the woman you were trying to assist. It would be a help if you could do your civic duty and bear witness as well, but we've seen enough."

"Waaaahhhhh," Butterbeans moaned in protest. "Now this here ain't right, officers. Don't jam me up this way."

Ollie looked over at Butterbeans, who was still bouncing on his toes. "Now it's 'officers', huh? Keep up that tone of respect. The jailer will use Vaseline for the cavity search." Ollie looked at Kraus and jerked his head towards Butterbeans. "Partner, put the bracelets on our friend."

"Fuck y'all," Butterbean shouted.

He stutter-stepped to his right, faking a run across the street. Kraus leaned in that direction to intercept him. Butterbean pivoted and sprinted towards the mouth of an alley ten yards or so in the opposite direction.

"Gordy, go get him. I'm cuffing her to the mailbox, and I'll be right behind you."

Kraus was already in hot pursuit behind Butterbeans. The pimp had ducked down the alley. Kraus could hear the slap of his shoes on the pavement. The alley was a dead-end and it cut into the back of buildings too high to jump.

He slowed down where the path took a blind turn to the right. Kraus didn't hear Butterbeans' running footsteps any longer. No sounds of heavy breathing. *Shit*, Kraus thought, "*Butterbeans must have found a spot to scale a wall and get away.*"

There were two weak light sconces in the alley. They cast more shadows than light. Low visibility. Kraus edged forward, thinking about the "Tarzan" movie he and a date saw the previous week. In one scene, a veteran big game hunter tells his safari party it was "always the dead rhinoceros that kills you." Was Butterbeans playing possum? Lying in the weeds ready to pounce? He started to put a hand on his service revolver.

In that instant, Butterbeans burst out of a dark corner and rushed Kraus. The pimp was taller than Kraus and had thirty pounds on him. He stuck out his left arm like a fullback stiff arming a linebacker. Making like he was trying to get past Kraus. Clearly a distraction ploy.

Kraus saw that the pimp also clutched a gravity knife in his right hand. He held the knife in a hammer grip close to his chest. Kraus anticipated the intended move would be to bring the blade in on him in a roundhouse sweep. A kidney shot.

Too late to draw his revolver, Kraus knew. There was a grizzled old hand-to-hand instructor at the academy. He'd fought with the Canadians during the Great War. The leader of a trench raider squad. He drilled into the recruits the principle of "The Widow's Circle". A recruit positioned in the center of a chalked circle. Nine-foot radius. Once a bad guy crosses inside that circle, there's no time to haul a twenty-four-ounce Colt Police Special from your holster and get off a stopping shot before the bad guy is on top of you. Butterbeans was about seven feet from Kraus. Way inside the "Widow's Circle".

Kraus saw his only chance was to deliver a hard shot to Butterbean's jaw. Back him off. Then he may be able to put some distance between him and the pimp. Pull his own weapon. Kraus braced himself, planning to put his full weight into the punch. The pimp was three steps away.

Butterbeans collapsed with the dumb resignation of a grain sack tumbling off a farmer's tailgate.

Ollie stood behind the prone, unconscious pimp. "Hot damn," Ollie shouted. "Ted Williams couldn't have swung that any better." Ollie was twirling his weighted rope. He called it a "Monkey Fist". Told Kraus he learned to tie it when he was a Port of Los Angeles stevedore. A loop of hemp rope with an elaborate knot tied with a triple-strand weave pattern at one end. The knot encased a pound or so of lead weight.

Butterbeans' Homburg had flown off from Ollie's blow and rolled to where Kraus stood. Kraus picked it up. The rope tore a jagged rip through the orange-trimmed pencil curl brim. He showed Ollie.

"Shit, when he gets out of stir, he'll have to head over to Club Bali for a new one," Ollie said. Club Bali was a notorious homosexual haunt on Sunset Boulevard. The waiters wore sarongs and many of the male patrons dressed in very flamboyant garb. "Where the Devil you think that orange feather came from?"

"They have something called 'orange duck' on the menu at Trader Vic's. Maybe the leftover feathers from those ducks," Kraus deadpanned.

Ollie shifted gears into training officer mode. He pointed at Butterbeans' motionless body. Blood had seeped into the pimp's processed hair, looking like a gory case of cradle cap. "What the fuck were you plannin' to do, partner? That wasn't some Speedry marker in his mitt." The cadets at the academy practiced knife defense with laundry markers. "Beans has been swinging a shiv that way since he was a youngblood at Whittier State Reformatory. Shanked his way up to barracks kingpin."

Ollie knelt, closed up the knife and tucked it away. He dipped into the pimp's pockets. He worked out a rubber, some crumpled KOOL menthol cigarette pack coupons and a flash roll. "Saves the coupons? Who would have guessed? The fuck he's saving them for? One of those fancy silver plated flasks?" He flipped through the flash roll. "Hundred sixty-five bucks! Shit! Just how many whores does Bean have on the string?"

The flash roll disappeared into Ollie's pocket. Kraus cleared his throat.

"Street tax, partner. These pricks would lose respect for us if we didn't collect the tariff." There was a voice at the mouth of the alley.

"McBride, you back there?" It was Lindsey, one of the other Newton cops on night patrol.

"Yeah, Lindsey. Get on back here, will you?"

Ollie told Lindsey to keep an eye on Butterbeans. He and Kraus would go back to the street, call in an ambulance and question the whore.

"Gordy, go to the squad and radio in for an ambulance. We'll send Beans over to County, then head back to the station and finish our report."

Kraus radioed for an ambulance, then reported their position and status to the precinct dispatcher. When he returned to the corner, Ollie was jawboning with Lindsey's patrol partner and a Herald Examiner stringer who happened on the scene. Ollie was finishing a joke.

".... there's skid marks in front of the dog," Ollie roared out a laugh.

All three men broke into raucous laughter. "Good one," the newspaper stringer said. "Ollie, I'm heading out. No real news here."

"Okay. See you later, Stan." Ollie turned to Lindsey's patrol partner. "Go back there and stand with your partner. If Beans wakes up, he'll be meaner than a bear with a toothache."

"Partner," Ollie said, "Let's go talk to the lady."

Kraus looked over. The man was gone. No surprise. Butterbeans' whore was still shackled to the mailbox. She gave the cuffs a defiant rattle and glared at the two policemen.

"Is BB gonna be okay?" The hooker asked as she rubbed the deep handcuff impression circling her wrist.

"Yeah," Ollie said while tucking the cuffs back into his belt pouch. "We've got him on assault and attempted murder of a police officer. Probably get talked down to reckless endangerment. Possession of an illegal weapon. Don't plan on seeing him for a month or so."

"Okay," the woman whimpered.

"Just what happened here? Why did Beans slap you like that?" Kraus asked.

"BB, he was just excited because when he came over to check trap, I told him I was expectin'. He got all emotional 'cause it'll be his first white baby."

"How do you know it's his?" Ollie asked.

"You think if this was some goddamned trick baby I wouldn't know? It's his for sure, awright. BB spunks like one of them fat icing bags they use to pump cream into the maple Long Johns down at Randy's. I'm moppin' his jizz up off my thighs for an hour after he dumps a hot batch in me. Oh, it's his ... a woman knows." The streetwalker nodded with sober conviction.

"Yeah," Ollie said, working his tongue against the inside of his cheek while rolling his eyes. "Okay. Nadene still his bottom bitch?"

"For now," she answered. The smug assurance of an office ladder-climber who knows a staff shakeup is on the horizon.

"Well, Nadene ain't gonna be too thrilled about the blessed event. Last one of Bean's girls set to poot out his previous first white baby got a free prenatal exam from Doctor Nadene. She used a sailmaker's awl."

"That bitch better think twice before she puts her hands on me and BB's baby!" She laid a protective palm on her belly. Even in the thin light you could see her nails were bitten down to the quick. Backs of her hands were spotted with red bug bites. "He'll give her the business end of that car belt of his, then turn her sorry ass out on North Main to work the Chink trade."

They let the hooker go and walked back to their squad car.

"You weren't thinking of giving her an early baby shower gift with some of your street tax, were you?" Kraus joked.

"Are you fuckin' kidding me?" Ollie grumbled. "After listenin' to all her crap, I should have run that dumbass hosebag in along with Butterbeans. Stupid tramp put me off maple bars for the rest of my life!"

<hr />

Arts District, Los Angeles - November 1956

Kraus' thoughts snapped back to the present. He rolled the Monkey Fist knot in his palm. "Gino, when Ollie's stuff gets released, get this over to me instead of Violet, okay?"

Laveroni trained his light on the bunched knot. "It doesn't look as though it came into play tonight, Gordy. Faint signs of dried blood but looks years old. It's a mythical relic in the department. Like a nail from the True Cross. It gets into Property, we'll never see it again." Laveroni looked over his shoulder. "Take it now before anyone sees it's here."

"Great. Thanks." Kraus gathered in the rope "That's probably Butterbeans' blood on the knot."

"Butterbeans?" Laveroni snorted. "Christ, I haven't thought about that puke in years. You know, before you got back from Europe, we found him in one of those SRO dumps on Jefferson he used for his girls. Sitting spraddle-legged on the floor. Back against the wall. An Eckherts ice pick rammed handle-deep in his eye."

"Dead?" Kraus asked.

"Dead as mutton. Pinned to the wall as neat as an undertaker's tie tack. I always liked that stable boss of his for it. Nadene. Never could pin it on her. She disappeared before we could stick her with it."

Despite the grim scene, they both guffawed at Laveroni's graveyard humor.

TWELVE

Kraus wanted to be the one to notify Ollie's wife, Violet. In person. He didn't make the offer, though. The spouse is always the first suspect in a murder. The entry wound angle indicated a killer shorter than Ollie. Small caliber kill shots are hard. The shooter was handy with a gun. Violet was shorter than Ollie and a cop's wife knows her way around handguns. Laveroni needed to be the one to notify Violet. Clock her reaction.

It was only ten o'clock in the morning, but Kraus didn't feel like working. Didn't feel like being around other people. He took an Oly stubby out of the fridge and started drinking it right out of the bottle. The cold beer tasted good. Washed some of the alley stink out of his mouth.

He took an album out of his stack, wiggled the record out of its sleeve and held it at an angle towards the window. Checking for dust. The lid on his stereo console stood open. He centered the album on the spindle and watched it shimmy down onto the turntable. Bill Evans' jazz piano rendition of "*Danny Boy*" flooded out of the speakers. Kraus flopped down on his couch, back propped up against the arm of the sofa. He closed his eyes and sipped his beer.

He had treated Ollie like shit at Desilu the week before. Ollie didn't deserve that. How many more loved ones will he let down? He rolled the cold beer bottle back and forth across his forehead. Flattening memories like grainy snapshots to be mounted in a scrapbook. Bill Evans moved into his interpretation of "*Lover Man, Oh Where Can You Be*?"

Thoughts about Charlotte danced on the musical notes. He reached into the built-in drawer beneath his coffee tabletop. He kept one thing in the drawer. An old, tattered book of poetry. The grime of brick dust coated the cover. Audrey Wurdemann Auslander's "*Bright Ambush*". Kraus flipped through the pages of poems. His Puppy Love inscription on the flyleaf. Charlotte's notes of desperation in her neat D'Nealian style on the margins. That's all that he saw.

Berlin - July 1946

"Sergeant Stuber," Kraus said, "why is the driver taking us through Wedding? Why aren't we going through Mitte to Prenzlauer Berg?"

"Captain," Stuber said, "we want to stay out of Ivan's backyard as long as possible, that's why"

Kraus was in a hurry to get to the Prenzlauer Berg location. Stuber instructed their driver to head west through the Tiergarten. North through Wedding in the French sector. Then turn back east to cross into the Russian zone. This route would add an hour to the drive. "Why do we want to do that?"

"Captain," Stuber said, in his professorial tone, "Abe Lincoln was walking down the street one day. He was holding both sons, one under each arm. They were squalling up a storm. A passerby asked Abe what the problem was. He said, 'The same thing that's wrong with the world. I have three apples in my pocket, and they both want two.'"

"Without the homespun parable, Sergeant." Sergeant Frankie Stuber was a born and bred Chicagoan. All Prairie Staters are never at a loss for an Honest Abe allegory.

"Captain, we only have so much swag with us. We cross into the Russkie sector too soon, we'll end up going through five different checkpoints. Have to bribe our way through each one. We'll be stripped clean before we get there. We need to keep our powder dry."

Kraus looked over at Stuber. The Germans referred to Americans as "Russians with pressed pants". He wondered what the Germans made of Stuber. His pants hadn't held a crease since the day the quartermaster issued them to him.

The sergeant was slovenly, short, overweight and observed military etiquette only when it suited his purposes. Kraus often wondered how Stuber got into the Constabulary Forces. While he clearly exceeded the intelligence requirements, the force also imposed height and weight standards his sergeant didn't measure up to. Still, Stuber was the best non-com Kraus had ever seen. That forgave a lot of the sins he committed against military customs. The jeep hit a pothole. Stuber moaned and put a palm to his head.

"Jesus wept. When are the labor details going to get to these? The tank traps at Fort Benning infantry school weren't that bad!"

"Long night?" Kraus asked.

"Stayed up with the boys listening to Armed Forces Radio. My Pale Hose took on the Yankees. Got their heads handed to 'em. Bill Bevens beat 'em for the second time in less than a week. For Chrissake, Bevens and Spud Chadwick will probably combine for over forty wins this season! How can my Sox get any traction in the standings against that?"

"Yanks look strong this season," Kraus agreed.

"Yep," Stuber shook his head. "Had some good groceries, though." 'Groceries' was Stuber's Chicagospeak for food and liquor. "Jeeze, my mouth feels like the bottom of a birdcage." He spat over the side of the jeep. "Criminy," the sergeant exclaimed, "it'll be good to get out of Berlin's center for a while. The last bombing raid was over a year ago and you can still smell the burnt hair."

Kraus smiled to himself. Nothing was too macabre about post-war Berlin to be doubted. But he knew this popular belief was wrong.

Berlin was a cesspool of disgusting smells. Human feces. Rotting canvas. Dead dogs and cats decomposed too far for even the most desperate Berliner to eat. Dried dung of every species burned for heat. Any remaining street trees had long ago been chopped to the ground, the wood used for cooking and heating. Now even the stumps were being dug up. The parts of the stumps below ground had the rancid odor of wet rot. When they were pulled out of the ground, the stench hung in the air for blocks.

People expressed the most disgust for what was mistaken as the smell of burned human hair. The bombing raids pulverized brick, mortar, plaster, concrete and cement sheeting into particles as fine as coal dust. Truck traffic, demolition work, and joyless breezes kicked up this powdery mixture into the air. It got into everything. Watches, canteens, radios, weapons. Motor pool mechanics kept busy replacing jeep air filters daily. Oil bath air filters, normally effective for thousands of driving miles. The Berlin miasma clogged them in a day.

Kraus was a builder's son. He knew most of Berlin's pre-war structures used mineral wool batting for insulation. The batting was an efficient insulation material. The added benefit was that it could withstand 1000 degrees centigrade.

A team of army scientists had been inserted into the 2nd Armored Division while it made its way across Europe. They were on the lookout for any Nazi installations involved in secret weapon research and development. During a poker game one night, a scientist told Kraus every bombing raid on Berlin unleashed the power of 300 lightning strikes. He explained a single lightning bolt heated the surrounding air up to about 50,000 degrees Fahrenheit. 300 lightning strikes transformed Berlin into Hell's boiler room.

More than hot enough to incinerate mineral wool batting. The burned wool smelled a lot like scorched hair.

Nothing about post-war Berlin was too morbid to be disbelieved. "Stuber, are you sure about the location?"

"Nazis were obsessed with keeping records, Captain. She registered for bread rations using the Prenzlauer Berg address in January of '45. I got this from my guy with connections in Zone Directories. If she's still there, we'll get her. If she's moved, we'll find her."

"This guy reliable?" Kraus asked.

"He owes me a favor," Stuber explained. He didn't elaborate. Kraus knew better than to pry. "His info is rock solid. He was a green badge guy. Now he's one of the main black-market players."

Kraus nodded his head. A green badge on a camp inmate signified professional criminal status. They survived in the camps like cockroaches will survive a tenement fire. Now they had connections in every part of the ruptured Berlin infrastructure. In a world where two cigarettes could feed a German family for a week, a top black marketeer had powerful clout.

They soon crossed the Wedding border. "Phillips," Stuber shouted at the driver, "be careful here. The French are taking apart German factories and shipping them back to Paris as quick as they can work a monkey wrench. Trucks barrel down the roads like bootlegger convoys. Won't stop for signals or other vehicles. They'd run us over like an empty C-ration carton."

It was true, Kraus thought. The French were determined to recover what they believed the Nazis had stolen from them. They passed by a group of German bystanders watching a team of French workmen. The workers were feverishly loading a dismantled printing press into the back of a military truck. The Germans looked over to the Constabulary jeep and immediately dropped their eyes to the ground.

The French in the ZOF treated the Germans with almost comic disdain. French soldiers in uniforms designed in the style of a Gilbert and Sullivan opera would bark orders at the Germans to walk in the roads, not the sidewalks. The sidewalks were for the French. There were eighteen overzealous French occupiers to pour abuse on every thousand Germans living in the ZOF. Only three nearly indifferent Americans per thousand in the American Zone.

The Germans hated the French occupiers. But they were deathly afraid of the American Police Constabulary. They called them *Blitz Polizeitruppe*. Lightning Police. For good reason. The U.S. Police Constabulary was the most professional, powerful law enforcement force in occupied Berlin. Likely in all of Europe. They controlled border points, investigated and broke up black market rings, tracked down escaped high-ranking Nazi prisoners and worked hand-in-glove with the nascent German Civil Police.

Kraus had been part of the 2nd Armored Division security force. An REMF who spent most of his time as a glorified traffic cop. Keeping order in the rear-guard supply lines supporting the frontline troops pushing their way towards Berlin. He saw sporadic combat action from straggling Nazi soldiers. True Believers trying to get their last licks in. Die for *der Fuhrer*. Kraus helped more than a dozen fulfill their dream.

The Division reached Berlin in the late spring but were instructed to hold up outside the city. They bivouacked in the Grunewald Forest. Conquering troops held up at the Rubicon. Then orders came to cross into Berlin on July 4th.

Many soldiers were eager to go home. Kraus had a different agenda. His sole purpose in joining the Army was to ultimately get to Berlin. But what next? Soviets had been ordered out of the American Zone, but continued to create problems with looting, raping, kidnapping, etc. No German police force. The U.S. Army copied its success maintaining control in the Philippines after the Spanish-American War. A mechanized security force to be known as the Constabulary was created.

Kraus saw his chance. He was a decorated military policeman. A former LAPD police officer. Spoke German with native fluency. He was the model of exactly what the new Constabulary wanted. His application was accepted on the spot. In less than two weeks he was at Sonthofen training academy in Southern Germany. It was quickly dubbed the "Constabulary West Point". His MP and LAPD experience exempted him from the first phase of the five-week training, which consisted of policing tactics, searching suspects, arrests and handcuffing. He was promoted to a Captain's rank and concentrated his training in the areas of military intelligence, self-defense and political relations.

Kraus was kept at Sonthofen Castle, the Constabulary HQ, to conduct training programs for the second wave of volunteers. He helped with the creation of the "Trooper's Handbook", the Holy Bible of Constabulary policy and procedures. Kraus was finally assigned back to Berlin in February of 1946 where he took command over a trio of patrol units. His topkick, Sergeant Stuber, was an encyclopedia of underground Berlin. Kraus told him who he was looking for and in less than sixty days, Stuber had a solid lead.

They crossed from Wedding into Prenzlauer Berg. Four candy bars got them through the Russian checkpoint. It was like Dorothy walking out of the tornado wreckage right into Munchkinville. The streets were clear of rubble and swept clean. Streetcars were in operation. Storefronts that had remained reasonably intact were open for business. The Nazis had removed all street signs ahead of the invasion, but the Russians had placed sawhorses with street names in German and Russian at most intersections.

"You haven't had much dealing with the Ivans, Captain," Stuber said. A statement, not a question.

"No, I've been involved in getting the Constabulary organized in the American Zone," Kraus said.

"I've had my share. I see these monkeys at the Tiergarten black market bazaar all the time. The enlisted men are as dumb as slaughterhouse mallets. Just as deadly. They don't know shit about any kind of machine made since the spinning wheel. I saw one jackass unscrew a light bulb from its socket and wrap it up in an old rag. He thought the light was held inside the bulb and he was going to send it home."

"Bullshit," their driver said from the driver's seat.

"Go to the Tiergarten on a Saturday and see for yourself", Stuber said. "They're queer for watches. Don't know from Adam how they work. That you have to wind one. When one runs down, they buy or steal another one. One Supply Battalion guy told me a Russkie could send a watch home and his family could trade it for a cow."

Stuber checked his notes and gave their driver directions to the building they were searching for. The smaller streets off the main roads were still being cleared. Slopes of smashed bricks and debris leaned against many building walls. Bombing raid fallout. The Germans packed dirt in the pockets of the rubble, then planted potatoes in the dirt. Protected them like Klondike gold claims. Kraus saw a woman in tattered clothes scrabbling up a scree of detritus with a tin of muddy rainwater and a wooden slat with dog shit on it. Going to water and fertilize her plants.

After a few wrong turns, they reached the spot they estimated the address to be. It was one of the buildings with the outer wall completely obliterated from bomb blasts, leaving the inner walls and floors intact. Desperate Germans, fearing the dire consequences of being classified as a "DP", or "displaced person", continued to live in their open-air flats. Kraus had heard Berliners call such buildings "*Sperling's-Lust*", meaning "Sparrows' Delight". A careless resident might unexpectedly take flight into thin air.

"Jesus," Kraus hissed, "do you think she still lives here with all the damage?"

"My guy said the address was a basement unit," Stuber said. He pointed to a recessed doorway next to a pile of shattered framework and bricks. "I'll bet that's it."

"Phillips, you stay here," Kraus said to the private, "Stuber and I will go in. Stay sharp."

"Yes, sir," his driver said.

The street was quiet with no Germans or Russians in sight. No glass in the street level hopper window. Stuber squatted down and peered through the bare rectangular frame. He shook his head.

Kraus and Stuber approached the basement apartment door. It was closed and the door frame looked in good shape. Three small steps led down to the small landing in front of the doorway. There were several little piles of very stubby cigarette butts in the corners of the alcove. Kraus knocked. No answer. He looked at Stuber. His sergeant shrugged. Kraus tried the doorknob. It turned. They both unsnapped their holster flaps while Kraus pushed the door open.

"Captain, let me go first. Wait for a second while I get in there, then you follow if there's no trouble."

Stuber walked through the door. "Charlotte Kahler," he called out, "it's American military police. You here?" No answer. No movement.

Stuber kept facing the interior but motioned behind him for Kraus to follow him in. Kraus stepped into the basement flat. Even with the door open, there was very little natural light. Gloomy with the musty smell of a turned garden bed. He called out, "Charlotte, it's Gordon. Gordy Kraus from Redondo Beach." Nothing.

The stillness was broken by a noise outside. The sound of a worn-out washing machine. A Russian GAZ-64 jeep. They heard the rattling wheeze of its four-cylinders struggling up the street. It braked with a metallic screech near the building. Stuber stuck his head out the basement door.

"Phillips, don't get out of the jeep. Unsling your M50, select full-auto and charge it. Don't shoot unless the Russkies point their weapons at you. If they do, spray them. I'll be out before you're empty."

Two Russian soldiers walked into the flat. They looked like two men familiar with the room pretending as though they'd never been there before. The leader was a tall, thin soldier with the chevron sleeve patch of a major. The red piping of Soviet transport troops on his cap. The second Russian had first lieutenant insignias. Probably the major's aide.

"What business do you have here?" the Russian major asked.

"American Police Constabulary. I'm Captain Kraus. I'm here to extract a German resident."

"Captain," the Russian major said in passable English. "Your papers, please," the major requested. He held out his arm to beckon Kraus. His palm faced the floor, and he moved his fingers in an open-and-close motion. Like sprinkling dirt onto a casket top.

The Soviet officer glanced over the credentials. "Captain, you're in the Soviet sector. You have no authority here."

"Is that right, Stuber?" Kraus turned to his sergeant. A mock naive tone.

"Captain, it's hard to tell. There are no street signs, and the Berlin registry shows this district clearly in the French zone."

"Well, major," Kraus said, turning to the Russian officer. "This may be an area still in dispute from the conference in Potsdam a few days ago. We'll just find who we're looking for and get going."

"Just who are you seeking, Captain?"

Kraus didn't see the harm in offering a name. "Charlotte. Charlotte Kahler." The Russian lieutenant snickered.

"Want to tell me what's so funny, lieutenant?" Kraus asked.

"He doesn't speak English," the Russian major interjected. "We've had this Charlotte Kahler under surveillance. She's suspected of spying on the Soviet liberation forces."

Stuber and Kraus looked at one another. "Captain, you stay right here. I'm going to look around."

Without taking his eyes from the two Soviets, Kraus nodded his approval. He heard the scratchy sound of floor debris being nudged by his sergeant. An alcove in the corner had been curtained off with a rough sheet of muslin. Kraus saw it when they entered and took it to be a makeshift closet partition. The fabric was polka-dotted by round, discolored rings about the diameter of a soup can. Hardened by sediment. A rainwater strainer. The Russians showed up before he could investigate. They looked antsy. Nervous. Defiant. Sounds of Stuber kicking the wall were followed by frenzied rat squeaks.

"Captain," Stuber said, returning from the alcove area. "I'll keep an eye on these two. You better take a look in that corner."

Kraus felt a cold flush of dread move across his chest and into his face. He stepped around to the corner niche. Hanging by a dirty, frayed piece of sash cord was what looked like a dry mop head atop a large piece of desiccated pork belly.

It took Kraus a moment to process what he was seeing. It was Charlotte's wizened body hanging from a rusty iron rigging hook. Dressed in rags. She must have been there for five or six days. Her feet had initially ballooned from the collection of blood and body fluids. Now they looked like salt cod hanging from a wooden drying rack to cure. A sticky-looking, yellowish stain had collected on the floor. Tatters of withered tissue dangled like buckskin fringe from the soles. Shredded by hungry rats that danced on their hind legs to gnaw on the shriveled flesh.

"Captain, you okay," Stuber called. He stole a quick glance at Kraus. His captain was as white as the poor thing he'd found hanging in that recess.

Kraus couldn't look at Charlotte's corpse a second longer. He ran his eyes over the walls. Dusty bricks. Many had fallen away from bomb concussions to expose ancient, splintered timber framework. One brick poked out from the others around it. The dried mortar on the brick edges didn't match the adjacent pattern. It was apparent the brick was pushed in upside down and stuck out a bit because it wasn't an exact fit. Kraus pried the brick out of its socket. This produced a harsh, deep scraping noise. A sarcophagus lid being pushed aside.

The cavity was above eye-level. Kraus gingerly felt around inside. He withdrew the only thing hidden inside. A dusty, well-worn book of poems by Audrey Wurdemann Auslander. Stuck between the middle pages was Charlotte's birth certificate and American passport.

"You found some reading material, Captain," the Russian major asked. Smug. Mocking.

"I found evidence of a crime, Major," Kraus said. "There are little mounds of cigarette butts on the steps outside. They've been collecting there for a few weeks."

"Untidy," the Soviet major deadpanned.

Kraus ignored him and continued. "No German would drop those butts or leave them there. They're called *Bessen*. Brooms. Four ounces of them stuffed in an old pepper tin can buy two weeks of food. Only people with an endless supply of cigarettes would leave them. People like Soviet soldiers taking bribes from black marketeers. Or strong-arming them."

"Inventive speculation, Captain. What are you suggesting?" the Russian asked.

"I'm not suggesting anything. You and your men have been coming here regularly. Taking turns raping her. One at a time. Waiting your turns out on those steps, passing the time with a smoke. She couldn't endure that any longer. About five days ago, she hung herself over there."

"Say this was true, Captain," the Russian smiled, "the raping, I mean. The body is self-evident. Just a German whore. They're all whores. She probably killed herself out of shame for what her people have done to Russia. All of Europe."

Kraus waved the passport. "She was an American citizen!"

"No wonder she was so good," the Soviet major sniggered. The arrogance of a conqueror.

Kraus didn't say a word. He let the book drop to the floor and took two aggressive strides towards the Russian major. The Russian stopped laughing. His contemptuous expression melted into panic. He fumbled with his holster flap. The Soviet lieutenant began to raise his rifle barrel.

Faster than many would have given him credit for, Stuber stepped into the Russian aide. He grabbed the rifle barrel with his left hand while delivering a savage chop into the soldier's throat with the flat of his right hand. The soldier tumbled back against the wall and slid to the floor. Stuber flipped the rifle across the rough floorboards. It skittered on the gritty floor and spun one rotation, coming to rest when the barrel thumped against the opposite wall. Stuber wedged himself between Kraus and the frightened Russian major.

"Captain, let's not," Stuber grunted. Kraus struggled to get to the Soviet, but Stuber stood firm. The sergeant had pinned the Russian officer against the wall with his stomach. He deftly plucked the Russian's Tokarev from its holster and slipped it into his own jacket pocket.

"Stuber, I'm ordering ..."

"Captain," Stuber said through gritted teeth. "I get it. But the orange ribbon on that bastard," Stuber threw a hand at the fallen

Russian aide. He was still sprawled against the wall, sputtering and gasping for breath. "That's the Order of Glory. Those don't come in Cracker Jack boxes. He's come through some real action. Those two in the jeep out there are probably his boys. All three are likely to be tough customers."

Kraus tried to reach around Stuber's stout back to get at the Russian major. Stuber pushed back with his butt, never taking his face away from the brass neck button of the Soviet's uniform tunic.

"Captain! Enough!" Stuber growled. "Look, I'm sure we can finish these two assholes," the Russian major blanched, "and get by the ones up there. But not without raising a ruckus that might get out of hand. Some other Red patrol shows up. You, me and Phillips? We're up Shit Creek in a chicken wire canoe."

Stuber sensed Kraus was calming down a little. Listening more than flailing. "Captain, you want to even this up, that's fine by me. I hate all these fuckers. We'll settle this. But not here. Not now."

Satisfied that his Captain had pulled himself together, Stuber stepped away from the petrified Russian officer. He walked over to the prone lieutenant. He bent towards him and grabbed the aide's chin, holding it up to make eye contact. Thick streams of saliva rolled from the corners of the aide's mouth. His chest was heaving, mouth open, exposing the dull stainless steel of Russian dental work. Barely able to breathe properly.

"Ivan, don't even think about making something of this right now." Stuber reached down with his left hand and removed the lieutenant's sidearm. "Trust me, chum, when we meet next time, I'll show you *exactly* how we do business on the North Side!" The lieutenant may not have understood English, but he got the meaning. He dropped his eyes, still clutching at his bruised throat.

"Captain," Stuber said while he unloaded the firearms he'd taken from the Russians, "it's time to get going." The sergeant shoved the magazines and bullet rounds into the little chamber the book had been hidden in, then stuffed the brick back in the opening as far as he could push it.

"I'm not leaving her here," Kraus said. Flat voice. Shock still evident.

"Me neither. Pick up the book and watch these two," Stuber said. He removed his jacket as he moved towards the alcove. He faced Charlotte's decayed body. "Come on, darlin'. We're gettin' you out of here," he whispered. Stuber reappeared with a small bundle wrapped in his field jacket over his shoulder. He held his own .45 automatic in his right hand. "Okay, let's move."

Stuber walked out and up to street level first, followed by Kraus. The temperature had risen and felt even hotter after a few minutes in the relative cool of the basement. The sky was cloudy, but they still squinted from the glare. The two Russian privates looked concerned that their comrades weren't out yet. Murmuring to one another.

"Phillips," Stuber barked, "wing a couple of chocolate bars to those two. They like to sip tea through the pieces." He looked towards the Soviets. "They'll be right out. They're collecting evidence," the sergeant yelled. The chocolate bars and reassuring tone calmed the privates down.

Stuber had already placed Charlotte's body gently in the rear storage locker behind the back seats. Phillips was behind the wheel and Kraus stumbled into the back seat. The jeep took off with a lurch while Stuber kept an eye on the Russians. Ready to return fire if they got frisky.

They had driven about a mile or so. The wind seemed to revive Kraus a little. "How did you know the two Russian officers wouldn't call out to their enlisted guys? Start a firefight."

"Are you shittin' me," Stuber laughed. "Admit they had their hats handed to them by a mutt sergeant looks like me?" He waved at himself. "Taken down by Bud Abbott? In the Red Army, that's the kind of fuck-up that'll get you marched out and plugged before evening chow. Cap, when I was a kid in Chicago, all the Russkies packed themselves into West Town. Pest Town, we called it. Peasants, Hebes, White Russians, every kind of Slav, all mixed together. They're all the same. None of 'em will sleep easy at night unless they've fucked over one of their own that day. Believe me, those two brushed themselves off, went up to the street and told their pals they gave us Yankees our walkin' papers."

Kraus saw the logic in it. He nodded.

"Let me know when you want to go after those pricks. I've got both their names. I'll round up two guys I know from the rackets, and we'll set things straight."

A week or so later, Kraus was still in a mild state of shock. He was sitting on his cot with his back propped against the wall, leafing through Charlotte's poetry book. He barely saw the verses. His focus was on the diary-like notes Charlotte had penned in the margins.

Kraus had been right. The Soviets had been raping her almost daily for weeks. She had been brave when it was clear the first wave of

Russian invaders were a few days away from Berlin. Like every other woman in the city, she had heard of the massive, remorseless raping the Soviet troops perpetrated. Tears welled in his eyes as he read her musing about where she might find a pair of eyeglasses. She had heard stories that the Russians were disinclined to rape women who wore glasses.

She was lucky for the first few weeks of the occupation. She managed to live quietly in her basement flat. Undetected. Then the crew found her. Probably betrayed by an unseen neighbor on the block. Traded for a cigarette or can of beans. Charlotte seemed optimistic at first. But as the weeks wore on, her words took on the flat tenor of someone resigned to death. Her last few notes speculated about the strength of the cord she was planning on using to hang herself with.

Without warning, a small orange patch plopped between the pages of the book on his lap. He started and looked up into the serious eyes of his sergeant.

"Cap, where you been the past two days?"

"Hanover. Regional conference. Updating training procedures. G-2. That sort of thing. Got back this afternoon on the Silk-Stocking Express." That was what the Americans called the Interzone train that ran from Osnabruck to Berlin. It carried all the supplies destined for the various PX depots. Kraus fingered the orange fabric. "What's this?"

"Order of Glory patch. Ivan won't need it where I sent him."

"What happened?"

"Captain," Stuber waved some documents. "I got my orders back home. I'm leavin' tomorrow, and I didn't know when I'd see you." Stuber lowered his voice. "I had to take care of those fuckers without you."

"How?" Kraus whispered.

"Me and a couple of boys from Ordnance Maintenance. Guys I knew workin' the Chicago rackets." Stuber said. "We snuck across into the Russian Zone. Brought along a *fraulein* we know who hates 'em worse than we do. She lured those idiots into a wooded area. Went down harder than Buddy Baer hit by Joe Louis. Got the lieutenant and both of the enlisted guys who were in the GAZ when we were there. Made it look like Gladow's gang playing catch-up for some black-market shit."

Werner Gladow had risen early through the underbelly of postwar Berlin's black market to become the "Al Capone of the Alexanderplatz". He was behind many of the brazen executions committed across all Berlin sectors. Kraus had little doubt Stuber could stage a convincing mob hit.

Kraus started to scold Stuber, but his sergeant held up a silencing palm.

"Hold up, Cap. I didn't know where you were. I'm leaving in ten hours, and I had no doubt those assholes were gearing up for a *Nacht and Nebel* snatch job on you. The Russkies don't like loose ends. I had to take care of them before I left. For your sake. And the girl's."

Kraus let his shoulders sag in capitulation. "Stuber, you're right." He waggled the strip of orange cloth. "Thank you for this. I owe you."

"Cap, you ever get to the Windy City, look me up. I won't be hard to find. Go to Uptown and tell anyone who you are and you're lookin' for Frankie Stuber. I'll hear about it same day and come find you."

Los Angeles - November 1956

Kraus never looked Stuber up but had heard he'd survived Chicago's post-war mob infighting. Story was that he owned one of Chicago's biggest garbage collection outfits.

He placed the Russian badge between the pages of the book and gently closed it. He put the book back in its drawer and slid it shut.

Charlotte, his father, too many squad mates to name, now Ollie. Kraus. He'd lost so many people in his life. Helpless to do anything to prevent their deaths. He thought about a line in one of the book's poems. *"A poultice on the shoulder of despair"*. A wet mound of herbs on a painful wound. A vague feeling of relief. Was that all that justice amounted to? It didn't seem like much, but if he could find Ollie's killer, he'd take it.

THIRTEEN

Kraus didn't want to waste any more time. He decided to pursue some leads while Laveroni handled the official notification and questioned Ollie's wife. Widow.

He made his way over to Sixth and Towne. Tucked back from the main buildings was a tavern called "the Bean Slot". Owned and run by his friend, Dave Hayashigawa.

The outside of the saloon was just a simple sign and an oak door with an opaque diamond-shaped bubble glass window. A row of transom windows with the same bubble glass panes were set near the roof line. Light got through, but offered no clear view of the inside.

Kraus pushed the tavern door open. The saloon had a boxcar layout. Long, twelve-stool bar on one side. Three naugahyde upholstered booths on the other side. The rear of the bar featured a tavern style shuffleboard table and a couple of round tables with chairs. Three old guys from the neighborhood played pinochle and nursed bottles of beer. A faded "No Wagering" placard hung unnoticed over the table from the back wall.

The tavern wall space featured memorabilia from Hayashigawa's time in the 442nd Infantry Regiment. The "Purple Heart Battalion". All Japanese-American soldiers. There was a 442nd Regimental Combat Team flag on the wall. A ribbon scroll below the insignia badge held the unit's motto, "Go For Broke". Wall-mounted frames displayed Hayashigawa's Bronze Star and Purple Heart medals.

A framed picture of his mother working on a sewing machine hung next to his medals. She was sewing a camouflage net at the Santa Anita racetrack WCCP internment camp. The relocation site for the whole family. Hayashigawa wasn't there for them. Not every family had Ollie to protect them from war hysteria.

Hayashigawa's war record and family history were only part of the story. Kraus and Ollie made his acquaintance fifteen years earlier by the slimmest of chances. This part wasn't memorialized on the walls of the Bean Slot.

———◆———

Newton and Hollenbeck LAPD Divisions, Los Angeles - August 1941

Kraus and Ollie were in the middle of their night shift when they received a radio call. Orders to leave Newton and drive across the L.A. River deep into the Hollenbeck Division. A hostage situation during a botched liquor store holdup.

"Just what we need, Gordy. A friggin' '*Merrie Melodies*' call."

"*Merrie Melodies*" was Ollie's new nickname for any call to leave Newton for another LAPD patrol district. Earlier in the year, each LAPD patrol car was outfitted with a cumbersome curtain roller contraption which held rolled up maps of each LAPD district. If a squad car was called to an unfamiliar beat to assist, the cops need only pull down the appropriate map from the roller.

A new Bugs Bunny cartoon had been showing in most theaters earlier in the year. Bugs reclined on top of the Warner Brothers shield during the opening credits. "It's the damnedest funniest thing, Gordy," Ollie told Kraus the day after he saw the cartoon. "Bugs looks out into the audience, sees he's being watched and pulls down the '*Merrie Melodies*' title screen like a window shade."

"Hit the lights and howler, Gordy. That was a run code."

Kraus took their patrol car onto Washington, crossing the river into the Hollenbeck division. The liquor store was on the far side of the district. He headed towards the district's eastern panhandle. Before they got five miles, the radio broadcast a Code 4. No further units needed. Return to regular patrol.

"Fuck me," Ollie groaned, "we'll probably miss dinner because of this. Gordy, turn into this neighborhood, I've got a shortcut back to Newton."

"Where that French Normandy house is?" Kraus asked.

"Where that house with the stucco silo is. Turn there! That reminds me. Quit putting that kind of shit in our reports."

"What shit?" Kraus asked.

"That fairy shit. 'We approached the Bawdy House gas station on foot.'"

"Bawdy House?" Kraus asked. "Oh. That's *Bauhaus*, Ollie. My dad's a builder. I grew up referring to buildings by their architectural style."

"Well, the skipper is already givin' me the stink eye after readin' your reports. Before you know it, the downtown brass will mark us as a couple of queers."

"Come on," Kraus laughed in protest.

"You laugh. We're about one 'Go-Karts' reference away from being yanked off the streets and finding ourselves workin' on a Vice grope-and-rope detail as urinal decoys at every jack shack in town."

"That's '*Beaux-Arts*', but fine," Kraus huffed.

"Good. From now on, just the color and type of building," Ollie flicked up his thick fingers, one by one, "house, storefront, gas station, diner. No homo stuff."

Kraus slowed down almost to a stop as they reached a sharp left turn on the residential street they were on.

"Partner, turn left at this elbow. It'll take us back to Soto. We can shoot down to Olympic and back to Newton for chow."

There was a station wagon backed into the driveway of the house on the left, right at the crook of the turn. "That Craftsman," Kraus began. Ollie shot him a look. "That woodsy looking house is right at the blind turn. No way would someone take the chance of maneuvering a back-up into that driveway."

Kraus pointed his flashlight at the station wagon's front license plate. "That front bumper only takes the top two bolts for the license plate. See the shiny circles around the bottom two bolt holes? That plate came off a different bumper."

"Christ on a hobby horse, Gordy. Let's not start snooping around another cop's beat. Let's go grab some tacos."

"Ollie, bolts have been holding that plate through all four holes. Pretty sure the plates have come off another car. Recently, too. Dollars to donuts that front plate was the rear plate of another car."

"You're just doin' this 'cause I bawled you out about the reports."

"No," Kraus backed the squad car up a few houses down and parked, "I'm doin' this 'cause we're cops."

"Hungry cops," Ollie grumbled as he piled out of the car.

It didn't take Kraus and Ollie long to find the side door of the house jimmied open. A pile of loot stacked up near the connecting door to the garage. A young Jap wedged into a dining area armoire.

The burglar gave up quietly enough. His name was Dave Hayashigawa. He worked at Hoegee Sporting Goods on Main Street near Little Tokyo. When he started talking, Hayashigawa wouldn't stop. The burglar had started out assembling tents in Hoegee's backroom factory. He got noticed. His outgoing personality and Japanese language skills landed him a front counter position. The Japanese are big fishermen. They would tell the garrulous Hayashigawa all about their upcoming family camping trip while he sold them two-dollar angling licenses. Hayashigawa had a steady supply of names, addresses and the dates homeowners would be out-of-town.

By his reckoning, Hayashigawa had pulled off a dozen of these burglaries so far. Tonight was number thirteen. Superstition was a central part of Japanese culture. Hayashigawa said he felt the thirteenth job was not going to end well. Not that he anticipated capture. Maybe cheap loot. He said that he doubted the LAPD would ever look hard at a burglary report from a Jap family. He didn't fear stakeouts or the likelihood of increased patrols in Jap neighborhoods. Kraus and Ollie nodded at one another. Hayashigawa's cynicism was well-founded. His M.O. was as easy to follow as the Yellow Brick Road. But no detective was going to put even that much thought into investigating these break-ins.

<hr>——◆——<hr>

Los Angeles - June 1947

Six years had passed since the night in the Hollenbeck Division. Kraus had been home from Europe for a few months when he got a call from Ollie.

"Gordy, you'll never guess what I got in the mail here at the station."

"Knowing you, it's a grand jury subpoena."

"Funny. It's an invitation for you and me to go to a tavern grand opening near Fifth Street."

"A tavern grand opening? Who sent the invitation?"

"Remember that little Jap house breaker we nabbed in Hollenbeck? The one who worked at Hoegee's?"

Kraus thought for a moment, "Yeah, Dave Hash-something."

"Hayashigawa. He drew a nickel for that beef. Don't know what happened after that, but he's opening a tavern. Guess what it's called?"

"I don't know. The Geisha House," Kraus said.

"From your lips to God's ear. No. 'the Bean Slot'!"

Kraus laughed. 'Bean Slot' was jail slang for the horizontal slot in a cell door that food trays slid through. "Jesus, I knew that kid had some moxie. Remember what a character he was?"

"Shit, yes. I almost let him go because he was so likable." Ollie rattled off the address, date and time of the grand opening. "Meet me there. We've got to see this."

Ollie met Kraus outside the new tavern. They walked into "the Bean Slot" together. Dave Hayashigawa was beaming. He looked almost the same as he did in forty-one. He trotted up to the two of them and embraced them like long lost relatives.

"Hey, you guys! I'm so glad you could make it!"

"It's not every day one of our busts invites us to a party," Ollie laughed.

"Are you kidding? You guys changed my life!" Hayashigawa made eye contact with one of the barmen behind the counter. The ex-burglar thrust two mugs of draft beer at the two men. "On the house, boys!"

"How so?" Kraus asked, taking a pull on his ice-cold beer.

"So, I end up being one of the first groups of inmates sent to Chino. It was brand new then, remember? They wanted it to be a progressive prison. Hell, at first, it seemed like a JACL summer camp."

"Sounds good," Ollie said. A plate of sandwiches sat on the bar. Ollie grabbed half a ham sandwich from the pile and shoved a corner of it into his mouth.

"It was, Officer McBride. After Pearl Harbor, I took a little shit, but by then I was a kitchen trustee. Kitchen workers have a lot of power, Jap or not."

Kraus shook his head in agreement.

"Next thing you know, the warden calls me and a couple other Niseis to his office. The War Department had a deal for us. Early release and our records expunged if we volunteer for the 442nd. What a deal! Next thing I knew, I was at Fort Shelby in Mississippi, then on to Europe with the greatest bunch of guys you could hope to fight with. But you know what the best thing was?"

"No more prison chow," Ollie offered.

"That wasn't it," Hayashigawa laughed, "I was a kitchen trustee, remember? Never ate so good. No. The rest of my family was already at Santa Anita. I visited them before I shipped out to Shelby. My old man was so ashamed of me when I went to the joint. Suddenly, I was his son again. Someone he was proud of. Restoring the family honor. Jesus, that felt good. Now I'm home with a clean record and," he swept his arm in an arc, "a respectable businessman. My mom loves me again. And it started when you guys cornered me creeping a house."

Kraus raised his beer mug and offered a toast, "Hayashigawa, here's to honor!"

Ollie clinked mugs with the other two, "Yeah, get on her and stay on her!"

The Bean Slot, Los Angeles - November 1956

Kraus pulled himself back to the present. Dave Hayashigawa came out of the kitchen in the back. He was wiping his hands on a dish towel. His black hair showed threads of gray, and he'd put on a few pounds over the years. He saw Kraus and tossed the towel on the bar. Sadness showed in his black eyes as he moved towards his friend.

"Gordy," he said, "I heard about Ollie. Jesus."

"Yeah. I was at the scene this morning and I'm wondering when it'll sink in," Kraus said. Hayashigawa gave an understanding head shake. Soldier instincts. You never had a chance to grieve or even react in combat. A friend went down, and you had to let it go or you'd be next.

"Any idea who did it?" Hayashigawa asked.

"Not yet. It's Laveroni's case for the present. He's with Violet right now. Was Ollie still keeping a locker with you?"

"Yeah," the barman said. Hayashigawa found an old locker at the flea market and mounted it in the back room of his tavern not long after he opened the saloon. It stood floor-to-ceiling and held nearly sixty file-sized drawers. He rented the drawer space out to guys fresh from the joint. Most ex-cons don't have a fixed address, which complicates life on the outside.

Renting a locker at the Bean Slot solved that problem. Their mail was delivered to Hayashigawa, who distributed it in the recipients' lockers. The guys could also store documents there. Birth certificates,

97

release papers, divorce papers, tax forms, probation receipts, etc. Things you didn't want to carry around but couldn't afford to lose.

"Ollie was here just a few days ago puttin' some stuff in." Hayashigawa went behind the bar, rummaged through a drawer near the register and withdrew a tagged key. The tag had the initials "OM" scrawled on it. "Come on back. Let's open his box."

Kraus followed Hayashigawa into the back room. The file cabinet sat amongst the mops, brooms, buckets, soap boxes and stacked chairs. Bolted to the floor and back wall. Despite the jumble of mismatched padlocks on its face, Kraus thought it had a certain Dickensian look. Something Bob Cratchit would reach into with frostbitten fingers to retrieve Scrooge's ledger books.

Hayashigawa required each drawer renter to give him a key. The renter had another and was allowed to open their box in privacy. The barkeep opened a padlock on a drawer near the center of the cabinet face. He grabbed the handle and pulled the drawer out of its slide panel. He handed it to Kraus.

The drawer wasn't particularly heavy. Kraus placed it on a stool top next to the cabinet. He lifted out the contents one at a time. A few unlabeled file folders and a handful of small, spiral-bound notebooks. Kraus recognized them as the kind Ollie always used for case notes. One folder had some bulk. A black Beretta 1951 automatic was sandwiched between the folder flaps. Kraus whistled and showed it to Hayashigawa.

"You let renters keep weapons in their lockers?" Kraus asked.

"No way. But Ollie was an exception. No one is going to get worked up about an ex-cop and licensed private eye keeping a gun in the drawer."

"Yeah," Kraus agreed. He released the magazine and pulled back the slide. One primed in the chamber. He ejected the round. Safety off. Single-stack handgun. Narrow profile. Unnoticeable if he pulled out a few file folders at the same time. Kraus sniffed the ejection port. Fresh oil, but it hadn't been fired recently. Ollie was taking no chances. What was he afraid of? "This one may have been off the books."

"I get you," Hayashigawa said.

"Dave, what was Ollie into? Do you know?"

"No. He'd been putting stuff in the drawer more often. I asked him if he was working a big case. Said it was real big. Maybe be his last one if he was lucky."

Kraus slipped the Beretta in his jacket pocket. "He was right about it being the last one. Dave, was he laying down bets?"

"Here? Not that I know of. A couple guys take some very small action, but hardly more than you'd bet with the guy on the stool next to you during a ball game. No one's making real book here."

"Yeah. What aren't you telling me? Come on, Dave. No sense covering for him now."

"Well, I know he's been spending a lot of time at the Cockatoo. He may have been gambling there."

"*The Cockatoo*?" Kraus cursed to himself. Had Ollie gotten in that deep?

FOURTEEN

Kraus called Laveroni from the phone at the Bean Slot. "How'd it go with Violet?" Kraus asked.

"Hard one to read. You know the relationship soured over the past few years. Ever since Ollie was defrocked. Forced out of the department," Laveroni said.

"Yeah. You think she's involved?" Kraus asked.

"I don't think so. But I haven't ruled her out yet," Laveroni said.

"Find the DeSoto yet?" Kraus asked.

"It was in the garage. Engine was ice cold, but after ten, twelve hours, that doesn't mean much. Violet said Ollie left in a cab yesterday evening. My guess is that whatever he was going to that alley for, he was planning on calling for a pick-up to get back home. Probably from the same booth I called you from. He knows the guys at Angel City Taxis."

"Wasn't taking any chances. Didn't want to get made by his car," Kraus said.

"Yeah, if that's how it played out. We're checkin' into it with Angel City," Laveroni said.

"I'm going over to see Violet. Anything I shouldn't mention? Subjects to stay clear of?" Kraus asked.

"No, but Gordy," Laveroni said.

"Yeah?"

"If you get anything, you bring it to me. You got me?" Laveroni cautioned.

"Sure, Gino," Kraus said, fingers crossed.

Kraus went through what he knew of Violet while driving to Ollie's small house in Gardena. He was Ollie's best man at their wedding. Spent a lot of time with them. Over the years he'd heard bits and pieces about her past from both. Where she came from. How they met, all the usual stuff.

———◆———

Violet was about ten years younger than Ollie. From Pierre, South Dakota. The state capitol. Population of about four thousand. Pierre's favorite son, Robert Gleckler, returned home in '36 for a family funeral. Gleckler had achieved reasonable success on the Broadway stage and then in Hollywood. Small town. Local boy makes good. He was asked to speak at the high school. Violet's family was friendly with Gleckler's, and she approached him for advice on making it in Hollywood.

Gleckler encouraged Violet to finish high school. After that, if she came to Hollywood, he'd help her get in front of casting directors. Jump start the process. He advised her to learn some secretarial skills. Get some waitressing experience. "It's a tough business even if you have an 'in'," he counseled.

Violet worked hard to finish high school. In '37 she got a weekend job in the basement cafe of The Hopscotch Bar, Pierre's first post-Prohibition saloon. She hoarded her tips like a miser. She committed herself to finishing high school and sacrificed what little time off she had to study.

She graduated with honors in the Riggs High School Class of '38. Stayed at home after graduation and continued working at The Hopscotch. She enrolled in a six-week acting course at Pierre's Grand Opera House. The day after New Year's 1939, Violet boarded a train bound for Los Angeles. She had saved almost five hundred dollars. Ready for Hollywood.

Violet reached Central Station in Los Angeles on a Saturday in early January 1939. She phoned Robert Gleckler from a station pay booth. Violet marveled at the sunlight streaming in through the station's three-story tall arched windows. In January! She knew she was here to stay.

Gleckler gave her instructions on taking the Red Car from the station to his home at the edge of Hancock Park. Violet had never seen so many people in her life. She kept her nerve and managed the trip without incident.

Gleckler was happy to see her. He introduced his wife, Adelaide, and their three children. Adelaide insisted that Violet stay with them for the first week or so. Bob, she explained, was busy with the role of his life. He'd been given the part of Jonas, the slave overseer at the Tara plantation, in *"Gone With the Wind"*. Gleckler, always quick with a witticism, said *"Gone With the Wind"* was going to give his career a second wind. Filming was underway and the sets were a madhouse. *"Gone With the Wind"* was the only thing the Hollywood community talked about.

The actor cautioned Violet that his time would be monopolized by the movie for a few months. He assured her he'd help her in every way he could after principal filming completed in June. Adelaide was sure that in the meantime Violet could find a job and learn her way around. She'd help Violet find a respectable place near the studios.

A week later, Violet and Adelaide found a suitable Fairfax neighborhood studio apartment. Ideal location. It was a block from a streetcar line. Two blocks from Paramount Studios. Three miles from the Gower Gulch strip of small movie producers. Canter's Deli was within walking distance. "You won't starve," Adelaide teased.

Violet found part time work at a nearby cafe. Adelaide gave her a list of reputable photographers. Violet would need a portfolio when she started to make the rounds. She joined the Gleckler family every Sunday for dinner. Gleckler looked more fatigued each week. David O. Selznick was running the *"Gone with the Wind"* production like his own slave plantation. Gleckler quipped that watching Selznick manage the production was all the inspiration needed for the slave overseer role. Tension on the sets was excruciating.

In late February, Adelaide put through a frantic phone call to Violet at the cafe where she waited tables. Gleckler had collapsed and died from heart failure. The news devastated Violet. She felt she'd made a place for herself in the world. Had a promising future. Accepted by a family she had grown to love. Mentored by a respected Hollywood actor. In the blink of an eye, all that seemed to evaporate. Literally gone with the wind.

Gleckler's sudden death received scant attention from the papers. It wasn't mentioned at all on the radio or in the trades. Non-stop reporting of Selznick's single-minded, all-consuming drive to make his movie left little room for minor sidebar stories. Even the Gable and Lombard elopement took a backseat to the daily coverage of the film's progress.

Without fanfare, veteran character actor, Victor Jory, took up the overseer role. Gleckler's funeral was in Pierre. The modest fame he'd carved out melted away. Adelaide and the children packed up and moved from California. The swift chain of events left little time for Violet to mourn. This was for the best. She now had to fend for herself and felt the need to put a new set of plans to work. She was on her own to make her own breaks.

She reinvented herself. Robert Gleckler was no longer a Dutch Uncle. In her revised backstory, he was her blood relative. Her mother's older brother. She visited agents and casting directors armed with the story that "Uncle Robert" had recommended them. She maintained "Uncle Robert" would have made introductions himself, but not for his untimely death while filming *Gone with the Wind*".

As ploys to open Hollywood doors went, it was better than most and worked to a point. She signed with an agent. A former child actor who ran a one-man shop in North Hollywood. He instinctively saw the potential in Violet's backstory and pitched it for all it was worth. Young aspiring actress. Her uncle-mentor sacrificed at the altar of Hollywood's most ambitious production. Perished before he could shepherd her through the treacherous switchbacks of the Hollywood movie business. Wouldn't you like to give her a part in your movie? Keep the torch burning? Think of the publicity!

Violet soon had a one-day walk-on as a co-ed in an RKO B-movie, "*Sorority House*". She also had a one-week stint at KRKD, a small, five-hundred-watt radio station in Los Angeles. Doing voices for various local ads. She felt her career was gaining momentum.

The country was gearing up for a war the industrialists knew was coming. Defense industry jobs were more plentiful every day. But Violet wanted her days free for casting calls and acting lessons. The cafe job required too many day shifts. Waitresses with more seniority staked out most of the evening shift slots. Bigger tips.

Another waitress showed Violet a help wanted ad in the Examiner for taxi dancers. "What's a taxi dancer?" Violet asked.

"Nickel-hoppers. Gals who dance with guys who come to the hall. They pay an entry fee, then buy tickets. Like movie admission tickets. Each one costs a nickel and that's how much a dance with one of the girls costs."

"Dancing? That's all?" Violet had been in L.A. long enough to ask.

"That's all if that's all you want. Some of the guys tip the gals. My friend, Sally, makes more than I do here and only works four shifts a week. I'd do it myself, but I have to be home nights for my kid."

Violet figured she had nothing to lose. She liked to dance, and it sounded safe enough. She took the streetcar to Spring and 9th the next day after her shift at the cafe ended. There was a stop right where the two streets split. A busy intersection in a canyon of tall buildings.

Violet saw the Los Angeles City Club, the California Bank building, but didn't see the Roseland Roof.

"What ya lookin' for, babe?" A man's voice. Coming from nowhere. Violet looked from side to side, then finally up. She saw a uniformed man perched in a stop light control tower suspended ten feet off the ground. The elevated kiosk looked a lot like a prison guard tower station she'd seen in a movie. She couldn't imagine a more boring job.

"I'm looking for the Roseland Roof."

"Yeah," the traffic cop said. A tone that said he'd taken her for a floozy at first sight. "It's on the fourth floor of the City Club building. Took over the old dining hall."

Two nights later Violet was dancing with every sad sack who came through the door. Like every girl on the floor, she collected a parade of regulars over time. Doll dizzy goofs convinced they've met "the one". Dreamboats out slumming. A few jive bombers. A lot of dead hoofers. Most guys were lonely. Less interested in dancing than simply connecting with a girl. Even for two minutes. Even if it cost a nickel and a two bits tip. Violet found many of them endearing in a sad way.

Three years later all she found about the job was that it left her with sore feet and a firm conviction that all men were *yucks* or worse. She had ample time to attend auditions and acting classes. Her number of roles dwindled despite this. She had only landed two more parts in the past year. Both one-liners. A troupe member in a "Ritz Brothers" picture. A walk-on in Griffith Park for a scene in the Republic serial, "*The Adventures of Captain Marvel*". She got an occasional radio ad voice-over gig. But wartime rationing was taking its toll on consumer goods advertising.

Violet often ate dinner at a cheap chicken joint down the street from Roseland. She would see the same man there from time to time. Big guy. Nice looking in an Irish way. Not in a hurry. Had the look of someone off work and on his way home. He started noticing her and would give her a polite smile. Didn't make a show of looking her up and down. He was different.

One day he walked over and said, "Hey, the manager keeps giving us the death stare. Probably 'cause we're always takin' up two of his tables when it's clear we're meant to sit together. How 'bout it? He's starting to give me indigestion."

She laughed at his confidence. Not arrogant. Sure of himself. She learned he was a veteran LAPD cop. Stopped at the cafe on the way home from his Newton district patrol shift.

He lived in a two-room flat near Bunker Hill. She told him about her sputtering movie career and dancing nights to pay the rent. He was the first man who didn't look at her like a prostitute after she told him about the dancing. She told him so.

"I like you. I like that you didn't look as though you'd sized me up as a streetwalker when I told you about Roseland."

"Well, I like you," Ollie said. "You didn't look like you were sizing me up as a Nazi brownshirt when I told you I was a cop." He waited for a beat, "Of course, that would be stupid. I look more like an IRA thug."

Violet liked his blarney. He talked her into driving up to Little Tokyo for what he called a "French Dip" at a place called "Philippe's". She loved it. Perfectly roasted, thin-sliced beef stacked between thick French bread rolls and dipped in warm roast beef drippings. Philippe's became a regular spot for them.

One night Ollie showed up at Roseland during her shift. Grinning like a kid on Christmas morning. His grapefruit-sized fist crushed a wad of dance tickets. The next song was a Glen Miller swing tune. Ollie took her into a neat promenade position. Led her into a crisp box step on the first beat of the song. He was very light on his feet.

"Ollie, you're a swell dancer."

"Yeah. I grew up with three sisters. If I practiced dancing with them, they'd take over some of my chores. I got to be better at dancing than dusting." He whisked her through a nifty Lindy swing out step.

"I'm probably the best dancer of all the girls here."

"Oh, yeah? Well, I've got a big roll of tickets here, sister. Might work my way through the stable tonight and decide for myself. That gal over there with the mustache? How's she at dancing the Merengue?"

She snickered and slapped his chest with the flat of her palm. "You just dance with who brung you, cowboy." Violet felt safe with Ollie. Life seemed so plain sailing with him. Movies, picnics, meals out at modest restaurants. What passed for her acting career was dead stalled. Lately, thoughts about her future felt distressing. The war made it worse. Ollie was steady and secure.

Agents who couldn't remember her name. Open auditions packed with ambitious hopefuls. Back stabbers desperate for their big break. Claws out. Casting directors on the make. Spending your days praying for vague half-promises to pan out. Call-backs that never came. Constant disappointment. Uncomplicated and solid seemed like a good trade by comparison.

Violet married Ollie in '42. The ceremony was at City Hall, followed by a big reception at a Knights of Columbus Hall. Kraus was Ollie's best man. It turned out Ollie had more than a little saved up. They bought a nice three-bedroom stucco house on Denker in Gardena. Violet had fun the first few years. Fixing up the house. Learning to cook for Ollie. Cop functions.

The war seemed to put everything on hold for everyone. After VJ Day, life seemed to take off with the sudden snap of a rubber band. Ollie made it into the detective bureau. Weekends off. No night or graveyard shifts. Vacation trips. Life seemed good.

The feeling didn't last. Violet saw so many people moving ahead in the world. The booming economy was providing many families with new luxuries. Two cars in the garage. Lake Arrowhead getaway cabins. Swimming pools. Whirlpool push button clothes washer. Ollie's pay envelope stayed the same. Violet felt as though they were being left behind. Life began to remind her of what made her so eager to get away from Pierre.

Having children may have changed things, but it didn't happen. Then Ollie's corner cutting tendencies got him pushed off the force. Violet had to find a job. She went to work as an office clerk for a bottled water delivery company. What seemed like a lifeline a decade ago had changed. The lifeline had become a rope lashing her to the pillar of a drab existence.

Violet opened the door before Kraus could knock. Looked as though she hadn't slept for a week. Frazzled hair. Red rimmed eyes. Runny nose. Usually a sharp dresser, she wore a ratty house dress under a snagged knit sweater. She clung to Kraus in a desperate hug.

"Gordy, Jesus. What happened?"

"I don't know a lot yet. How are you doing, Violet?" Kraus asked.

"I'm a mess. Gordy, I could barely stand the sight of him yesterday and now I'd give anything for him to walk through that door." She started weeping. Kraus felt her back heave in a fierce spasm with each sob. He gently walked her to one of the stuffed chairs in the living room. The house smelled of Ollie's cheap cigars and lemon furniture polish. Violet sat forward. Elbows on her knees. Head cradled in her hands. One hand clutched a soggy lump of facial tissues.

"Violet, I'm not going to ask you the same questions Gino must have just asked. But is there anything you've remembered since he left? Anything you'd rather not tell the police?"

"Gordy," she said, "we barely talked anymore. He was up to the same old crap." She waved her hand around. "Some blackmail case for a squirrely guy at Desilu. Tracking down welchers for guys at the Cockatoo. Things like that. Nothing that should have gotten him shot in an alley."

"*Shit*," Kraus thought, "*The Cockatoo. Second time that place has come up.*" "What'd Gino take?" Kraus asked.

"Some street maps he used. He writes notes on the margins. Two months' worth of phone bills. Some random crap he kept in a cigar box on the dresser. I don't know where his case notebooks are."

Kraus looked around. Ollie's wide-armed, stuffed chair. Threadbare fabric. The floral pattern upholstery on the seat cushion was thin from wear. A catalog was on the walnut side table. Slick front and back covers. "*Allied Radio. Everything in Electronics from One Dependable Source*".

"What's this? Ollie taking up ham radio?"

"Some crap he's been obsessed with for a few weeks. He would sit there flipping the pages and adding figures half out loud. Almost chanting like a damned monk. I thought he was toting up the cost of making a do-it-yourself color television. My friend at work, Agnes, her husband made one for peanuts and it works better than the Curtis-Mathes they have on the floor at Sears."

Kraus flipped through the catalog. Yellow newsprint pages. Three columns per page. Several pages were earmarked. Section headings displayed the name of a part type with a drawing of the item. Below each drawing were tight columns crowded with rows of part numbers, specifications, and unit prices. Crystal diodes, whatever those were, going for eleven bucks each. P-N-P transistors, another unfamiliar term, listed at seven bucks a throw. Page after page. He looked at the cover. Chicago address and phone number.

He pointed his chin at the old ten-inch Philco perched on a maple cabinet across from the couch. Lifted his shoulders. A *what-happened* shrug.

"I know," Violet laughed through her tears. "No color television. He never brought home a single part. Just like him."

"Violet, can I take this with me?" He slapped his palm with the catalog.

"Yeah. I was going to throw the thing out. It was only going to collect dust."

"I'm sorry I didn't make it for Thanksgiving, Violet."

"He just asked you because he knew you wouldn't come. You think it was going to be like some Norman Rockwell magazine cover? Ha! More like those awful paintings that artist, what's his name, Anonymous Boss, made," Violet spat out.

Kraus didn't bother to correct her. What was the point? He knew who she meant. "Yeah, you're probably right. Okay," He started towards the door, "Violet, I'm heading out, but I'll check back with you every day or so."

He hesitated when he spotted some papers on the tiled kitchen counter. Kraus recognized the logo on a buff-colored envelope. Eureka Mutual. The insurance company that underwrote LAPD cops' life insurance policies. Violet followed his eyes.

"Yeah," she said in a near whisper. "I've got to get things started with those bastards."

"Nice to have something to fall back on," Kraus said in a flat voice.

"Get off it, Gordy," Violet spat out. "You think I killed Ollie for a lousy two-thousand-dollar policy? I'm going to have to fight like hell to settle the claim! I'll need every dime of that just to keep the house. Gosh, that and the thirty-eight bucks a month for widow's benefits. I might take a cruise!"

"Hey, Violet, I wasn't thinking anything," Klaus said, hoping that was only half a lie.

"Bullshit," she barked, "you're thinking why I'm so up on Social Security benefits." Cop's wife. She knew the thought process. "I bring on new hires at the office. I go over these things with the drivers all the time. I know the numbers!"

"Okay, okay," Kraus held up his palms in surrender. He dropped the sham of thinking otherwise. "Look, Violet. You know you're going to be on Gino's short list for a while. Right? Nothing personal." He didn't need to add that he'd approach the investigation the same way. "I'm going to go, but I'll stay in touch. Call me if you need anything."

"I'm sorry. I'm just on edge with all this," Violet said. "I'm gettin' some money from my Gramps. He cashed in his war bonds and is giving the money to me and my sister. His heart's going and he's not long for the world. Sweet of the old coot. I'm going to invest most of my share, see if I can make it last."

Kraus nodded his understanding.

"Thanks, Gordy," Violet held the sweater closed at the neck while she stood at the door to see Kraus out.

A '51 Packard convertible glided up to the curb behind Kraus' Lincoln. A man looking barely thirty swung out of the car. On the short side. Tanned. Dirty blonde hair. High and tight on the sides and swept back at the top. Quiff style. Clean shaven. Strong chin. Self-satisfied smile. He wore a snow-white polo shirt with tartan on the collar underside and button panel. A shiny leather belt held up cuffed chinos. His shoes were two-tone black-and-white oxfords tied in a snazzy ladder-lace style. He skipped over the curb with the supple grace of an athlete.

To Kraus he looked like the assistant manager of a golf course pro shop. One who moonlighted as a nightclub sax player. He noticed the man's left hand wasn't tanned. Frequent golf glove wear would cause that. Kraus thought the pro shop job may have been more than a flight of fancy.

"Hey, doll," he called out. His smile faded when he got a look at the condition Violet was in. "What gives, babe?" He took a long look at Kraus. "This guy a bill collector or something? Some jam your old man is in?"

"Oh, Tommy," Violet said, "get in here. We've got to talk." She opened the door a little wider.

Kraus was standing on the narrow walkway leading from the sidewalk up to Ollie's front door. Only wide enough for one man. Tommy seemed reluctant to walk in the damp Bermuda grass bordering the concrete path. He bumped a contemptuous shoulder into Kraus' as he walked past, flashing an ineffectual scowl as he made his way into the house.

"This isn't what it looks like, Gordy," Violet said.

Kraus cocked his head and raised an eyebrow. "What does it look like?" He didn't wait for an answer. Got into his car. He noted down Tommy's license plate number before he began his drive back to the office.

FIFTEEN

Almost four o'clock, but the guy on the radio said it was eighty-seven degrees. Kraus thought a turkey dinner would have roasted fine on his car's roof. November in California. He rolled the windows down. There was a faint breeze coming from the west. Kraus wanted to catch it while he was stuck in the traffic on Wilshire.

"Tommy," Kraus said to himself. What on earth was Violet up to? He hated thinking of her as a suspect, but this playboy showing up at Ollie's house changed the way everything looked. The timing stunk to high heaven. Correct height. Right-handed. But so were eighty-five percent of L.A. males.

The congestion on Wilshire bunched up traffic. The collective exhaust heat from the cars suffocating. He fanned himself with the electronics catalog he took from Ollie's. He looked at the cover again. *"What was this about,"* he thought.

He decided to put off telling Gino about this golf course gigolo until he found out more about what Ollie had been up to. There were a few leads he had to follow up on before he crossed that bridge. Burned it more likely. If Kraus dimed her on the boyfriend and she went to the top of Gino's list, she'd never speak to him again. Strange as it seemed, Ollie and Violet were family. Kraus wasn't ready to lop that branch off of his family tree just yet.

Melinda met Kraus at the office door and held him in a warm hug for a minute or so. She didn't say anything. She understood Kraus didn't need to hear anything comforting. He liked that about her. He told her what he knew so far.

"Violet was having an affair?" Melinda couldn't believe it.

"He wasn't passing out Jehovah Witness pamphlets with Mickey Spillane," Kraus said.

"Do you think Ollie knew?" Melinda asked.

"I'm not sure. He wasn't easily fooled. But how many of our clients are poleaxed by the news their spouse is cheating on them? A lot. Plus, Ollie may not have been a saint himself as the marriage broke down. There's no reason to believe that playing around was a one-way street. Maybe they both just decided to look the other way."

"Do you think this 'Tommy' had anything to do with the shooting?"

"Not sure," Kraus said. "Hard to picture him getting the drop on Ollie. He described what 'Tommy' looked like. What he drove. How he carried himself.

"Sounds dreamy," Melinda sighed.

"Yeah, That's probably the idea. Very calculated look. Like he just stepped out of a studio wardrobe fitting. My money says he's all cackle and no eggs. But I liked that golf shirt with the plaid accents. Know where I could pick one up?" Kraus asked.

"You can look around the May Company on Wednesday. Remember, you have a date with Margaret Woodward."

"I haven't forgotten." Kraus placed a slip of paper on Melinda's desk. "Here's his plate number. Find out everything you can about him. Don't go to Gino. I don't want him to know about 'Tommy' yet. Call Wyatt Dugan, the desk sergeant at Harbor Division. He owes me a favor and doesn't know Gino."

"Will do," Melinda said. "What are you going to do now?"

"I'm going to pay a visit to the Cockatoo. The joint keeps coming up in connection with Ollie. I want to find out what was up with it," Kraus said.

"Oohh," Melanie groaned. "Don't you have some history with the owner?"

"A little. Nothing serious, anyhow. I want to know if Ollie had a worse history."

"Just be careful, Gordy," Melinda pleaded.

"Always. Seriously, though. If you don't hear from me in the morning, get Gino on the horn and tell him everything," Kraus said.

Melinda shot him a worried look as Kraus worked on his shoulder holster and headed out the door. "Gordy, call me at home when you get back. I want to sleep tonight."

"Nothing to fret about, but I'll give you a buzz."

Traffic was light on LaCienega. People staying in holiday mode. Kraus had promised himself he'd never set foot in the Cockatoo again.

Melinda was right. There was a little history between him and Andrew Lococo, the owner of the place and a low-level gangster in the L.A. mob scene.

Lococo was in his late-thirties. Born to Sicilian immigrant parents. Raised in Milwaukie. His father, Felice "Phil" Lococo, was an active player for the local Italian blackhanders, the criminal society that had taken root there at the turn of the century. He specialized in extortion and enforcement.

Andrew Lococo grew up in Milwaukie's notorious Sicilian Third Ward. His family often shared evening meals with other apartment tenants. Neighbors included Capone button man Angelo LaMantia, and Isadore Aiello, the son-in-law of Mafia boss Vito Guardalabene. Many nights they both joined the Lococo family on the front stoop, balancing plates of pasta *con le sarde* and *cassata* sponge cake on their laps. Raisin wine, a neighborhood specialty during Prohibition, was poured from straw-swaddled fiasco bottles.

Phil Lococo gave his son an early start in the rackets. At eight years old, Lococo worked Saturdays as a lookout for several of the rum-holes his father had an interest in. Frank Cunningham, Milwaukee's zealous prohibition agent, deployed tuxedo-clad agents to the Third Ward. The agents posed as visiting toffs out to "do the Ward". On the prowl for clandestine saloons and wine cafes to shut down.

The boy proved to be quite skillful at singling out these imposters and alerting the speakeasies. Lococo told his father the agents were easy to spot. Unlike authentic well-heeled swells roaming the Ward, the undercover men wore clip-on tuxedo bow ties. No agent wanted to have a ready-made strangulation cord around his neck when tussling with hoodlums. Breakaway ties made more sense.

Lococo served a six-month sentence at the county House of Corrections in 1940. Soon after, he and his entire family relocated to San Diego. They joined the Sicilian fishing operations starting up on the West Coast. After the war, Lococo moved north to L.A. He went into business with two partners, one being an LAPD detective. They opened a lounge in Hawthorne, calling it the "Cockatoo Cafe". Food, liquor and a jazz trio in the front, gambling and bookmaking in the rear. A 1946 ad in the Times announced the promise of "It's showtime all the time at Andy Lococo's ultra-swish Cockatoo Cafe".

The post-war boom was good for Lococo's new enterprise. Business grew. After a couple of years, Lococo elbowed out his silent partners. The detective member of the dissolved triumvirate was not so sanguine about the breakup. He dropped an anonymous tip and the L.A. Sheriff's Office raided the Cockatoo Cafe in 1949. Lococo was arrested for running a gambling den. Money changed hands. County charges were dropped. It was determined the City of Hawthorne had jurisdiction over the establishment. Lococo ditched the "Cafe" part of the name. The new "Cockatoo" flourished. The former detective partner did not fare as well.

Kraus parked a block down off of Hawthorne. He didn't want to valet his car. He might need a quick exit. The outside of the Cockatoo looked like any number of roadhouses you'd see dotting the interstates. A square, lighted Pabst Blue Ribbon sign topped a twelve-foot pole near the sidewalk. A smaller horizontal plank hung below the Pabst sign. It read "The Cockatoo" on both sides.

The face of the Cockatoo was a single story of red brick. Heavy oak front door. The four windows facing the street featured heavy velveteen cafe curtains. Kraus walked in and looked around. The air conditioner was running. The room felt comfortable after the scorching car drives throughout the day. Banquettes ringed the lounge walls with some two-tops scattered around the center. It was early. The Cockatoo didn't see a lot of action in the dining room until eight or so.

A hostess stood behind a greeter stand inside the door. Kraus cocked his head towards the bar. She smiled and waved him through. The taproom was livelier. A long bar occupied a place against the far wall. Half the bar stools held patrons. Two busy bartenders.

A barman filled a pilsner glass from the Pabst tap and ran a beer comb across the mouth to remove the excess foam. He pushed it across the countertop to a lone patron on a stool. The customer pushed two singles and a fifty across in return. The bartender rang up the one-dollar beer and dropped the other single in the tip jar. He slipped the fifty under the counter.

Kraus watched the exchange out of the corner of his eye. He figured the customer was paying off a bet. The Rams lost big to the Colts the day before. Didn't beat the spread. A guy who bet with his heart and not his head was Kraus' guess. Along with the table games run in the back, the Cockatoo ran a big book operation. Baseball, football, basketball, horses, boxing. Lococo would take all the action a bettor wanted to lay down.

"What'll it be, buddy," the bartender asked when Kraus settled into his stool. His name tag read "Bob".

"Oly on tap." The beer was swiftly drawn. Kraus pushed a fiver across the bartop. "Andy in? I'd like to talk to him."

"Yeah? Who're you?"

"Tell him Gordy Kraus needs a word with him." The bartender turned and picked up the receiver of a house phone on the wall. He murmured into the mouthpiece.

"He says 'okay'," the bartender said. The barstool legs scraped the floor as Kraus stood. "I'll need your piece," the tapster added. He nodded his head at the bulge under Kraus' left armpit.

"And you'll need some new teeth if you try to take it," Kraus said in a low voice.

"Come on," the bartender pleaded. He pulled an *it's my job* shrug.

A door marked "Under Renovation" a few feet from the end of the bar cracked open a few inches. A voice came out of the opening. "Bobby, it's okay. We know him."

The bartender jerked his head towards the door. Kraus tossed him a *nothing personal* nod and went through the door.

"Gordy, come on in," Andy Lococo called from a horseshoe-shaped bar on the far side of the back-room casino. "Bring your beer or I can pull you a fresh one in here."

A decent-sized gambling den. Well insulated to hold casino noises inside. No plungers in the place yet. A handful of poker and blackjack tables. A roulette and craps table. The hourglass birdcage of a Chuck-a-Luck game sat next to the bar. Serious drinkers could lose money without leaving their stools. The dice cage obscured the sight of two of Lococo's men horsing around with the game. They rotated the cage and watched the three imprisoned dice rattle their way to the bottom. Each turn ended in a scatter of profane wisecracks about the results.

Lococo was a big man. A little too fond of his restaurant's food. Not yet fat. Heavier than in the pictures of him alongside various celebrities that hung on the walls. He had a head of thick, black hair left a little longer than the fashion. A stray forelock curl was forever tormenting his forehead. Thick, heavy eyebrows as black as his hair, stretched across a protruding brow.

His dark eyes looked sunken and bracketed a wide, fleshy nose. Lips as thin as prison blankets. They pressed together into a ruler-straight seam balanced above a broad chin. A bluish black beard growth covered his jowly cheeks everyday by noon.

In unguarded moments, all his features combined to create a surly look. But Andy Lococo had a certain animal charm that emerged when he put on the smile of the Genial Host. That smile almost made it to his eyes as he watched Kraus come through the door.

Lococo was favoring the California casual style of an expensive sports coat over an equally expensive cotton polo shirt. The shirt was tucked into pleated linen slacks. A thick tassel of curly black chest hair poked out over the top button of his shirt.

The lounge owner held out his hand to Kraus. He grasped it in a firm handshake and placed his other big hand on Kraus' left shoulder. A fraternal clasp. "Kraus, I'm so sorry to hear about McBride. We thought a lot of him here."

"Thanks, Andy. Pretty big shock. He was like my big brother."

"I can imagine," Lococo studied some nonexistent grime under his fingernails. "You're not here for a few hands of poker to take your mind off things. You want to know if I know anything about it." Not a question.

"If you do, I'd appreciate the info. The Cockatoo has come up several times while I've asked around about Ollie today. Was he gambling here? Owe you money? What?" Kraus asked.

"He gambled on the money we owed him," a voice came from the Chuck-a-Luck table. Sal "Two-Loop" Moretti. He walked a few steps to close the distance between him and Kraus.

Moretti was about fifty or so. Average height. Stocky build. Big, strong hands. Wrists like a butcher. Kraus believed he was one of the most dangerous men he'd ever met. He was Lococo's second-in-command. Ran every aspect of the gambling part of the operation. In some circles the word was that he had ambitions not completely aligned with his boss's.

Moretti came up in the underworld under the tutelage of "Pep" Strauss. "Pep" was one of Murder Inc.'s most prolific button men and known for never carrying a weapon of any kind. He'd suss out his target and when the time was right, murder him using any tool or method handy at the moment. Tire iron, drowning in a toilet, shooting the mark with his own gun. You name it.

"Pep" grew up in Brooklyn. Mobbed-up family in the Jewish Bugs gang. "Pep" came of age at the height of Prohibition, when the Italian Mafia co-opted the main Jewish mobs. He met an ex-Foreign Legionnaire who'd settled there. The retired mercenary taught "Pep" a strangulation technique. A double coil of rope, electric cord, anything, is dropped over a victim's head to encircle his neck. Even if the victim yanks on one of the coils as pressure increases, the other still tightens.

"Pep" Strauss passed this skill to Moretti. The double-loop garrote method became Moretti's favorite way of taking out a mark.

Hence the moniker, "Two-Loop". Lococo called him *"Doppio"*. The Italian word for "double".

"You guys owed Ollie money? What for?" Kraus asked.

"This and that. He'd sometimes take the payments in house credit. Get a little over-extended. He's down about five bills at the moment. But we trusted him to work it off," Moretti said.

"Work it off," Kraus said, "what does that mean?"

Lococo broke in. "McBride was a pretty good guy for, what would you call it? A line of communication. He knew guys downtown. I trade information with guys downtown. But it's always better to have a go-between. Sometimes he'd visit a guy doing a jolt at Lincoln Heights or Chino Men's. Folsom and Q a couple of times. Kite a message. Worked good."

"So Ollie was their bagman," Kraus thought. *"Great."*

"Yeah," Moretti picked up the thread. "He'd play some cards, place bets. Sometimes get a little upside down. Like I said, we trusted him. He wasn't some rat bastard snitch who comes in here askin' a favor and calls the cops down on us the same fuckin' night!"

Moretti raised his voice for emphasis on the last line. The other hood edged forward. Heard the dog whistle in his master's voice. Kraus recognized him. Rico-something. A mediocre ham-and-egger who bled all over Olympic Auditorium undercards for a couple of years. Nose like a Bull Durham pouch. Kraus saw a couple of his matches. Dirty fighter. Never hesitated to give his opponent the laces or head-butt him when he thought he could get away with it.

The mood wasn't developing the way Kraus had hoped. If it soured much more, he'd have to do something. No way could he handle both Moretti and his goon, even if he could draw his weapon in time. He'd have to do something he didn't want to do. Have to hold his Colt on Lococo's head. Take the boss hostage and bluff his way out of the building. After that? Who knew? But it was his only play.

Lococo stopped the spiraling tension. "Doppio, we've gone over this. Gordy had a job. One of our guys was fleecing Gordy's client. Gordy did us a favor. I run a clean joint. The punters know they have a fair shake at the tables here. That we give the best odds of any slaphouse in Southern California."

The previous year, Kraus had gotten a job from a frequent Cockatoo gambler. He was certain a particular poker dealer was holding back some of the pot on big hands. The client didn't believe it was a house fiddle. He believed the dealer was in business for himself. But he wanted an unbiased opinion before taking it up with management. His client was right. Kraus informed Lococo, who pledged to make it right with the client. Kraus left and later that night LAPD vice showed up. It wasn't a good look. It was a convenient reason for Moretti to raise a ruckus about Kraus. Distracting Lococo from the embarrassing fact a rogue dealer was skimming on Moretti's watch.

"Doppio," Lococo continued, "the cops showing up was a coincidence. They were just trying to shave off some of Hawthorne P.D.'s kickbacks. The two things were, what do you call it, mutually exclusive. We got rid of a bad apple. That guy!" Lococo swept a hand in the air like he was swatting a gnat. "Best ratholing artist I've ever seen. We tuned him up good. Right now, he's probably runnin' a three-card monte game at Union Station from a furniture dolly. Settled up with Gordy's client. Gave him some generous house credit, which he quickly lost. But lost on the square! Didn't cost us a thing. Everybody wins."

"Yeah," Moretti continued. Not wanting to let it go. "The next time something 'mutually exclusive' happens, one of Kraus' brother's houses might end up a pile of charcoal."

Kraus heard the threat against his family. Now he didn't care about Moretti's reputation. His thug sidekick. His two-stranded garrote. Kraus reacted without thinking. He stepped forward towards the hoodlum, "You fucking, two-bit lowlife, you ever ..."

That was as far as he got. Lococo put one of his big paws on Kraus' chest. He had strong arms. Years of reeling in fish laden nets onto the decks of deep-sea boats had left his forearms like belaying pins. He stopped Kraus in mid-step.

"Gordy, that's enough." Lococo then turned a baleful eye on his number two guy. "Doppio," he put a strong emphasis on the 'dope' part of the pronunciation, "leave it alone. It was a coincidence. Plain and simple. No talk about people's families. Never. That's not who we are."

Moretti looked as though he was going to protest some more, but Lococo dialed up the volume of his glare.

"And no talk about torching someone's property. You think we're in Mississippi or something? You wanna burn something down, put a match to this place. I could use the insurance money to build a roomier place." Lococo swung his free arm around the room. A few of the casino workers had drifted in. Getting the craps table ready. "Christ, look at that. So crowded, the croupier has to choke up on the fuckin' stick."

Moretti backed off a half-step. Kraus settled back on his heels.

Lococo looked at both men. He took his palm off of Kraus' chest. Satisfied the flare up had cooled below boiling point.

"Gordy, the kitchen's bringing in some chow in a minute. Have some with us." Lococo sounded sincere. Sharing food. An Italian peace offering.

"Know what? I could eat. Sure, Andy." Kraus realized he was starving. He hadn't eaten all day. What was it about a Thanksgiving meal that made you famished for the following week?

A kitchen worker brought in a platter covered with a stainless-steel restaurant cloche. He placed it on the bar and whisked the cover off with a magician's flourish. Lococo eyed the platter and nodded approval.

"Gordy, you like sardines?" Lococo asked.

Kraus caught the aroma coming off the platter before he recognized the food. Long row of fat sardines. Fresh from the oven smell. Slit open and stuffed with a mixture of anchovies, breadcrumbs, garlic, parsley, raisins, and pine nuts. Olive oil drizzled over the top. His mouth was watering.

Lococo scooped one up, plopped it on a small dish and handed it to Kraus. "Fresh caught off Baja. One of my cousin's boats. Best sardines on the West Coast."

"*Sarde a beccafico,*" Kraus said. He stabbed a forkful in his mouth and chewed. He only used his left hand. Didn't want his right oily if he had to draw his piece. He groaned from the rich taste. "God, I love this dish. Ate it all the way across Sicily in '43. I was there with the 2nd Army."

"No shit," Lococo sounded impressed. "I want to get to Sicily one of these days. Take my ma. See where the family is from."

They all chatted about Sicily. Kraus told them about some of his war experiences there. The sardines were washed down with cold draft lager. No one was feeling any pain by the third helping of beccafico.

Kraus had a thought and took out his photo of Anna Bjorkquist. Showed it to Lococo. The gangster looked at it and whistled. "Nice lookin' dame."

"So everyone says. History of working gambling joints. No hooking. Runs cons." Lococo looked at the photo for another moment, then handed it to Moretti. Moretti peered at it. His eyebrows went up.

"Yeah, I've seen her in here. Swell lookin' broad. Virginia Hill, on her best day, couldn't have held a candle to her."

"You don't say? Remember when she was here?"

"Let me think," Moretti said. Trying to be helpful. Showing the boss there were no hard feelings. Could control his emotions. "Yeah," he snapped his fingers. "Two weeks ago. She was with a couple of guys. Chumps. Looked like the type who couldn't get themselves in hot water fast enough. Skinny guy runnin' with a thumb-breaker type."

"Know 'em?" Kraus asked.

"I asked about 'em. Looked like they were casing the place. Guys that dumb, I want to know who they are. You know?"

Kraus nodded. Mickey Cohen was released last October. Cohen was putting on a show of opening men's clothing stores, gas stations, and flower shops. Joe Citizen. At almost the same time, Jack Dragna, L.A.'s top crime boss, had keeled over from a heart attack. His successor was Frank DeSimone. Licensed attorney. Looked and acted more like a Rotary Club president than a mobster. Received little respect from his peers.

Rumors were there was a power struggle between the Italian mob and Cohen to gain full control of L.A. There had been some blood spilled here and there. Laveroni told Kraus it was more Cohen settling some old scores than signs of a full-blown war. Kraus figured Lococo was kicking up to both gangsters. Not letting either side know he was sharing action with the other. Waiting to see how it played out before choosing sides. He and Moretti had to be on high alert. Any new faces got special scrutiny.

"Guys were lettin' it be known they were from Detroit. Former Purple Gang members. Shit, these birds weren't even out of diapers when the Purple Gang was still in business. I asked around. Turns out one of the two, Hebe named Lester Fox, did a deuce at Jackson State. Ended up a biscuit boy for another Hebe. Harry Fleisher, one of the last Purples to go down. Probably learned all about the Purple Gang when he and Fleisher were cellies."

"Make any trouble?"

"At first I wanted to make sure those two were kosher." Moretti laughed at his own joke. "Kosher. Two Hebes. Funny, right? Nothin' against 'em. Hell, 'Pep' was a Yid. Anyhow, I didn't want any Cohen people in here nosin' around. Seemed okay. Wanted everyone to think they were bigger fish than they were. You know?"

"Yeah," Kraus said. "What about the girl?"

"She caught my attention at the craps table. Got herself wedged in next to one of the shooters who was holdin' heavy. I thought she was going to pull some railbird stunt, but I didn't spot her snag any of his chips. Real cool customer. Classy. Shit, the guy was obviously so keen on her, he would have *given* her his fuckin' stack."

"Did they talk anyone up? Let on what their game was?"

"This one Hebe, Fox? I didn't know his name at that point. Had eyes so close together he was almost a whadda call it? A Cyclop. He was askin' about runnin' broads in town. Who gets the pungle. That kind of thing. I asked him if he already had a stable."

"What'd he say?"

"Said he didn't yet, but he and his partner had plans. I asked him if the dame at the craps table was part of the plans. He said she was, but she didn't know it yet."

"Think he was serious or just bullshitting you."

"*He* thought he was serious. Kept lookin' at that brunette like Rico's lookin' at that last beccafico."

"*Christ*," Kraus thought. He doubled his hope the May Company gambit on Wednesday paid off. He sensed she was running out of time.

SIXTEEN

Kraus was sitting at his desk drinking coffee and eating a Helms Bakery chocolate covered raised glazed donut. He was paging through his notes when Melinda walked in.

"Hmmmm," she said, "is that a Helms?"

"Yeah," Kraus said, "I flagged down a truck before I left the house this morning."

"Yumm," Melinda said as she tore a piece off his donut and primly popped it into her mouth. "I'm glad you called last night and everything went okay." She reached for another piece.

Kraus play-swatted her hand away. "Me too. I think we can rule out Andy Lococo and his people as suspects. Plus, we've got some more good info on our missing car thief." He popped another piece of the donut in his mouth and drank some coffee. "What did you get on 'Tommy'?"

"Your friend was very helpful," Melinda chirped as she settled into her desk chair. She pulled a steno pad out of her top drawer and flipped it open. She started reading from her notes. "Thomas Adam Thorp. No 'e'. Turned thirty-one last month."

"I told you he looked young," Kraus said.

"Umm," Melinda hummed, scowling at Kraus for the interruption. "Grew up in Oxnard. Started having trouble as a teen. Truancy, vandalism, driving without an operator's license. Kid stuff. Barely finished high school. Expelled from Oxnard High and finished up at a Ventura County continuation school."

"All-American boy," Kraus cracked.

"Now, now," Melinda scolded, "Robert Mitchum was expelled from high school. I read about it in '*Modern Screen*'."

"Yeah," Kraus continued, "and he went on to make that '*Night of the Hunter*'. Jesus, what a stinker."

"Really? What kind of reviews did your last picture get?" Melinda asked in a wry tone.

"Okay," Kraus surrendered, "Go on."

"Right," Melinda flipped the page of her steno pad with a crackle, "Continued getting in trouble. Oxnard is a small town. The cops got to know him by sight. Parents kicked him out. He moved to Santa Barbara. Ten times the size of Oxnard. Got in ten times as much trouble. Trespassing. Public intoxication. Caddied at the Montecito Country Club. That's where he made his fatal error. He was stealing from members' golf bags and lockers. Caught taking an expensive watch from a councilman's locker."

"Sounds like there's more to the story," Kraus said.

"Oh, this is the best part," Melinda said. Relishing the surprise element. "His defense was that he was having a fling with the councilman's wife, and she said he could take the watch."

"No kidding? Audacious defense. How did it play in the courtroom?"

"The judge liked it as much as you liked '*Night of the Hunter*'." Kraus laughed. "He got the choice of two years in jail or a stint in the Army. He chose the Army."

Kraus peered at the dates Melinda had jotted down. "The Korean War was in full swing. Don't tell me he's a vet?" Kraus asked in disbelief. He crammed the rest of the donut in his mouth.

"Gordy, you look like you're swallowing a fat, chocolate fishhook. Smaller bites, please."

"Too late," Kraus mumbled through the donut he was chewing.

"He served in the Army, but I'd stop short of saying he was a 'vet'," Melinda continued. "Stationed at Camp Zama in Tokyo after basic. Made corporal. Ended up assigned to the camp golf course."

"Guy has a pattern, doesn't he?"

"Maybe more than we know," Melinda said, flipping another page. "He got out with a 'general discharge'. I asked your friend, Sergeant Dugan, about that. He said it was usually a sign that there was some tit-for-tat. 'You leave quietly, and we won't court martial you' kind of thing."

"Sounds like he got next to an officer's wife or two," Kraus mused. "Brass wanted to avoid a scandal. Those can be career killers."

"I was thinking the same thing. Nothing much on his record since. Couple of traffic citations. He settled in the Windsor Hills area. Works as a golf pro at Sunset Fields Golf Course off Crenshaw. Sticking to that pattern. Maybe added a new wrinkle or two."

"What's that?"

"Our boy was named as a co-respondent in a '54 divorce petition. Husband claimed Thorp was dallying with his wife. Also accused him of trying to scam money off her. Thorp maintained he just gave the wife golf lessons and had suggested she talk to a friend of his about an investment possibility. Inclination and opportunity couldn't be established for adultery. He was removed from the petition as a co-respondent and the dissolution was granted six months later. The wife ended up filing a civil suit against Thorp for fraud. Settled out of court."

"Hmm," Kraus murmured, "Got the ex-wife's name and address?"

"Right here," Melinda tapped a finger on her notepad.

"Mel, type all that up, please." Melinda shot a cross look at Kraus for the 'Mel'. "Also type up Thorp's address and plate number on an index card. I'll give that to Gino. If he's interested, he can sniff out anything else that interests him. I'm going to make a couple of calls to get ready for the May Company tomorrow, then I'm going over to the Department."

Kraus left his car in a lot off Temple Street and walked to the PAB. Once through the doors, he started towards the detective bullpen when he saw Laveroni making his way down the corridor with some files in his hand. The two men stopped in front of one another.

"Gino, how's it going with Ollie's case?"

"Got the post results a little earlier. The headshot killed him. Bullet was too banged up for comparison purposes. Slug broke apart a little. Total weight of the main slug and other fragments the M.E. could extract points to a .32."

"Any other leads?" Kraus asked.

"Uniforms got a weak hit during their canvas. Old guy dossed down in a doorway on East 4th. Said he saw a dark sedan peeling off out of the Arts District about the right time. The noise woke him up. Couldn't make out the driver. No plate number, naturally. Did say the plate had a symbol on it next to the numbers."

"Physician plates?"

"Nope. Said it looked like the plates on the CCC trucks that took the guys to construction jobs during the Depression. Of course, that was a couple thousand gallons of Wild Irish Rose ago. Who knows?" Laveroni said.

Kraus took the index card with Tommy Thorp's info out of his breast pocket. "Gino, I think Violet may have been spending time with this character. He came up to the house just as I was leaving. Violet was flustered and it didn't look good. I got his name and took down his plate number." He handed the card to Laveroni.

The sound of brisk footsteps slapped on the marble floor tiles towards the two men. They halted when a young man in a sharp suit parked himself next to Laveroni's right shoulder. The younger man was shorter than both Laveroni and Kraus. Dark, stringy hair that looked like horsehair stuffing plastered to his scalp with lanolin. Close-set eyes peered with suspicion on everything in view. Liver lips set in a perpetual smirk held a shaky perch atop a weak chin.

This was John Gowan, Laveroni's assigned partner for the past year. Gowan was the son-in-law of one of the eighth-floor mandarins. One of the prices Laveroni paid for having a powerful rabbi in the byzantine LAPD command structure. Kraus had met him one or two times. He loathed the little weasel.

"We'll add that to the murder book, Kraus," Gowan butted in. "Don't hold your breath, though. Gino and I have a full plate right now. McBride's case has a second priority status."

"Second priority status? For a cop's murder? Since when?" Kraus demanded.

"McBride wasn't a cop any longer," Gowan shot back in his snottiest tone. "Some say he wasn't much of one when he was on the force."

"You little prick," Kraus said. "On his worst day, Ollie made you look like a trainee crossing guard."

Gowan edged a fraction further behind Laveroni's shoulder. Laveroni put up his hand. "Okay, you two. Enough with the pissing contest. Gordy, the brass has looked this one over and don't think we have enough to go full throttle on it yet. We'll just be spinnin' our wheels until some break comes our way." Kraus started to protest, but Laveroni raised his palm another quarter inch. Demanding silence. "We'll work leads as they come up. I'll look into this one," he tapped the index card, "but we're not at the 'all hands on deck' stage yet."

"You know what, Gino. That's just fuckin' eighth floor fimble-famble. They're scared shitless about what might come out of this investigation. Ollie may not have been squeaky clean," Gowan snorted at this. Kraus scowled at him. "But he wasn't bent like the bastards who were all too happy to see him coming when he was toting fat envelopes with their names on it."

"That's it," Laveroni stepped away from his partner, took Kraus' elbow in a firm grip and walked him down the hallway. "Listen, Gordy. Enough. I'm no more happy about this than you are, but that kind of bullshit here in the goddamn halls of the department isn't going to help your cause."

Kraus took a deep breath. Composed himself. "You're right, Gino. Thanks. But that fuckin' partner of yours ..."

"I know. I know. He's my cross to bear. Not yours." Laveroni let go of Kraus. Made a show of smoothing down his suit jacket. "Gordy, stay out of this. I swear to you I'll work this on my own time until I get enough traction on the case. But I have to contain this. Can't let this pot boil over. I'll keep you up to date, okay?"

"Yeah," Kraus said. "Just don't let this one die on the vine, Gino. Ollie deserves better than that."

"Agreed," Laveroni said. "I'll call you."

"Yeah," Kraus said. He patted Laveroni's shoulder, turned and walked away towards the exit doors.

Kraus hadn't gotten ten yards down the long hallway when a side door opened. A detective rushed out the door and nearly collided with Kraus.

"I'm sorry, man, I wasn't watching ..." the man stopped as he got a clear look at Kraus. "Shit, Gordy. I haven't seen you in a coon's age." He pumped Kraus' hand. "I'm sorry to hear about Ollie. We had facing desks in G-2. Solid guy."

Kraus struggled for a moment to come up with the detective's name. "Lyle Norwood. Of course." Kraus had run into Norwood several times during Ollie's stint in Parker's G-2 unit. "Ollie mentioned you several times. Liked working with you."

"Jesus," Norwood sighed, "those were the days. One more year and I'm pulling the pin," Norwood gave Kraus a dreamy smile. "I saw Ollie in here just the other day. Told him when I retired we'd bowl a few frames and swap lies."

"Ollie would have liked that," Kraus said. "Lyle, what did he come to see you about?"

"Good question. I don't really know. Wanted to know if I was still working G-2. Had some questions about the Russians messing around with the studios."

"Russians," Kraus said.

"Yeah," Norwood went on, steering Kraus to a bench against the corridor wall. Avoiding the hallway bustle. He looked around and lowered his voice. "G-2 doesn't just dig up dirt on Parker's targets anymore. Not all the time, anyhow. One of the newer jobs is keeping tabs on the Russians. Their efforts to organize unions in the studios and defense plants. That sort of stuff."

"That goes on a lot?" Kraus asked.

"Seems so. Parker uses the info to horse trade with Hoover's boys. You scratch my back. You know." Kraus nodded, letting him go on. "I'm not in G-2 anymore. Set myself up with an easy glide path out the door, you know? Missing persons now. Paper chase mostly. But I've still got friends in Intelligence. In fact, Ollie was going to see one of them. I suggested a guy after I told him I couldn't help him. Larry Butler. Good egg. Knew Ollie back then. Works the Russkie desk now. He's on vacation. Not back until the first part of December. Fishing in Mexico, the lucky bum."

"Yeah," Kraus agreed. "Lyle, would you leave word for Larry Butler to call me when he gets back?" He handed Norwood his card. "I promised Ollie's wife I'd help her track down any fees clients may have owed him. He wasn't great at keeping records and it would help to find out what he was working on. If he has any info Ollie asked about, maybe I can close out a case or two and get her some money."

"Will do, Gordy," Norwood said as he tucked the card in his pocket. "Got to run. You hearin' any news about what happened?"

"Not much. But Gino's workin' the case. He'll turn something up."

"Yeah," Norwood pushed himself away from the wall. "Listen, Gordy, I'll look you up after the holidays. We can get together and hoist a few in Ollie's memory."

"Sounds good, Lyle. Take care."

Kraus walked out the doors of the Police Facilities Building. He stopped to breathe in the fresh air. The lower altitude of the November sun took the bite out of the eighty degree heat.

The mildness softened his mood. He mentally organized the information he'd gathered. Ollie's scullion work for Lococco. Police brass smothering the investigation in the cradle. Laveroni reluctant to say anything in front of his snitch partner.

He turned to make his way back to Temple Street. An unmarked police car honked its horn as it pulled out of the department parking garage. Announcing it was crossing the sidewalk. It turned onto Los Angeles Street. Kraus noticed its rear end license plate. A capital "E" stamped in the middle of an octagonal frame on the left side of the plate. "Exempt" designation. All cop cars and city vehicles had them. He noticed how much from a distance the cop plates could be confused with CCC plates, which had "Cons. Service" stamped into their left sides.

SEVENTEEN

"Beauty Salon" was spelled out with black, foot-high molded Bakelite letters. The backlit Art Deco style letters sat at the front edge of a transom recess above the entryway to the May Company Wilshire beauty parlor.

Kraus was in one of the rounded shell lobby chairs placed off to the sides of the salon entrance. Discreet waiting area for husbands. He was making a show of reading the L.A. Times. A spouse killing time while his wife gets beautiful.

It was approaching one o'clock. A busy time of day for high-end salons. Affluent housewives had already played tennis and shared lunch with their friends. Enough time left to pamper themselves. Make it home before their husbands returned from the office.

Two or three women waited at the reception desk for check-in. Kraus figured Anna Bjorkquist timed her appointments for these time slots. The crush of inbound patrons would give her a chance to check the surroundings while she waited. The mild chaos and confusion would give her cover if she needed to exit the premises unseen.

"Why don't you just scout around for the Studebaker while she's in the store, Gordy," Melinda had argued earlier that morning. "It would be easy to spot. You've got the key and could drive away with it without any fuss."

"Normally I would," Kraus explained. "But this gal is in trouble. Bad guys are looking for her and I'm not going to leave her twisting in the wind without wheels. She wouldn't last an afternoon trying to make her way around town by bus or streetcar."

"Gordy, you sound like you're working for her, not the guy she stole the car from," Melinda lectured.

"I work for myself, and I want to be able to look at my face in the mirror. I'll get the car and the girl, don't worry."

"Sure you don't want me to go along?"

"Not this time, Mel," Kraus said. "If she gets away and I need to put another plan in action, it may involve you. I don't want her seeing you this time around. It will limit my options." The entire May Company store was decorated for the Christmas season. Soft holiday music. Festive adornments. Faux garland. Tasteful and understated. An aluminum Christmas tree was set up in a corner of the boutique. Curved tin foil strips sprouted from each metal limb. The fake branches looked like skewered metal sea urchins. The foil spines reflected a continuous rotation of holiday colors. A little machine on the floor aimed a tri-panel disc at the tree. Each panel held a different colored lens. The disc rotated in front of an encased light bulb. Optimistic hues of red, green and blue fell across the bright foil tassels.

Gift wrapped boxes filled the space under the tree. Wrapped lids leaned against open boxes to reveal the contents. Hair care and home beauty product gift assortments. An avocado green handheld hair dryer shaped like a giant teardrop. Kraus thought it looked like a ray gun prop from a science fiction movie.

Anna Bjorkquist appeared from the elevator. It seemed anticlimactic. Kraus spotted her in the reflection of the brass frame of a fire extinguisher cabinet beyond the elevator doors. He turned a newspaper page and caught sight of her coming towards the salon entrance above the top edge of the Times.

She crossed his field of vision from under the brim of his hat as she walked into the salon. He could only see the confident tread of her low-heeled black pumps passing by. A faint scent of French milled soap floated on her slipstream.

Once she was inside, Kraus lifted his head to take a good look at her. Raven black hair brushed her shoulders as she walked to the reception area. She was wearing a smart rayon dress. Green the same shade as her eyes. Sheath top with a drop waist that flared into a pleated petticoat from her hips. The hemline was at the top of her calves. Sheer dress stockings. Younger style but nothing outrageous. Nothing to set her apart. She looked chic and poised. The wife of a bank executive getting ready for the firm's Christmas party. She held a small bag from the store's book department. A conscientious woman getting some holiday shopping done.

Kraus knew the next minute or so was the riskiest part of his plan. He was counting on luck to prevent the receptionist being the same one Melinda and her friend spoke with. If the receptionist mentioned to her that two "friends" had asked about her, she would bolt. If his luck held, he planned on approaching her once she was seated at a manicurist's station. If her treatment today included a pedicure, so much the better. He'd corner her with her shoes off and toenails wet.

Anna chatted with the receptionist for a couple of seconds. The manicurist appeared out of the back. Her crisp white salon smock gave off the impression of a professional nurse. The beautician flashed her a warm, welcoming smile. A smile reserved for repeat customers who were big tippers. They exchanged a few words. The two women walked together towards the back end of the beauty parlor.

The duo disappeared into the rear of the salon. Kraus settled into his chair. He wanted to wait a few minutes. Let the treatment get into full swing before he approached. Catch her unawares. A minute or so had passed. Kraus saw the manicurist appear at a glass etagere centered against the rear wall of the back area. Fussing with little bottles of nail polish and manicure accessories on the shelves. She had the air of someone trying to look busy. Waiting for someone.

"Shit," Kraus muttered to himself. He tossed the newspaper aside and leapt from the padded chair. He ignored the sputtering of the receptionist as his long strides took him towards the rear of the salon. He spun around one customer who had stepped out from a hair dryer station and sped towards the manicure section. A halfback pounding for the end zone. He cleared the low divider separating the manicure area from the front of the salon. The burnt onion odor of filed nail dust mingled with the smells of wet paint and acetone. Both chairs at the manicure table were empty. The small bag from the bookstore rested on the tabletop. The manicurist gave Kraus a shocked look.

"Where is An ... Margaret?" Kraus demanded.

"She said she had to use the restroom before we got started. She went to the one we use outside the rear door." The girl lifted her arm towards the shadows deep in the rear of the salon space.

Kraus sprang towards the back door. It opened onto a narrow hallway that connected all the units on the Mezzanine level. Deliveries, trash removal, employee restrooms. One end of the hallway led to stairs and the other to a freight elevator.

"*She wouldn't have taken the elevator,*" Kraus thought. He raced to the stairs. "*Which way?*" Debating with himself. Up one level was a large women's department. Easy to get lost there. Easy to get trapped, too. One floor down was street level. Many departments. Exits to the streets and the rear parking lot. A large millinery department was down there. She would be difficult to pick out amid a flock of women trying on hats. Kraus took the down staircase two steps at a time and burst into the costume jewelry department. He scanned the surroundings as he walked deeper into the store. He saw the heavy glass doors that let shoppers out at Fairfax and Wilshire. Front display windows curved around the corner of the building outside those doors. A lot of shoppers bunched up there. Holiday goods and apparel on display beneath the store's signature gold tower cylinder. A woman could melt into a loose huddle of gawkers, but then what?

The rear parking lot made the most sense to Kraus. He trotted to the rear doors that opened onto the asphalt lot. He looked around. Cars entering the parking lot from Wilshire, exiting onto Fairfax. Many were circling around, looking for a space they liked or the driveway leading off the lot. There was movement in the corner of the lot closest to the store building. Long afternoon shadows made it difficult to pick out details from the part of the lot still fully sunlit. Kraus reasoned that had been the intent.

Once his eyes adjusted, Kraus saw Anna Bjorkquist near the Azore green Studebaker. She was struggling with a tall, lanky man in a blue cotton suit. Bareheaded with scuffed Weejuns worn down at the heels. The man was pulling on Anna's elbow. He was trying to get a grip on her arm with both hands, but she squirmed like an eel. Anna pivoted away from the man and raked his face with the car keys in her hand. The man howled and slapped a palm to his cheek. A thin dribble of blood leaked from under his hand.

"Bitch," he yelled. He whipped a wild backhand swing with his free arm, but Anna had already scampered around the car. In an instant she was sliding into the driver's seat of the Studebaker. Kraus was within a few feet of the man when he made a move towards the passenger door.

"Hey," Kraus yelled, shouting over the roar of the Studebaker as Anna gunned the engine. The car primed to flee the scene.

The man turned. Eyed Kraus up and down. Saw he wasn't a cop. Not store security. "Butt out, pal. Family business."

"Step away from the car and leave, Lester." The man's eyes widened. Surprised Kraus knew his name. "Yeah, I know who you are. No one needs to get hurt here," Kraus continued. A reasonable tone. Calm. Meant to infuriate the man. Invitation for him to redirect his rage. Lester Fox looked over his shoulder. The Studebaker was already a few feet away from its parking spot. Rolling towards the Fairfax exit. He shrugged his shoulders like a man who knew another chance would be around the corner.

"Oh, I'm not worried about getting hurt," Fox said. Full attention on Kraus now. He reached into his pocket. His hand came out holding a switchblade knife. Mother of pearl handle. A thin blade flipped out of the side and locked into position with a snick. It looked sharp. Fox took a step towards Kraus. Brandishing the knife. His nicotine-stained forefinger looked mustard yellow wrapped around the white handle. "You stick your nose in, buddy, you're apt to lose it."

Fox held the knife in front of him. Crouched to lunge forward without warning. Arm slightly bent. A maniacal courtier presenting a rose. The kind of pose he'd probably seen in a movie. Dexie-addled high school hoodlum pointing a knife at a strait-laced teacher. Unpredictable. Threatening. Fox had a long nose dividing a longer face. A chin nearly as sharp as his knife blade. His close-set eyes gave him a spiteful look.

Kraus tossed his hat to the side and squared up to meet his assailant. Fox was way inside the "widow's circle", but this wasn't Gordy Kraus, the rookie cop in an alley.

Most of the criminal elements in post-war Berlin carried knives and truncheons. Few firearms. Kraus' Constabulary training concentrated on close-order-combat. His hand-to-hand combat instructor was a disciple of the legendary William Fairbairn.

Fairbairn had been a Royal Marine attached to the Shanghai Municipal Police in 1907. Fairbairn headed up the anti-riot squad created to police colonial Shanghai's infamous red-light district. The British officer spent a decade developing hand-combat skills for use against the drunks, vicious pimps and ruthless agitators. Kraus spent countless hours practicing Fairbairn's knife defense techniques. Ten years later, he could still execute the moves in his sleep.

Fox shuffled a half-step closer to Kraus. He waved the blade in a tight lateral motion. Trying to intimidate. This was a textbook scenario. Kraus took him down in three heartbeats.

In almost a single motion, Kraus moved the palm of his right hand under Fox's knife hand. He clasped his left hand over the back of Fox's, clear of the blade. He had the knife hand firmly encircled. A brotherly handshake. Kraus lifted Fox's arm a few inches while twisting clockwise. This bent Fox's hand in towards his wrist, loosening the grip on the knife. Kraus lifted the blade out of his hand. Easy as plucking a toothpick out of a Langer's club sandwich.

Fox was now disarmed. Kraus looped his left arm around Fox's right. Slapped his palm on the back of Fox's head. A bar lock. He bent Fox at the waist and drove his right knee into his face. Fox went limp and Kraus let him slither to the pavement.

Kraus put a knee on Fox's back and looked over to see the Studebaker entering the traffic on Fairfax. He could see Anna Bjorkquist looking back at him. She may have been looking to see if her rescuer was hurt. More likely gauging how much of a head start she had gotten.

Fox moaned when Kraus leaned his palm into his head, grinding it into the gritty asphalt. "Fuckin' get offa me," he snarled.

"Sure," Kraus said without conviction. He continued pushing Fox's cheek into the ground. He folded the switchblade with his other hand and dropped it into his coat pocket.

"Hey," Fox protested. He tried to buck his body out from under Kraus' knee.

Kraus gave his head a pop with the heel of his hand. "Fuck! I think you busted my nose."

"I wouldn't be surprised," Kraus said. "You made a mess out of my pants leg."

"Fuck you!"

"Lester, you and your buddy got noticed by the wrong people. You've heard of Frank DeSimone." Not a question.

"So what?"

"People think you're teamed up with Cohen. Former Purples brought in to shore up his team."

"What people? I wouldn't know Cohen if I took a piss next to him."

"You know, I don't think that matters. DeSimone is looking to pad his rep. Taking out a couple of *gonifs* like you two sounds like just the ticket to him. No one cares about you. The perfect patsies. Big status boost. No consequences. That's the word, anyhow."

"Wat word?" Fox sputtered. His voice was muffled from being pressed into the ground. Blood plugged his swollen nose.

"Foxy, no one in DeSimone's camp buys your Purple Gang tales. You did a skid bid at Jackson State. Got lucky. Celled with Fleischer. Ran errands. Held his place in line for the stress box. Who knows what else. He filled your head with all that Purple *bubbe meises.*"

"Hey, how'd you know …"

"Shh … shh," Kraus hushed his captive. "The important thing is DeSimone burns you two. Cohen will figure DeSimone's people took you two as his people. It looks to Cohen like DeSimone's not afraid to hold his territory. Kind of a validation." Kraus could see a knot of people gathered on the walkway outside the store. He had to speed this along. "You two need to clear out of L.A. Forget about the girl. Portland. Seattle. Dallas. Frisco, even. They're all nice. Leave today. L.A. isn't safe for you."

EIGHTEEN

Lights blinked on inside many of the tidy houses in the Hyde Park neighborhood north of Slauson. November days were short. It was getting dark outside.

A man sauntered up the walkway of a small, single-story, Spanish-style stucco home. He was wearing a dark suit. No hat. The falling darkness made it hard to identify the bulky object he held in his right hand. A weak light glowed behind the closed blinds of the front window. The man knocked on the door of the modest home.

An attractive brunette in a green dress opened the door. She had a striking face. Beautiful, but at that moment showing signs of fatigue. A woman tired of running. Resigned to her capture. Prepared to accept the very worst.

"You left this behind, Anna," Kraus said. He held out the bag from the May Company book department.

Anna smiled. Perfect white teeth. Smaller than Kraus would have guessed. Each tooth separated from the other by an almost imperceptible gap. They suited her looks. She took the bag from his hand. Shook a book out of the open end. Examined the cover as though she suspected it may have been different from the one she'd purchased.

"I took a look at it," Kraus said. "Hadn't heard of '*Beast in View*' before. Read the first page. Grabs you right away."

"That's what I thought," she said as she slipped it back into the bag. "It just came out and caught my interest," she said. Anna looked up from the book to watch a taxi drive past the house. "That your ride?" She had the slightest hint of a lisp. It added to her charm.

"Not anymore," Kraus said. He watched her eyes follow a second taxi making its way past. "That was the cab that followed you here from the department store," Kraus said, not turning around. "The driver was watching the house until I could get here."

"So, that's how you found me," she said. "He was good. I never spotted him." Anna stepped to the side and opened the door a bit wider. "You may as well come in."

Kraus stepped by her into the small living room. He picked up the scent of French milled soap that seemed to always waft around her. It would have been generous to say the house was sparsely furnished. The living room had two webbed aluminum patio chairs set up between an upended milk crate. A beach towel was draped over one chair to serve as a crude slipcover. A cheap thrift shop lamp atop the crate provided the only light.

"I love what you've done to the place," Kraus said. "Is this the newest bait for your rental scam?"

"You must be the guy with the lock and chain," Anna said. She took a step further away to give herself a better look at Kraus.

"My name is Kraus. Gordy Kraus. You must be the gal with the lock picks," Kraus replied.

"Lock picks? The man at the pawnshop said they were quality dental tools. I'm enrolling at that new Bryman College on Wilshire. I'm going to study to be a dental assistant."

"Oh, you're good," Kraus laughed.

"Not good enough, it seems," Anna said flatly. She sat down on the patio chair with the towel. "Lester Fox almost nabbed me. You found me. Have my real name and seem to know a lot about me. You're probably here to arrest me."

"I'm a private investigator. I don't arrest people," Kraus said.

"Then what are you here for?" Anna asked.

"Ostensibly, to repossess the Studebaker."

"It's right over there. In the garage. I'll give you the keys if you don't have a set."

"It's gotten more complicated since you gave my padlock a dental exam," Kraus said.

"Complicated? What's complicated to a man who uses 'ostensibly'?"

"Look, Anna. We can sit here all night trying to out-charm one another."

"You were trying to be charming?"

"As comfortable as this place is," Kraus ignored the jibe and continued, "we need to get going. I might not be the only person clever enough to find you here. I'd rather neither of us be here if your friend Lester and his sidekick show up."

"Louie. Louis Applebaum is the name of the other lug. I'd rather not see them again either. What do you have in mind?"

"I'm taking you to my place. They don't know who I am or how to find me. You'll be safe there and we can work out the next steps."

Anna stood up from the patio chair. "And leave all this?" She waved her arm at the expanse of the darkened house. Kraus watched her weighing the options. "Okay. Okay," she said. Decisive. Confident. "I'm just pulling your chain. I'll get my things from the bedroom."

"I've got the book," Kraus called, picking it up from the milk crate.

"Don't flip back and read the ending first. I hate it when people do that," she called back.

NINETEEN

Anna and Kraus spoke very little while he drove the Studebaker. His Harvard Heights home was only three or four miles from where he found Anna. He'd left his Lincoln parked on the street so the path to the garage was clear. Kraus eased up the driveway, stopping before the closed garage door.

"Here we are," Kraus said. "You were almost in my backyard. Stay inside the car. I'm going to open the garage door and park inside. Kraus exited the Studebaker and unlocked his garage door. Its heavy-duty springs groaned as the door tilted up into the open position. He drove it inside and pulled the door back down. Only then did he tug on the light cord to switch on one of the garage lights.

Kraus walked to the passenger side and opened the door for Anna. A fourteen-foot-long polished wooden board sat in padded cradle hooks on the garage wall. It looked like a long, teak cutting board.

"Are you making a dining room table?" Anna asked.

"That's my surfboard," Kraus laughed.

"Surfboard? Those things the boys at the beach wade into the ocean with?"

"Yes. Then ride them on waves back to the shore. I've been surfing since I was about twelve."

"How does it stay on top of the waves? It looks like it weighs a ton."

"It doesn't. It's hollow inside," Kraus said, thumping the board's polished surface. "This is an early Thomas Rogers board based on a Tom Blake design," Kraus said.

"Am I supposed to know who they are?"

"Probably not when you're from Minnesota," Kraus chuckled. "Tom Blake is the Babe Ruth of surfing. I knew him a little but was never a good enough surfer to keep up with him or his friends."

"Do you still use it?"

"Now and then. I love the ocean. Water is in my blood. In the blood of my whole family. My mother was a competitive swimmer in Germany. She made the women's Olympic swim team in 1914 when she was only sixteen years old. Beat out Louise Otto, who was a top German swimmer."

"Did she win a medal?" Anna asked.

"Nope," Kraus sighed. "The 1916 Olympics were called off because of the Great War. She married my pops in 1916 and came to America. But we all have the water bug. I surf. My younger brother, Rudi, is a top swimmer and diver. He was a swimming instructor at Camp Pendleton during the war. Won the Marine diving competition one year. My little sister, Austie, is on the girl's swim team at El Camino College."

Anna allowed herself a faint smile, amused at how people take so much pride in their family legends. They walk around bragging about them. Advertising them like the people who wear those signboards on street corners. She didn't relate to the feeling herself, but took advantage of it in others to connect with them. Win their confidence.

"'Austie'", Anna said, that's an unusual name.

"Her actual name is Astrid," he emphasized the 'ass' in 'Astrid'. Anna giggled. "I know, it would have been a hard name to grow up with. I started calling her 'Austie' before she even got into kindergarten. That way she wouldn't get teased for her name."

"That was sweet of you," Anna said, surprising herself with her own sincerity.

Kraus flushed and shifted conversational gears. "This is how I ended up an LAPD cop," he said, placing his hand on the edge of the surfboard.

"I can't even imagine how one led to the other," Anna said.

"I was in college. I worked summers for my pop's building company. Three years of hanging drywall during the summers. I barely had time to surf, and it was killing me. I decided I'd get a job as a seasonal county lifeguard," Kraus said. "Let's get your things in the house while I explain," he said. Kraus heaved her big wardrobe trunk out of the car and carried it towards the side door leading into the house.

"Let me open the door," Anna said, moving ahead of Kraus. She opened the door for Kraus and he wrestled it into the house.

He set it down near the kitchen counter and drew a glass of water from the tap. "So," he continued after taking a long swallow, "in those days the county would deputize lifeguards. I was walking to Room 5 at Los Angeles City Hall. That's where new lifeguards were sworn in. I saw an LAPD recruitment sign. 'Join the Finest'. I don't know. The whole thing appealed to me all at once. I walked into Room 3, the LAPD recruitment office, applied and got accepted. They let me finish my final college term. Graduated in May and was in the Academy in June."

"But you're not a cop now?" Anna asked. Still concerned about facing an arrest.

"No. Long story," Kraus said. He looked down at his right pants leg. A lengthy blood smear ran across the fabric at the knee. "Shit," Kraus said. "I forgot about the mess your friend Lester's nose made of my pants leg. I'll be right back. Sit down. Get some water or I've got juice and beer in the fridge. The glasses are in that cabinet."

Anna watched Kraus walk up a hallway and heard him open a door. She removed a glass from the cabinet shelf and filled it from the tap at the sink.

A minute later he returned wearing a gray sweatshirt and chinos. He cradled the slacks as though he was carrying a wounded soldier off the battlefield. Kraus pulled open the fridge and rummaged around. He withdrew a bottle of Schweppes club soda and scooped up a bottle opener that was on the counter. Popped open the bottle and started dribbling the club soda onto the pants leg. He stopped every now and then to rub the fabric together.

"One of my favorite pairs of slacks. I don't want the blood stain to set," he rubbed the fabric together some more. A camper trying to start a fire by rubbing two sticks together.

Anna smiled. It was rare to see a man be so fussy about his clothes. "You must have been in the service," she said.

Kraus looked up from his task, then looked down at his stain removal efforts. "Yeah. And before that, the LAPD. Both organizations were strict about keeping your uniform spotless. Old habits die hard, I guess." He held the wet pants leg up closer to the ceiling light. Getting a better look. "That did the trick," he said. "My dry cleaner will take care of the rest." He carried them back to the room down the hallway.

When he emerged again from the hallway, Anna was walking around the kitchen and dining area. She looked at the paintings on the wall, the books in the built-in cabinetry, the crown molding and dark window casings.

"You have a beautiful home," Anna said. "I remember some homes like this in St. Paul. My mom cleaned houses and took me with her during the summers. How long have you lived here?"

"About four years," Kraus said. He motioned for her to follow him through the wide opening into the living room. "It didn't look like this when I bought it," he explained.

"Gosh, it looks like it's always been like this."

"That was the idea. I was working a sort of missing persons job in '52. An old man in New York was convinced a son he had from the wrong side of the sheets had settled in Los Angeles. The man was rich and owned property all over the country. He intended to leave a trust fund and this house to his son."

"What happened?"

"His son had started drinking heavily the minute he mustered out after the war. By '48 he was living rough. Skid Row. Panhandling. Menial day jobs. Every penny went towards the next bottle. He was found dead near Chinatown one May morning in '51. His birthday had been the day before."

"How sad," Anna said. "How did you find this out?"

"Same way most detective work gets done. Leg work. Paperwork. L.A. doesn't have a potter's field. Evergreen Cemetery on the other side of town has been cremating unclaimed bodies for fifty years. The remains are all buried in the same plot. It's a good place to start looking. Eliminating possibilities."

"Sounds like that was the long and short of it in this case. That's where the missing son ended up?"

"Yeah. His ashes and a lot of paperwork. Only knew his name. His Army discharge papers and a few photos from his wallet were the only things left in a folder in the mess that passes for the cemetery archives. Buried deeper in the files than he was in the ground."

"How did you find out the details you just told me? When he started drinking? That stuff."

"I didn't want to get back to the old man with a two-sentence report. 'Your son is dead. His remains are in East Los Angeles.' Would have been too harsh. You can't treat clients that way," Kraus explained.

"So what did you do next?"

"Well, you've probably gotten a good idea that I can find out a lot about a person. I worked the skid row food kitchens. The corners where day workers hang around waiting for a one-day job. That sort of thing. Found other guys who knew him. Managed to build a complete picture of the guy. He was a regular guy who couldn't readjust to civilian life after a crummy time overseas. A lot of guys ended up like him."

"How did the father take it?"

"As well as can be expected," Kraus said. "He was crushed that he couldn't connect with his long-lost son. Wanted to make good on something before he checked out himself. Settle a debt. That kind of thing. Turned out he was so grateful to hear the story I pieced together about his son that he offered to sell me the house he was going to give him. This house. At a fraction of market value."

Anna had wandered over to one of the built-in bookcases near the entrance to the dining area. She scanned the titles, tipping one out for a better look every now and then. "So, you remodeled the house."

"Well, Rudi, my brother, did most of the work. The house was fundamentally sound, just neglected. Rudi preserved most of the Arts and Crafts touches. Just restored and modernized when necessary. Take a look at this," Kraus said.

He approached one of the box-like pedestals flanking the wide entranceway to the dining area. A tapered support column rose from the top of each pedestal to a ceiling beam. Kraus waited until Anna was beside him, then pressed a spot under the lip of the decorative molding on the pedestal base. The entire facing section silently swung open.

"Open sesame," Anna giggled. She bent down to peer through the open door. "What is that? A secret passageway? It smells like my grandmother's hope chest."

"My brother and I think it was a hiding place for booze during Prohibition. He found it by accident and kept the door in place. Lined it with thin cedar strips after finding it. Prevents termites. I'm looking for the right size safe to fit inside."

"Well, I'm impressed," Anna said. She turned slowly in a circle while looking the house over.

"So, are you hungry? I'm starving," Kraus said.

"Yes, I haven't had a thing since breakfast," Anna said.

"Okay," Kraus grabbed the handle of her trunk, "let me show you where you're going to sleep."

Anna gave him a hard stare.

"Don't worry," Kraus said. "I haven't mistaken you for your friend, Penelope Westgate. You have your own room."

"You *have* been on my trail, haven't you, Nick Charles," Anna laughed. "She was something else, boy. That chippie would have tripped you and beat you to the floor."

"I'm not sure she had the patience for that long of a mating ritual," Kraus said as he lugged the trunk down the hallway. "Here's the guest room," he said as he opened a hall doorway and flipped the light switch. "The bathroom is directly across."

Anna looked inside, taking in the neatly made double bed. A radio and lamp sat on the maple bedside table. Some nice prints on the wall. A small writing table and padded chair sat against another wall. "Nice," Anna said.

"I have a bathroom attached to the master bedroom, so this bathroom is entirely yours. Feel free to spread your French milled soap cakes all around."

"I'm gaining more respect for your investigative skills every moment," Anna said. "Is there anything you *don't* know about me?"

"I know you only chew half-sticks of gum," he said, getting another laugh from Anna. "I don't know how you like your eggs," Kraus said. "I'm going to whip some up with some sausage links. I've got toast and English muffins. Raspberry jam."

"Eggs the way you're having them. Toast, please. A little butter. No jam," Anna said.

"Fine. I'll get busy. You take your time getting squared away. Change if you want. There're fresh towels and washcloths in the bathroom," Kraus said.

"Okay," Anna said. Kraus took a step towards the kitchen. "Mr. Kraus," Anna said, stopping him.

"Gordy, please," Kraus said. "Yeah?"

"Thank you, Gordy" Anna said.

"Don't thank me yet, Anna. You haven't tasted my cooking," Kraus said.

Kraus took four eggs out of the fridge and placed them on the counter. He wanted them at room temperature. He busied himself chopping onions and bell peppers. The sounds of Anna changing and using the bathroom issued from the hallway. Just as he was cracking the eggs into a ceramic bowl, she padded out into the living room. She was wearing a light, sleeveless cardigan over a crisp white t-shirt. Neat slacks and a pair of canvas espadrilles. She walked into the kitchen area and leaned against the counter, watching Kraus work.

"Need any help?" Anna asked.

"Not now. You're the guest. Please relax. Want anything to drink?"

"I wouldn't turn down some orange juice," she said.

Kraus pivoted around, took a pitcher of orange juice from the fridge and filled a tumbler. "Here you go," he said.

"Thanks," she took a sip.

"So, how did you end up splitting off from your two partners in crime? Get on the outs with them?"

Kraus watched Anna take a breath while he sprinkled the sliced green onions and scraped the pieces off the cutting board into the bowl. She was deciding whether to tell him the truth. How much to tell. What would work to her advantage.

"You've already guessed I was working a rental scam with Lou and Lester. I met them while I was in Denver. I dealt blackjack for a guy who operated a floating crap game operation. Nosebleed stakes. One night the Oxford, next the Magnolia, next the Crawford. You know the routine."

"Yeah," Kraus said.

"So, the Denver sheriff was a guy named Enlow. He was pretty friendly with the big gambling syndicate in town. Run by the Smaldone brothers. Without warning, Enlow gets nabbed on a tax evasion charge and a new sheriff gets into office."

"There's a new sheriff in town," Kraus said in an exaggerated Texas drawl.

"Oh, exactly," Anna laughed. "Art Wermuth. Starts a big law and order campaign. Going to clean up the gambling, the vice."

"You get caught up in this?"

"No, but the handwriting was on the wall," Anna said. "A lot of people stopped coming to the hotels for craps and cards. Tips were horrible. I met Lester and Louie. They were heading for Los Angeles. L.A. sounded good to me. I had been toying with the idea of a fake landlord operation, but needed a partner or two to run it at the scale that made it worthwhile. Denver was too small. Los Angeles is such a sprawling place, I figured a well-run operation could keep going for two years or so without any trouble."

"Probably a good guess. What happened next?"

"I met back up with Louie and Lester here in L.A. about a month later. Got the lay of the land and everything started out fine. I would rent a house, then put notices up in these new laundromats springing up everywhere. Supermarket bulletin boards. 'House for Rent'. I'd list the rent about ten or fifteen dollars below market. Louie and Lester would handle the phone. Take the calls and make the appointments. Rope in the suckers. I'd show prospects the places. The asking price was so cheap, they couldn't wait to give me their deposits. Then wait for the next bumpkins to show up."

"How much did these marks pay you?" Kraus asked.

"Averaged almost one-fifty a throw. First and last plus a cleaning deposit," Anna said.

Kraus whistled, "Must have added up quick."

"It did when it got going. I had rented out a string of houses. Not all at the same time. Staggered out, you know. You can only milk one for a few days. Maybe a week. But that's enough time to break even and turn a good profit before moving on to the next. I had a good run in late October. Everyone wanting to get moved and resettle before the holidays. In a rush."

"Busy time of year," Kraus agreed.

"I had over three thousand dollars in accumulated deposits hidden in my car. A young couple showed up to see a house I'd rented in Carson. They looked like they'd tumbled out of Life magazine. Office worker husband. PTA wife. I turned my back on them to open the kitchen cupboards. Show them all the storage. The whole drill."

Kraus nodded his head as he started to whisk the eggs.

"I turned back around and was looking down the barrels of two thirty-eight revolvers."

TWENTY

Los Angeles Russian Consulate - November 29th, 1956

Kuznetsov read through the notes Balabanov had given him a second time. He didn't need to. But Balabanov sat squirming in front of his desk. Kuznetsov knew it can be very discomposing for a KGB operative to sit by while a superior scrutinizes his work. Kuznetsov could scarcely believe anything could alarm Balabanov. The KGB man had been a fierce Soviet partisan fighter during the early days of Operation Barbarossa, the Nazi Germany invasion of Russia.

Balabanov had been part of a particularly brutal partisan squad in eastern Belorussia. These paramilitary resistance groups harassed the front lines of the advancing Wehrmacht. Their mission focused on disrupting German communications, destroying fuel and ammo dumps, and blowing up railroad lines and airfields. Guerilla warfare and sabotage. Balabanov specialized in scouting German targets the night before a planned action. He worked alone, often equipped with only his sidearm and a vicious-looking combat knife. Many nights he returned to his partisan encampment with German medals, patches and field caps. Kill trophies.

Now this fearsome night fighter fidgeted in his chair like a schoolboy. The headmaster reviewing his classwork. Kuznetsov looked up from the notes Balabanov had given him.

"Balabanov, it strikes me as a fortuitous coincidence that the very man who posed such a risk to one of our country's most vital operations is now dead," Kuznetsov said.

The KGB agent sat rigid. Unsure how to answer. "No thoughts on the matter?" Kuznetsov asked.

"Sir, America is little more than a society of gangsters and hoodlums. My contact tells me the man was a former police officer. He fraternized with the lowest criminal elements in the city. I was also told that his police colleagues are surprised it hadn't happened before now."

"Your contact is a policeman?" Kuznetsov asked.

"Our West Coast labor union section is working on the creation of a labor dispute at a small film studio," Balabanov explained. "A small part of a larger operation aimed at the heart of the industry. A guard on the studio lot is a retired Los Angeles policeman. His family is Lithuanian. He's been very helpful to our cause."

"I see," Kuznetsov said in a skeptical tone. "Just so I'm completely clear on the matter," he looked back at Balabanov's notes. "You discovered who this extortionist was before his death?"

"Yes, sir," Balabanov answered. "I observed him meeting with the studio clerk you identified as a possible weak link."

"According to your notes," Kuznetsov nodded at the papers in his hands, "you then maintained surveillance of this agent provocateur."

"Yes, sir," Balabanov confirmed. "He fit your description. I watched him for several days. He made contact with two others on your list."

"Quite so," Kuznetsov said. "That is made clear in your notes. Here is what is not so clear. You lose track of him on the very night this American hooligan turns up dead in a deserted alleyway. It appears more to me as though you acted on your own, Balabanov."

"No sir," Balabanov broke in. "This man was slippery as an eel. He always acted as though he suspected he was being watched. I'm not proud to confess that he eluded my surveillance."

"On the very night he met his death," Kuznetsov said in a tone of disbelief.

"Sir, I would never exceed the limits of my orders," Balabanov declared.

"I hope so, Balabanov. I hope so. I will not report this. For now," Kuznetsov emphasized. "In the meantime, keep looking into the background of this dead American. Find out if he was working for someone. If he worked alone. Who he may have confided in. He may be dead, but his activities before his demise may continue to pose a threat to our operation."

"Yes, sir," Balabanov said. He stood to go.

"Report your progress to me on a regular basis. Continue to keep your work in the strictest of secrecy. The Kremlin has made it very clear that no local consulate personnel are to be aware of our project."

"Yes, sir," Balabanov said. "I'll have another report for you the day after tomorrow."

"See that you do," Kuznetsov said. "And Balabanov," the retreating operative stopped in his tracks. "No liquidations without express orders from me. You're not hunting Nazi sentries in a Belorussian forest any longer."

Kuznetsov smiled at the sight of a retreating Balabanov. The poor man still didn't know whether he was suspected of killing the American or not. That should keep him under control. Of course, Kuznetsov knew quite well that his KGB subordinate didn't kill the American. Because he had done the job himself.

TWENTY-ONE

"Pointing guns at you? Unhappy with the storage space?" Kraus joked as he poured the egg mixture into his skillet.

"Ha, ha," Anna said. "They came there to rob me," she exclaimed. "They looked so normal. Both of them had me fooled from the moment they got out of their car. I never suspected a thing until they pulled their guns."

Her exasperation amused Kraus. It was so funny that crooks are often the most incensed when the tables are turned on them. "What happened next?"

"Dumped my purse onto the kitchen counter. Took the cash I had in my pocketbook. Then they tied me up, stuffed my own hankie in my mouth and left. I got loose after a few minutes and saw they'd taken my car keys."

"Boosted the car?" Kraus asked while he moved the eggs across the warm skillet bottom. "How'd you get it back?"

"They didn't steal the car," Anna explained. "But they found my big bankroll in the trunk space under the spare where I kept it. I could tell they hadn't searched anywhere else. Knew right where to look. Nothing inside the car was touched. Thank God they didn't find my private stash under the driver's seat. They left the keys on the windshield under the wiper."

"Sounds like an inside job," Kraus said, pushing some of the finished scramble onto Anna's plate.

"Just what I thought," she said. "I figured Lester and Louie had set me up. I just couldn't see why. I know they'd never seen that much money drop into their laps on such a regular basis. They killed the golden goose to get my third of the past two weeks take?"

"What do you think they were up to?" Kraus asked as he buttered the bread he'd rescued from the toaster.

"I wasn't sure," Anna said, taking her toast and cutting it into neat triangle quarters. "I figured they got greedy. Set up the robbery, then planned to demand I give them a bigger cut to pay back what I 'owed' them. But I wasn't sure. Before I was robbed, I had thought it was funny that they kept dodging our meetups. Up until then we met up every few days to split the take. I realized afterwards they wanted me to be holding a lot of money for the stick-up. I felt things taking a turn for the worse and I got clear of them."

"They told some people at the Cockatoo that they were planning on setting up a call girl operation. Lester hinted to the pit boss that they were going to make you their star employee," Kraus said. He poured some more orange juice into Anna's tumbler.

"Thank you," she said. She carried her plate and glass to the dining table. "The Cockatoo? You were right on my trail, weren't you, Dick Tracy?"

"I read the paper bobbing behind in your wake. You don't have to be Einstein to figure you'd show up at a betting parlor at one point or another."

"A call girl operation," Anna blurted out. Incredulous. She forked up some eggs, "These are good, Gordy!"

"Thanks," he lowered his voice into a whisper, "I fold in some sour cream. Makes them creamier."

"I'll keep your secret. They're delicious," she said before biting off a small corner of a toast piece. "Those two couldn't organize a Red Cross sock hop. What suddenly makes them think they can be Brenda Allen?"

"Small time hoods fantasizing about the old days. Seeing themselves as big players. I imagine they planned to force you to work off your 'debt' as a prostitute. Wouldn't be too much of a stretch to figure they planned on getting you hooked on horse and working pretty much for free after that. Lucky Luciano playbook."

"Fat chance," Anna said scornfully. She picked up her plate and glass, depositing them in the kitchen sink. "You think they're still looking for me?"

"Dreams die hard," Kraus said. "I tried to put a scare into Lester when I had him on the pavement. Told him he'd caught the attention of the new local mob boss. Gave him the idea that he and Louie would be the perfect pigeons to kill. Use them to make an example."

"Did he buy it?" Anna asked. She walked back into the living room while Kraus added his dish and glass to the pile in the sink.

"Maybe. But these aren't bright fellows. They're probably still out looking for you. Like I said, dreams die hard."

"I really don't want to leave L.A. I like the weather here. People seem nice. But if you turn in my car," she began.

"It isn't your car," Kraus reminded her.

"You know what I mean," she shot back. "If I don't have a car and have to get around town on the transit lines, they'll catch me pretty soon."

"I know that. I'm at a crossroads with you," Kraus said.

"Oh?" Anna asked. She nibbled on a corner of her toast. Hiding her anxiety, Kraus thought.

"I could turn you in to the LAPD. Build up some credit in the favor bank. Return the car. Collect my fee and bonus."

"What's stopping you?"

"I really don't want to do that. Steer you into the arms of the law, I mean. The car is definitely being returned. But I've been thinking about how we can help each other out."

"How's that?" Anna asked. Suddenly suspicious. She saw the Monkey Fist on a small table near the couch. It was holding down some mail Kraus had opened and hadn't yet filed away. "What is that evil-looking thing?" Anna asked. She touched it with the tip of her finger as though it might snap at her.

"That was a sort of sap my old patrol partner used to use. He was the main reason I was at the Cockatoo the other night. I asked about you on the off chance they might have seen you in there. My old partner, Ollie McBride, is the thing I think you can help me with," Kraus said.

He told her about Ollie. About his murder. How he thought she could help.

TWENTY-TWO

"So, we're going to interview a woman who had an affair with the man you think shot your partner?" Anna asked. She took a stick of spearmint gum from her purse, tore it in half and unwrapped it. Popped it in her mouth and offered the other half to Kraus.

"No, thanks," Kraus said. "My mom won't let me chew that kind." She laughed. He was driving south on the Harbor Freeway. Their appointment was at eight and the morning rush hour traffic was heavy. He got off at Century and started working his way west towards the Lennox Park neighborhood. "I have my suspicions. About him being the shooter."

"And you want me tagging along because you think it'll soften her up?"

"Her name is Emily. Emily Matz. This is a woman who was betrayed by a man she sacrificed her marriage for. I'm guessing having a woman in on the interview will offset the natural distrust she probably has for men. She may be more forthcoming with the information we need."

"I don't think it takes a divorce and a romantic disappointment to make a woman distrust men. If she's like most women, she was there well before all that happened."

"Sounds like the voice of experience," Kraus said.

"You're forgetting the situation you lifted me out of. Not that I trusted them in the first place. Not that men have *ever* given me a reason to trust them."

Kraus could tell there was a bigger story there. He let it go for now. He was looking for the killer of his friend. No time for distraction from the task at hand.

"I don't have an exact idea of how we're going to approach her. She agreed to meet with us readily enough when my secretary called her. Let's just play it by ear. Take my lead, then feel free to jump in with any question that occurs to you. If she responds better to you, run with it. I'll just listen."

Kraus drove deeper into the neighborhood south of Century, looking for the right street. "What's that?" Anna asked, pointing at a large commercial building with cages set up on the parking lot next to the main walls.

"That's a parrot aviary. Supposedly the largest in the world. This all used to be agricultural land. Big poultry farms. We'd go with my mom sometimes when she drove here to get eggs. She'd let us wander around looking at the parrots. It felt like we were in Central America with all the colorful birds squawking and flapping their wings."

Little square houses were scattered along the narrow streets. Chain link fences surrounded many of them. Most of the houses started off as temporary homes for the migrant labor working the Lennox farms. Most were now single-family homes for the blue-collar workers at the aerospace factories popping up around the airport. At that moment, a large DC-6 passenger plane roared overhead.

"We must be close to the airport. That thing sounded like its wheels were going to scrape the car roof," Anna said.

"L.A. Municipal Airport is just a couple of miles west of here. Lately, most people are imitating radio and television announcers by just saying its airport code, 'L-A-X'. A huge bond was passed this year to expand the airport. Support businesses are moving in. This whole neighborhood won't be the same ten years from now. There's a high school going in just a few blocks away. It's going to start growing. Rudi, my brother, considered buying some lots here to develop, but he thought the airport noise would always hold values down."

"That's what I like about this place," Anna said. "Always growing. Changing every day."

"Yeah. There is an energy here," Kraus said. "I'm not always sure I like the growth. Here we are."

Kraus pulled up in front of a small stucco house sitting towards the rear of a narrow lot. A short chain link fence ran around the front yard. No garage. The driveway consisted of two gravel-topped strips leading from the dip at the curb to the area beside the house. A yellow Mercury Monterey with a dusty black top sat next to the house. Pretty fancy for a Lennox one-bedroom, Kraus thought. He figured it was her car prior to the divorce.

"Let's go," Kraus said. He climbed out of the Lincoln and went around to open the door for Anna. "I'll start the talking," he reminded her.

They walked up the driveway and Kraus flipped open the horseshoe latch on the chain link gate. No screen door. Kraus knocked. A little dog started yapping inside the house. The door opened to reveal a woman in her forties with hair the color of cinnamon. She wore an A-line plaid flannel dress. Pleated skirt with a wide, solid color belt and matching cuffs on the three-quarter sleeves. A little brown chihuahua squirmed in her arms.

"Emily Matz?" Kraus asked. "I'm Gordon Kraus and this is my associate, Anna Bjorkquist. My secretary, Melinda, arranged for us to meet with you."

"Of course," the woman said, "please come in."

Emily Matz turned and bent down to release her dog into the house. She shooed him away. "Go to your bed, Carlos." The dog's long toenails made frantic scratching noises on the hardwood floor as it scurried out of the room.

"Please, sit down," she said, sweeping an arm toward a charcoal-colored sofa against one wall. It was a three-seater with a walnut base. Almost too long for the small living room. Another part of her divorce settlement, Kraus thought.

He and Anna took a seat while Emily Matz settled into a simple stuffed armchair opposite the sofa. She leaned a little forward in the chair. Ready to stand back up and bolt.

"I told your girl that I could only see you for a few minutes this morning. I'm a bookkeeper at the Von's in Inglewood and have to be there by nine."

"Mrs. Matz, we'll only take a few minutes of your time," Kraus said. "We just have a few questions."

"Your girl told me you had questions about Tommy Thorp. Is that right?"

"Yes. We've been asked to look into a recent situation your previous acquaintance, Mr. Thorp, may have been involved in," Kraus said.

"Mr. Kraus," Emily Matz said, "you can just say you're looking into another one of Tommy Thorp's conquests. By now I'm well aware of the kind of man he is." She lowered her voice, "the kind of woman I am."

"He was a selfish exploiter, Mrs. Matz," Anna said. "That kind only prey on people who have a basic innocence. Decency. That's what made you vulnerable. It was fun for him," Anna continued. "So yes, I know full well what kind of woman you must be. You're so brave to talk about this all over again, so we won't take up too much of your time."

Emily Matz gave Anna a mixed look of surprise and gratitude. Unaccustomed to being treated with sympathy and understanding. "You're right about Tommy. He had some charm, but underneath he was a user. I look back at it now and wonder how I ever fell for him and his malarkey." She had a pretty enough face. The bridge of her nose was a bit wide, as was her chin. She knew how to use makeup to her advantage. Her round, brown eyes began to water.

Anna took a tissue from her purse and handed it across to Emily Matz. The divorcee dabbed at her eyes. "Now, Mrs. Matz," Anna began.

"Emily, please."

"Okay. Emily," Anna continued, "we need to know a little bit about Mr. Thorp. How did you meet him?"

"My husband and I had a home in View Park," Emily explained. She looked around at the worn floorboards and cracked plaster walls of her present home. "I know, I've come down quite a ways. This was all I could afford with what I received from my divorce."

"Not at all," Anna said with a soothing tone.

"My husband was so busy all the time. He owns three swimming pool supply stores in the Valley," Emily said. "Chemicals. Cleaning equipment. Pool toys. Even a home pool service. The operation of the stores and the pool maintenance end of it kept him away twelve hours a day, seven days a week. I begged him to take on a partner or at least hire a manager he could trust, but he refused. Said he was doing it for us."

"Sure," Anna said. "I understand."

"I was bored. I joined a women's club. We had group luncheons. Played tennis. Golfed. I began taking golf lessons at Sunset Fields Golf Course on Crenshaw. It was easy to drive to. Women's club members received discounts in the pro shop and instructions. Tommy started giving me lessons. He was a good teacher. Made me feel comfortable. Never criticized me. Praised my progress. I enjoyed the lessons."

"Sounds like a break from being home waiting for your husband to come home, wolf down dinner, go to sleep and leave again," Anna suggested.

"Just that," Emily said. "Tommy was interested in spending time with me. Listened to me. Paid attention to me. We started spending time together between lessons. Then more time. Not just lessons."

"Emily, don't beat yourself up for being human. Men do this every day. There's nothing to be ashamed of."

"Thank you for that, Anna," Emily said.

"I mean it, Emily," Anna said. "What happened that made everything go off the rails?"

"Tommy kept telling me he wanted us to be together. I was so besotted by him, I think I would have done anything he asked at that point. He told me he was so angry at how my husband had enslaved me. He never wanted me to have to financially rely on someone again. Not even him. He wanted me to have some financial independence."

"I see," Anna said. "What did he suggest?"

"He knew I had some money from my great aunt. Not much. A few thousand dollars. Tommy said he had a friend who had invented a sure-fire electronic device. It was going to make millions, but the friend was looking for private investors. He said that the friend was afraid if he tried to sell the patent to an established corporation, he'd be cheated and never see a fraction of what he deserved."

"*Electronic device*," Kraus thought. That instantly brought to mind the catalog he'd taken from Ollie's house. He almost jumped into the conversation but held back. Anna had gotten Emily Matz talking and he didn't want her to stop. He wanted to hear the whole story.

"Sounds like an attractive opportunity," Anna said in a soft voice.

"It did," Emily said. "I agreed to meet Tommy's friend. See a demonstration of what he'd invented."

"Practical, cautious approach," Anna said.

"I met them at a hotel room in Culver City. Tommy's friend had the demonstration all set up. Very professional. The invention was a little box. About the size of a box of margarine cubes." Emily held her palms about eight inches apart to show the dimension. "It had buttons. The little box would turn the television in the hotel room on and off without wires. Change the channels. Make the sound louder or quieter. He let me use it. It worked very well."

"Really," Anna said. "I've never seen such a thing. It does sound like something everyone would want."

"Precisely my opinion. Tommy's friend told me that a company in Chicago, a big company, had already developed one. But Tommy's friend said they were way behind the curve on what this kind of thing could do. He pointed it at the little radio on the bedside table. Turned the radio on and off. Just like the television."

"Wow," Anna said.

"That's what I thought. Tommy's chum told me he'd developed a way for the electronics to work on not just televisions. Radios, record players, light switches. He said the possibilities were unlimited and people would be lining up to buy one."

"Okay," Anna said. "What did he say next?"

"He said that he was recruiting investors because he wanted to go into production right away. Get product on store shelves by the next Christmas. He said all the hard work had been done, but he needed capital for a building, materials, packaging, advertising. Start-up costs. He said that Tommy had told him I had some money I wanted to invest."

"Hmmm," Anna said. "Did you tell him you were interested?

"I did. I told him I had three thousand dollars and I could get it to him by the end of the week."

"I'll bet he told you he was looking for much larger investors," Anna smiled gently. "He already had three investors willing to put up ten thousand each. He felt the fewer investors the better and he couldn't start accepting small investment amounts. Something like that."

"Exactly like that," Emily Matz exclaimed. "He told me he'd already turned away several people who wanted to buy shares for five thousand dollars. The lowest buy-in was set at ten thousand. And he only had room for two or three more investors. He couldn't let me get in on the ground floor for even less. He said it wouldn't be fair."

"What did you say?"

"Anna, I was so crushed. When I saw the demonstration, I saw myself divorcing my husband, striking out on my own, enjoying my life with Tommy. Returns on my investment making me rich. Independent. Happy. I was desperate. I saw it as my one chance to break free."

"I'm guessing Tommy noticed your distress. He cared so much for you."

"He cared alright," Emily Matz barked out a laugh. "But you're right. At that moment, he was my knight in shining armor. He scolded his friend for belittling the amount of investment money I offered. Tommy said that if his friend was so determined to have a ten-thousand-dollar block of investment capital, he'd write a check to his friend right there for the other seven thousand."

"Very generous," Anna said. "Tommy must have seemed quite committed to his relationship with you right at that moment."

"Oh, you said it, sister," Emily Matz said. "I thought it was perfect. The love of my life and me investing in our future together. A team. Definitely not the relationship I felt with my husband."

"And you had the money for him by the end of the week," Anna prompted.

"Oh, I couldn't wait to put it in his hands. Afterwards is when it all started to fall apart," Emily whispered. "My husband found my bank statement. Made me tell him what I'd done with 'our nest egg'. Made me tell him about Tommy. God, the names he called me." She started to weep again. The dog padded over and put its head on her foot.

"Now, now," Anna soothed, "that's all in the past and your husband had a mistress long before you met Tommy Thorp. His pool business. Emily, it's not all that different. Like I said, don't beat yourself up for this."

"Thank you," Emily hiccupped and choked on her tears. "My husband did some digging. He found out that Zenith, the television and radio company? They had developed a television remote that was coming out soon. He figured Tommy's friend had gotten hold of a test model somehow and was using it to cheat people. My husband enjoyed rubbing my nose in my own stupidity. I did try to sue the so-called inventor after my divorce. I couldn't find him. I tried to sue Tommy for fraud. He told the judge he had been duped just like me. He claimed he lost twice as much in the swindle. Nothing came out of it. You know the rest."

"We do, Emily. Thank you. But we have a better idea of what Tommy Thorp is capable of."

"Emily," Kraus broke in, "do you think Tommy was the violent sort underneath all his slickness? Would he have harmed you or your husband if he thought you were going to get him in trouble?"

Emily Matz thought for a moment. "It's hard to say. He's such a devil in my mind now. Maybe I'm not the best person to judge his true character." She seemed to reach an opinion, "Mr. Kraus, I hate that man, but I don't think he was the violent type. He did own a gun. A pistol of some sort. He made a big show of taking it with him when we drove to give his friend my money. For protection. He told me he was a Korean combat veteran. Knew how to use a gun. Practiced with it at some gun range in the valley. Irish sounding place. But no, I don't think he was violent. Just a liar and a cheat."

"Good enough," Kraus said. He and Anna stood to leave. "We've taken up enough of your time. You've been very helpful." He handed Emily Matz his business card. "If you think of anything else, please call my office."

"And, Emily," Anna reached out her hand and placed it on Emily Matz' shoulder, "you haven't done anything horrible. All of us have used poor judgment during our lives. Don't beat yourself up for the rest of your life over one mistake."

"Thank you, Anna. You've been very kind."

"Not in the least. And you haven't fallen as far as you think. Mr. Kraus' brother is a real estate expert, and he thinks the houses in your neighborhood are going to be worth a lot more before long." Anna waited a beat, "But list it with a reputable broker when you decide to sell."

Both women shared an understanding laugh.

TWENTY-THREE

It was a beautiful day at the golf course. The end of November. The sun was shining, and the noontime temperature was in the low-eighties. Kraus was not an avid golfer. He played a round once or twice a year with his brother, Rudi. His brother was a nut for the sport and was in the men's club at two L.A. golf courses. He wrote the dues off as a business expense.

Despite his lack of enthusiasm for the sport itself, Kraus loved the atmosphere of a golf course. The ripe melon smell of freshly mowed grass. The etiquette rituals. The sporty-formal way men and women dressed for the course. The rattle of golf clubs bouncing around in their bags. The pure thwack sound of a driver making solid contact with a ball. His brother would say, "hitting it right in the screws". A white dimpled sphere whisked cleanly off the tee to sail down the fairway. Polite, hushed whispers of other players waiting their turns.

After meeting with Emily Matz the day before, Kraus decided he needed a more thorough look at Tommy Thorp. Gauge the accuracy of Emily's opinion of Tommy's peaceful disposition. He and Anna chatted about it on their way back to his home.

"What did you make of Emily and her story?" Kraus asked Anna.

"I think she wasn't holding anything back. I was impressed with how candid she was with us," Anna said. "All stories like hers sound the same, but there were some interesting insights."

"Like what?" Kraus asked.

"This Tommy Thorp is a pretty good flim-flam artist. That get-rich-quick scam he ran with his partner was a masterpiece. Impeccable timing. Inventor insults the amount of money the woman offers. Boyfriend rises up and vows to make up the difference. First-rate."

"You sound envious," Kraus said.

"I've steered for several confidence teams over the past few years. Good ones. The ruse she fell for was watertight. You have to respect a gambit like that. Tommy must be quite the Lothario. Emily didn't have a chance."

"Lothario? So, you read Shakespeare as well as new mysteries," Kraus remarked.

"I never finished high school. Left St. Paul when I was sixteen. I thought I hated school. Turns out, I just hated my life there. I discovered I love to learn. I read quite a lot."

"Well, tomorrow you're going to go to Sunset Fields Golf Course and read Tommy Thorp a little bit more," Kraus said. He called his office and asked Melinda to call the course and arrange a lesson for Margaret Woodward. She called back fifteen minutes later. A noon appointment had been set with the club's assistant pro, Tommy Thorp. "It's on," Kraus announced. Anna protested that she didn't have the appropriate clothes. Kraus called his sister, who was all too happy to rush over to the rescue.

"Not to worry. About three boyfriends ago, Austie dated a guy who golfed. She took up the sport with a passion. She probably has golf clothes she's never worn."

Kraus' sister arrived an hour later with an armload of skirts and blouses. Kraus introduced her to Anna. Austie gazed at Anna, looking her up and down. "Aren't you lovely," she sighed, casting a raised eyebrow at her oldest brother. "I would die for your figure," Austie continued. "Hell, I'd die to just step into your skin," she gushed. "Your hair! Do you have your eyebrows shaped?"

"Why, thank you, Austie," Anna replied in a gracious tone. "You're too kind. I think you are quite beautiful yourself."

"I definitely was the kid who got the looks," she giggled, looking at her brother with a mischievous grin. "Are you staying in the guest room?" she asked. Half-cautious. Half-suspicious.

"Of course," Anna said.

"Austie," Kraus said in a stern voice.

"Oh, hush up. You know Mom is going to ask," Austie laughed. "Let's go to your room and see how these things fit you." She took Anna's hand and dragged her towards the guest bedroom. "This is going to be so fun!"

Austie and Anna came out a half hour later. Both women giggled like school girls on a sleepover. Anna did a nifty pirouette to show off the outfit, finishing with a model's little back leg kick. She was wearing a peach-colored sleeveless blouse tucked into a green plaid skirt. The skirt had the generous cut women golfers need for their swing. Matching peach-colored socks rolled down in a neat reverse cuff. She looked enchanting. Vibrant. No shoes. Austie saw her brother look at the socks.

"No way can Anna wear shoes the size of my clompers," Austie declared.

"She almost got thrown off the El Camino College swim team. The coach thought she was wearing swim fins the first day," Kraus said.

"Meanie," Austie said, sticking her tongue out at her brother. Both women broke out into more titters. "We're going to go shopping and get her some new golf shoes." Before her brother could protest, Austie cut in, "Gordy, she can't show up for new lessons in slingback pumps!"

"Where are you going? I don't want you two going anywhere near the Miracle Mile."

"Don't worry. She told me she's avoiding a jealous boyfriend. We're going to go to Hoegee's for the golf shoes. If they don't have the right ones, Bullock's in Westwood Village. We might both get manicures while we're there," shooting Anna a conspiratorial look. "At some point we're going to drop into Clifton's for a bite. Anna's going to change back into her street clothes now," she said. Kraus' sister held out her hand, "I think forty dollars should cover the whole trip. Throw in an extra five for that swim fin crack."

"Just be careful," Kraus said as he pried his wallet out of his jacket pocket.

Kraus had let Anna out way in the back of the course parking lot. Thorp had already seen him, and he didn't want to chance being spotted with her. His sister's golf club bag was lashed to a collapsible cart. Anna scooped it out of the Lincoln's trunk, expanded the wheel legs and towed it in the direction of the clubhouse. Wheels squeaking. Kraus waited in the car.

After enough time had passed, Kraus strolled to a deserted area adjacent to the driving range. He peered east towards the busy traffic moving up and down Crenshaw. A hedgerow of trees grew on the other side of the boulevard. Norton Avenue ran along the other side of the file of trees. Tidy little Leimert Park houses were visible through the treeline.

He spied one house that had been a vacant lot when he came home from the war. One early January morning in 1947, a woman's body turned up on that lot. Completely bisected and left in the open. Carved up like a jack o'lantern. Carefully posed. Pregnant when she died. The pregnancy was one of the police holdbacks for eliminating false confessors. Only the true killer would have known her condition. Ten years later and the public still wasn't aware of it.

The LAPD ultimately figured out who the killer must have been. One of the department's litany of poorly protected secrets.

The identity of the unborn child's father was a different matter. The police were confident the father and the killer were not the same man. "Mutually exclusive" as Lococo would say. The mystery father *did* have clout. Anonymous clout. Potent clout. The kind of clout that gummed up the works of an investigation. Clout to bury the facts. Clout to bury the career of an ambitious police investigator. Maybe bury more than the career.

The news business abhors a void. Newspapers and radio didn't need facts. The victim had been an enigma. A laundry list of contradictions. Needy but resourceful. Clingy but aloof. Insecure but confident in her ability to manipulate men. She used a stick of paraffin wax to fill in the imperfections of her teeth. She wanted men to see her as beautiful. Desirable.

The public fell in love with this mysterious, striking woman. The press trumpeted every new theory about her life and her death. No one knew her but previously unpublished pictures of her cropped up every week. Many of her posed next to notable Angelenos. As perplexing and irresistible in death as she had been in life. More so. There was a firestorm of continuous news coverage. A scandal bomb waiting for the powder to ignite. Half of Hollywood dove for foxholes. Kraus had only returned from post-war Berlin a few months before. Getting his investigation business off the ground. The inevitable explosion of the scandal bomb was feeble. Muffled by an invisible blanket of influence. Nevertheless, the heat of the relatively minor blast burned a lot of people. It even managed to scorch Kraus.

Like Charlotte, this woman had been alone in her final days. Scared and in danger. The murdered woman had dyed her black hair red a few panicky days before her murder. Another police hold-back. She had naturally raven black hair in all her photos. Impossibly thick, obsidian curls that lent her a starlet quality. People became infatuated with her, like people were with Anna.

Kraus was not going to let Anna become another victim like Charlotte or the poor girl in that field.

"What are you looking at?" Anna asked, startling Kraus. He was so lost in thoughts of the past he hadn't heard her come up behind him.

"I was looking around," Kraus said. "Where's Thorp?" he asked. He didn't want to tell her about the tragic fate of the other black-haired woman.

"My lesson doesn't start for another fifteen minutes or so. The guy in the clubhouse told me he was on the course with a group but will be back in pretty soon. I'm supposed to meet him at the driving range." Anna pointed at the line of tee boxes under a metal canopy. "I spotted you and walked over to see what you were doing.

He came up with something almost at once. "I was thinking about coming right here with my family back in 1932. This is where a running event was held for the '32 Olympics."

"I thought the Olympics took place at the Coliseum. I read that it was built for the games."

"Oh, it was," Kraus agreed. "But events were held all over L.A. The cross-country track event was here," he waved his arm, "right here on the golf course. We went to see it because ... well, it was the Olympics ... and it was free to watch." He laughed.

"Was it fun?" Anna asked.

"Yes. But not as fun as going to the L.A. Swimming Stadium. That's next to the Coliseum. Built at the same time for the swimming events. My mom knew a lot of the German swim team coaches. Old friends from when she was on the German Olympic team. Rudi and I were flabbergasted by how she was treated like a celebrity. Saw our mom in a different light. We got to watch several events from poolside. Races. Men's water polo. I saw Buster Crabbe win a gold medal."

"Buster Crabbe? '*Flash Gordon*' Buster Crabbe?" Anna asked.

"In the flash," Kraus quipped.

"Ouch. That one was beneath even your sad sense of humor. You really love Los Angeles, don't you?"

"I guess I do. I grew up here. I've seen a lot of the world. Nothing compares to the magic of L.A. Nothing."

"Well, you better magically make yourself scarce, buster," Anna mock scolded. "My instructor is due to be here at any time."

"I'm going to go to the bar they have in that adobe building over there," Kraus said. "Dig around for information. The bartender may know some useful things about our boy. Have fun."

Anna chuckled and strode towards the driving range in her new two-toned golf shoes. Her hip motion caused her skirt to sway back and forth in a hypnotic movement. Kraus could see why she captured the heart of every man she crossed paths with. Just like the doomed woman who ended up dumped on a patch of dirt a thousand feet from where he stood.

TWENTY-FOUR

Kraus sauntered around inside the clubhouse saloon for a few minutes before taking a seat at the bar. He looked at the trophy case display of club champions dating back twenty-plus years. Tommy Thorp was the men's club champion for two years running. The walls were decorated with pictures of tournament winners, junior golf teams and club luncheons. Missing were the usual clipboards holding sign-up sheets for next year's men's and women's leagues, tournaments and charity events. 1956 was the club's last year. The entire golf course facility had been sold to a development company and next year at this time the area would be littered with foundations for new subdivisions. Kraus shook his head. The kind of growth he didn't care for.

He took a seat near the end of the bar. There was one guy at the other end of the bar reading the sports page and drinking a highball. A foursome was seated at one of the floor tables. They drank beer out of schooner mugs and ate shelled peanuts out of bowls while talking about their game. Every few minutes, braying mule laughter would erupt in reaction to a story of a bad shot or missed putt.

The driving range was in full view from his vantage point. Kraus saw Tommy Thorp in the midst of giving Anna her first golf lesson. Her cover story was that she and her husband had recently moved to Los Angeles from New York. Her husband was a production manager at one of the studios and was never home. She decided to take up golf as a hobby. Bored. Well-heeled. Slightly naive. That was the backstory they worked out for her.

Anna didn't look bad at all. Solid stance. She had the confident, easy takeback and downswing of a natural athlete. Graceful. Unhurried. Her hips rotated through her downswing as though she'd been golfing for years. Smooth follow-through. She looked almost as though she was dancing. After her first couple of swings, she regularly drove the ball a hundred-fifty yards or so out onto the range. Kraus was certain she could beat him without a minute more of practice.

"What will you have, boss," the bartender asked. A balding guy in his fifties. Tall and skinny as a golf flagstick. Small ears like tortellini shells set high up on the sides of his face. He wore a white long sleeve sports shirt with the club's logo patch on the breast pocket. Green and red sleeve garters with quarter-sized Christmas wreaths on both arms. They were the only visible concessions to the holiday season in the whole place, which made them seem sad rather than playfully festive.

"Pour me an Oly, will you?" Kraus asked.

"You got it, admiral," the bartender said. He almost grudgingly pushed a bowl of pretzel sticks and a small ceramic pot of hot mustard towards Kraus. He proceeded to pop open a cold bottle of Olympia. Kraus watched him deftly pour the beer into a tipped cold mug he'd taken from the bar fridge. A copy of the L.A. Times sat on the rear counter. Folded open to the want ads section. Looking for an escape hatch with earth movers rumbling up over the horizon. "You play today?"

"No. I've played here a couple of times over the years, though," Kraus said. "I read that Sunset Fields was being torn up for a housing development and I wanted to get a last look."

"Lot of good memories here, that's for sure," the bartender said without conviction.

"I was here in '32 with my family to watch that Olympics cross country track event. Old times sake. You know." Kraus pointed at a framed photo hanging behind the bar. It pictured a lone runner loping down one of the fairways. He dipped a couple of pretzel sticks into the hot mustard and chewed on them. Stale. No need to cultivate repeat business at this point.

"Yeah," the bartender groaned. He wiped the bar with a damp rag. "It's progress. This land is just too valuable to hold on to. Not enough money to justify it. Golfers payin' two bucks a round and thirty-five-dollar annual club dues. You know what I mean?" the bartender asked. It sounded like a grumble he recited often.

"I sure do," Kraus commiserated. "Have anything lined up?"

"I already work nights part-time at the Tam O'Shanter up near Glendale. I just need one more decent gig and I'll be fine," the bartender explained. "A good barman can always find a job in this town."

"Tam O'Shanter, huh," Kraus said. "Isn't that one of Walt Disney's favorite places?"

"It was, yeah. Not so much since he opened Disneyland down in Anaheim. I used to see him at the Tam a few times a month. Stingy tipper."

"What about the pros? I was here with two friends during the summer. The starter filled out a foursome with Tommy Thorp. Good ball striker," Kraus said, parroting a term his brother often used.

"Yeah, he's not bad," the bartender agreed. "Club champ a couple of times," waving his rag at the trophy case. "I heard he was getting on at Harding Memorial over at Griffith Park. Seems young to me for that stuffy crowd, but maybe that's why they want him. Attract some new blood."

"He seemed like a smooth kid when he played with us. Real Romeo. Must get a lot of action with the ladies," Kraus said.

"Oh, he's a cake eater alright," the bartender laughed. "Big cooze hound. He's over on the driving range right now with a looker," another wave of the rag. "That dame wouldn't look at me once, let alone give me a second look. Jesus, look at her," he moaned. "But that boy will be in her knickers before Christmas. Mark my words."

"Ladies' man, huh," Kraus remarked. "Ever get in any trouble over it?"

"There was some kerfuffle a year or so ago," the bartender said. "Blew over quick. He's a cocky one, but it seems to work for him. More power to him, I say."

The bartender didn't offer up any other dirt on Thorp, so Kraus let it go. They switched to talk about the Rams and the USC Trojans. Kraus figured there wasn't any real juicy stuff about Thorp. The bartender was the type who wouldn't have been able to resist sharing it. He munched on some more mustard-dipped pretzels. The lesson was over and Thorp had escorted Anna over to one of the outdoor benches near the range where they sat close to one another chatting and laughing. Thorp was very animated. Anna paid him back with encouraging laughter and fond gazes.

"See what I mean," the bartender said. He flapped his rag towards the scene at the redwood table. Vindicated. "It's only a matter of time now."

"Good for him," Kraus said. He was pleased that they were spending time together after the lesson. Thorp didn't know it, but he was the one being played. By an expert. He downed the last of his second beer and exited his barstool. He left a half dollar on the bar. Enough for the beer and a Walt Disney-sized tip.

TWENTY-FIVE

Kraus went straight back to his Lincoln after exiting the bar. He was careful to keep the building between him and the outdoor table Anna and Thorp sat at. Almost a half-hour went by before Anna wheeled the clubs into the parking lot and towards his car. Kraus left the trunk lid unlocked. Anna was able to heft the clubs into the trunk and jump into the passenger seat.

"I don't see him. Do you think he's watching you from some hidden spot?"

"No," Anna said. She settled into the seat and checked her makeup in the side view mirror, "he went right into the clubhouse. Said he was going to shower. He's too sure of himself to watch me leave. He had no reason to think I was anything but the movie studio widow I put myself up as. He's confident he has me nibbling on the bait. Believe me."

Kraus rapidly drove towards the exit and merged into the traffic on Crenshaw.

"You hungry? The only thing I've had since breakfast were some pretzels and mustard."

"I'm starving. Did you see me on the range? That was so fun. I hit that ball a country mile."

"You looked great," Kraus said with enthusiasm. "I mean, you had great form," Kraus laughed at himself. "That didn't come out much better, did it? I meant that you looked like you've golfed before."

"I know what you meant," Anna said with a touch of a smile. "Our boy was impressed, too. Austie gave me a few swing tips yesterday," Anna explained. "I'll tell you all about it when we sit down for lunch. Where are we going?"

"You like Mexican food?"

"*Si, senor*," Anna said with an exaggerated Katy Jurado accent. "I practically lived on Mex food for six months in Tucson."

"Well, we're going to go to the oldest Mexican restaurant in Los Angeles. They serve Sonoran Mexican food that will knock your little peach socks off."

"El Coyote?" Anna asked. "I've heard about it."

Kraus snorted. "El Coyote is the Disneyland of Mexican food. Nice enough place for the atmosphere. Food isn't bad. But it feels like a movie set. CBS studios is just down the street and tourists flock there hoping to see a star or two."

"So, where are we going?" Anna asked.

"El Cholo," Kraus swung onto Western. "It opened up in the early-20's. Moved around between buildings over time. Always stayed near Western and Pico. You're going to love this place."

They soon pulled in the parking lot off Western. Anna looked up at the restaurant sign atop a streetside pole. Moorish style shape and lettering. It read, "*El Cholo Spanish Cafe*".

"This looks great," Anna said.

The restaurant was quiet. It was between the lunch rush and dinner service. Several employees were busy hanging garland and decorating a Christmas tree in the lobby. Christmas music with a Latin flare was playing through the speaker system.

Kraus and Anna were seated in one of the booths. The booths were end-capped with quarter-partitions, giving diners a sense of privacy. Their waitress brought glasses of water and menus, then bustled off to another table to give them time to decide.

"Know what you'd like?" Kraus asked after a few minutes.

"It all looks good. Why don't you order for me. The only thing I don't like is shrimp. I hate the feeling of the crunch when I bite into them. *No comidas de marisco, por favor*."

"*Claro*," Kraus said. "You didn't waste your time in Tucson, did you?" The waitress returned and flipped open her pad. "We'll start off with a couple of Victoria lagers and an order of your guacamole with chips. For the main meal I'll have a cheese enchilada and rolled beef taco. My friend will have chile relleno and pork tamale."

"Sopas or salads?" the waitress asked.

He looked at Anna who gave him a small shake of the head. "No, that will be plenty," Kraus said, handing her the ashtray that was on the table. "You can take this. We'll need room for the chips and guacamole."

The waitress retreated with their order. "We can share portions of each other's plates so you can get a taste of everything," Kraus suggested.

Anna nodded her approval. "You don't smoke?"

"I used to when I was in college and my first year on the force. But I worked a lot of night shifts. You light up and your night vision is gone. Dangerous thing to lose when you're a cop. It was a good habit not to have when I was in the war. I notice you don't either."

"No. I smoked when I was still in high school. It was a dirty habit, and I didn't like it. I would have stopped later anyhow. In my line of work, you need to have your hands free at all times. Not draw attention to yourself by waving a cigarette around."

The waitress brought their beers and guacamole along with a wicker basket of fresh tortilla chips. Anna dipped a warm chip into the thick avocado mixture and bit off a piece. She rolled her eyes in approval.

"Okay," Kraus said. "What was your overall opinion of Thorp?"

"Well," Anna patted her mouth with her napkin and took a sip of beer, "he's pretty smooth. Charming in a smarmy sort of way. Knows how to talk to women."

"Knows how to talk to women? What does that mean? Does he speak Esperanto or something? Secret hand signals?"

"If you have to ask, you don't know how," Anna mock-scolded. "He's good working a con. Dips the hook in the water and waits for his mark to nibble at the bait. Like Emily Matz told us, he shifts right into the Judas Goat role when the situation calls for it. You can see his mind chugging away, running through all the percentages like a card counter."

"Interesting," Kraus said. "Do you think he's capable of a cold, calculated murder?"

"There's something just under that thin layer of charm he puts on. Selfish. Ruthless. Greedy. Angry." Anna stopped to consider for a moment. "I believe he wouldn't stop short of killing someone under the right circumstances. Someone who was standing between him and a big payday, for instance. That's the good news from the way you're looking at it."

"What's the bad news?" Kraus asked.

"He's got a solid alibi," Anna said.

"Christ, you didn't ask him about where he was that night, did you?"

Anna gave Kraus an irritated look. "Of course not, silly. What do you take me for?" She took another bite of guacamole. Just then the waitress appeared with their platters of food. The steam rising from the plates carried mouthwatering aromas of melted cheese, chili powder, oregano and cilantro.

Kraus was restless in his seat. Impatient to hear the bad news.

"Thank you," Anna said to the waitress. "I think we have everything we need right now."

"Well?" Kraus pressed once the server was out of earshot.

"Thorp was setting the table for our upcoming golf outings. The course is closing. Did you know that?"

"Yeah," Kraus said with a brusque tone.

"Goodness, you are a grouchy one. Take a bite of your enchilada. It'll make you feel better," Anna laughed. "Thorp was hinting that we could take a weekend trip to Santa Barbara and play at a course or two there. He painted such a beautiful picture," Anna sighed like a besotted schoolgirl.

"Yeah, he's quite the romantic," Kraus groused. "What's the rest?"

"He told me he was in Santa Barbara for Thanksgiving Weekend. He missed playing his favorite course there because he had to cut that part of the trip short to spend all Sunday at his mother's home in Oxnard. Spent the night. Didn't get back to L.A. until Monday afternoon." Anna cut into her chile relleno and forked a piece into her mouth. "Ummmm, this is wonderful!"

"Pretty weak alibi," Kraus mused. "Oxnard isn't all that far from Los Angeles. Ollie was killed in the middle of the night."

"On the face of it, yes," Anna conceded. "But he was just talking to me. Volunteered the information as part of a conversation. He had no reason to lie. No need to plant the idea so I could corroborate his story later. It had the ring of truth to it. Told me about his mother's special cranberry pancakes she made him Monday morning. It would be easy enough for your police friends to check out. But you'd look like the Hardy Boy who cried wolf. It would be harder for you to make your case with our next discovery."

"*Our* next discovery," Kraus emphasized the 'our'. "You're enjoying this, aren't you?"

Anna considered that for a moment. "I have to say I am. It's fun being Torchy Blane for once. Looking for the bad guy instead of being looked for."

"Well, you were a big help today," he said. "After hearing what you got out of him, I'm thinking the same thing about Thorp. Damn. All the pieces seemed to fit so well. Ollie's wife having an affair. Ollie tumbling onto both the cheating and the scam. He confronts Thorp and our boy kills him. I wanted it to hang together. Wanted it to be Thorp. The cardinal sin of investigation. Forcing the facts to fit your theory."

"I know. It happens on my side of the fence, too. You always pray your marks will react exactly the way they're supposed to," Anna said. "Slice off a piece of that enchilada, brother. It looks scrumptious. I'll trade you with the rest of my chile relleno."

"It looks like all that's left of that is the pepper stem and some egg coating. I'll take some of your tamale, too."

"If I get a bite of your taco," Anna said. "It looks like we still have a mystery on our hands. So what now?"

"The best course of action is to revisit Ollie's last case. The guy at Desilu Studios. The one who was supposedly being blackmailed. His address is in Ollie's case notes I've got in the Lincoln. We'll see if we can catch him this evening when he gets home from work."

TWENTY-SIX

Russian Consulate, Los Angeles - November 30th, 1956

The Russian billiard balls on the pool table were nearly a half-inch in diameter larger than their American counterparts. The pockets of an American pool table looked huge to Russian billiards players. Corner pockets on a Russian pool table were barely wider than the object balls. Adding further to the incongruity was that the numbered object balls were solid white. The cue ball was red. A homesick consulate member had contributed them to the consulate game room.

"Number fourteen in the side pocket," Kuznetsov murmured to himself. He pistoned his pool cue with practiced strokes, then accelerated the forward motion to strike the red cue ball, sending it rolling across the felt with a whisper. It struck the white object ball with a solid crack. The white ball marked with the number fourteen caromed off the side rail to roll straight into the opposite side pocket. It dropped into the silk pocket net with a soft swishing sound.

The KGB man looked up to see his legman, Balabanov, entering the billiard room with two thin file folders in one hand. Balabanov wore his standard issue factotum black suit, white dress shirt and black tie. The knot of his tie looked as though it was made by a blind man wearing oven mitts. The operative's dress shoes were scuffed and worn, like footwear fished from a soup kitchen rubbish bin.

"Ah, Balabanov," Kuznetsov said, "right on time. Please close the door behind you. What do you have to report?"

Balabanov looked around the large room. Georgian style mahogany panels with Greek revival molding covered the walls. Old World copper wall sconces. A bright chandelier hung above the plush billiard table from a ceiling plastered in the Jacobean style with intricate strapwork.

"Don't worry, Balabanov," Kuznetsov said, seeing his subordinate's eyes darting around the open space. "We're in complete privacy here. As you can see, the walls and ceiling are well insulated." He placed the cue stick in the wall rack and sat down on one of the club chairs in a corner of the room.

Balabanov took a seat on the cushioned chair next to his superior. He never felt comfortable in the confines of the consulate compound. The opulence was astonishing. He couldn't have imagined the most lavish tsar living in such luxury. Being exposed to such Western decadence was politically dangerous. Balabanov knew Red Army soldiers sentenced to prison after the war for being pictured in the American military newspaper, "Stars and Stripes", sharing an American army field ration at the Elbe River. A denouncement for enjoying himself in this grandeur could end with him on a Gulag forest logging team cinching choker chains on fallen trees until he was seventy years old.

"So, comrade," Kuznetsov said, "what progress have you made?"

"It's all in here," Balabanov proclaimed. He handed both file folders to his superior. "It appears the American was working alone. I cannot find a single clue that indicates otherwise."

"Good news," Kuznetsov mumbled as he thumbed through the pages of the report.

"There *is* a complication," Balabanov said, "I have discovered the man who was killed has a friend who is trying to discover the identity of the murderer."

"This is very quick work. You are to be commended," Kuznetsov said as he brought the second file to the top of the order.

"We have intelligence on this friend," Balabanov declared triumphantly before his superior could read the contents of the folder.

"Is that so," Kuznetsov said as he opened the folder. He hid his alarm behind a stoic poker face. "Hmm," he read some of the contents aloud. "Gordon Kraus. Los Angeles Police Department. U.S. Army. Captain in the Lightning Police in Berlin from '45 to '47. Multiple commendations. I wasn't in Germany during the war, but the Berlin Constabulary Police had a fearsome reputation. Other American military units referred to them as the '*Circle C Cowboys*'." Kuznetsov continued. "Licensed private investigator since returning from the war. Suspected of the murders of three Soviet soldiers in 1946." He looked up at Balabanov. "Is this true?"

"I sent an inquiry to one of my contacts," Balabanov said. "In 1946, Kraus had evidently taken a squad into the Berlin Soviet Sector in search of a woman he knew before the war. A *Vernugen Frau*," Balabanov said with a shrug. "He was too late to find her alive. A few weeks later, three of the Red Army soldiers he had confronted at the woman's flat were found dead in a remote Soviet Zone field."

"Was he charged," Kuznetsov asked.

"Initially the death of the soldiers was thought to be the result of a black market transaction gone bad. Clashes with German gangsters weren't uncommon," Balabanov said. "But when the squad's remaining officer was finally questioned, the militia learned of the earlier confrontation with the American. By the time the incident with Kraus was uncovered, he had already rotated home. The Red Army decided it would be both complicated and fruitless to levy allegations against him."

Kuznetsov continued to hide his concern. A skilled investigator with an ax to grind against the Soviet Union. If he was close to the woman he sought in the Berlin Soviet Sector, nine years might not be enough time to dull a desire for revenge. He thought back to what the Soviet invasion of Germany was like in 1945. Kuznetsov considered Balabanov's use of the phrase, "*Vernugen Frau*". German for "*comfort woman*". A polite term for a perpetual rape victim. He had been an intelligence officer stationed in Vienna, where the behavior of the Soviet troops was not as high-spirited. But he had heard stories about Berlin in the days immediately following occupation.

It must have seemed as though Satan himself had emptied a jungle's worth of wild, rapacious primates onto the Berlin streets. No woman was safe. He *had* heard the odd tale of female Berliners employing creative contrivances to escape abuse by Soviet troops. One pretended to be a deaf mute. Another feigned mental feebleness. Yet another was saved by declaring herself to be a Jew. This ruse gained popularity. Before Russian troops arrived and German currency lost all value, Star of David medallions were selling for 500 DM. Enough to buy a week's worth of cooking oil. In the end, these were isolated cases. Nearly myths. Nothing could stop the crude horde of Soviet soldiers engaging in the age-old practices of a conquering army. The few women who may have actually avoided rape were not unlike newspaper photographs one saw of a community flattened by a swarm of tornadoes with one lone building pictured standing upright amongst the wreckage. Miraculously untouched.

First a greedy extortionist, now a friend of the blackmailer with a strong prejudice against the Soviet Union. Kuzentsov was frustrated.

So close to his goal and yet these constant impediments. It seemed as though the closer he came to reaching his goal, the more obstacles were thrown in his way. "*Well,*" he thought, "*This will be the end of it.*"

He gazed at the billiard table for a minute or two. Thinking. A solution came to him. One that would keep his strongman, Balabanov, in the dark as to his true goal. Yet one that would keep this meddling investigator out of the way while he could complete the final steps to free himself from whatever dire fate the Kremlin had in store for him.

"Balabanov, we must safeguard our vital mission for the Rodina from interference by this American detective. The extortionist wanted money or threatened to expose our efforts to the authorities. His friend may be a more dangerous foe. One who only seeks revenge. Allowing him to pursue his quest would still result in the failure of our mission."

"What would you suggest?" Balabanov asked.

"This is us." Kuznetsov picked up the red cue ball and held it up to show Balabanov. He placed the ball on the table and held up another. "This represents our anonymity from our American detective." He placed the ball six or seven inches away from the cue ball.

"So that ball is hiding us from others," Balabanov said.

"Just so," Kuznetsov said. "This is a trigger." He placed this ball ahead of the shield ball, closer to the side rail. "And this is our pesky American." Kuznetsov placed another ball near a corner pocket.

"I am following you," Balabanov said.

"Our plan is to initiate a chain of events. Like falling dominoes, to mix game metaphors. None of the other balls can see where we've started." Kuznetsov took up his cue stick and struck the cue ball with enough side spin to curve around the nearest ball, carom off the cushion near the second ball, striking it and sending it into the ball nearest the pocket. A crisp plant shot that neatly potted the ball representing Kraus.

"You see?" Kuznetsov said after making the complicated combination shot. "Our Detective Kraus is taken out of the game with no other ball seeing it was us setting off the series of events. Understand?" He looked to Balabanov for a nod of understanding. His henchman moved his chin up and down.

"Very well. These are the steps I wish for you to undertake." He began to outline his plan.

TWENTY-SEVEN

Delbert Blanchard was the name of the man Ollie had met with at Desilu Studios. He lived in a small apartment building below Melrose in the Fairfax District. Kraus and Anna watched the entry to his complex from across the street in the front seat of the parked Lincoln. It was a simple building constructed in the Spanish Colonial Revival style. Wrought iron features, red tile roof, buff-colored stucco walls. A wide entrance that opened onto a lighted inner courtyard.

The end of the workday brought a steady stream of occupants into view. Many returning residents walked from nearby bus stops, others drove into the rear parking area. Many stopped to pick up their mail from the warren of aluminum boxes set in both entryway walls before making their way to their apartment doors. The large foyer was well lit. They could see the tenants clearly.

"So, this guy was the last case your friend mentioned in his notes?" Anna asked. "Do you think he's connected to Ollie's murder?"

"I've been trying to remember Ollie's exact words when I saw him at Desilu. He was there to meet with this bird. Ollie said someone had been 'leaning' on his client. I asked him if he had solved the problem for the client. His answer was pretty vague, then he launched into one of his fever dream stories about striking it rich. I mostly tuned him out at that point."

"But you saw the client?"

"Just for a second. I'll know him when I see him again. He looked a little 'fay', as my mother would say."

"Fay?" Anna asked.

"Means kind of sprite-like. A fairy. You know. My mom was from Kassel, Germany. The Brothers Grimm were from there. All Kasselians use Old World folk-story terms. It's in their bloodstream."

"I always liked the *Rapunzel* story," Anna said. "What did *you* mean by saying he looks a little 'fay'."

"A little light in the loafers. He had the look," Kraus said.

"The look?" Anna asked.

"Hard to define," Kraus said.

"It must be nice to have such a reliable 'faydar' system," Anna said. Archly. Not in a joking way.

"You sound peeved. I'm just telling you how he comes off. I'm not passing judgment on him," Kraus said.

"If you say so," Anna said in a flat tone. "I know what it's like to be sized up by how I look and hounded by people who 'aren't passing judgment'."

"Okay. Okay," Kraus surrendered. "Point taken. What I'm suggesting is - regardless of where you stand on the subject - the reason he needed Ollie's services was that he was probably being leveraged. Probably involving something he doesn't want people to know about." Kraus' attention was caught by a person entering the apartment breezeway area. "That's our man. Let's go ask him exactly why Ollie was helping him."

Kraus and Anna piled out of the Lincoln and walked briskly across the road. Delbert Blanchard had placed his briefcase on the pavement and was fishing around in his pocket for keys. He pushed a key into one of the mail slot locks. The door emitted a torque squeak as it swung open. He wiggled out a stack of mail. The box door made a tinny, clanking sound when Blanchard slapped it shut. Pocketed his keys. The studio worker thumbed through his mail with the jaunty confidence of someone who pays his bills on time and is on decent terms with his relatives.

Delbert Blanchard looked like Kraus remembered him. Early thirties. Ginger hair was cut short. Average looks with dark brown eyes. Medium height and build. Tweed sports jacket over a light sweater vest. Light blue shirt with a button-down collar. Dark necktie with a loose Kelvin knot. Pleated trousers and gleaming patent leather Oxfords. Blanchard tucked his mail under his left arm, swept up his briefcase and headed towards the interior of the complex.

They caught up with Blanchard as he was opening the door to his second-story apartment.

"Mr. Blanchard," Kraus called out.

The youngish man pivoted back towards the walkway at the sound of his name. He looked over Kraus and Anna as they approached. Kraus figured it was Anna's presence that kept him from jumping inside and bolting his door. It was good she'd come along.

"Do I know you?" he asked. His face broke into a half-smile of recognition. Kraus and Anna stopped a few feet away from Blanchard and his front door.

"No," Kraus said. "I saw you at Desilu before Thanksgiving. You were meeting with Ollie McBride."

Blanchard's smile evaporated at the mention of Ollie's name. He shifted to move completely into his apartment, but his briefcase got hung-up on the framework. Blanchard struggled with the case. A Thrifty Drug Store advertising circular came loose from the pile of mail under his arm and fluttered to the concrete. Kraus took a step closer and planted his palm on the door.

"Mr. Blanchard, we just need your help in finding out why Mr. McBride was killed," Anna said while stooping to retrieve the throwaway. Kraus figured it was the calming effect of Anna's voice and the fact she was a woman that stopped Bowers from abandoning his briefcase altogether and darting into the safety of his apartment. Whatever the reason, he stopped moving and gave each of them a closer look.

"I didn't have anything to do with Mr. McBride's murder," Blanchard said in a low voice. Several newly arrived neighbors on the outer walkways paused outside their own apartments to view the scene developing on Blachard's doorstep.

"Mr. Blanchard, why don't you let us in? Right now, we just look like two solicitors or friends. Any longer out here and it becomes grist for the mill."

"We're not here to do you any harm," Anna added.

Blanchard's shoulders sagged. He righted his briefcase and stepped inside his apartment, leaving the door open behind him. "Please come in," he said.

The young man put his briefcase down by the side of his couch and deposited the mail on a glass-topped, distressed driftwood coffee table. His entire apartment was made over in what Beverly Hills decorators call "coastal style". Turquoise and beige color scheme. Wicker chairs at a small breakfast table made from old barnwood. His couch looked as though it were made from old warehouse pallets with nubby fabric cushions and awning striped throw pillows. Sea glass nick-nacks were scattered around the room.

Blanchard shrugged off his sports coat and hung it in the entry closet. "Please, have a seat," he urged. "Can I get you something to drink?"

"No thank you," Kraus said. He and Anna took seats on two padded, birchwood frame chairs across from Blanchard's couch. Blanchard sat on his couch and fidgeted with a letter he had placed there without looking at it.

"Mr. Blanchard, my name is Gordon Kraus. This is my associate, Anna Bjorkquist. Oliver McBride was a colleague and a friend."

"I can't tell you anything about Mr. McBride's death," Blanchard reasserted.

"No," Kraus said, "I don't think you were involved in his murder. But if you can tell us why you hired Mr. McBride, it may go a long way towards helping us find who killed him. Completely confidential," Kraus assured.

"Jesus, I'll never put this behind me," Blanchard almost wailed. "I haven't slept well for six months or so. I feel as though I'm in a trap with no way out."

"The fact that you're dealing with this alone probably makes it feel hopeless," Anna said. "Why don't you tell us what has happened to you? We'll hold your information in the strictest of confidence, Mr. Blanchard. Please believe me."

Blanchard closed his eyes and bit his lower lip. He crossed his arms. Hugging himself while unconsciously rocking back and forth. Mentally struggling to decide what to do. When he opened his eyes, he took a deep breath. Ready to make a leap of faith. "Okay, what do you want to know?"

"Start at the beginning," Kraus said. "First of all, what do you do at Desilu?"

"I don't technically work for Desilu Studios," Bowers said. "I work for Zanra."

"Zanra?" Kraus asked. "I do work for Jess Oppenheimer, and I've never heard of it."

"Zanra is 'Arnaz' spelled backwards," Blanchard explained. "Desi and Lucy own and operate it as an independent company. Zanra designs and builds very sophisticated editing equipment. Even if you've spent time at Desilu, it's unlikely you've seen the apparatus. We call it '*The Monster*'. It's so big, the only place it fits is in the props room. It's a giant, multi-screen editing machine. An editor can watch the show's footage from all three camera angles at once and choose which one for a particular shot or scene."

"And what do you do for Zanra?" Anna asked.

"I'm their purchasing agent. '*The Monster*' is a complicated machine with a lot of moving parts. Mechanical and electronic. Desilu is expanding its production all the time and we need to build more of the editing machines. Plus, CBS wants to lease a few. Between new builds and replacement parts, I'm buying hundreds of parts per week for 'The Monster' and all the other studio equipment. Receiving inspection, inventory control, material requisitions, expediting. All the activities of a purchasing agent. I really need an assistant."

The hair on the back of Kraus' neck stood up when Blanchard used the word, '*electronic*'. "How did Mr. McBride fit in?" he asked.

"In late April I was grabbing a quick lunch at the Farmers Market. A gentleman appeared and took a seat opposite me. No introduction. Nothing. He just sat down and smiled at me. At first, I thought he was someone at Desilu who recognized me. Wanted to sit with someone he knew. Make a friend. You know."

"But he didn't work at Desilu," Kraus said. It wasn't a question.

"No. He got right to the point. He said that he had some pictures of me taken at a couple of parties. He said that it looked as though I was having such a good time, it would be a shame to keep them from my friends at work. From my family."

"Didn't beat around the bush," Kraus said. "Did he prove he had any photos or was he just talking?"

Blanchard squeezed his eyes shut and turned his face towards the ceiling for a moment. Then he turned a damp-eyed gaze towards Anna. A pleading look.

"Go on," Anna urged.

"Oh, he had them, alright. A manila envelope with several prints. He was quick to assure me they were just copies. He pushed the envelope across the table. I peeked inside it. Couldn't believe my eyes. I couldn't imagine how they were possibly taken."

"But they were authentic. They were real photos of you at a party," Kraus said.

"Oh, yes. At two parties, actually. *Confidential* would call them '*limp wrist parties*'. All the photos caught me in the bathroom with other party goers," he whispered. "My face was as clear as a bell."

"Okay," Kraus said. "What did he want in exchange for keeping these photos from getting out?"

"That's the funny part. Nothing really illegal. At least not on my part. He said that he knew where I bought some of the electro-mechanical and electronic components for Zanra."

"*There it was again*," Kraus thought. "*Electronic parts.*"

"He was right," Blanchard continued. "He seemed to know a lot about my vendors. He said that every week or so, when I received a delivery, there would be products in the consignment I didn't order. He wanted me just to separate out the material I didn't order and wait for the next delivery. If the delivery man asked for the items I had set aside for return, I was just to give them to him."

"Just a minute," Kraus said. "I'll be right back." He left the apartment and rushed out to his car. He returned a minute later with the catalog he'd taken from Ollie's home. He placed it on the coffee table in front of Blanchard. "Is this the kind of product you'd receive and give back to the delivery guy?"

Blanchard took up the catalog and flipped through the pages. He looked up at Kraus and Anna. "Allied Radio. Sure." He turned the catalog around towards Kraus. "Connector cables," he flipped a few pages, "transistors, diodes, resistors, capacitors. I buy all of these components and a lot more besides."

"From this place? Allied Radio?" Kraus asked.

"Yes. Well .. not much anymore," he corrected himself. "For the last year or so I've been buying from a local distributor in Culver City. Milestone Electro Supply. Everyone just calls them 'Milestone'."

"Why the switch?" Kraus asked.

"Allied Radio, Newark, others. All catalog houses are basically the same. See these sections," Blanchard asked, pointing a manicured finger at a page section headed by a drawing of what Kraus would have called a "thingamajig". The name, "Germanium Diode" was printed next to the picture. "See this first part number for a 'high peak diode'? You can see the unit price is right here. Five dollars and thirty-seven cents. Same unit price no matter what quantity you buy."

"Okay. How many high peak diodes do you need?" Kraus asked.

"I bought a total of two hundred this year. You know what the exact same diode costs me from Milestone?"

"Surprise me," Kraus said.

"Two dollars, sixty-seven cents," Blanchard said. Sounding proud. A shopper bragging about a shrewd bargain.

Kraus smiled inwardly, thinking of how quickly Ollie would have come up with the total amount of savings. "So, Milestone offers the better deal."

"A much better deal," Blanchard insisted. "Allied and Newark ship from Chicago. Zanra pays the freight. Then wait for the Parcel Post delivery. We used to pay in advance with a money order or have it sent C.O.D. Zanra ultimately opened an account. They give you ten days to pay the invoice. No discounts. No volume discounts. Even without the process time of a pre-paid transaction, it still takes forever to receive an order."

"Milestone gives you a discount?"

"Yes. Two percent off an invoice that's paid in ten days or sooner. They have price columns for each part. The more you buy, the less a part costs. FOB destination. That means free shipping. They make most of their own deliveries and can get product to me the same day if it's an emergency. I can pick it up at their warehouse if I need to."

"This all sounds great," Kraus said. "But where do the blackmailer's demands come into play?"

"I have no idea what happens behind the scenes," Blanchard said. "Every few days I receive a shipment from Milestone. I check the contents myself. Almost every time there are more parts than I've ordered. Different parts not on the packing slip. I place these in a brown shopping bag, staple it shut and place it on my 'returns' shelf with 'Milestone' written on the outside."

"Then what happens?" Anna asked.

"A day or so later, the Milestone delivery man shows up. Sometimes he has a new order for me. Sometimes not. In either case, he takes the shopping bag from the 'returns' shelf and leaves."

"Does Zanra get billed for the parts you've returned?" Anna asked. Trying to see the mechanics of a scam.

"No. We've never been invoiced for any product I haven't actually ordered and received."

"So, Mr. Blanchard," Kraus said, "it appears as though the only thing you're being asked to do is what you'd normally do. Zanra receives a shipment that contains some material you didn't order. You separate them out upon receipt and return them to Milestone. Do I have that right?"

"Exactly," Blanchard said.

"No escalated demands? Always this set-up," Kraus pressed.

"No. Exactly the same thing. Week in. Week out," Blanchard insisted.

"Why call in a private detective then?" Kraus asked. "It's a little dodgy, but it doesn't seem as though you're doing anything strictly illegal."

"After a couple of months of dealing with wrong shipments several times a week, others began to notice. I have my own office and receiving area, but I don't work in complete isolation. Dann Cahn, the operations director, asked me about the regular returns back to Milestone. I explained it away. New company. New people learning the ropes. He's a busy man and dropped it. For now."

"And I imagine the blackmailer gave you strict instructions not to contact Milestone about these incorrect shipments. No asking for a return authorization number," Anna said. Getting a stronger sense of the way the scam worked.

"Exactly," Blanchard agreed. "I'm walking on eggshells, Mr. Kraus. Miss Bjorkquist. Every day I get to my desk I expect my boss to be standing there with that envelope in his hands. I'd lose my job. My employability. My parents. Everything. The Milestone outside salesman who calls on the studio will occasionally talk to my boss about new products. I knew all it would take is for him to mention the overages to the salesman. It would be a disaster."

"Would it be that serious?" Anna asked. "You're in show business, but not a known personality. Would anyone at the studio even care."

"Oh, they'd care, alright," Blanchard replied. Nearly a shrill tone. "After Lucy's HUAC run-in a couple of years ago, she's super-sensitive to even a breath of scandal. I'd be out on my keister the same day. It would only grow worse after that. Like a brush fire in the canyons."

"So, you called Ollie," Kraus said.

"Yes," Blanchard said. "An acquaintance of mine had some dealings with Mr. McBride. He told me I could trust him."

"Well," Kraus said, "I inherited his case files, and he didn't make any notations about your situation. So, your trust was well-founded. You can trust us as well."

"What next, then?" Blanchard asked.

"I have some more questions about the blackmailer. What did he look like?"

"I told Mr. McBride he was average," Blanchard chuckled nervously. "At the time my head was really spinning from all of this. I've had more time to think back on those few minutes at the Farmers

Market." He closed his eyes for a moment. Gathering his recollection. "Brown hair and eyes. Shorter than average. Five-six. About one-sixty or so. Squarish face with a strong chin. Almost oriental eyes. Dressed well but not expensively. Unforgivably boring shoes. Something a junior IRS auditor would wear."

"How did he talk? Did he sound educated? Any accent?" Kraus coaxed.

"Good question. Strong voice. Good diction. Maybe had some stage training. Sounded as though he was educated. English was definitely not his first language, though."

"How's that?" Kraus asked.

"He used very precise grammar. Fluent but rigid. Deliberate. Now that I've gotten past some of the shock, I recall he struck me as the way the movies portray a Nazi officer. Often with a cultured British accent. He spoke in a very formal way. I wouldn't say German. Definitely not French or Spanish. Maybe Polish. Hungarian. Eastern Europe."

"Is it always the same delivery guy who collects the returns?" Anna asked.

"Yes. Milestone only has two delivery men. One older man. Retired school bus driver for the L.A. district. Supplementing his income, you know. There's a younger man who always takes the returns. Early twenties. Tall. Lanky. Pale blue eyes. Hair so blonde, it's almost white. A scruffy little beard. Looks like one of those hipster bums you see wandering around Venice lately. They're drifting down from North Beach in Frisco. Better weather here. You see them standing on corners reciting atrocious free verse." Blanchard wrinkled his nose as though he'd found himself downwind of a slit trench.

Kraus laughed. Blanchard seemed curious and intrigued despite his show of disdain. If the younger delivery man hadn't been involved in the blackmail scheme, he'd have gotten some party invitations from Blanchard, Kraus thought. He decided to keep that observation to himself. Odds were the humor would be lost on Anna.

"Okay, I think we've got what we need," Kraus said, looking at Anna to see if she had any other questions. She shook her head. "Mr. Blanchard, the wisest thing right now is for you to keep following the blackmailer's instructions."

"For how long?" Blanchard asked.

"Not very long," Kraus said. Hoping he was right. "We'll get a solid line on this guy very soon. Also, it is very rare for a blackmailer in this sort of situation to follow through on the threat. He wouldn't want the police involved. As long as he thinks you're dancing to his tune, you'll be okay."

"Will you let me know when it's over," Blanchard asked.

"Absolutely," Kraus said. He handed Blanchard a card. "Please jot down your home number for us so we won't have to contact you at work. If you get any new demands, please contact me."

"Mr. Kraus. Miss Bjorkquist. Mr. McBride was a very kind man. I hope you get the man who killed him."

"We will," Kraus said. He thought about how much trouble kindness or greed could get a person in. Ollie had equal measures of both. Kraus wasn't motivated by either in pursuing Ollie's killer. He hoped that was to his advantage

TWENTY-EIGHT

Kraus and Anna spent Saturday locating and interviewing two more of the shakedown victims he found in Ollie's notes.

The first was a man who worked in the parts warehouse of a small electronics company. He was pretty deep into a local bookmaker. Knee-breaking deep. The company made wireless transmitters for shoulder-mounted television cameras and bought a lot of material from Milestone Electro Supply. Blanchard's blackmailer approached this luckless gambler. The blackmailer told the man he'd bought up his markers. He'd no longer have to make weekly payments on the principal and the juice. Instead, he had to follow the same steps Blanchard was demanded to follow.

Kraus called the Bean Slot from a phone booth before he and Anna drove to their second interview. He asked about the bookie this man named during their interview. Dave Hayashigawa told him the bookie was found unconscious in his own office. Savagely beaten. He was currently in the hospital. Both arms in traction. One leg that would never work well without a hinged brace.

"I don't think the blackmailer paid cash for our man's paper," Kraus told Anna after he hung up.

The second was a woman who was the purchasing clerk for a company designing and manufacturing electronic controls for industrial food handling machinery. She was secretly living with a man, which was damning enough. Being unmarried and living with someone was enough to get a woman fired from a lot of companies on the spot. This particular woman was committing the ultimate indiscretion. She was a white gal shacked up with a Negro. Once again, the same blackmailer told her he would allow her unorthodox domestic situation to remain secret if she abided by his instructions.

Both told Kraus and Anna the shipping overages were only from Milestone and always picked up by a very young man with very blonde hair and a goatee beard.

It was already six o'clock when they got back to Kraus' home. Anna changed while Kraus began preparing dinner. He took two thick pork chops from the fridge so they could get to room temperature while he mixed up a marinade. He peeled a garlic clove and minced it with his favorite knife. He put some soy sauce, brown sugar, Worcestershire and hot mustard in a shallow glass dish. Added the minced garlic and whisked it around. Kraus laid the two pork chops in the dish, stabbed them several times with a fork, then covered it with a kitchen towel.

Anna came out of the guest room wearing a sweatshirt and jeans. The house was warm, and she was barefoot.

"Want a beer or some wine?" Kraus asked.

"I'll have a beer," Anna said.

Kraus retrieved two cold Pfeiffer's Extra Specials from the fridge and poured them into pilsner glasses. He brought the beers to the couch where Anna had planted herself.

"The pork chops have to marinate for a little while. I'll turn them in a few minutes." "Okay," she sipped her beer.

Kraus sat on the other end of the couch, shifting his body so he could face her. "Well, what was your take on our interviews today?"

"No question they've all been pressed by the same man. Very professional bamboozler. He'll be hard to get next to. The blonde delivery boy is the Duke Man." A pickpocket term for the man who takes the handoff from the pick. "He's the common denominator."

"Yeah, I was thinking the same thing," Kraus said. "But we can probably think of him more as the dip. My guess is that the delivery boy is the one who fills the orders at Milestone for delivery. Later, he takes the shopping bags full of returns to a cut-off man before he returns to Milestone. The cut-off man is the real Duke Man. He'll be the one who delivers the goods to our extortionist."

"Possible," Anna agreed. She tucked her legs up under her and sipped some more of her beer. "What's our next move?"

Kraus got up to turn the pork chops. "I'm thinking that over." He returned to the couch.

"There's one thing that really stands out about the whole bilk," Anna said. "What is the point of all this? I get that these electronic parts are expensive. But it doesn't seem like there's a big enough market for stolen electrical components. There are thousands of people who would buy a hot television set. How many people would open their wallets for a handful of stolen 'high peak diodes'?"

"It is puzzling," Kraus agreed. "But if Ollie thought the profits were big enough to take huge risks for, trust me, there's some serious money somewhere along the way. Our primary objective is to get to the boss of the operation. Odds are he's the one who clipped Ollie. Once I have my hands on that character, I'll find out the rest." He got up to continue the dinner preparations.

"I'll get the side dishes going and then put the chops in the broiler," Kraus said.

"What are you making?" Anna asked.

"Creamed spinach and roasted carrots," Kraus said.

"Yummy," Anna exclaimed. She got up from the couch and sat down at the counter breakfast bar. She let the common household kitchen sounds wash over her. The rattle of pans. Clinking of utensils. The rhythmic thunk of a chef knife on a butcher block. This symphony of domesticity sparked memories of a lost time. Bittersweet comfort. "What are you planning on doing when you catch the guy?"

"It all depends on the circumstances," Kraus said. He cut open a package of frozen spinach and dumped it in a colander to drain in the sink. He then began dicing half an onion while melting a stick of butter in a saucepan on the stove. "I'll turn him over to Laveroni if I find enough evidence for the charges to stick. If I don't have the goods on him, I may make the decision to go another way."

"That's what I figured," Anna said. She sensed Kraus didn't want to elaborate. Didn't want to make any remarks that would come back to haunt him. She busied herself helping with the dinner. Kraus told her where to find the ingredients needed for the roasted carrots. She arranged the various items on the counter. "Maple syrup?" she asked, just to make sure she heard him right.

"Trust me," Kraus said as he finished prepping the creamed spinach. "It will knock your socks off. Pass me the cayenne pepper, please."

Kraus and Anna kept off the subject of their investigation while they ate. He told her stories about growing up in Los Angeles. She told him stories about the different places she'd been over the years. After finishing their meal and clearing the dishes, they returned to the couch to discuss their theories.

"Gordy, that was delicious! You were right. I loved the way you used the maple syrup. What did you say it did?"

"Caramelizes. Roasting them in the oven causes the sugars to form a sweet crust over the carrots. Great flavor."

"What were those crunchy things in the creamed spinach?"

"You want me to give away all my secrets, don't you? Pine nuts. I discovered them in Europe and kept using them in recipes when I got back to the States. I have some oatmeal raisin cookies in the kitchen if you'd like dessert."

"Maybe later," she said, taking a sip of the water she'd brought from the dinner table. "Isn't it funny about blackmail?"

"How's that?" Kraus asked.

"These people we talked to. All three of them are doing things that will likely get them into worse trouble than the stuff the guy is threatening to reveal about them. It astonishes me how people will trade one problem for a bigger one just to avoid dealing with the original."

"Your follies fight against yourself. Fear and be slain. No worse can come to fight. And fight and die is death destroying death. Where fearing dying pays death servile breath," Kraus quoted with a dramatic flair.

"Richard II," Anna giggled.

"That's right for the thirty-point bonus," Kraus said in a GE College Bowl announcer voice. "Hey, you're not the only one who's read Shakespeare," Kraus said with a smile. "Another beer?" he asked.

"Sure," Anna said. "I like this Pfeiffer's beer," she said after taking a sip. "Hamm's was the only beer in town when I was in school. From what I remember, it tasted like bilge water compared to this." She waved the glass. "I grew up in Swede's Hollow and our house was almost in the shadow of the brewery plant. You could see it from our front stoop. Yeasty smell in the summer." She wrinkled her nose.

"Swede Hollow?" Kraus asked. He thought about the childhood snapshot of her in a Swedish folk costume he'd found in her car. "Where's that?"

"St. Paul, Minnesota," Anna said. "Swede Hollow is on the East Side where a lot of Round Heads lived. Our house was on the northern fringe. Hamm's brewery was there."

"What did your folks do?"

"My father was a points man for the MN&S Railroad. He worked there for years," Anna had a tone of pride in her voice, then it softened to almost a whisper. "He was killed on the tracks when I was about nine or ten. A railcar jumped the track right where he was working a yard switch. He was crushed to death."

"I'm sorry," Kraus said.

"Yeah, so was I," Anna muttered. "Of course, the railroad claimed my father was negligent. The railroad was blameless, and his widow didn't qualify for any survivor's benefit. We got the spare set of Sears overalls, a cap and a lunch pail left in his locker."

"So, what happened? Is that why you left school?"

"At ten?" Anna sniggered. "No, that was later. No, my mom was determined to keep us together. There was my mom, me and my two younger sisters. The Depression was on. It wasn't unusual at all for families like ours to be split up. Destitute widow with no means of support. Kids sent to country farms where they could earn their keep. My mom started cleaning houses. Took the trolley to Highland Park where she cleaned houses for rich folks. Two transfers both ways. Long days. On the weekends she took in laundry and mending."

"Very brave woman," Kraus said.

"Yeah," letting out an ironic chortle, "until she wasn't. She started doing the laundry for a man. A foreman at the Hamm's plant. Big Irish guy. Tufts of orange-red hair poking out of his shirt neck like a Paddy scarecrow. Prohibition was just over, and the plant had gone from one shift making soft drinks back to three shifts churning out as much beer as they could. Good money. My mother still had her looks," Anna said. It came out as an accusation.

"*I'll bet she did*," Kraus silently mused, seeing how naturally beautiful Anna was.

"Before you knew it, my mom was doing his mending and everything else he wanted. They got married." She took a sip of her beer. "Looking back at it, I can't blame her. She must have felt as though that railcar flattened her life along with my father. Then along comes a steady paycheck. One hundred and thirty-eight dollars a month. A lot of overtime. My mother could stop cleaning houses," Anna stretched her legs out for a moment then tucked them back under her haunches. "I think she came out the loser in that trade-off."

Kraus decided not to press Anna any further. These were not happy memories. "Gordy, that was a delicious dinner," Anna said, changing the subject. "Where did you learn to cook so well?"

"I was outside Berlin when the Germans threw in the towel. Instead of lining up to get rotated home, I volunteered for the U.S. Constabulary. It was a special force created to police Berlin."

"I thought you were already a military policeman," Anna said.

"I was. But law enforcement in post-war Germany was a tough nut to crack. When the Nazis were defanged, Berlin turned into the Wild West. Chief Parker likes to talk about being from Deadwood, South Dakota. What a wild place it was, even in the early 1900s. Let me tell you, Berlin in '45 and '46 was like fifty Deadwoods. Black market gangs, protection racketeers, counterfeiters, rapists, smash-and-grab crews, dope peddlers, hugger-mugger teams, looters, the odd crazy murderer. You name it."

"Sounds like the war didn't end when Hitler topped himself," Anna said.

"The war turned in on itself. Like an ingrown toenail. Anyhow, the U.S. Constabulary was created to embed a large, specially trained force in Berlin. We were trained at an actual castle in the extreme south of Germany. In the '30's it had been a training academy for up-and-coming Nazis, so you can imagine how plush it was. The U.S. Army took it over and turned it into a training school for the Constabulary. It was called 'The Constabulary West Point'. The kitchen was like something you'd see in a classy Paris restaurant. Teams of us took turns making dinner for the whole facility. Like a firehouse. Living alone, I don't have much of an excuse to cook, but it's been fun fixing meals for the two of us."

"It's been fun eating them," Anna said. "Weren't you in a hurry to get back to the states? The war was over. You weren't going to make a career in the service. Why stay? Did you get some sort of bonus?"

"No bonus, but I had a reason to stay," Kraus admitted. He told her about Charlotte. His adolescent love for her. His determination to find her and get her out of Berlin.

"Wow," Anna said after he finished his explanation. "That was so terrible. For you and her. I'm sorry."

"It's been a long time," Kraus said quietly. "So," changing the subject, "Swede Hollow to Los Angeles. You've had quite an adventure yourself. I can tell by the way you handle yourself during interviews that you have great people skills. Solid instincts. How did you learn those?"

"Flim-flam people are the best psychologists in the world. They read people like a book. You run a few cons and you pick up the knack pretty quick."

"You obviously love to learn. You're talented. Attractive. Charismatic. Why stay on the outside of the law?"

"You mean, why is a nice girl like me wasting herself?" Anna asked. Slightly acidic.

"*That was quick*," Kraus thought. "No," he said, "I didn't mean it like that. You're the one who said it was nice not being the one on the run for a change."

"You're right," Anna said in a softer tone. "I left home when I was fifteen. A runaway truant. I didn't want to risk getting sent back to St. Paul. In those days, no one wanted you. If you found a church or rescue mission, their first goal was to get you off their hands by figuring out where you came from and sending you right back."

"And you didn't want to go back?"

"No," Anna said. She sat a bit straighter on the couch. Took a deep breath. "My stepfather was a pig of a man. I had blossomed out and believe me, he noticed. Pretty soon he was finding excuses to get me alone. In the back shed. In the bathroom. He told me he was the head of the family now. It was his job to 'see that I reached womanhood the right way'."

"Jesus," Kraus said. He had heard this story dozens of times when he was a patrolman and in Berlin. In those roles, you had to maintain a certain detachment. Hearing this from Anna was a different kettle of fish. He found he cared for her, and this was disturbing in a personal way. "What did you do?"

"Oh, I told my mother," Anna huffed. "She completely turned a blind eye to it. Told me I must have been leading him on. I had to quit tempting him. It was the Irish way of things. She was desperate not to lose that Hamm's pay envelope."

"So, you left," Kraus said.

"Not right away," Anna said. "My mom made me feel guilty at first. I almost bought into the notion I was this wicked temptress. Then, one day when he didn't see me watching, I noticed him take my younger sister into the bathroom. I listened at the door. He was telling her that my mother was getting tired and after her big sister left home it would be her job to step in as the woman of the house. He told her to open her blouse. He said she'd know the time had arrived when her 'woman pillows' swelled up. It was nature's way of signaling it was her turn. She was to come to him when the Lord made her ready. God, I ran out the back door and vomited into the garden bed."

"You stayed to protect your sisters?" Kraus asked.

"No," Anna said, "I knew I couldn't protect them, and my mom wouldn't. I decided to leave. To make enough money to send for my sisters. Take them away from there." Anna clutched one of the pillows to her stomach and looked into the middle distance with wet eyes.

Kraus knew the end of the story without hearing it. No need to ask. "You know, Anna. We could go downtown to the Redwood any night. You couldn't swing a dead cat without hitting at least two top defense lawyers who would trip over themselves to take your case. Solomon, Ringgold, Pacht, Haller, Matthews, Geisler. You'd have the pick of the litter. They'd pencil whip your record into mint condition and you could go completely straight. Get some more schooling and a job. Bring your sisters out here."

"Oh, and how would I pay for one of these litter mates?" Anna asked. Harshness in her tone.

"I know most of them," Kraus said, "we would work something out."

"Work something out, huh," Anna barked. "Would it involve me moving across the hall," she demanded as she threw an arm out at the rear hallway.

"Hey," Kraus said, astonished at how quickly this conversation went sour. "What kind of guy do you think I am?"

"I know full well the kind of guy you are," Anna said. "The kind of guy who knows exactly what kind he is, but still wants to hear it from someone else."

"Hey," Kraus began, but Anna kept on.

"You men! You think you can just fix things. Make it all better for little old me. Don't you?"

"Anna, you're taking this ..." Kraus started to say.

"No!" Anna stopped him. "You know, I'm sure you didn't imply I had to spread my legs for you to help me, but that makes it almost worse. You lead this charmed life. Surfer boy with your custom board. College. Brave policeman. Heroic Berlin Centurion in your fancy uniform and sporty armored car. A private eye like out of the movies. All the while you live in this fancy house with money coming in from your building company. You live like a little boy who's found his way into an adventure comic book and closed the cover behind you."

"All I wanted to do ..." Kraus tried to interrupt.

"Oh, I know, all you wanted to do is be the hero in your own story. You couldn't rescue your teen crush in Berlin and now you want to make up for it by rescuing me. Brother, I don't need rescuing."

With that, Anna stormed off the couch, stomped down the hallway and slammed the guest room door. "I guess no oatmeal cookie, then" Kraus mumbled as he went into the kitchen to get one from the jar for himself.

Kraus munched on his cookie and sipped his beer. He wasn't upset by Anna's explosion. She clearly carried a lot of anger around with her. He couldn't blame her after hearing her story.

He thought about losing Charlotte. Ollie being murdered. Anna's predicament. It was true that he wanted to rescue her. Even with all her experience, Anna didn't know how fast and remorseless evil can be when it has you in its sights.

He went into his bedroom and got ready for bed. Still thinking everything over. Kraus thought about Anna's favorite Grimm's tale being "Rapunzel". He would bet money it was the version in which the prince is blinded after falling into a patch of thorn bushes. That sounded about right after hearing her tirade.

Kraus drifted off into a thin sleep. He dreamed of Sonthofen Castle. Its stone clock tower jutted up like a tombstone from the roof. Long hair braids dangled from the top. They transformed into a rope with a twisting, desiccated corpse hanging from it.

A squeak of door hinges roused Kraus from his sleep. He peeked at the lighted alarm clock face on his bedside table. He'd only been asleep for an hour or so. Kraus heard a rustle at the foot of his bed. It was Anna. She was wearing a lightweight silk robe. Mid-thigh length.

"Everything okay?" Kraus asked. His eyes adjusted to the faint light his alarm clock emitted.

"I'm sorry, Gordy," Anna whispered. "I was a real pill. So much has happened all at once. I was mad at myself. I took it out on you, and you don't deserve it. You're trying to help, and I appreciate it."

She shrugged and the silk robe fell from her shoulders. It dropped to the floor in a soft puddle around her feet. She was wearing a black lace bralette and matching French-cut lace panties. Kraus thought she looked like a goddess. Raven black hair spilling down over her shoulders. Lacy black lingerie against her smooth, firm porcelain skin. The hemispheres of her breasts bubbled up above the bra line. Her legs were sturdy and shapely.

"Anna," Kraus said. "You don't have to apologize ..."

"Shhh, shhh," Anna softly hushed him. She reached behind her back and unfastened the bralette. The spaghetti straps slithered off her shoulders. The bra clung to her breasts a moment before falling completely away, as though reluctant to part from her. She had large, heavy breasts. Womanly. Small, pink rosette nipples protruding from ginger areolas. Next, she hooked her thumbs under the waist of her panties and pushed them down over her wide hips. She stepped out of them and onto the bed in one motion.

"You are ..." Kraus started as he sat up.

"Shhh," Anna hushed him again, leaning into his chest. Kraus felt the firm crush of her breasts. Soft scents of French milled soap radiated from the heat of her body. She tilted her head and pressed her lips against his. He tasted the sarsaparilla sweetness of her toothpaste as the tip of her tongue nudged into his mouth. Her kiss was firm. No urgency, but insistent. He kissed her back. Harder. Their tongues swirled together.

Anna kissed his neck, moved her lips to the furrow of a gunshot wound scar near his shoulder, and then teased one of his nipples while licking and sucking on his other. She worked the fly of his pajamas with a warm hand and pulled his stiff member out. Kraus leaned back and moaned.

"You know, as apologies go, this is one of the best I've ever gotten." She was still busy teasing his nipples with moist, suckling sounds. He stroked her hair and shoulders.

"You know, I didn't plan this to happen," he said.

"Gordy," she whispered, lifting her head for a moment, "when a woman comes uninvited into your bedroom wearing a lace bra and scanty knickers, it's *her* plan, not yours." She ran her wet tongue down his stomach, pausing when she reached his pelvis. She made solid eye contact with him while taking him into her mouth.

"My God," Kraus moaned, "that feels like you're wrapping me in warm, buttered silk. God, that feels so good."

After a minute or two, Anna lifted her head from him, scooted up and swung a leg over his hips. She moved the tip of his manhood against her, found the right position and eased herself down on him. She moaned as she settled onto him and began slowly rocking back and forth. Grinding her mound against his pubic bone. Little gasps of delight.

"Keep still," she whispered in a hoarse voice, "let me do the work for a while."

Kraus caressed her breasts, feeling their heft in his palms. Her nipples and areolas had swollen like engorged plums. He lightly pinched them. She threw back her head and whimpered.

"Wait," Kraus said in sudden realization, "I don't have a ..."

"Yes, you do," Anna giggled. "I slipped it on while I was tasting you."

"Really?"

"Yes, silly. I'm that good," Anna laughed. "Remember, this was my plan. I came prepared."

TWENTY-NINE

It was Sunday. The second day of December. The radio said it would be a little cooler, with highs only near seventy. Despite the cooling trend, Violet had several windows open while she cleaned the house. Her world had turned upside down since Ollie's murder, but she reasoned that the only way to keep sane was to stick to her routines. That meant cleaning on Sunday. Deciding about getting a Christmas tree. Holiday decorations. All those commonplace things she used to take for granted. Enjoyed. She wondered if there was any meaning in them any longer. She thought that once the police released Ollie's body and the funeral was held, things might begin to sort themselves out. God, the details.

The Gardena neighborhood where she and Ollie lived was one of those mixed dwelling areas. Houses sharing the streets with those quick-and-dirty apartment buildings which had sprouted up after the war.

Ollie and Violet bought a small house on Denker Avenue near Normandie and Artesia after they were married. A string of apartments now sat across the street. Two-story, four-unit, oblong stucco boxes. They were called dingbats. The front portion of the upstairs units squatted on top of open carports or enclosed, street-level garages. Some were decorated in a tiki motif, others in a preposterous French Chateau style. All looked cheap and ugly. The ones across from the McBride house went up four or five years ago but already looked decades old.

First a row of four-unit apartments. Next a Honeywell plant popped up around the corner on Western and Artesia. All combined to create a lot of traffic, curbside parking, car door slamming and pedestrian activity. So, Violet didn't pay much attention to the sound of footsteps coming down the sidewalk. Heavy sounds. A man's footsteps. Then she heard the footfalls turn up the cement path leading to her front door. She put her dust rag down and went to the front window, but she wasn't quick enough. The visitor had already reached the small concrete slab that formed her front stoop. Outside her field of vision from the picture window.

Violet heard the screen door creak open and a firm knock on the door. "Jesus," she muttered. *"It's Sunday. A solicitor on Sunday. A Jehovah's Witness? It better not be Tommy after I told him not to come around anymore,"* she thought. Violet opened the door a crack to see who was on the porch. The interruption annoyed her. She intended to shoo away anyone who stood there.

The door exploded into her with a force she'd never felt before. Like being struck by a moving car. The doorknob punched into her stomach like an iron fist. Violet toppled backwards, landing flat on her back. The wind was knocked out of her, and she was dizzy. Her chest heaved as she tried to catch her breath. She watched helplessly as a man in dark clothing crossed over the threshold and softly shut the front door behind him. He stepped over her and slid the front window closed then pulled the drapes shut.

THIRTY

Kraus woke up to clattering sounds coming from the kitchen. He must have been dead asleep when Anna left the bed. *"Did she leave in the middle of the night to sleep in her own room, or did she just get up?"* he wondered.

It had been a night of surprises. Not the least of which was the small tattoo he'd noticed on Anna's right buttock, near the hip. About the size of Franklin half dollar. Even the skimpiest bathing suit would have hidden it.

The tattoo was inked in the fashion of a pirate flag. A dark pink heart positioned in front of crossed white bones. *Heart and Crossbones* instead of *Skull and Crossbones*. Hard to guess how old it was, but the outlines and colors were crisp. Top notch work. Meant to last.

There was nothing whimsical about the tattoo. Stern and forbidding as a minefield warning sign. Affection and love were strictly off-limits. He wondered if the message was intended as a cautionary reminder for her lovers or herself. Maybe both.

It was Sunday morning. What was she doing in the kitchen?

"Good morning," Kraus said when he came out of the hallway. "How long have you been up?"

"About an hour," Anna said. "I'm an early riser." She waved her arm across the counter. "I thought I'd do the cooking for a change." She had her hair tied in a ponytail and was wearing a sweatshirt and jeans. Her feet were bare.

"Sounds great," Kraus said. "Coffee?"

"In the percolator," Anna said. "I used the last of your cream for the eggs, so you'll have to make do with milk."

"I've gotten by with a lot worse," Kraus said as he took a cup down from the cupboard. "What are you making?"

"Denver omelets," Anna said. "I took some things from your pantry. Hope that's okay," she added.

"That's what they're for," Kraus assured her.

"What are we up to today?"

"I thought we'd go and take a look at some furniture," Kraus said. He stirred some milk into his coffee cup.

"Hey, buster," Anna exclaimed with a chuckle. "Last night was nice. Really nice. But I'm not looking to set up house with you."

"Take it easy," Kraus laughed. "I have a friend who runs a wholesale office furniture business. Met him in the service. He has his finger on the pulse of L.A. businesses. I have an idea how we can push this Milestone Electro Supply investigation along. Besides, I like the furniture I have."

The phone rang. Sunday morning. Never a good sign. Kraus picked it up.

"Yeah," Kraus said. He listened for a minute. "It's for you," Kraus said. He held out the handset to Anna.

"Me?" she whispered.

"It's okay," Kraus said. "Not Fox or Applebaum. Someone more dangerous. It's my sister."

"Hello, Austie," Anna said. She listened for a minute, then smiled. "Just a minute," she held her palm over the transmitter cap of the handset. "Austie is planning a baby shower for your sister-in-law this Tuesday. It's the only day that works for everyone. She wants me to help her with the planning and decorations. Do you need me for today?"

Kraus was amused. His sister had a dozen friends she could ask, but she'd sensed Anna needed a friend. A female friend. That was pure Austie. Heart of gold. "Yeah, why not? I think you'll have fun, and this errand could be a little boring. Let me talk to her."

"Austie, Gordy wants to talk to you for a moment," Anna said. She was still smiling. "Sis," Kraus said, "Anna is happy to help out, but you remember the rules. Keep off the Miracle Mile. Do all your shopping in Redondo or Santa Monica, okay? Keep your eyes peeled for anyone who seems to be paying too much attention to you two."

"Right," Austie said in a sarcastic tone. "I'm sure no one usually gives Anna a second look. She's so homely and plain."

"You know what I mean," Kraus said.

"I know, I know," Austie said. "Tell Anna I'll pick her up at eleven."

"She'll pick you up at eleven," Kraus said, placing the receiver in its cradle. "You too, Anna. Keep your eyes open."

"I will," she said. She gave him an appreciative smile, dimples on full display. Then she pivoted and skipped back to the kitchen, ponytail flying behind her. "Does all this furniture you like include that lumpy mattress of yours?" Anna asked over her shoulder. A smile in her voice.

"All complaints must be submitted in writing," Kraus said.

THIRTY-ONE

Kraus made his way southeast to the City of Vernon. Vernon sat about five miles outside Los Angeles. Its motto was "Exclusively Industrial". Actual residents were thin on the ground. Vernon voting rolls clocked in at four hundred-odd souls. Instead of citizens, Vernon housed numerous heavy industrial manufacturers and large warehouse operations. Too big to operate within L.A. city limits.

In its heyday, Vernon had a 7000-seat boxing arena, a baseball stadium for a Pacific Coast League minor-league team and the world's longest bar. "*Pretty good combination,*" Kraus thought.

He drove past the Studebaker factory on Loma Vista. It pushed out sixty cars a day until recently. The plant shut down earlier in the year and already looked like a ghost town. Kraus pulled into the parking lot of a huge building. "*Diamond Wholesale Office Furniture*" was painted on the wall in vivid red lettering. Its slogan rested under the name. "*Diamond Quality at Rhinestone Prices. Guaranteed.*"

Kraus met the owner of the company, Norman Diamond, in Berlin. Diamond had been a navigator in B-17 bombers that flew daylight bombing raids over Germany. As navigator, he was responsible for one of the cheek guns in the forward part of the plane. He shot down four Messerschmitt 109's during his time on B-17's. Diamond was proud of the four Nazis he'd personally sent to Hell. Even prouder than the thousands more his squadron annihilated at the bombing targets pinpointed by his navigation.

Diamond stayed on after the German surrender in 1945. He was a visionary and saw opportunity in the post-war occupation. He finagled his way into a quartermaster role. He was placed in charge of one of the biggest supply depot sections near Tempelhof Airfield. Diamond put together a personnel staff who all shared his entrepreneurial spirit. Like their new leader, all his men were Jewish. He called them his "G.I. Jews". His section was the best-run, most-efficient supply unit in the American sector.

The newly minted supply master reasoned that a reliable stream of toothpaste, shoelaces and other simple luxuries would keep American officers satisfied. An officer would never crack down on petty cases of pilferage and black-market activities if by doing so it meant his weekly delivery of sirloin steak would be screwed up.

Kraus met Diamond during an investigation of a stolen painting. A well-connected American colonel issued a complaint that a valuable painting he had purchased from a refugee was waylaid and never shipped back to the States. The colonel believed the painting had disappeared while stored in Diamond's depot section. Diamond, like Kraus, was a native Angeleno. Kraus discovered he and the supply sergeant had a lot in common. He liked Diamond. He listened to the supply sergeant's explanation of how the painting came to be missing. Kraus sympathized with the sergeant's situation. Together, they hatched a plan to mollify the American colonel and keep Diamond's dilemma a secret. This alliance blossomed into a friendship. The two kept in touch after the war.

When Diamond returned to L.A. from Europe, he used his connections to buy up Army surplus office equipment pennies on the dollar. He warehoused the massive inventory he'd built up and started a wholesale new and used office furniture business. Post-war L.A. was bursting at the seams with businesses of all types starting up or expanding. There was pent-up consumer demand in the new, unrationed peacetime. American enterprise was gearing up to feed the hunger for new goods.

Diamond's office furniture business offered immediate delivery of inexpensive desks, chairs and other office trappings. Businesses getting underway appreciated the convenience and low prices. Word got around. Diamond Wholesale Office Furniture was soon the starting point of hundreds of emerging L.A. basin businesses.

Norman Diamond was a veritable encyclopedia of the Southern California business scene. He had been a reliable source of tips and inside information for many of Kraus' investigations.

Seeing it was Kraus, Diamond's secretary waved him right back into her boss's office. Dull yellow filing cabinets filled one wall. Another held a chalkboard filled with a complicated grid pattern. Each square held cramped notations about the week's deliveries. A Thomas Guide map of Southern California, the size of a bed sheet, hung next to the schedule grid. Beneath the map, a dusty plastic Ficus gave an unconvincing performance of being alive in a plastic pot brimming with fake Spanish moss.

The furniture mogul was sitting behind a large, ornate mahogany desk. Not exactly a floor model in Diamond's warehouse. Neither was the tufted leather executive swivel chair he sat on. A large print hung behind his desk. A piece by the Jewish artist, Man Ray. An odd picture of an unrecognizable shape covered by what looked like a horse blanket and trussed up with twine. His desk blotter calendar was covered with scribbles and flanked by a heavy green glass ashtray, two empty mugs and cartons of Chinese food.

"Gordy," Diamond exclaimed. "How's the shamus business?" He lifted one of the cartons and pointed its open flaps at Kraus. "Egg roll? I've had all I can handle."

"Don't mind if I do," Kraus said. He plucked out one of the deep-fried cylinders from the box. "Full stomach, huh," he said, lifting a paper napkin off the desk to hold the egg roll with. "You must be eating up a storm during Hanukkah."

"Oh, don't get me started," Diamond said. He pointed at a plastic cup of hot mustard next to the food carton. "Every *nudnik* freeloader who can hold a fork is lined up at my door minutes before we light the first candle."

"That bad, huh," Kraus laughed, humoring his friend.

"You don't know bad," Diamond moaned. "The Pharaoh didn't suffer like this from the locusts of the Ten Plagues. Kids screeching. Dreidels skittering across the floor. Food disappearing so fast you'd think Linda put out empty platters. I walk downstairs during the night for a glass of seltzer? My bare feet are chewed apart by those wadded up foil discs from the chocolate gelt."

"But you're enjoying your family," Kraus urged.

"Family? These *shnorrers*?" Diamond waved a dismissive hand. "I'm enjoying them the way street sweepers enjoy a ticker-tape parade. The final night is the sixth and I'm counting the hours. Gordy, if people wouldn't think I was celebrating Pearl Harbor Day, I'd throw a party for myself on the seventh!"

"That I might come to," Kraus said, pushing the final bite of the egg roll into his mouth. "I heard about Ollie. My condolences. That man was a real *Mensch*. A bit of a *goniff*, sure. But a *Mensch* all the same."

"That'll make a good epitaph for him," Kraus said. "I've been looking into his murder. I'm hoping you can help me with some information."

"Anything," Diamond said. He pushed a paddle switch on his desk intercom, "Bonnie, would you bring us a couple of Cel-Rays? Thanks, darling." He pushed back in his chair and looked at Kraus. "Shoot."

"What do you know about Milestone Electro Supply?" Diamond's secretary came into the office with a couple of cold bottles of celery soda. They were an acquired taste, but Kraus was thirsty after the egg rolls and hot mustard. He declined a glass and guzzled some right from the bottle.

"Milestone," Diamond said. "New outfit. Over near Venice and Overland. Sold 'em most of their office furniture when they first opened up."

"When was that?"

"Over a year ago. Owner is Eddie Stone. A real *macher*."

"What exactly do they do?" Kraus asked.

"Great question. Here's how Eddie got started," Diamond said. He poured the bottle of Cel-Ray into one of the mugs on his desk and took a gulp. Diamond worked a pack of Camels from his shirt breast pocket and shook one out. He held the pack towards Kraus, who shook his head. "You still don't smoke?" he asked.

"Nope," Kraus replied.

"Good for you," Diamond said as he flicked a gold lighter to life. "Ever see Stone's Radio Repair over on Culver? Radio repair, parts, sales. Randall Stone, Eddie's father, owned the place."

Kraus thought for a moment and snapped his fingers. "Yeah. My old man took our radio there to be fixed one or two times when I was a kid. My brother and I went with him once. Great place. Tubes and panels with knobs and needle gauges everywhere. Felt like I was in a Buck Rogers movie."

"That's the one. Two story place. Stone family lived above the shop. There's a barber shop and beauty salon in the space now. Randall retired in fifty-four. He and his wife live in Palm Springs now."

"Okay, where does Milestone come in?"

"Eddie went to college. Graduated. Comes back to help his father build up the business."

"Sounds like something you might experience before long," Kraus said.

"My son? Duddel? Come into this business?" Diamond swiveled his head around, gazing protectively at his office through a cloud of cigarette smoke. A ship's captain peering through the fog and spying a

Brigantine flying the Jolly Roger. "I wouldn't wish that on my worst enemy. The only time he's shown any kind of enterprising spirit was when he was selling those Mexican nudie comics in his dorm."

"God, I'd forgotten that," Kraus chuckled.

"Wish I could say the same. Don't ask me how much it cost me to keep him in school after that *balagan*," Diamond flapped a hand as though he were swatting at a pesky gnat. "No, I've got him in medical school. New med school in the Bronx." Another gulp of Cel-Ray. "Albert Einstein College of Medicine, if you can believe that. Just opened last year. I made a sizable donation, and they made a sizable compromise in their admission standards to take Duddy. With any luck he'll graduate. Open a general practice where he can't do much harm. I'll load him up with malpractice insurance and find him a real *chaleria* for an office manager. Keep him in line."

Kraus laughed. "Okay. No Diamond and Son in the future. How does Eddie Stone go from the radio repair business with his father to starting Milestone Electro Supply?"

"So," Diamond continued, "Eddie comes into the business. Makes a few changes here and there. Nothing earth-shattering. He's checking out the competition one day. Sees a tube tester at a radio shop in Chatsworth."

"Tube tester," Kraus said, "what's that?"

"You've probably seen them. Sort of a cabinet. Looks a little bit like a pinball machine. The bed of the thing has a bunch of sockets fastened into it. The vertical section has a few lights and a big meter. Your radio starts acting up, you bring in the tubes and test them. If they test bad, there are drawers underneath holding new ones you can buy."

"Okay," Kraus said, "good way to draw in customers for a repair."

"Exactly," Diamond snapped his fingers at Kraus. "The *shnooks* pay money for the replacements. Nine times out of ten, the new tubes don't entirely fix the problem. Voila. They leave the radio for a full repair or buy a new one."

"So Eddie gets one for their store," Kraus prompted.

"Yes. Eddie sees how well the gimmick works. RCA and Sylvania buy the machines and put their own stamp on them. Place them at stores and radio-television shops for free. Like photo booths or cigarette machines. They make their money from providing the replacement tubes for sale. Worked great. Repair business and new radio sales rocketed. Old man Stone had to hire an extra bench technician. But after a while, Eddie didn't like having a passive partner taking such a big cut."

"Let me guess. He found out where the machines were made and bought his own. Put the Stone's Radio Repair sign on it. Bought the tubes independently in bulk and kept more of the profits."

"Yes, sir," Diamond said. He drained his mug and slapped it down on his desk. "But he didn't stop there. He bought more of the testers. Set 'em up all over L.A., the valley, Orange County, San Diego. Little corner stores, bodegas, barber shops. Had a guy who regularly restocked the tubes and maintained the testers. Paid the stores a small percentage of the sales. Every customer who bought a tube got a coupon offering ten percent off for a repair or new purchase at the shop. Customer could leave his set at the place where he tested the tubes. The guy who stocked the drawers would pick it up, take it in for repair and return the fixed unit to the location for a will-call. Slick program and the cash started rolling in. Like a license to print money."

"Sounds good," Kraus said. "But I still don't see how Milestone Electro Supply sprouts out of that"

"I'm getting to that. Great story," Diamond said with a glint of admiration in his eyes. "Heard this directly from Eddie Stone himself. One day he notices his guy had to restock an entire inventory of tubes all at once. Donut shop in Norwalk. He gets curious. Pays a visit to the place."

"Shoplifting?" Kraus suggested.

"No," Diamond said. "Stone has a cruller and coffee while he listens to how one of the shop's regulars came in earlier in the month. Didn't test any tubes. Just scooped up almost all the inventory in the drawers and paid for them at the counter. Full price. No haggling. Stone said it typically took one of his locations over a month to go through that many tubes."

"Wow," Kraus said, "what was it all about?"

"The guy who bought the tubes worked at a place called Bendix-Pacific. They build assemblies used in radar and sonar equipment. Turns out they were continually running out of inventory. Had to wait for parts they ordered from Midwest wholesalers who shipped by a slow boat from China."

"Place called Allied Radio?" Kraus asked.

"That's it," Diamond said, pointing his cigarette at Kraus. "The guy from Bendix was desperate. They had orders to fill. Couldn't wait. The tubes they needed were right there at the donut shop, so he bought all of 'em. Stone hears the story. Looks around. Sees all these companies springing up in Southern California. All of 'em needing electrical and electronic parts. All of 'em buying from joints two or three thousand miles away, waiting weeks on orders they're charged the freight for. And paying in advance or C.O.D. for the privilege of it. Paying top dollar, too."

"Believe it or not," Kraus said, "I've heard a similar story about how painful it is to buy from these vendors."

"You have? Good. Then you'll understand Stone's brainstorm. He asks himself, 'Why not keep loads of the merchandise here? Stock locally. Sell it cheaper than the competition. Offer payment terms. Deliver for free.' Milestone Electro Supply is born. Bendix-Pacific became his first customer. Now he is a franchised stocking distributor of most of the major electronic product lines. RCA. General Electric. Westinghouse. Sylvania. Raytheon. A couple dozen others."

"Fast growth," Kraus remarked.

"It's a fast industry. What does all this have to do with Ollie," Diamond asked.

Kraus told Diamond about the guy at Desilu. The other blackmail victims. The Allied Radio catalog on Ollie's table. The kid from Milestone Electro Supply who picked up the overages.

Diamond ran his fingers through thinning hair. "I can come up with a half-dozen ways someone could make money that way. But anyway I cut it, there just doesn't seem like there's enough headroom for a decent profit to offset the risk. At least for an outsider."

"What do you mean," Kraus said, "you think it could be Stone?"

"It would make more sense as an inside job. You pilfer from your own company. No real costs, because you're blackmailing the primary accomplices. Chump change for the delivery kid. You're basically skimming at no cost."

"How so?"

"Back in Prohibition, a drug company, McKesson, was taken over by a shyster. He installed family members in the firm. Set up a dummy corporation as a straw buyer. Looted the place down to the petty cash box with every scam in the book. Fake purchase orders. Overstating inventory value. Siphoning cash from sales. This guy took millions right under the nose of a fuckin' Big Five accounting house. It can be done."

"You think that's what's going on at Milestone Electro?"

"Not really. I just don't see enough meat on the bone for that kind of thing. What does Stone really have to gain? He does have some competition coming in. I've had feelers from a New York concern, Avnet. A local guy, too, Tony Hamilton. Both looking to set up the

209

same kind of operation here that Stone has going. They're coming and want office furniture. Maybe Stone's figured out a way to fund a war chest to fight off the competition. Gordy, you have an accounting degree. You know figures can lie and liars can figure."

"I just don't see it," Kraus said.

"Me neither. The blackmail part smells like an outside job. Getting free products to resell. But there's still the limited gain problem. The McKesson scandal netted millions. Why this scam? This is mice nuts in comparison. Worth murdering for? You couldn't offer warranty coverage on the product. Certainly no exchange or return privileges. To turn the parts into money, you'd have to sell them on the gray market to *hondlers*."

"You think there's a gray market for these types of things?" Kraus asked.

"Gordy, there's a gray market for any kind of commodity. But the buyers are guys who know the product fell off the back of a truck. You couldn't get fifty cents on the dollar from those types."

"Yeah," Kraus agreed. "But Ollie was like a Bluetick Coonhound when it came to sniffing out illicit money. He told me he was onto something big. There's money in this somewhere. I'm just not seeing it right off the bat. I really need to scope out the operation without tipping Stone that I'm an investigator. Maybe if I get inside, I can discover something I'm missing."

Diamond smiled. "I may have a way in for you," he said.

THIRTY-TWO

Kraus mulled over his Sunday morning as he drove home. Diamond had promised to arrange a meeting with Eddie Stone tomorrow morning. Kraus' cover story was as the owner of a newly-formed electronics company. He was looking for a steady, cheap supply of electronic products. He wanted to conduct a "vendor survey" at Milestone Electro Supply. Diamond was going to tell Stone that if Kraus liked what he saw, he would open an account with the distributor.

In the meantime, Diamond called one of his newer customers, Jeff Katz. A guy fresh out of Carnegie Mellon. Electrical engineer. Electronics specialist. He came to L.A. to set up shop as a consultant. Outfitted his new office with Diamond Office Furniture goods and befriended Norman Diamond in the process.

Jeff Katz was a tall, lanky man with a head of tight curls and inquisitive eyes made even more so by thick-lensed glasses. An easy smile revealed a slightly crooked row of upper teeth. The imperfection gave him an innocent look. They discussed Norman Diamond for a few minutes, using their mutual acquaintance for the introduction ritual.

Katz was genuinely fond of Diamond. The transplanted Easterner clearly saw Diamond as a surrogate father. Katz bought a home near Diamond's Palos Verdes residence. He joined Diamond's synagogue, Temple Beth El, in San Pedro. He was a guest at Diamond's home for their Hanukkah observances. Kraus figured Diamond viewed Katz as a surrogate son. The son he'd always wanted.

The electrical engineer listened to what Kraus wanted. He had some reservations. "Milestone is a very useful resource for my business. I know Eddie personally. He allows me full access to their catalog room. All the specifications for new products are there before they appear anywhere else. Of course, Eddie knows I will steer my clients to him for product purchases, so it's a two-way street, but I'd hate to lose his cooperation. Are you trying to get him in trouble?"

"No, Mr. Katz. He's a link in the chain leading to someone who murdered my friend. I doubt Eddie Stone had anything to do with that." Kraus wasn't certain that was completely true, but he needed help from this engineer.

"From what you've told me, I can't imagine what Eddie would have to gain. You're wanting a closer look."

"Correct. My friend saw something going on somewhere along the way that was worth a lot of money."

"And you think if you get close enough, you'll see the same thing."

"I'm hoping for that."

"Okay," Katz said, "let's get to work." The engineer pulled some files from his desk drawer and laid them out on the desktop. "These," he said, pointing to schematics and brochure pages, "are what the most advanced hearing aids were like just after the war."

"Looks like a large transistor radio," Kraus said.

"Precisely," Katz agreed. "But no transistors. This unit hangs by a chain or lanyard from the user's neck. The earpiece leads from the side of the case. Weighs about five pounds and was built with small vacuum tubes. The vacuum tubes provided better clarity, but the battery life was extremely short."

"Not very practical," Kraus said.

"No," Katz said, "and the vacuum tubes made the unit very hot. So, along comes the transistor. Do you know about them?"

"Little bug looking things," Kraus offered. "I've seen drawings of them in the Allied Radio catalog."

"Good," Katz beamed. Praise for an ambitious student. "They're soon going to be all around you." The engineer swept his hand around his study. "Televisions, radios, toasters, refrigerators, cars. You probably used the term, 'transistor radio', before you even knew what a transistor was or what it did. Unseen and largely unknown but making things possible that weren't dreamed of twenty years ago." Kraus thought he sounded a little like a fairy tale wizard.

"And how do these unseen miracle workers make hearing aids better?" Kraus asked.

Katz laughed. "I sound a little like that inventor chicken character in the Disney comics, don't I. Gyro something? I'll admit, the speed of technological advancements since the war sometimes takes my breath away." Katz pulled another brochure out of the file. "This is the Sonotone 1010. It came out four or five years ago."

Kraus lifted the brochure and looked it over. "It looks much smaller than the other one."

"It is," Katz said. "It uses a combination of small vacuum tubes and one transistor."

"Why not all transistors?" Kraus asked.

"At that time, they would have produced too much electrical noise," Katz said. "Low-level static, if you will. Interferes with the output of the hearing aid."

"A limited miracle," Kraus said.

"For a time," Katz said in a clipped tone. Defending his religion from a heretic. "Technology is an evolution, Mr. Kraus. The first wagon probably came along quite a while after the first wheel."

"Point taken" Kraus conceded. "I'm guessing your college project was centered on making a better mousetrap."

"Just so," Katz said. "The addition of a single transistor extended the battery life. But the unit rests against the body of the user. Heat and humidity builds up in the case. The transistor got damp and died altogether. Sometimes in just two weeks. My experiments proved that transistors could escape humidity damage by being treated with a thin coating. Other design revisions reduced the electrical interference. I built a lab prototype of an all-transistor hearing aid. Crude by industrial design standards, but it performed well."

Kraus looked at a photograph Katz produced from the file. It pictured a simple open-topped plastic box containing a black card piece with little bug-like transistors soldered onto it. "This did the trick?" he asked.

"For what was available at the time," Katz said. "Transistors are beginning to be made with silicon now. Better performance. Smaller. Cheaper. If I were designing one today, it would consist completely of the silicon components. This is the story you'll use for your visit to Milestone."

"What's that little black card with the hole pattern drilled through it?" Kraus asked.

"That's a standard Bakelite circuit board. The thru holes are commonly called 'sockets'. The wire transistor leads are poked into the sockets and soldered in place. Little flat brass traces on the rear of the board connect the circuit design. A device that goes into production uses custom-designed circuit boards and the socket connections are embedded into the board."

Kraus spent the next three hours learning all about the engineer's concepts and jargon for a new type of electronic hearing aid. Miniaturization. Component density. Battery life. Electric sound amplification. First-to-market. Product evolution projection. Economies of scale. He was reminded of a Sherlock Holmes story he and Rudi read as kids. Watson had to learn everything he could about Chinese pottery in one night in order to pass himself off as an expert.

"Here," Katz said as Kraus got up to leave. He handed Kraus a thin comic book. "This is something General Electric published a few months ago. Ingenious bit of marketing, really."

Kraus looked at the cover. It was titled, '*Adventures in Electronics*'. "This is what I could call the investigation." He thumbed through it. Some know-it-all was showing his younger brother and his brother's dumbfounded girlfriend the wonders of the new Electronic Age. It looked to Kraus as though the guy was trying to make time with his brother's gal. The man took the two on a tour of how a modern television camera was put together. Kraus thought about Delbert Bowers at Desilu.

"General Electric is trying to get the guy on the street used to the idea of how electronics are going to change things," Katz added. "Consumer education. Brilliant. If you learn everything in this twelve page comic book, you'll possess the equivalent of the first year of a double-E program."

Kraus was confused for a moment. A strip joint in Little Tokyo advertised their headliner, Sugar Flame or Sugar-something, as having a double-E bust size. "Double-E. What do you mean?" Kraus asked.

Katz chuckled, "Electrical Engineering. You'll have the knowledge every double-E student gets in their first two terms. All packed into that comic book. What did you think I meant?"

Kraus laughed. "I'd rather not say. Let's see if I can hang on to this education you've given me until tomorrow," Kraus said. "Mr. Katz, thank you for your time."

"Will you let me know what happens?" Katz asked. "You've got my curiosity up about this."

"I'll do that," Kraus promised. "Thanks again."

Kraus walked into his house and plopped the material Katz had given him on his kitchen counter. There was a note held by a magnet on the fridge. It was from Anna. Austie wanted her to spend the night in Redondo Beach so they could get up early on Monday to keep working on his sister-in-law's shower. He'd call her later. He wondered if Anna was ready to meet his mom. For that matter, he wondered if his mom was prepared to meet Anna.

Kraus decided to reread the General Electric comic book. He'd pop open a beer to drink while studying. He was reaching for the handle of the fridge when a loud knocking came from his front door.

"Damn," Kraus muttered. "Who could that be on a Sunday?"

THIRTY-THREE

The knock was the thunderous, knuckle-bruising, "Rent's Overdue" variety.

"Okay, okay," Kraus hissed under his breath as he went to the front door. Standing on his front porch was a hatless man in a tailored Southwick suit. Two uniformed patrol cops stood a few paces behind him on the edge of the lawn.

It was John Gowan, Gino Laveroni's partner. Gowan's horsey hair was slicked down with a greasy pomade. His forehead was beetle-browed, causing it to overhang and cast a permanent shadow across his close-set eyes. A weak chin added to the Neanderthal look. On the rare times Gowan expressed smug humor, the set of his mouth became slack-jawed, giving him a look of impotent contempt. He had that look now.

"I'm sorry, I bought my Girl Scout cookies from the troop selling outside the grocery store," Kraus said.

Gowan switched to a scowl he must have thought looked menacing. Kraus thought it made him look constipated. "Very funny, Kraus. You're coming with us." Gowan jabbed a thumb over his shoulder at the two young patrolmen standing on the lawn just behind the detective. Too young to have known Kraus while he was on the job. Kraus figured Gowan picked them for just that reason.

"Where are we going?" Kraus asked.

"I'm here to take you in," Gowan spat out.

"Wow, you sound like Kirk Douglas in 'Detective Story'," Kraus deadpanned.

"Smartass no matter what, huh, Kraus," Gowan said.

"Smartass? No, I meant it, you almost sounded like a real cop for a moment," Kraus said.

Gowan swiveled his head around to look at the two patrolmen he brought with him. He gave them a 'can you believe this guy' look. "Kraus, get your jacket. You're going with us."

"Going where? Where's Laveroni?"

"I'm taking you in for questioning. The lieutenant's out of town. You don't have your old buddy here to run interference for you."

"I don't need Gino to protect me from the likes of you," Kraus said.

"We'll see," Gowan said. "You can get your jacket and come with me, or I'll have the officers take you into formal custody."

Kraus shrugged and grabbed his jacket from the back of his couch. He stepped out the door and locked it behind him. He stepped past Gowan and off his front porch onto the narrow walkway that led up from the sidewalk. He gave Gowan a 'what now' look.

Gowan pointed at Kraus as though he'd just seen him. "You two take him in the squad. Follow me." The patrolmen escorted Kraus to their black-and-white. They let him in the back and climbed into the front. Gowan drove past them in his plain wrap and the squad car pulled from the curb to follow.

The squad car went east on Venice and followed Gowan's turn north on Figueroa. But Gowan didn't veer towards the PAB when they came to 1st Street. When both Gowan and the patrol car stayed on Figueroa, Kraus knew what the little martinet was up to. He didn't want to bring Kraus into the new headquarters. Gowan wanted to keep his shenanigans out of sight of the people who'd report it to Laveroni.

The squad car crossed the river and turned into the Lincoln Heights Jail parking lot. They made the familiar button hook turn past the imposing front of the five story Art Deco building to the little parking area that led to the booking room entrance door. When Kraus was a cop he'd made the same maneuver hundreds of times. The facility was expanded after the war, but to Kraus the general feel of the place was the same as it was in 1940.

The holding vestibule hadn't changed much. Old wooden benches and seats covered with graffiti and carvings. Institutional green walls. Barred windows and doors. An ancient cigarette machine sat next to one of the benches. A mirror was set into its upper case. Its silvering was thinning at the edges like a receding tide. The machine was so old it still accepted just a dime for a pack of smokes. Legend had it that Al Capone spent some time at Lincoln Heights. He supposedly combed his hair in that mirror. It was said he bought everyone in the room a pack of cigarettes while waiting to be booked.

Kraus knew this tale was pure bunkum. Capone *was* in L.A. for a few days in '27 or '28. The LAPD ran him out of town almost as soon as he stepped off the train onto the Santa Fe Railroad depot platform. Chief Jim Davis was a no-nonsense type in those days. He didn't like a midwest bootlegger sniffing around his town. He had his fiercest detective, Ed "Roughhouse" Brown, give Capone and his entourage the bum's rush back to the train station. Even if Capone had been in custody for a few hours during the roust, it wouldn't have been here. Lincoln Heights Jail didn't open until '31.

But the myth endured. Kraus often wondered why the average person was so quick to believe the best about criminals and the worst about cops. He watched Gowan talking to an admitting officer through a barred window, trying to be affable and intimidating at the same time. Looking exactly like what he was. An officious prick. Kraus thought he understood the cop part if that was how the public saw the police. He glanced over to see the patrolman's face next to him. The cop was rolling his eyes.

"Been runnin' with him long?" Kraus asked.

"What's it to you, Kraus?" the uniformed cop retorted. Defensive. Half-embarrassed.

"Hey, I know how it is," Kraus whispered. "I was on the force. A guy wants to get ahead in the department? He needs a sponsor. But take a good look at this guy. You hitch yourself too close to his wagon and there'll come a time he'll back it over you. Get ahead but watch your back."

The cop shot Kraus a look of mild gratitude mixed with resentment.

Gowan turned and motioned for the patrolman to bring Kraus along. They walked single file into the area where prisoners were processed. Like the outer seating area, the booking room smelled like bleach, cigarettes, and vomit. Two milk glass light globes hung from the ceiling over the counters. They seemed to restrain the illumination, casting a dusky gloom over the window counters, like a thick marine layer.

Kraus was escorted past the booking windows. The two clerks didn't give him a second glance. He was marched directly into the drunk tank. Sunday afternoon. The tank was packed as solid as a Metro bus at quitting time. A jail guard opened the barred door of the tank for Gowan. The detective grabbed Kraus' shoulder and made a show of steering him through the door.

"You cool your heels in here for a while, Kraus," Gowan said.

"How long you think you'll keep me here," Kraus said.

"As long as I want, Kraus," Gowan answered. He turned on his heel and walked away, the patrolman following behind.

Lincoln Heights was originally designed to hold about six hundred inmates. The post-war addition was meant to give it the capacity for another twenty-five hundred. At any given time, the facility housed over six thousand inmates and detainees. The drunk tank was always overcrowded. It reeked of sickly-sweet fortified wine and sour body odor. Two barred windows at one end of the rectangular space offered little light and no ventilation.

Kraus draped his jacket over his arm and looked around the room. Easily fifty men in a space meant for twenty-five. Some sat on their heels with backs against the wall. Others were curled on the bare floor trying to sleep it off. There was little room to walk, but he made his way a few feet down the wall from the door and used his elbows to clear a place to lean.

There were a handful of Mexicans squatting in a rough circle near the center of the room. He couldn't see what they were doing, but there was a steady clicking sound coming from the center of the scrum. It sounded like badly played castanets. The clicking stopped and a rowdy chorus of voices lifted out of the pack. Kraus moved his head to one side to get a better look between two of the men. They were hunkered around an open floor space with flat, oblong tiles scattered across the linoleum.

A spirited game of dominos was underway. The click-clack noise was from the domino tiles being swirled around. Mixing them up before a new game. They hooted and insulted one another in that curious fusion of Spanish and English one hears on Olvera Street. Others standing closer to the circle laughed and kibitzed as the game was played.

The tank door swung open. Kraus looked but didn't move. Putting him in here was Gowan's ham-handed attempt to soften him up. For what, Kraus couldn't guess, but it was too soon for Gowan to spring him. A new arrestee had been brought in. He looked over the tank's newest inductee.

A wiry Negro teen was ushered into the tank. The youth had closely shorn hair and chestnut brown skin. He was wearing a snow-white t-shirt with a sharp crease ironed down the center. His pants were baggy blue dungarees like the ones issued to inmates at Wayside Honor Ranch in northern L.A. County. Street gang uniform. Young street gangsters called the pants their "counties". Posing as *veteranos* even if they'd never been incarcerated a single day.

"There sure are a lot of fuckin' beaners in this place," the kid half-shouted as he pushed through the crowd.

Kraus saw a fresh tattoo of "IV" on the inside of his left forearm. Roman numerals for "four" inked in the ornamental Latin lettering style favored by 15th century monk scribes and Latino gangs. It was ringed by red, swollen skin and his forehead was clammy from tattoo fever. The youngster must have gotten jumped into the Fourth Street Flats, a small gang that had splintered off from the larger Flats gang in the Aliso Village projects. Kraus had heard the Fourth Street faction was allowing Negro membership. Both groups were heavy into the narcotics trade and destined to clash. Fourth Street Flats needed all the soldiers they could recruit to survive a sustained feud.

This new member of the Fourth Street clique clearly craved more validation. A black eye and a few bruises from a *chingasos* while in the tank would be just the ticket to gain respect. He aggressively bumped a few of the Mexicans standing near the domino game, then gave them a challenging look when they pulled an annoyed face.

Kraus looked at the man standing next to him. His neighbor was an older Mexican in a tattered sweatshirt and torn jeans. Kraus noticed the faded tattoo of a four-leaf clover on the top of his left hand. Eastside Clover alumnus. A large gang. About two-hundred strong. Held turf around Union Station. Big drug dealers. This one probably left the life years before. Familiar story. Knocked up his girlfriend. Got married. Got a job with a moving company or concrete outfit. Co-workers probably thought he was a Notre Dame fan.

"*Pendejo*," the man said in a soft voice.

"*Verdad*," Kraus snickered, nodding his agreement.

None of the *vatos* in the tank were going to give this *nueva perra* the satisfaction of a tussle. They all wanted to get home to the pots of Sunday menudo simmering on the stove. Settle down on the couch tonight with a cold glass of Tecate. Tune in to the Sunday night fights broadcast from the Olympic Auditorium. Get up on Monday and go to work. They weren't looking for a fistfight to add an overnight stay to their detainment. A few minutes of fruitless aggression sent the Negro teen into a vexed crouch near the rear corner of the room.

Kraus contented himself by watching the activities in the tank. How the men interacted. The rites of the dominos game. He'd been in the tank for over an hour and was lost in thought when he heard his name.

"Kraus," a jail guard yelled from outside the tank door.

"Yo," Kraus yelled. He pushed himself away from the wall. "*Buena suerte*," he said to the former Eastside Clover hood. He got to the door as the guard pulled it open.

"Guy wants to talk to you in the box," the guard said.

"Gowan?" Kraus asked. "Looks like a ferret with indigestion."

"Come on," the guard laughed. He led Kraus out of the booking area and down an inner hallway. "In there," the turnkey said.

Kraus walked into the Lincoln Heights bullpen. It was a boxcar shaped room with four library tables in a row from one end of the room to the other. The facility did have interrogation rooms, but those were reserved for prisoners who'd been booked. This room was a catch-all. Journalists interviewing cops. Prisoners meeting with their lawyers. Patrolmen bringing detectives up to speed. Gowan and the other patrolman were sitting next to one another. Kraus took a chair opposite them. No one else was in the room.

"Like your little visit, Kraus?" Gowan sneered.

"Learned how to play dominos," Kraus said. "Gowan, you haven't started any paper. Don't think this kind of stunt can bother me. Is this how you're killing time while you're waiting for that transfer to the Rat Squad?"

The LAPD created the Internal Affairs Group six or seven years ago. Getting posted to that division had become a fast-track to promotion in the LAPD. Kraus figured Gowan for the kind of weasel who yearned for an IAG transfer.

Gowan ignored the jibe. "When's the last time you saw Violet McBride?"

"On Monday. I went to see her after Gino did the notification," Kraus said.

"You didn't see her today?" Gowan pressed.

"No," Kraus said. "What gives here, Gowan?"

"Someone forced their way into her house this morning."

"Is she okay?" Kraus asked. His stomach dropped at the news.

"Guy beat her nearly to death," Gowan said. "Probably the only thing saved her was that it was interrupted. Two of the delivery guys at the bottled water place she works for came by to drop off some flowers and a card from the office. Rang the doorbell. Scared the perp off."

"Where is she?" Kraus asked.

"Angelus Hospital, over on Trinity," Gowan said.

"I'm going to go see her," Kraus said as he started to rise from his chair.

"Sit right there, Kraus, or I'll have you cuffed to the table," Gowan growled. "She's in surgery. They're not sure when we can talk to her."

"You know who did it?" Kraus asked.

"Kraus, I'm askin' the questions. You're givin' the answers. Knowing you, you've got a good picture of all of this. It's time to come clean, or so help me, I'll ring you up on obstruction."

The door to the interview bullpen flew open. "What the fuck is goin' on here?" a booming voice asked.

All three of the seated men cranked their heads around to see who had barged in the room. It was Gino Laveroni, LAPD senior detective and Gowan's supervisor. He was wearing a felt pastry hat, sports shirt, cardigan sweater and loose pleated slacks. His off-duty driving duds.

"For Chrissake, Gowan, what the hell are you up to?" Laveroni demanded. "I take one weekend off to go to my fucking in-laws in Escondido. Forty-eight hours! And this is the shit you pull when I'm out of sight? Takin' two patrolmen off the street for no reason other than to piss on a fire hydrant!"

"Lieutenant, I know this chump knows more than he's letting on. I chased him out of the PAB when he tried to bog us down with his stupid tips. Chapped his butt. He's been sniffing around when you told him not to," Gowan said.

"Gowan, you couldn't chase a rat off a sinking ship. I'm going to show you what chapped looks like," Kraus shouted. He shot up out of his chair, knocking it over in the process. Gowan took a half-step backwards, bumping against the end wall of the room. The patrolman started to stand.

"Enough," Laveroni shouted. "Gordy, sit your ass down. As hard as it is to believe, he's a sworn law officer. Hands off." The lieutenant turned to Gowan and the patrolman. "You two get out of here. Go help out with the door-to-doors on Denker." Gowan started to stammer something and Laveroni pointed his finger at him, "No talk. Leave. Now."

"Gordy, you almost bought yourself three days in this place," Laveroni said after Gowan left. "It's not like you to lose your cool that way."

"Shit, Gino, I'm pissed about the news about Violet. First Ollie. Now this."

"Yeah," Laveroni said. He pried a pack of cigarettes from his shirt pocket and offered it to Kraus, who shook his head. "Still not smokin'? Good for you," he said as he lit one for himself with his banged-up U.S. Navy Zippo. *USS John Hood* was engraved on its side. "My wife insists these are goin' kill me. Thing is, she says it with the sound of hope in her voice. Let's get out of here."

"You know much yet?" Kraus asked as they walked out of the interview bullpen.

"Not a lot. Gardena P.D. were called to the scene. They made the Ollie connection right away and gave the LAPD a call."

"Any witnesses?"

"Latchkey kid looking out the second story front window from across the street said he saw a white male go to the front door. Impossible angle to get an accurate description. Not even the height. Whoever it was had some muscle. Knew how to dish out a beating. Left a couple of smudged shoe prints in Violet's vomit. Gardena cops said it looked like he was starting to toss the place when he was interrupted."

"Jesus," Kraus said, "know anything about her condition?"

"She's in surgery. Or was when I checked on my way here. I've got a uniform there keeping an eye on her. Angelus is a top-rate hospital, Gordy. My nephew was born there last year. Premature. Tricky delivery. Doctor was the husband of that actress, Rhonda Fleming. He and the staff were first-class."

"No kidding?" Kraus remarked. "Ollie and I saw her at Desilu just before he was killed."

"Small town," Laveroni said. They exited the gloomy jail interior into the brightness of the rear parking lot. Despite the diesel fumes and sulphury asphalt, the air smelled cleaner. The sunlight made Kraus sneeze. Laveroni took another drag on his cigarette. "Gordy, is there a connection between the attack on Violet and Ollie's murder?"

"Gino, if there *isn't* a connection, it would be a helluva coincidence," Kraus said. "I just don't know what the connection is." He watched Gowan turn his city ride out of the parking lot onto 19th. The sunshine played on the edge of the diamond shape stamped into the side of the government plate. "*Yet,*" Kraus thought. "*I don't know, yet.*"

THIRTY-FOUR

"Well, hello, Philo Vance. How are you this morning?" Melinda said. "You called in on your own line for a change."

"Don't want to tie up Stanley's phone during tax season. I had quite a Sunday, Melinda," Kraus said. "Learned all about hearing aids and spent a couple of hours in jail."

"Did one lead to the other?" Melinda teased.

"No, they were mutually exclusive," Kraus said.

"My, such a fancy term. Where did you pick that up?"

"Long story," Kraus said. He told her about Violet. How Gowan ran him in. His appointment at Milestone Electro Supply coming up later in the morning.

"How terrible," Melinda said. "Do you know how her surgery turned out?"

"Gino told me this morning they took out her spleen and are treating her for a collapsed lung. Broken ribs and a couple of fractured fingers. The attacker was trying to get something out of her."

"God, Gordy," Melinda gasped.

"I know. She's barely lucid with all the medication and has a tube down her throat. Arrange for that florist we use to send her some flowers this morning. I'll keep you updated during the day."

"Are there any leads on this?" Melinda asked.

"None I know of. I'm sure it's directly related to Ollie's murder. Cops found a couple of footprints and figure the guy for six-one, six-two. Probably too tall to have pulled the trigger on Ollie. Could be two guys working together, though. If I find one, I'm bound to find the other."

"You think Milestone Electro Supply is involved?"

"The place is the common denominator of everything I've traced from Ollie's case. It's playing a big part in some way," Kraus said.

"Gordy, be careful," Melinda said.

"I always am," Kraus said. "I'll check back with you later today."

Kraus headed west on Venice towards Culver City. Milestone Electro Supply was on Washington Boulevard near the new Veteran's Memorial Park. He mentally combed over the details of the hearing aid he'd be pretending to take into production. He looked to make sure he'd brought his prop along. Katz let him borrow one of his plastic boxes with a Bakelite board fastened inside. The board bristled with mounted transistors, resistors and small vacuum tubes.

"Take this along when you meet with Eddie. It'll boost your credibility. Makes it look like you've got something beyond the drafting table. Close to needing parts in production quantities."

"Is this a hearing aid design?" Kraus asked as he turned the box in his hands.

"No," Katz chuckled. "It was an early version of a circuit for a burglar alarm. I've built a better one. Don't worry. Unless an engineer looks it over, it'll pass as a new hearing aid prototype."

Washington crossed over National and Kraus glanced south. He thought about the nights he'd spent at the Cotton Club. The building had burned down four or five years before, but it was a swinging place when he was in college. In the early-20's, a local restaurateur, Frank Sebastian, opened a West Coast version of Harlem's famous nightspot. He boldly named it Sebastian's Cotton Club. Like the Harlem original, Culver City's counterpart served liquor until dawn, even during Prohibition. Louis Armstrong performed there. So did Lionel Hampton and Artie Shaw.

It was still a hot joint fifteen years later. He'd spent quite a few evenings there with college friends, not long before it closed for good. Sebastian was the picture of a charismatic speakeasy host. He had a standing offer right to the end. Any patrons who stuck it out the entire evening until dawn would be served a free, hearty breakfast of ham and eggs.

One night, he and his friends decided to go the distance. While the sun peeked over the San Gabriel mountains, exhausted cooks wearing stained, limp toques served breakfast to the intrepid revelers. Bowls of thin oatmeal drizzled with molasses along with fried pieces of Spam sliced thinner than Artie Shaw's clarinet reeds.

The memory made him laugh. They took the letdown in stride, eating with such gusto you would have thought they were at the Pantry Cafe. Empty promises were in the Hollywood bloodstream. Taking them seriously would make you look like one of the rubes.

It was after nine and morning traffic had thinned. Milestone Electro Supply occupied a low-slung, brown brick building that had once been the home of a large, independent costume design company. It had collaborated with many of the old-time Culver City studios. They were a full-service shop, turning studio concepts into sketches and patterns, making samples and custom-fitting stars. Their high-volume cut and sew operation quickly outfitted large casts of extras. Hundreds of films dating back to the silents featured their work. Thomas Ince, RKO-Pathe, Hal Roach and many others had been clients.

The company relocated to Burbank years before, but traces of its glory days were still evident. Norman Diamond told him Thelma Todd's signature could still be seen etched in a cement sidewalk slab near the entrance. Katz said Milestone used one of the old fitting rooms for a literature library. Catalogs rested on the same slanted shelves that once held custom-made shoes for many stars. He said he'd seen the names of Gilbert Roland and Tallulah Bankhead written in ink on shelves emptied of the last brochure.

Kraus handed a pretty receptionist stationed behind a boomerang-shaped lobby desk one of his generic business cards. He told her he had an appointment with Eddie Stone. She pressed a button on her phone.

"Sheila, it's Candy. Gordon Kraus is here to see Eddie. Thanks." She looked back up at Kraus, "He'll be out in a minute. Can I get you a coffee or some water?"

"No, thank you," Kraus said. "How long has Milestone been here?" he asked.

"About eighteen months. I started almost a year ago. I replaced a receptionist who moved to the inside sales department." A young woman carrying a stack of catalogs bustled into the lobby through an inner door.

"Candy, would you type mailing labels for these?" the woman said as she plopped them on the end of the receptionist desk near where a typewriter sat. "The address info is on the notepad sheets separating each stack. Make sure each catalog has a Milestone sticker on it, please."

"Will do," Candy said in a lively tone.

"Growing company," Kraus said.

"Yes," Candy said. "Very fast-paced. I worked at a welding supply company before coming here. It was like watching the lawn grow there compared to this place."

A man about Kraus' age burst through the same door the other woman had used to come and go. He was about five-seven with a fair complexion. His left cheek was slightly scarred from chicken pox or bad acne. Dark auburn hair neatly cut but unruly. Good dove gray suit. New and nicely tailored. Right amount of cuff showing at the sleeves. A stripe of porcelain white handkerchief was visible above the edge of his breast pocket. The initials "ES" were monogrammed in the center of it. He walked with an air of confidence. An easy smile that won respect and kept up his dentist's boat payments.

"Gordon Kraus?" the man asked in the deep voice of natural authority.

"Gordy," Kraus replied, extending his right hand.

"Eddie Stone," he shook hands with a firm, dry grip, "nice to meet you."

"Thank you for the time on such short notice," Kraus said.

"We don't do anything slow around here," Stone said. He looked at the receptionist who was beaming at them both. "You've met our sweetest team member, Candy," Stone chuckled. Candy blushed and giggled before regaining a professional composure. "Let's go," he said, "I'll give you the cook's tour."

Kraus followed Stone through the door at the rear of the lobby into a long, wide hallway. "How long have you known Norm Diamond? Great guy. Knows his onions," Stone said.

"I met him in Berlin right after the war," Kraus said. "We stayed friends after coming back to the states."

"Berlin, huh?" Stone said. "You go that far back. Were you part of Diamond's flight crew?"

"No," Kraus said. "I was attached to a unit of combat engineers. I stayed in Berlin after the surrender. More work to do." Not a complete lie and it helped with his engineer-businessman masquerade.

"I was in the Coast Guard," Stone said. "Stationed at a base in Petaluma. It was made up to look like a dairy farm. We called it 'Two Rock Ranch'. Didn't want any prying eyes. It was actually a radio signal intercept operation. Picked up signals from the Japs. Kept tabs on Russkie traffic, too. The Reds were our ally then, but you know what the Bible says about friends making the worst enemies. I was a warrant officer responsible for keeping the workshop supplied with all the gear needed to build and repair the equipment. Vacuum tubes, wires, hardware, soldering equipment."

"Sounds interesting," Kraus said.

"It had its moments," Stone said. "Basically, the same thing I do now. Pay is better nowadays," he added with a wink. "Diamond said you're building a new kind of hearing aid."

"Yeah," Kraus said. He waved the plastic box around, tilting it so Stone could see inside. Kraus began putting his hours of study to work. "I'm using all transistors and charging capacitors to improve battery life. By getting away from the wound resistors and using high-frequency transistors, I'll get superb pure-tone ...."

Stone swept his hand towards the box as though he was swatting it away, "Gordy, I'm a pusher, not a user. How it works is Greek to me." He peered into the box. "It looks as though you have a lot of sockets. You came to the right place. Let me show you around."

Before they could take another step, a hallway door swung open. A young man wearing a suit and clutching a briefcase hustled out in front of them.

"Hi, boss," the man said.

"Hey, Jerry, hold up," Stone said. "Excuse me a second," he said to Kraus.

"What's up?" Jerry asked.

"Paul showed me that quote you brought in from Packard Bell," Stone said.

"Yeah, I won two-thirds of the line-items," Jerry beamed.

"Which was a quarter of the other third's total value. You lost the best part of the quote," Stone said. "Let me tell you what happened. That prick-buyer, Danny Salgado, let Newark cherry pick the list first. They sucked the cream right off the top of the bottle and left you with gristle and bones. Newark probably has some sweet-talking phone gal working that poonhound for all he's worth."

"You think?" Jerry asked. Sheepish now.

"Jerry, I *know*," Stone said. "What's more, you gave Salgado last-column pricing for everything. Unconditionally. Twenty-two fucking percent margin. I'm losing money on the deal just taking the time to talk to you about it."

"The product managers set the pricing," Jerry protested.

"They probably thought you had better control of your account," Stone countered. "Here's what you're going to do. Set up a lunch with that asshole. Take Susan from inside sales along. Let her bat those eyelashes and shake her bazooms in his face."

"Susan isn't their inside salesperson," Jerry said.

"She is now," Stone said. "I don't want to get the shitty end of the stick on the next quote from that guy, or it's *you* won't be handling the account."

"Yes, sir," Jerry stammered. He practically ran away.

"Sorry about that," Stone said as he turned back to Kraus.

"No problem," Kraus said. "It was instructive, actually. Who's Newark?"

"Great question," Stone said. Shifting into sales mode. "They're another catalog house. Like Allied Radio. Also out of Chicago. They print a catalog once a year. Size of the Monkey-Ward's catalog. Most customers get it right after New Year's. Once a year! You know how fast this industry is moving? By St. Patrick's Day, it may as well be those Dead Sea scrolls, for all its worth. Half the shit in it is obsolete or impossibly overpriced. What's worse, it's missing every new part that's come out since it was printed six months before."

"How are you different?" Kraus asked, knowing the answer, but wanting to seem like a neophyte.

"Gordy, we're different in almost every way. Different? Make that '*better*'. No catalogs. Our product managers and inside salespeople have manufacturer's price sheets updated immediately whenever there's a price change or a new part is added."

"But Newark and Allied must get the same updates from their vendors," Kraus said. New prospect playing Devil's Advocate.

"Sure. They'll probably show up in the next year's catalog. If it's a top-mover. Call Newark for a quote on a newly released part. You know what happens? If it's not in the catalog or in their price books, they call it a '*NIC-NIC*'. Means '*not in catalog, not in cost book*'. Takes an act of Congress to get them to order one of these for a customer, and they require a huge minimum with no return privileges."

"What do *you* do about a NIC-NIC? In the design phase I'm always going to need the newest parts in small quantities," Kraus said. "How'll you handle an order you don't stock?"

"Milestone doesn't have NIC-NIC's," Stone insisted. "You want a part? If it's available from one of my vendors, we'll get it for you. No minimums. Full return privileges."

"Aren't you afraid of getting stuck with product?" Kraus asked.

"Gordy, Milestone isn't a catalog house. We're a distributor. There's a difference. These catalog shops all answer to the same heartless bitch. RONA," Stone declared.

"Say again?" Kraus asked.

"RONA. *Return on net assets.* They can't afford to get sludged up with slow-moving products. Fucks up their balance sheet. Their board of directors would throw a fit every quarter," Stone said. "Heads would roll."

"Accounting principles are the same for everyone. Doesn't slow-moving inventory hurt *your* balance sheet?" Kraus asked.

"Don't care about that. It's *Milestone* Electro Supply. Not *Stone Age* Electro Supply. Right now, this racket is about service, volume and market share. This industry is on the crest of a huge wave. Norm told you how I made my money?"

"Yes, tube tester machines, right?" Kraus said.

"Right. Made a fortune. *Still* makes a fortune! I own Milestone outright. Cash flow like I have a printing press in the basement. My board members are in the crotch of my Jockey shorts. I don't answer to a bunch of hidebound coupon-clippers who wear suspenders with their belts. You know what my dad told me when he gave me my first car? *'Take care of the oil and the water. The gas will take care of itself'.* Know the market. Keep on top of the technology changes. Service the hell out of our customers. We do those things and the goddamned bean counter crap will take care of itself."

"I like what I hear so far," Kraus said.

"Come on, let's tour the rest of the place, see if I can bring you onboard," Stone said as he led Kraus to a hallway spur off of the main one. They came to a door with a sign that simply read, "*Eddie*". Stone opened the door and steered Kraus through into an anteroom.

An attractive, red headed secretary sat at a desk with a name placard reading '*Sheila*' on it. Low-cut dress. Long legs crossed, sending the hem of her skirt skidding up to her thighs. The walls were paneled with sheets of mahogany. A small, padded bench was placed against one wall. Sheila was Stone's gatekeeper. Probably more. Corporate geisha. Her desk stood guard before a set of large double-doors with ornate backplates and brass knobs. His father called them Victorian Eggs.

"Sheila, this is Gordy Kraus," Stone announced. "He's our newest customer."

"Nice to meet you," Kraus said, offering his hand.

"And you," the secretary said in her breathiest, starlet voice. She leaned towards him for the handshake, allowing a lingering view of her cleavage. It was a nice view. The most ambitious vamp in the Paramount typing pool couldn't have done it better.

"Gordy, come on in," Stone said. He swung one of the doors to his inner sanctum open. It was a large office with a picture window looking out on Washington Boulevard. Exotic teak paneling covered the walls. A desk was the centerpiece of the office. Also teak. There was a tufted leather Chesterfield couch against one wall and matching chairs for the desk. Stone saw Kraus eyeing the couch. "Like it? I had it and the chairs custom made. Looks like leather, but it's buffalo hide. More durable. The frames are made from mango wood. Harder than oak. Heirloom quality stuff." A man who likes his luxuries.

"*Likes telling you about them more,*" Kraus thought.

"They're beautiful," Kraus said. Meaning it. He looked around the office and approached a far wall where a college diploma and a dozen or so pictures and plaques hung.

"Gordy, I've got a packet of stuff for you here," Stone said. He rummaged through a desk file drawer. "There's a credit application in it. You're a friend of Norm Diamond, you're family. Just a formality. We'll need your bank information, shipping and billing addresses, that sort of thing. But I'll tell you right now, I'm giving you 2% 15 days or 3% 10 days terms. FOB destination."

"Eddie, that's very generous of you," Kraus said. He was looking at a picture of Stone shooting a small-caliber pistol. Probably a thirty-two. It was taken from behind. Stone was in a one-handed Bull's Eye shooting stance. Standard combat position dating back to duels with flintlock pistols. Giving your opponent the slimmest profile for a target. His off-hand on his left hip. Right-handed shooter. Below the framed photo was a framed medal won a year ago in a shooting competition at the McCambridge Park Small Bore Range in Burbank.

"*A gun range with an Irish-sounding name,*" Emily Matz had said.

"You shoot?" Stone asked, interrupting Kraus' train of thought.

"Not really," Kraus said. "It looks as though you're pretty good."

"I have my moments," Stone said. "I do it to blow off steam. A lot of work here. A lot of pressure. My wife calls the place 'Millstone'."

"Success is hard work," Kraus said. He pointed at another framed photo of Stone with three other men, all wearing golf clothes. They posed with their drivers held in front of them at an angle. Like

Medieval knights with their swords. "You golf, too," Kraus added, pointing to the photo.

"Yeah. More steam than one hobby can handle," Stone laughed. "I'm in the men's club at Sunset Fields on Crenshaw. *Was* in the men's club, I mean. They're closing at the end of the year. I'm scouting around for a new club. Thinking about Harding at Griffith Park. Know it?"

"No, never been there," Kraus said. His gaze fixed on another member of the foursome. Same height as Stone. Dirty blonde hair. Self-satisfied grin. Polo shirt with plaid accents at the collar. Was there a suspicious tone in Stone's voice? "I don't play much. Or well," Kraus went on. "Busy like you. Not as successful, though" he chuckled.

"We're going to help you with that," Stone said. He slapped Kraus on the shoulder.

"My business or golf game?" Kraus asked.

Stone laughed. "You're a sharp one," he said. Almost an accusation. "I like that. Come on, I'll show you the floor."

Kraus considered what he'd just learned while he walked alongside Stone to another part of the building.

Stone goes to the same gun range that Tommy Thorp frequents. Thorp is the club pro at Stone's golf club. They've played together. Stone is thinking of joining the same club Thorp is going to work for. Thorp pretends to be involved in electronics in order to bilk people. Customers of Stone's company are being blackmailed into participating in some shady shell game with electronic parts.

Kraus had been a cop and investigator long enough to know the world is full of strange coincidences. *"Hollywood is a small town,"* Laveroni had said. Still, there's a point when a pile-up of related events challenges the notion of coincidence.

He had to find out more while he was at Milestone Electro Supply.

THIRTY-FIVE

Stone led him to another part of the building. They walked through a door into a spacious room full of people seated on padded, metal office chairs at gunmetal gray desks. Standard bargain issue from Diamond Wholesale Office Furniture. Wide metal catalog racks sat on the laminate desktops, tilted like a book stand display. The racks appeared to hold dozens of catalogs and price books printed on cheap, salmon pink and baby blue newspaper stock. Kraus could hear a ventilation fan running, but it wasn't keeping up. Clouds of cigarette smoke hung in the air.

The room had the frenetic energy of a movie scene set on the floor of the stock exchange or a busy newsroom. Phones jangling. Men and women shouting questions to others. People shooting out of their chairs, trotting out through swinging doors, while others raced back in through the same doors and jumped back on their phones.

Stone produced a kazoo from his jacket pocket and started blowing out a show tune of some sort. It was familiar, but Kraus couldn't put his finger on its name. Others started humming along with the buzz of the kazoo. Some clapped. Kraus saw a window on a far wall that looked into an adjoining room. Four or five office workers were in the room, looking out onto the sales floor. Several phones were mounted on the walls. Long receiver cords hung down, like hangman's nooses made from pig's tails. No actual sound could be heard coming from the room, but the workers inside were laughing and clearly humming along with the rest. One person clapped.

The kazoo buzzing stopped. Workers treated him to a last round of applause and returned to the jobs at hand. Talking into their phones. Leafing through the catalogs in their desk racks. Scribbling on order pads. Multiple phone conversations overlapped. Kraus heard portions of the gabble as Stone walked him across the sales floor.

"Milestone Electro Supply. This is Larry ..."

".... axial or radial leads?"

"... let me check the warehouse to make sure we have that many ..."

".... I can get to that price for two hundred units ..."

"... you have a purchase order number for this?"

"... the hundred microfarad unit has ten percent tolerance, the two-fifty microfarad ..."

It didn't seem as though the competing conversations distracted any of the salespeople. Kraus figured it was like cops in a squad car. They can always hear their own call number out of a cacophony of static-filled radio traffic.

Stone approached a man sitting on the edge of a desk talking to a seated salesperson. The man wore a short-sleeved dress shirt and slacks. Half-bald from a receding hairline. He looked around at Stone and Kraus and flashed a good-natured smile. Small teeth stained from years of nicotine. Intelligent eyes tinged with humor behind metal-framed glasses. Kraus noticed that while the man presented a calm exterior, he chewed his fingernails. The thin edges of his fingernails stopped far short of his fingertips. Rough furrows of calluses covered the exposed nail beds.

"Hey, boss," the man said. A baritone voice which lent him a commanding air. Firm and easily heard in the middle of a noisy call center.

"Gordy, I want you to meet Brent Manning. He's the inside sales manager and will help get your account up and running."

The sales manager stood up. Tall with broad shoulders. Developing a bit of a spare tire, but he had the look of a former athlete.

"Good to meet you," Kraus said. "Gordy Kraus." He shook hands with Manning. Confident grip.

"Nice to meet you. That was our *welcome aboard* song. You're official now."

"Brent, I'm going to leave Gordy with you. Show him how we do things here," Stone said. Stone turned back to Kraus, "Gordy, it was a pleasure meeting you. Welcome aboard! I know you're small now, but we'll grow with you." Even though it sounded like a stock line to Kraus, Stone's charisma made you want to do business with him. The electronics mogul turned and walked towards the exit door. He stopped two or three times to say a few words to assorted salespeople as he made his way out.

Manning pointed at the presentation folder Kraus was carrying. "It looks like you got the intro package. There's a credit application and a couple of our line cards in there. We're franchised for all the major lines. One-stop shopping." He turned towards the main part of the sales floor. "This is where it all happens," he said.

"Looks busy," Kraus said. "Sounds busy."

"Yeah," Manning agreed. "We have field salespeople with assigned territories and accounts, but most of the actual quoting and buying happens over the phone. The field guys are out there to win us share-of-mind. Talk to design engineers. Keep buyers supplied with freebies. Pick up quotation lists."

Kraus looked more closely at the activity. Many of the phone receivers had extension arms sprouting off of them. Like Tiny Tim's crutch. The salespeople placed the curved ends on their shoulders and wedged the receiver between their shoulders and chins. Hands-free operation. Several of the people were working cardboard discs crowded with small numbers. A smaller wheel disc, also dense with numbers, was centered on top of a larger one, fastened with a grommet. The salespeople rotated the wheels as they discussed parts and pricing with customers. Manning saw Kraus looking at the little discs.

"Those are profit wheels. We have most of the price books in those racks, but there are times when a part is so new it isn't in the latest price books."

"Nic-Nic's," Kraus said.

Manning laughed. "Exactly! Eddie's given you his '*we're different*' speech. We use those wheels to calculate an acceptable profit margin. Also to set a decent profit margin when we break price."

"Break price?" Kraus asked.

"Give a price lower than last-column. Don't tell Eddie I said we did that," he joked.

"Tell him what?" Kraus quipped.

"You're alright," Manning said. "We're going to like working with you."

"What is that?" Kraus pointed towards the window looking into the adjacent room.

"The fishbowl. Did you know this building was a movie costume factory before Eddie bought it?"

"Now that you mention it, I remember seeing it once or twice a long time ago," Kraus said.

"Yeah. Worked for everyone on Poverty Row over the years. Even some of the big guys subbed out to them on occasion," Manning said. "That was a soundproof fitting room. At that time, all the windows were curtained. Privacy fittings. Pictures a studio didn't want word to get out about. We've turned it into a sort of central nervous system."

"How so?" Kraus asked.

"This is Milestone's headquarters and biggest stocking facility. Over the past six months, Eddie has opened a large facility in the Bay Area. Redwood City. Smaller branches in Santa Ana, San Diego, Seattle, Denver, and Phoenix. We have sales offices in Albuquerque and Portland. Rumor mill says Dallas is next."

"How does your *'fishbowl'* come into that?" Kraus asked.

"Quite a ballet goes on here," Manning answered. "Say an order is taken at that desk," he pointed at the nearest sales desk, "A copy goes out to the warehouse to be pulled for shipping. Another copy goes to accounting for billing. A third goes to the fishbowl. That tub-looking thing in there? It holds large inventory cards. One card for each part we stock or have on order. The parts sold at this desk are recorded on the cards minutes afterwards."

"Very efficient," Kraus said. "Do they track inventories for all the branches?"

"No, just for the inventory here," Manning said. "Those phones you see on the wall? The other branches call them directly to check for inventory they need. If we have it to spare, we ship it out as an inter-company transfer. The transferred quantities are recorded and the total on-hand amount is adjusted on the cards."

"Non-stop action," Kraus said.

"Posting every transaction. Continuous calls. Dispatching branch transfer orders. It's quite a pressure cooker in there. If the room hadn't already been soundproofed, we would have done it ourselves. The noise in there added to the noise out here would combine to sound like a prison riot."

"So, when I need parts, I call one of the people in here?" Kraus asked.

"Exactly," Manning said. "I've just met you, but I think Vergil Fleming and you have complementary personalities. That's important. Like Yogi Berra says, *'half this game is ninety-percent relationship'*. Getting along with your salesperson makes it so much easier. Don't get me wrong, any of the people in here would treat you right. I just can tell Vergil will like you and keep a close eye on your account. Let you know when new products are announced, that sort of thing."

"Sounds good. It's Vergil then," Kraus agreed.

"Let me show you the warehouse operations," Manning said.

"Okay," Kraus followed Manning out a door and down another hallway. A sign taped to the outer face of the door reminded everyone that a company named *"Bourns"* was coming Thursday night for a Christmas tree-trimming party.

"That box you're holding. Prototype design?" Manning asked while they made their way down the hall.

"Yeah," Kraus said. "I wanted to have it handy in case anyone is interested."

"A lot of parts," Manning said. "Looks to have a lot of sockets. You'll be glad you found us when you get going."

"Is that a Pasadena Junior College ring?" Kraus asked.

"Yeah," Manning said. "I graduated in forty-eight. Business degree."

"I went to El Camino before UCLA," Kraus said. "We had swim meets against PJC."

"Sure, I remember," Manning said. "Track and field meets too. That was my sport. But I was mainly there for the turkeys."

"Huh?" Kraus said.

"Turkeys. Chicks. Girls. Every spring, hundreds of the best-lookin' chicks you've ever seen enroll at PJC. Clockwork. Like the Capistrano swallows. They all want to apply for the Queen of the Tournament of Roses Parade competition. Being enrolled at PJC is one of the requirements. Ones that don't make it are mainly gone after the September interviews, but what a spring and summer."

Manning led Kraus through double aluminum swinging doors like you'd see leading into a restaurant kitchen. The doors opened onto a large warehouse with eight-foot metal shelving covering about eighty percent of the floorspace. The ends of each row displayed large signs identifying what product lines were down the row. Like library stacks. Instead of *"Fiction A-G"*, names like *"Belden"*, *"Cinch-Jones"* and *"Cutler-Hammer"* were fixed to the end caps.

Two loading bay doors were open onto the back parking lot. Stacks of various-sized cardboard boxes stood next to long tables with rolls of sealing tape and newspapers. Two young men were busy boxing up electronic parts, stuffing them with newspaper and taping them shut. A little paperwork pouch was fastened to the top of the box.

"This is where the orders are pulled for shipping," Manning said. "We ship out over a hundred boxes a day. One-fifty on the last day of each month. Our error rate is less than one-half of one percent. That means we make a mistake on a shipment once or twice a week. Eddie wants it to be zero, but that's impossible. A Q.C. guy checks every order for accuracy before it's sealed up. But part numbers are small on lots of these units. Sometimes they only differ by a couple of letters or numbers. It's easy to mistake '10%' for '1%', screw up reading the color-codes on the resistors, etc."

"I'm impressed. That's real precision," Kraus said. He wondered what Manning would say if he knew the rate of overshipments going to Desilu and eight or ten other firms. Maybe he did know. At this point, Kraus knew he couldn't rule anyone out at this point.

"It's quite a machine, I'll say that," Manning agreed.

"Not every box is shipped parcel post, it looks like," Kraus said. He pointed to a shelving unit near the back door to the warehouse. Its shelves held boxes and stapled paper bags with company names on them.

"Will-call, yeah," Manning said. "Some rush orders for buyers who need it immediately. Most are for schlockers paying at pick-up."

"Schlockers?" Kraus asked.

"Brokers," Manning said. "Deal in excess inventories. Obsolete parts. Things like that. Real bottom-feeders. But there's a market for everything and they're a great outlet for getting rid of dead inventory."

"Like day-old bread stores," Kraus offered.

"Pretty good comparison," Manning admitted. "That other shelf with the boxes are ones we deliver ourselves. We have two delivery guys who cover the territory within a twenty-mile radius of the office. Saves us a ton, actually. One of the guys is getting ready to head out right now."

Manning pointed to a young man with white-blonde hair and a wispy goatee loading boxes into a small panel van with *Milestone Electro Supply* printed on the side.

"Hey, that guy looks like Bobby, the kid who delivers my newspaper," Kraus said, pointing at the delivery van.

"Not unless he's moonlighting under an assumed name," Manning laughed. "That's Calvin Wersky. He's been with us almost from the beginning. Kid from Porterville. Trying to make it in the big city."

Kraus watched the delivery boy named Wersky load the boxes into the back of the Ford panel van.

"How many overshipments are in that van today?" Kraus silently wondered.

THIRTY-SIX

Kraus exited Milestone Electro Supply and turned towards the parking lot. A Pontiac Star Chief was parked in the space marked with a sign reading "Eddie". Last year's model. Shiny two-tone paint job. Dark maroon and white. He slowed as he passed the Pontiac.

The rear license plate had a custom chrome frame. "*Milestone Electro Supply*" was engraved into the frame's flat upper face. A large tab extended from the frame's left side. A piece of chromed metal art in the shape of a roadside distance marker. "*Milestone*" was engraved on the tab. Two edges of the metal ear had rippled to give it a three-dimensional look. Like a carved roadside stone marker. It looked like a gravestone to Kraus.

Kraus wondered if a drunk would only see the maroon color in the dark. Ignore the white. What's more, would the same drunk see the milestone emblem protruding from the edge of the license plate frame. Register it as a "*CONS SERV*" symbol stamped onto the side of the plate. "*Hell*," Kraus thought, "*with drunks anything is possible. The D.T.'s can do crazy things to your mind.*" Once, while staking out the King Edward Hotel downtown, he chatted with a wino outside the L.A. Mission. The bum insisted the curb face storm drain across the street was a Guadalcanal Jap pillbox.

He drove out of the Milestone lot and parked a block west. Kraus looked up and down Washington until spotting what he was looking for. A bar nestled in between two nondescript buildings. The name, "*Carby's*", was painted on the front window.

Carby's was one of those joints that are permanent watering holes for the surrounding office buildings and factories. Firms come and go, but the place where their office workers retreat to extinguish the hardships of the workday is always there. A decompression chamber for stressed out workers surfacing from eight or ten hours in the turbulent depths of Corporate America.

It wasn't yet noon, but Carby's opened at ten. Kraus walked into a dark cavern of a saloon. A long bar, covered with a sheet of hammered copper and edged with a cracked red leather elbow bolster. A lone customer sat at the end of the bar. He wore a Yellow Cab jacket and was drinking a Boilermaker. A cluster of small tables and chairs were spaced out over a scuffed and sticky linoleum floor.

Multi-colored bubble tubes on a Wurlitzer jukebox lit up one corner. Evelyn Knight's old hit, "*A Little Bird Told Me*", was playing. An area on the other side of the room was set up with a dart board and chalk slate. Chalked names and hash marks attested to Steve losing against Randy four games to two. Maybe they'd pick back up tonight. Maybe the tally was from last year.

A barkeep wore an enameled name tag reading "*Simon*" pinned to his breast pocket. He looked in his mid-fifties and was scrubbing the zinc surface with a damp rag. Simon gave Kraus a nod of acknowledgement when he took a stool near where the bartender stood.

"What'll it be, bud?" Simon asked.

"Got Oly on draft?" Kraus asked.

"I do, but I haven't changed out the keg yet. Get mostly foam from the one in there until I do. How about a Burgie?" Simon said.

"That'll do," Kraus said.

Simon worked the tap handle, tilting a frosted mug under the spout. Kraus saw green veins of Bon Ami packed into the deeper ripples of the copper. They reminded him of the tracers he'd seen from Russian guns during a couple of firefights he'd been in against them in Berlin. Russian tracer rounds were made with barium salts during the war. Produced a distinctive green trajectory path. American and British tracer ammo colors were white or yellow. "*Goddamn Ivans,*" he thought. Had to be ready to draw down on them at the drop of a hat. What was it Stone had said? "... *friends make the worst enemies ...*".

"Haven't seen you in here before," Simon remarked as he finished pouring. He set the mug down in front of Kraus then whisked a bowl of potato chips from under the counter and placed it next to the mug.

"Thanks," Kraus said. "First time here. I was across the street at Milestone and thought I'd grab a drink before heading back."

"Milestone, huh," Simon said. "Doin' business with them?"

"Maybe," Kraus said. He crunched on a potato chip. "I was there checking them out. What do you know about them?"

"A lot of the sales and office people come in after work," Simon answered. "Probably my steadiest customers. Not like when the costume place was there, though" he added.

"How so?"

"The costume place's cutters and seamstresses would come in at all hours. Creative folks. Kinda show people. Fun. You know?"

"Yeah," Kraus said.

"Plus, you never knew who'd walk in that door," Simon pointed at the front door. "Five or six years ago, Bill Bendix walked in. Big guy. Tall as you, but wider. Stocky. He was making an RKO picture with Victor Mature and needed to be fitted out special with sports coats. Big shoulders."

"I think I saw that movie," Kraus said. "Gambling yarn."

"That's the one," Simon said. "Well, Bendix goes right over to that table where the pinball machine is. Takes on all comers for arm wrestling. Fifty cents a match. Won every one. Christ, he had wrists like tree limbs. Bought everyone a couple of rounds with his winnings. Sat right where you're sitting and told us about when he was a bat boy for the Yankees. Saw Ruth hit forty, fifty home runs. Jesus, what a guy."

"Sounds like great times," Kraus said.

"Yeah," Simon sighed. "Don't get me wrong, though. The Milestone folks are a good crew. Steady. Come in with a lot of energy on Thursday and Friday nights. Lot of pressure workin' there. They call the place '*Grindstone Electro Supply*'."

"*Wow*," Kraus thought. "'Grindstone', 'Mill Stone', the place picked up some telling nicknames in less than two years. It takes a generation for nicknames to take root at the LAPD or in the service. Must be some place to work."

"Course, they must pay 'em pretty good there," Simon admitted, "if the money they drop in here is any sign."

"I took a tour of the place with the owner, Eddie Stone," Kraus said. "Think I should consider buying from them?"

"Eddie Stone," Simon whistled through his teeth as he resumed his scrubbing. "Now there's a showman. He'd be right at home workin' for one of the studios. He showed you around? You get the song treatment?"

"Yeah. At least I think," Kraus chuckled. "Stone started playin' a kazoo to the tune of a song I thought I knew. Everyone joined in."

"Old Crosby musical," Simon hinted, "sang the song to Ethel Merman." Simon hummed a couple of notes, then sang in a nearly atonal melody, "*You're the top ...*"

"Cole Porter," Kraus snapped his fingers and picked up the refrain, "*you're a Brewster body ...*"

"*You're the top,*" Simon came back in, "*you're a Ritz hot toddy.*" Both men laughed. "Speakin' of hot toddies," Simon said, turning his head towards the end of the bar, "Nate, you need another one?"

"Naw," the cabbie said. "My old lady doesn't like it when I come off shift with a load on. Take some more chips. Better eat now. God only knows what the old biddy'll be cookin' up tonight."

"You got it," Simon said, sliding a fresh bowl of chips down the bar. He turned his attention back to Kraus. "You see that fishbowl room when they were serenading you?"

"Yeah," Kraus said. "Busy part of the operation."

"You can say that again," Simon said. "It's like a Turkish steam bath in there from the pressure, what I hear. When the fishbowl workers sing along with that '*welcome aboard*' gimmick? They ain't singin' no Cole Porter, mister. That's their chance to get it out of their system. They yell curses and insults all through the song."

"You don't say," Kraus said.

"Yeah," Simon confirmed. "I've heard 'em talk about it lots of times. They were callin' you everything but a white man. But Stone's not that bad. He'll come in on the last business day of the month, 'specially if it's Friday. Stand his people a couple of rounds. Give a little speech."

"Sounds like him," Kraus said.

"Yeah. I've learned a lot about their business over the past year or so. All the people talk about is '*sockets*'. '*He's got a lot of sockets.*' '*That quote had a lot of sockets.*' Stone is in tall cotton right now. No real competition."

"That's what he said. I really don't think I have many choices other than do business with Milestone," Kraus said.

"For the time being," Simon agreed. Sounding sly. Cocky. A man with inside information. "From what I hear, a couple of outfits are comin' in soon. Place called Hamilton. Another one, too. New York operation. Avnet, I think it's called. I hear they're already trying to poach some of Stone's salespeople. You don't get the oil fields all to yourself for very long, boy. Doheny found that out the hard way."

"I saw one of their warehouse guys during the tour," Kraus said. Changing course while Simon was chatty. "Blonde kid. Little goatee. Shifty looking. I thought I knew him."

"That's Calvin. Skunk of a personality. Little prick used to slink in here on busy nights. Tried cadging drinks off one or another of the sales guys' tabs. They've had to kick his ass out more than once. This place is for Milestone sales and office people. No grunts allowed. I heard he hangs out at 'Shooters'. Pool joint south of here. Side street between Sepulveda and Sawtelle. There most nights unless they've run his skinny ass out of there already."

"I think I know the place," Kraus said, crunching down on a fresh potato chip.

THIRTY-SEVEN

Kraus drove north to a library a few blocks off Venice. He needed to make some phone calls and the Palms branch was nearby. Two enclosed phone booths were near the reference desk.

Manning said Calvin Wersky was from Porterville. A farm town about 150 miles north of Los Angeles. Kraus kicked around what he knew about the Porterville authorities while he drove. In '52 he'd spent time staking out the town's Southern Pacific depot station.

The Miracle Mile Merchants Association bought freight space on an entire forty-foot boxcar twice a month. Merchandise for two dozen of Miracle Mile's smaller stores was consolidated in the Midwest for shipment to L.A.. This tactic drastically reduced shipping costs for the merchants. Each shipment was like a rolling department store. Everything from specialty meats to small appliances in a single boxcar.

The first three shipments that year were looted before reaching L.A. Kraus examined the route and thought theft during the Porterville stop was very likely. Never more than one railroad police officer on duty and the town was policed by a five-member force. The town had a screwy law enforcement system. Police officers were "constables". There was another classification, too. "Night watchman". It was considered a promotion for a constable if the city council appointed him a night watchman.

Based on his experience in the town, Kraus was confident he could work the Porterville police department for some information. His first call was to Dave Hayashigawa at the Bean Slot.

"Bean Slot," Hayashigawa answered on the second ring.

"Dave, it's Gordy," Kraus said. "Hey, I need a favor. I have a strong line on the guy who pulled the trigger on Ollie. Will you check with your guys to see which of their P.O.'s are on vacation this week?"

"Can do," Hayashigawa said. "There's only one guy here right now, but I'll make a couple of calls. You somewhere I can call back?"

Kraus gave him the payphone number. He had learned you can get a lot of information about people in the guise of a probation officer. Impersonating a vacationing P.O. makes the ploy more reliable. The person being pumped for information can't double-back and check up on the caller. The L.A. probation office won't divulge to anyone where an officer is or who his clients are. Many *Bean Slot* regulars were on probation. Inevitably, one or another of their officers were on vacation. Hayashigawa would check with his people and call back with a name. While he waited, he got the Porterville P.D. number from the information operator. The payphone rang two minutes later. Kraus grabbed the receiver. "Kraus," he said.

"Gordy," Hayashigawa said. "Mulcaster. Mike Mulcaster. He's out for the week. Year-end use it or lose it time." He read off the probation officer's badge number.

"Thanks, Dave," Kraus said. "I owe you one."

"Just get the guy," Hayashigawa said. "I heard about Violet. You know how she's doing?"

"I'm going over there in a little while," Kraus said. "I'll let you know."

Kraus dropped some coins into the payphone and dialed the Porterville number. "Porterville Police Department," a male voice answered. No name offered.

"Yeah. Name's Mulcaster. Mike Mulcaster. I'm an L.A. P.O.," Kraus read off the officer's badge number. "Who am I speaking to?"

"Baker," the man said. His tone was edged with irritation. "Constable Roger Baker."

"Look, Constable," Kraus said. "I inherited a new report-to on my backlog this week. This squint is full of more shit than a chicken coop. Says he's from your neck of the woods and I was hopin' I could fill in the blanks on this blockhead before I get my ass handed to me by the boss for an incomplete profile."

"Sounds like half the town, officer," Baker laughed. He was enjoying the salty banter. "What's this guy's name?"

"Wersky. Calvin Wersky," Kraus said. He rustled the pages of the booth phone book. "Shitbird says he's twenty-four. From Porterville. Won't get specific about any trouble he's had there. But this assbite? He's been in trouble, or I'll eat my badge."

"Oh, God," Baker said. "Cal Wersky. Twenty-four sounds right. No need to start nibblin' on your badge. You've got that boy figured."

"Seen enough of 'em. What can you tell me?" Kraus asked.

"Good family. Farm people. Raise turkeys. Grow melons. Cal is the black sheep. Got started early with truancy and vandalism. Stopped goin' to school and became a pool hall bum. Stepped up to a couple of D-n-D's. Shoplifting. Tulare County judge finally sent him to a CYA probation farm for a year. Down in Lancaster. Came back and started up where he left off. Assault. Picked him up on a burglary after that. People wouldn't press charges out of respect for the family. Final straw was we suspected him of stealing a truck. We think he unloaded it at a greaseball strip-down garage in Fresno. Couldn't get enough to pick him up for it."

"When did he leave town?" Kraus asked.

"His folks will tell you about six years too late," Baker said. "But he's been gone about two years. Miss him like a wet sock."

Kraus laughed. "Constable Baker, you've been a big help. I'll touch base with Lancaster for some more info. That'll keep my shorts in one piece. You ever need any skinny on someone who's got an L.A. County sheet, give me a ring."

"Will do," Baker said.

THIRTY-EIGHT

Kraus spent a few hours at Angelus Hospital. Violet was still too out of it to be questioned. He sat with the uniform patrolman Laveroni had stationed outside her room. The cop told him that neither the LAPD or Gardena P.D. got much else from the door-to-door.

"There was one thing, though," the veteran cop said. "Old guy about three doors down from the victim told them he'd heard someone clambering over his back fence, opening his side gate and trotting down the walkway to the sidewalk."

"Did he get a look at him?" Kraus asked.

"No," the cop said. "The citizen was madder than a hornet about it, though. Suspect stepped right on his dichondra lawn while hot footing it away. Guess when you step on that kind of grass, it kills it. Left a partial shoe print. Lab boys think it matches the size of the one they found in the victim's house. No stride length to zero in on how tall he is, but I heard the guy must be pretty heavy to leave a print as deep as the one in the lawn."

"That's all?" Kraus asked.

"The man also says he might of seen a car pull away just as he walked outside to check on the racket. Old coot. Failing eyesight. Said it was a dark sedan, anyways. Either pulling away or driving up Denker from Artesia. Said the license plate looked funny to him."

"*License plate again,*" Kraus thought. He kicked all of it around while driving back to Culver City.

Shooters was a bar tucked away on a side street south of Sepulveda. One of those neighborhood places that used to be a local market or upholstery shop before the Depression. A neon sign in the window read *"Billiards"*. Smaller signs proclaimed *"Cold Beer"*, *"Sandwiches"* and *"Six Tables"*. Only a few cars in the parking lot on a

Monday at four o'clock. Kraus figured Calvin Wersky wasn't there yet but would be pulling in before long. He went inside.

The neon sign was flashing "*Billiards*". A throwback to an earlier time. All six tables were regulation pool tables. Up until a few years ago, it was hard to find a pool table in L.A. bars. The city was still a billiards or snooker parlor town. Pool started to catch on when 1950's production fully shifted away from wartime needs to meet the entertainment demands of the public.

Straight pool was fast. Nine-ball even faster. The quick rotation gave idle players time to visit the bar. Drink booze while waiting for their next game. More money for the joints offering pool tables. Snooker and billiards tables all but disappeared. Only two of Shooter's tables were in use when Kraus walked in. The bar ran the shorter length of the rectangular space, tucked back away from the playing floor. Lighted signs on the walls reminded customers to drink Oly, Burgermeister and Schlitz beers. A few wall placards read: "*No Sitting or Cigarettes on the Tables. Keep Your Butts Off*". Other signs were tongue-in-cheek declarations that gambling was prohibited.

"What's your pleasure," the barkeep asked Kraus as he swung a leg over a barstool.

"Looks like you've got Burgermeister," Kraus said. "I've had one Burgie already today. Better stick with it." Kraus put on his tipsy act. He hoped the bartender worked contracts with the regulars. Signaling the hustlers when a pigeon landed in the coop.

"Haven't seen you in here before," the bartender said when he slid a glass of beer in front of Kraus.

Kraus caressed the cold tumbler of amber liquid with an affection reserved for heavy drinkers and undercover investigators. He took a long pull on the glass, then spoke. "No, I'm out cold-calling houses. Sellin' vacuum cleaners. The way my day went, you'd never guess I won a hundred-buck spiff just yesterday for most sales. Couldn't take one more '*no*' today before havin' one of these." Kraus took another greedy gulp.

"Welcome to Shooters," the bartender said. "Open tables right now. Fills up quick after seven. First drink buys you a free half-hour. Fifty cents an hour after that. Cue racks are over on that wall. The two pinballs over there take dimes. A quarter buys four plays on the jukebox. I can make change for you if you need it."

"Thanks," Kraus said, "but I think I'll have another one of these first," he tapped the glass. "What kind of sandwiches you have?"

"Tuna, chicken and roast beef. Choice of white or rye," the bartender said. "Sixty cents. Comes with some dill pickle chips."

"Any cheese?" Kraus asked.

"American or pimento. Nickel extra. Got horseradish for the roast beef."

"Roast beef on white. American. Horseradish on the side," Kraus ordered. "And don't forget my beer."

A young man walked into the bar and settled into the end stool. Not Wersky. He ordered a beer and nursed it while paging through a week-old Herald-Express left on the neighboring stool.

The bartender rattled a plate down in front of Kraus. The sandwich wasn't bad. Freshly made and cut on the diagonal. Nice grid of grill marks on both sides. He popped a dill pickle chip in his mouth and chewed. Crisp and tart. He lifted the top bread slices to spread the horseradish. Adequate pile of hot roast beef. No onions. Cheese only half-melted. Not Melody Cafe caliber, but then again, this wasn't Wilshire Boulevard.

Kraus had gotten through most of the sandwich when a tall, gangly youth carrying a pool cue case walked through the front door. Tousled pale-blonde hair. Cigarette wedged behind his right ear. Scruffy goatee to match. Almost invisible white eyebrows above eyes like robin's egg shells. He had a little color. Tulare County farmer's tan. The same young man Kraus had seen at Milestone Electro Supply. Calvin Wersky.

Wersky was wearing a black-and-white checkered Gaucho shirt. Black ribbed waistline hem clung to his hips, making him look even lankier. Jeans. Worn Chukka boots with grease smears. Delbert Bowers was right. He looked to Kraus like a lot of the hipsters he'd seen at Venice Beach. Hanging outside in clusters around places like the Gas House.

The young man at the bar walked over to Wersky. They obviously knew one another. Wersky removed the cue halves from their case and screwed his stick together. The other man appraised the ones in the wall racks. He lifted one out and held the butt of the stick to his eye, like he was sighting a rifle. Satisfied with his choice, he returned to the table. He and Wersky chatted for a few minutes.

They lagged for first break. Wersky won and fussed with the cue ball placement. He settled on a point back of the head string, off the first diamond, close to the right cushion. Pro position. Power break shot. Kraus watched him carefully. With a pool cue in his hand, Wersky was no longer all elbows and ankles. He worked the cue with a practiced grace. Comfortable. Confident. He leaned forward, knees slightly bent. Sawed the cue back and forth a couple of times then hit the cue ball with a smooth stroke. An explosive break. Balls burst from their triangle and scattered across the table. A solid-colored ball dropped into a corner pocket.

Kraus munched on his sandwich and sipped a third Burgie while he watched Wersky run the table. The next game was more even, but Wersky's opponent was overmatched. The Milestone delivery driver had a good game. Played safe shots. Rarely overreached. Consistent. Kraus saw that he was the worst kind of good player. A good player who thought he was better than he was. He did recognize that Wersky was probably a better player than him. But Kraus wasn't interested in beating Wersky at pool. He didn't need to be the superior player for what he planned.

Police detectives will tell you that a lot of invaluable information can be gathered in pool halls. They attract a criminal element. Crooks like to gossip. Good leads can come your way If you know your way around a pool joint. The officer's club at Tempelhof in Berlin had a couple of billiards tables and Kraus became an avid player. The skill was a tool he took to the post-war Berlin streets while investigating crimes. Kraus spoke German like a native. He often dressed like a common *Berufstätige* and visited many of the seedier pubs that had risen from Berlin's ashes. He was able to collect a great deal of intelligence just by playing pool, listening and buying a few beers.

Kraus continued with the same technique after coming home and getting his private investigator license. He began frequenting Hollywood Billiards, the center of the L.A. billiards and snooker scene. It was a good place to study the people and the culture. He learned where all the L.A. pool haunts were. Kraus improved his game. He took some instruction from Cuban Joe, one the best players on the scene. Not to get good enough to win tournaments and trophies. Kraus wanted to look and talk as though he fit in. It worked.

Rudi, Kraus' brother, had put a pool table in what was meant to be the cabana next to his backyard swimming pool. When his wife, Louise, objected, Rudi joked, "What's more natural than a pool table in a pool house?" He and Kraus often shot pool while discussing their construction business. Kraus felt his game was good enough to keep up with Wersky for a while. If everything went as planned, that would be all that was required.

Wersky's friend evidently had enough. He handed Wersky a few singles, shook hands and left. The blonde hipster stuffed the singles in his breast pocket and started practicing some shots.

"I think I'll take on your local champ. Guys at the Elks Lodge say I'm kind of a shark," Kraus said to the bartender. He stood up and laid his jacket across the seat of his stool. "You want me to pay up now or can I use my winnings in a little while?"

The bartender laughed, "You can pay me after you play. Your jacket's here. I know you won't skip out."

Kraus deliberately wobbled a step as he moved towards Wersky. He caught the bartender out of the corner of his eye, getting Wersky's attention and making a scissors motion with his hand. A sheep ready for shearing.

"Hey," Kraus said to Wersky, "up for another game or two?"

"Always," Wersky said. A sharp, twangy voice. "Go get a cue. I'll rack the balls."

Kraus favored cue sticks with heavier handles. He found one. "Flip for the break?"

"Yeah," Wersky said.

Kraus fumbled in his pocket for some change. He drew out the contents of his pocket, careful to let Wersky see the pile of folded bills he was carrying. "Here's a quarter," Kraus intentionally slurred his words a little. The "here's" came out "*hersh*".

"Call it," he said as he flipped the coin into the air.

"Tails," Wersky said.

It came down tails. "Story of my life," Kraus said. "The table's yours."

Wersky set up his breakshot much like before. Weak break this time. The cue ball missed the nose of the rack by a quarter inch or so. None of the balls dropped this time. Probably deliberate. Setting Kraus up. Lulling him. "Oh, well. Happens to the best of us. It's your shot."

Kraus went to the side where the cue ball had rolled to. He deliberately bumped the table a little with his pelvis. Faking impaired depth perception. He leaned into a shooting stance, then looked up at Wersky. "Want to make it more interesting? Dollar a game?"

"Didn't you see the 'no gambling' signs, friend?" Wersky said. Before Kraus could react, he let out a shrill croak of a laugh. "Just fuckin' with you. Yeah, a buck a game is fine."

Kraus placed a dollar bill on the one-top closest to the pool table. Wersky fished a one out of his breast pocket and slapped it on top of Kraus'.

Wersky lost the first game when he scratched while potting the eight-ball. Almost certainly on purpose. "Goddamn it," he mumbled, "I didn't think I'd hit it that hard." They went on, Kraus winning two or three, over the course of several games. In the fifth game, Kraus lined up for a long corner pocket shot.

"That's a lot of green, buddy. Even if you make it, it's a sure scratch shot," Wersky heckled.

"For some people, maybe," Kraus said. "Five dollars says I don't."

"You're on," Wersky said.

Kraus potted the object ball, but the cue ball careened into the opposite corner pocket. Like he had planned. "Shit," Kraus said. He took up the beer he'd ordered two games earlier and threw back a swallow. "Here," Kraus snarled, slamming a five-dollar bill on the table. Wersky laughed and stuffed it into his pocket.

During the next game, one of Wersky's misses left Kraus with the cue ball frozen to the rail. An object ball was sitting in a decent position for a side-pocket bank shot. Another was closer but sat in an awkward spot for an angle shot into the corner pocket. Particularly with the cue ball firmly hugging the rail.

"*This is the one,*" Kraus thought. "Four-ball, corner pocket," Kraus announced.

"Are you kiddin' me, man? Makin' a shot like that off the rag?" Wersky mocked. "The bank shot is your obvious choice."

"You sayin' I can't make this?" Kraus asked. "I lose a couple of games to you, you think I'm no good?" he snapped. "Listen, you miserable punk. I was sinkin' shots like this when you were shittin' yellow."

"Well, you ain't showin' me anything makin' me shit my pants tonight, buster. How 'bout you shut your trap and take your shot," Wersky growled.

"How 'bout we make it interesting," Kraus demanded. A drunk who won't let it go. "How much you won off me so far?"

"Five bucks on your last weak-ass bet and five more on the games," Wersky said. "About to be six more."

"Yeah?" Kraus said. "Let's add a little yeast to the pot." He jammed his hand in his pocket and brought out a fifty-dollar bill, clumsily spilling three or four coins across the floor as he did. "My fifty against your ten says I can drop that ball."

Wersky hesitated, but it was all show. This was the moment he had also been waiting for. "You're on," the delivery man said. He pulled some bills from his pocket and placed them on the two ones already on the little table. "Show me what you've got."

Kraus reached over and let the fifty flutter down to settle over the other greenbacks. He stepped back to the table and lined up his shot. He noticed the bartender watching the action with a great deal of interest. Licking his chops over the share he figured he'd get from Wersky.

The cue ball *was* in a tough position. Joe Cuba made Kraus practice frozen rail shots over and over. Many novice players instinctively tilted the cue stick handle way up, as though the higher angle would somehow allow the cue tip to dig the ball off the rail. Miscues were common with that approach. Most of the time, the shot called for a short, firm, precision stroke. No need to elevate the stick handle much higher than a normal shot.

It was true that from a certain standpoint, the bank shot was the better choice. But Joe Cuba and other old-timers had a saying. "*Not every table banks the same, but every table cuts the same.*" This particular sharp angle shot looked harder than it was. A perfect set-up for Kraus.

He looped his index finger over the stick shaft for added stability. Lifted the butt of the cue fractionally above his hip. Held his breath and stroked the cue. The cue ball cleanly shot from the rail and collided with the extreme outside edge of the four-ball. The four-ball was sent on a sharp left-turn towards the corner pocket. It plopped into the pocket with a satisfying thunk. Kraus dropped all pretense of intoxication. He scooped up the money from the little table and put it in his pocket. He moved in close to Wersky. Almost touching noses.

"How long did it take the short, foreign guy to hamstring you, Wersky? My guess is he came in to play several days running. Strung you along with little scores a few days in a row, then went missing for a day or so. Made you anxious. You thought you could milk him dry but the cow didn't come back to the shed. Then he showed back up and took you for the real ride."

Wersky's jaw was open, and his eyes were almost the size of bar coasters. "How did ...how ...," he stammered.

"Yeah, he plucked you like one of your folks' prize Tom turkeys," Kraus went on. "Trussed you up and hung you in the display window."

"Turkeys, my folks ...," Wersky faltered. "How ..."

"Oh, I know it all, Porterville Kid," Kraus said. "Let's go outside and talk." He snagged his jacket off the stool and tossed a five and two singles he'd taken from Wersky onto the bartop. "Keep the change," he said to the bartender. "Calvin here doesn't have anything to cut you in on." He took Wersky by the elbow and steered him to the front door.

THIRTY-NINE

Russian Consulate, Los Angeles - December 3rd, 1956

"I took the boat out on the *wooder* yesterday."

Kuznetsov was using a low voice while perfecting a Baltimore accent. "Wooder" instead of "water". The KGB operative wanted to sound like a native when he made his departure from the consulate. Baltimorese was one of the most subtle regional dialects on the eastern coast. Most consulate staff couldn't distinguish a Mississippi Southern drawl from a Connecticut "Yankee Nutmegger" accent. Nonetheless, he didn't wish to be overheard.

A firm knock sounded on his office door.

"Come in," Kuznetsov said. He was careful not to pronounce *"come"* like *"calm"*, in the accent he had just been practicing. No sense giving away any clues before he disappeared.

Balabanov loomed in the doorway, checking the room before fully entering. Always on high alert. A dangerous man. "I have something to report, comrade," the Russian enforcer said.

"Balabanov, come all the way in," Kuznetsov said. "You make me nervous standing on the threshold like *Koschei* out of a fable, ready to pounce."

"Old habit," Balabanov offered in the way of an apology. He stepped all the way inside the office and closed the door behind him. "I have news to report on the American detective."

"Go on," Kuznetsov said. A trickle of ice water began dribbling down his insides.

"His inquiries have brought him to the doorstep of Milestone Electro Supply. Somehow, he determined the delivery boy's involvement," Balabanov said.

"What do you know?" Kuznetsov demanded.

"I just heard from one of my contacts. He spent an hour or more at Milestone this morning and he's with the boy, Wersky, right now."

"Damn him," Kuznettsov muttered. "Why hasn't the next phase of our plan taken place?"

"The target is away from home. It is too risky to put the next step in play until the return."

"When will that be?" Kuznetsov asked.

"I believe sometime tonight. I will be able to execute the next step of the plan by tomorrow morning."

"Balabanov, this is a critical phase of the mission. The first blackmailer who tried to scuttle our plans has been replaced by an even more dangerous foe," Kuznetsov lectured. "Our success - Russia's success - depends on the faithful completion of this task. Have I overstated your ability in my last report to Chairman Serov?"

The question was almost laughable. Kuznetsov had never communicated with anyone even two levels removed from the State Security Chairman. But Balabanov needn't know that. Fueling his fear was the best way for Kuzentsov to control the man.

"No, sir," Balabanov almost shouted. He straightened to attention as though he was on a parade ground lined up for inspection. "I will carry out my instructions successfully."

"See that you do," Kuznetsov said with an air of quietude he did not feel. "Keep me informed."

Balabanov strutted out of the office. Kuznetsov leaned back in his chair and closed his eyes. *God in Heaven*," he thought. "*So close. So close.*" He was ordered to leave the consulate and return to Moscow on the twelfth, barely a week away. But how many times had he seen an order of that sort turn out to be a red herring? A man believes he has a week to prepare an escape only to be scooped up by security personnel five days ahead of time? Kuznetsov could feel the hot breath of impending Doom licking at his neck.

He was slipping away on Wednesday, less than two days from now. As he had planned. Kuznetsov had killed one man already to keep that plan alive. He would kill again if it was necessary.

FORTY

Kraus hustled Wersky out Shooter's front door. It was after six. The sun had been down for over an hour. The daytime high had been in the mid-sixties. The temperature had dropped to the mid-fifties but felt warmer. It had been a smoky day. The smog held the heat in.

Traffic noise from nearby Sepulveda Boulevard rumbled across the pool hall parking lot. There was a small gas station a block or so to the north. Its canopy was lit by fluorescents. Kraus saw the dim figure of a man leaving a phone booth and climbing into the driver's seat of a large sedan. At that distance, the artificial light and grainy air combined to make visibility hazy. Like looking through a layer of dingy gauze. He couldn't swear it was Eddie Stone or his car. He couldn't swear it wasn't.

"Hey," Wersky protested. Kraus roughly guided the delivery man to the outside corner of the bar furthest from the door. "What's your problem, man? You a cop or something?"

"Something," Kraus said. "You're the one with a problem. A big one. Right now, I'm the only guy standing between you and a bullet to the head or a long prison stretch."

"Bug off, man," Wersky said. He yanked his elbow out of Kraus' grasp but didn't try to bolt. He took the cigarette from behind his ear, planted it in his mouth and lit it with trembling hands. A man who saw his options drying up. "I'm just a package carrier, man." Less peevish now. More scared.

"Oh, Calvin," Kraus said, "we both know you're a lot more than that."

"I'm going by '*Kip*' now," Wersky insisted with the preening juvenile pride of reinvention.

"You can call yourself anything you want, Wersky," Kraus said, "you're in hot water by any name."

"Listen," Wersky said. A pleading tone that came out as a wheeze. He drew hard on his cigarette. His cheeks caved in, giving him a cadaverous look. "I'm nobody, man. No one's interested in shooting me. Putting me in jail."

"Calvin, I don't have time for your horseshit," Kraus said through gritted teeth. "Let me tell you where you're at."

"Yeah, you tell me man," Wersky said with squeaky bravado.

"You got in deep with the little foreign guy," Kraus said. "He makes a deal with you. You can work off the debt. He gives you shopping lists. Tells you to put extra parts in shipments to specific customers. Places like Desilu. Then you pick up the returns. But you don't bring the overshipments back to Milestone. How am I doing?"

"Prove it," Wersky said. A school kid accused of stealing milk money.

"I don't have to prove it," Kraus said. "I'm not a cop. I'm not building a case. But the foreign guy has all the proof he needs. It's not about the money you owe him any longer. He has a stronger grip on you. He can turn you in for stealing from your employer."

"He wouldn't do that," Wersky said. Impulsive reaction. Didn't care he was confirming his guilt. "He'd be cutting off his supply."

"Yeah, for some reason, I don't think he's going to need you much longer. One, maybe two more runs. I have a hunch he's closing up shop."

"What makes you think that?" Wersky challenged.

"A friend of mine dead in an alley. Shot in the back of the head. Another friend beaten to within an inch of her life. The foreign guy wanted to know what she knew. *You* know a lot more than she does. How long before someone plants one in your skull? Best case, he drops a dime on you. You end up in jail."

"Jail," Wersky snorted. "For what? Boosting a few parts?" He flicked his cigarette butt into the parking lot with a practiced insouciance. The way a movie tough guy would do it.

"Theft. Larceny. Conspiracy," Kraus listed. "Eddie Stone doesn't strike me as the type who'd go easy on someone who stole from him."

"So what," Wersky said with a sneer. False courage. An attitude that didn't make it up to his eyes. "I've jailed before."

"Jailed?" Kraus laughed. "Listen, Dillinger, that little stint you did at Lancaster is like summer camp compared to what's waiting for you. First adult offense. Five-to-eight. Probably Chino. If you're lucky."

"Shit, you know about Lancaster, too?" Wersky said. "Yeah, I've heard things about Chino. Don't seem so bad."

"You have, huh?" Kraus said. "Here are some things you haven't heard. First day. Bus pulls into the yard near the intake entrance. Inmates are watching from the baseball field bleachers about fifty yards away. Not just any yard dogs. Hard cases. Barn bosses. You and the other cherries are herded out of the bus. Chained together. Prodded single file down a gravel path leading towards processing and orientation. Inmates call it *"Split-Tail Alley"*. You'll hear the whistles and catcalls as you shuffle to the door."

Wersky had turned his face away from Kraus. Feigning disinterest. Captivated by what he could see through the pub's window. Head in the sand. Kraus could see his panic-stricken face in the window's reflection.

"Pay attention, Wersky," Kraus insisted. "I'm reading your future right now." He waited until the farm boy ratcheted his face back around. "Your name won't be Wersky, Calvin or Kip. You're a fresh-fish. A tight-squeal. A bitch-boy. You'll be bought and sold three or four times before you cover the twenty yards to the door."

"Fuck you, man," Wersky spat out. "Ain't no one gonna set me up for a fall like that. If the short guy don't need more parts, he won't take the extra trouble. He'll want to just disappear. Get away clean." Said with more hope than conviction.

"Maybe," Kraus conceded with a dubious tone. "I might set you up, though. Just for the satisfaction of seeing a little prick like you take a hard fall." Kraus paused a second for the threat to sink in. "There's a *viejo* at Chino. Can't even remember his actual name. Everyone calls him 'Segovia'."

"A flamenco player," Wersky exclaimed. "That supposed to scare me?"

"No," Kraus said. Impressed the little shit even knew who the real Segovia was. "He's called that because he's an artist with a guitar string. Whichever shot caller ends up owning you will hire 'Segovia'. I think the fee nowadays is two or three packs of Lucky Strikes. The old Mex will take a sharpened end of a nylon string and tattoo tits on your back. Hear they look pretty real."

"Whaaaa ..." Wersky protested. "Why the fuck that?"

"Think it over," Kraus said. He saw the realization come into Wersky's widening eyes. "He mixes the ink with soot, charcoal and a little bit of baby oil. Guitar string point goes deep. Lasts a lifetime. Don't need to be a genius to figure out what the rest of the baby oil is for."

Wersky's forehead was speckled with beads of sweat. He nervously pushed up his sleeves and unconsciously started plucking hairs from his forearm. Nervous habit. There were already decent-sized bare patches on both arms.

"Why should I tell you anything if you're just going to turn me in?" Wersky asked. Probing for possible bargaining room.

"Tell me what I want to know. Then I'm not the guy who dimes you out. I'm the guy who'll stand up for you in court. Testify you were being blackmailed. Ninety days in county lock-up. Probation. No unwanted tattoos."

"How can I trust you?" Wersky asked.

"You can't. But you *can* count on me to grass you if you don't spill to me," Kraus said. "Your choice. I know most of the prosecutors in town. I can help you skip hard time. Maybe skip any time at all."

"I need to think this over," Wersky said. Rattled. Racking his brain for another way out.

"Sure," Kraus said, glancing at his wristwatch. "You've got thirty seconds, then I'll leave you to the foreign guy or *Segovia's* guitar string."

FORTY-ONE

Wersky took fifteen seconds to decide to talk.

"Okay, okay," the delivery man said. A child sulking about eating vegetables. "You're right."

"Right about what?" Kraus asked. "That you're a little shit? I already know that."

"Hey," Wersky whined, "You wanna know how it was or just take pot shots at me?"

"Both, actually," Kraus said, "but you're right. I'm pressed for time. So, talk."

"Pretty much happened the way you said," Wersky admitted. "Short, foreign-sounding guy comes into the bar. Snappy threads except the shoes. Those looked like the mail-order brogans farmers wear to church. We shoot a few games. Decent enough player. Loses five or six bucks. Buys a round. Says he's comin' back the next night."

"Did he?" Kraus asked.

"Oh, yeah. Two more nights in a row," Wersky said. "Second night, lost ten bucks or so. Third night, a double sawbuck. Bought a round and some grub for us both."

Kraus whistled through his teeth, "Pretty nice scores. You must have thought you'd struck oil."

"Yeah," Wersky grunted. "He didn't get mad like some do. Acted like he was havin' more fun than he'd had in a long time. I figured him for maybe a queer. Willin' to lose money while he cruises me, you know. It's happened before. Said he was gettin' a big paycheck the next day. He'd return that night to win back his losses, and then some. Fuckin' guy wasn't kiddin' about that part."

"So, let me guess," Kraus said. "He doesn't show the next night. You're a little antsy. Figured you had a big payday coming yourself."

"Got that right," Wersky said with an ironic laugh. "He's a no-show. I come in the next night. Still not there. Next night after that I almost decided I'd be the one not to show up. But that money he mentioned. He'd baited the hook, you know. Then he walks through the door."

"You must have been relieved," Kraus said. "Not a dry well after all."

"You can say that again," Wersky said. "We start playing. He keeps losing. If anything, he was worse than before. Not a horrible player. Just couldn't make two decent shots back-to-back. He's down three C-notes. Says he's nearly tapped out, but really wants a chance to win his money back. Takes his watch and a diamond ring he's wearin' off and puts them on the table. Claims together they're worth four bills. Wants to bet the jewelry, three hundred he has left plus the three hundred he'd already lost. One large altogether. Says he's good for it. Nice stuff. I showed 'em to Myron. That's the bartender. He looks 'em over and gives me the nod. I tell the foreign guy it's okay. I gave him the next break even though he lost the last game."

"Pretty confident," Kraus said.

"Oh, yeah," Wersky said. "He was playin' like crap. I wasn't even worried about the extra three hundred he wanted on credit. Knew I'd win. I was already thinkin' about whether I'd keep the watch or let Myron move it." He looked wistfully at his bare wrist.

"Go on," Kraus pushed.

"All of a sudden, he's Willie Mosconi. Fucking breaks the rack like he hit it with a bazooka. Two stripes drop. He sinks the next five stripes. Potted a combination shot I'd never seen made before. Lined up for the eight-ball shot. Said, *'For all the marbles'*, and looked me in the eyes as he stroked the cue. Didn't even look at the damn cue ball."

"I take it he dropped the eight-ball," Kraus said.

"Shit yes," Wersky groaned. "Now his happy queer act is nowhere in sight. He's more like the guy at the feed store still carryin' your balance at the end of harvest time."

"No offers for a chance to win your money back," Kraus said. Not a question.

"Hell no," Wersky said. "He said, *'Mr. Wersky, it appears as though you owe me a thousand dollars. I'll finish my drink while you gather up the funds'*. I was surprised he knew my name. Talked fancy like that limey who plays '*The Falcon*" in the movies."

"What did you do?" Kraus asked.

"Told him I didn't have it," Wersky nearly screeched. "He let out a big sigh. Said that was unfortunate. Said I'd have to deal with his 'associate'. A big guy was sitting on a corner stool. Almost in the dark. Must have come in while we were playing, and I didn't notice. Ugly. Mean-looking. Even his hair looked pissed off. He stood up and took a few steps towards the table. I begged the little guy to give me some time."

"He made a counteroffer," Kraus said.

"Yeah," Wersky confirmed. "He said all debt could be forgiven if I 'performed some tasks' for him at work. I could even keep the three hundred he'd lost." Wersky lowered his voice a little. Sounding a bit cowed, "You already know what he wanted me to do."

"Yeah," Kraus agreed. "Tell me more about how it worked."

"He told me to keep my car's passenger window cracked a little all the time. Some mornings I would go to my car and a little envelope would be on the passenger seat. It was a list of parts and quantities he wanted added to shipments that day."

"That your '39 Slipstream over there," Kraus pointed his chin at the white, shark nosed Willy's sedan parked at the edge of the lot. It had seen better days.

"Yeah," Wersky said. "Found a list in it every other day or so."

"No one ever caught on at Milestone?" Kraus asked.

"Naw," Wersky said. "Too much chaos. I've been there almost from the start and pretty much have the run of the place. No questions asked. I wait until the order fillers take their morning break. Go down the aisles and pull the parts on the lists. Takes five minutes or so. Most of the stuff is stocked on the same aisle. Keep them in my lunch sack and stuff them in the shipping boxes when I get them in my van."

"What happens when you pick up the overshipments?" Kraus asked.

"I take the bags over to the picnic area at that new park over from Milestone. Right off Culver. Stuff them under a park bench and leave immediately."

"Then what?" Kraus asked.

"Whadda ya think?" Wersky said. "I practically run out of the park. Jump in my van and head back to Milestone."

"Ever see what happens to the bags afterwards?"

"Well," Wersky said, "One time I got hung up at the curb when I was trying to leave. Traffic had backed up from Overland and I was blocked in. In my side mirror I saw the same lug who was about to bust me up when I lost the money."

"The foreign guy's muscle?" Kraus asked.

"Yeah," Werksy insisted, "No mistaking that guy. It was like seeing Frankenstein walking through the park. He grabbed the bags and turned right around. Walked back across the lawns. Probably left his ride on Coombs."

"Didn't see what he drove?"

"Nope," Wersky said. "Didn't see it the time I spotted him at Milestone, either."

"He was at Milestone? The big guy?" Kraus asked. "When was this?"

"Four, five months ago," Wersky mused. "One of the shop guys was helping him sign-out a box off the schlock shelf. I saw him from across the warehouse. I was going into the break room and didn't see him drive away."

"Schlock shelf," Kraus said. He thought about the tour Brent Manning had given him. "The shelf where the broker orders are held for pick-up?"

"Yeah," Wersky said. "Rag men. Guys who buy surplus stuff and resell it."

"You see who he was picking up for?" Kraus asked.

"Not exactly," Wersky said, stretching out the '*exactly*'. "I do remember there were only two schlocks on the shelf that day. One of the regular pullers was sick and I was helping out. I pulled one myself and put it on the shelf next to the other one."

"Give me their names," Kraus demanded. "I'll look them up and go check out both of them."

"Look 'em up? Shit man," Wersky chuckled, "these guys aren't in the phone book or anything. They're fly-by-nighters. Got a notebook from work in my glove box. It has all the customer addresses. I'll get it for you."

"Wersky," Kraus said as the hipster started for his car, "did the foreign guy shoot right-handed or left-handed?"

"Right-handed," Wersky answered. "Why?"

"Just checking. Got anywhere besides home to sleep the next few nights? Some place no one else knows about?"

Wersky paused to ponder the question for a moment. "Wop diner," he said, "other side of Sepulveda. They know me there and I can park 'round back. Sleep in my car. Wash up with their hose-pipe in the morning."

"Do that for a couple of nights," Kraus suggested. "Ounce of prevention. You should be safe enough at work. Watch you're not followed."

"You think they'll come for me?" Wersky asked. Frightened.

"Not sure," Kraus said. "But it hasn't been good for the ones they've come for already."

FORTY-TWO

When Kraus approached his home, the outside lights were on, and he could also see lights on in the kitchen.

"Lucy, I'm home," Kraus said in an exaggerated Cuban accent as he opened his front door. He walked into the kitchen to see Anna in a sweatshirt and jeans checking a bowl that was in the oven. She was barefoot and her thick, raven black hair was held with a wide, French barrette.

"You pick that accent up while you were on the set watching 'Superman'?" Anna giggled.

"Oh, Austie told you about that, huh?" Kraus said. "Is that beef stroganoff you're making?"

"It is beef stroganoff I'm heating up," Anna corrected. "Irm sent it home with me. Said it was one of your favorites."

"Irm, is it?" Kraus asked. A little relieved that Anna and his mother must have gotten along.

"That's her name and she wouldn't let me call her 'Mrs. Kraus', or anything else," Anna said.

Kraus stepped closer to the oven, next to Anna, "Mmmm, that does smell good."

"That's the only thing that does," Anna said. "You smell like a pool hall. Why don't you go take a shower and change while I finish up?"

"You must be a soothsayer. I just came from a pool hall. I did some fortune telling myself while I was there," Kraus wrapped a kitchen towel around his head like a swami. "No visions of beef stroganoff or a shower, though," Kraus said.

"Just get cleaned up," Anna insisted, laughing at his antics.

Kraus walked through the hall to his bedroom. He passed the open doors of the guest room and guest bathroom. Both rooms threw off scents of spearmint gum and French milled soap. He'd miss that when Anna had to leave.

Anna looked up when Kraus returned from the shower. His hair was damp, and he wore a gray cotton sweatsuit. The word "Constabulary" was printed in curved script across the chest. She was impressed that it fit him perfectly after what had to have been twelve or thirteen years. She liked the way he looked at that moment. Boyishly handsome and happy. She was going to miss this world of his she'd stumbled into.

"It was nice of my mom to send home some food," Kraus said.

"Irm's been cooking for days. She's very upset about Ollie, and I think that's how she's coping with her anxiety."

"Ollie meant a lot to the family," Kraus said.

"She told me the story. Sounds like he was a great guy. Any progress on our case?"

"Maybe," Kraus said. He took a beer from the fridge and poured the bottle into a glass. "Want one?"

"Yeah, please, and take out the sour cream," Anna said. "What have you learned?"

"I went to Milestone Electro Supply. Spotted the delivery boy there," Kraus said. He told her about Eddie Stone. The delivery boy, Wersky, getting ensnared by the pool game loss. How he took parts from Milestone and ultimately handed them off to the blackmailer.

"You've found out a lot about the 'how', but not the 'why'," Anna said. "And you haven't connected Ollie to the whole thing at all."

"True," Kraus agreed, "but there's a connection. I can feel it. Right now, I could make a decent argument for any one of four guys having pulled the trigger. I feel like I'm this close," Kraus said, holding up his hand to show forefinger and thumb separated by an eighth of an inch.

"Four guys?" Anna asked.

"Yeah, Gowan. Laveroni's partner. He's a queer duck, but still, his behavior about Ollie is just off. Ollie was a bagman for Andy Lococo. Maybe the brass was afraid Ollie was about to get a conscience and decided to silence him permanently. Gowan wouldn't be the first cop to make his bones at the behest of one of top brass. It makes a certain sense, but even if the brass wanted Ollie out of the way, I can't see Gowan getting the drop on him that way."

"I think it's improbable, too," Anna said.

"Then there's Thorp. Con artist lover boy. Right height to be the shooter. He's involved in electronics. Yeah, just as a scam, but the parts are real. Maybe his partner got parts for the props from Milestone. Thorp has connections to Eddie Stone." Kraus told her about the golf club and shooting range. "He tried to rope Violet into a con. Maybe Ollie got in the way."

"I don't see it?" Anna asked as she sipped her beer and nibbled on a piece of bread. "Why kill Ollie over some small-time sham? It would be plausible if the shooting happened during a struggle in the middle of an argument. This was more like an ambush."

"I know," Kraus said, "I don't see it either. Next there's Eddie Stone. He and Thorp are loosely connected. Same golf course. Same small caliber shooting range. Maybe coincidences, yeah. But the coincidences are stacking up. Odd-looking license plates fit both Eddie Stone and Gowan. All three are the right height for the shooter. But like you said, 'small time'. Where's the profit?"

"Who's the fourth?" Anna asked.

"The best prospect. The short, foreign guy. The blackmailer. In most investigations, the most likely suspect turns out to be the one you know the least about. Been described as the right height for the shooter. Right-handed, according to Wersky. Capable of playing rough, but it sounds like he has a goon to do the heavy work. He's not doing this as a hobby. Have to believe he's the one who's found a way to make money with all this."

"What next, then?" Anna asked as she put oven mitts on and took the bowl from the oven. "I've got green beans in there, too," she said.

"I'm going to check out the two brokers Wersky pointed me towards. One of them is the one the foreign guy's knee-buster picked up parts for. If I can figure out which one, I may break this case." Kraus stood and helped Anna set the plates and flatware on the table. "I'm paying both surprise visits tomorrow morning. You can go with me. One of them has the nickname, 'Dirty Neck John'."

"Sounds charming. But I'm still helping Austie with the set-up. Remember that the shower starts at three," Anna said.

"I'll be back in plenty of time," Kraus said. He stood next to her as he placed the beer glasses on the table. He breathed in her scent. It was getting addictive. "Smells delicious," he said.

Anna turned to him and smiled at the double-entendre. "Maybe after we eat and clean up the kitchen, we'll go try to smooth down the lumps on that miserable mattress of yours," she said. She brushed her palm against the front of his sweatpants. "Oh," she whispered, "it seems that not every lump is in the mattress."

FORTY-THREE

Kraus got up early the next morning. He and Anna ate breakfast together then he drove her to his mom's house. His first stop was the office. Tax preparation season was in high-gear, and he knew Melinda would be in early to help Hodges with the workload.

When he dropped Anna off, his mother gave him a pan of apple strudel that had finished baking minutes before. It was still warm as he parked near the office. His car smelled like cinnamon and spiced apples. He carried it into the office where Melinda was grinding away on her adding machine.

"Is that warm apple strudel I smell," Melinda gasped.

"Fresh from Mutter Kraus' kitchen," Kraus said.

"Well, bring some over here, young man," Melinda said.

Kraus placed the pan on a little cabinet in the back of the office. He found a small plate and fork in a drawer of his desk and pried a piece out for Melinda. "Here you go, *fraulein*."

"*Danke*," she said, stabbing a raisin that had fallen from the edge of the strudel slice with her fork and munching on it. "Hodges isn't here yet. He wants to talk to you before the end of the week."

"Sounds ominous," Kraus said. He sat on the edge of Melinda's desk and picked another stray raisin from her plate. "Am I being evicted?"

"No, and you didn't hear this from me," Melinda whispered. "He's going in with another CPA in Pasadena. Early next year. Guy he went to school with. He's hated the drive here ever since he and Gloria moved out to Glendale. He thinks there's a great future in the new partnership for him."

"Great," Kraus said. "I'll take the whole office over. After they have the baby, Rudi won't be able to run the construction business from home. I'll share the office with him."

"Sounds like it'll work out fine," Melinda said.

"Yeah," Kraus said, "How do you feel about making your way to Pasadena every day?"

"That's another thing," Melinda said. "I was hoping I could stay on here and work for you. Get more involved in the business."

"I'm all for it," Kraus said. "Louise isn't going to stay on as office manager and bookkeeper. The baby will keep her busy enough. How do you feel about working for both companies? Sort of like you do right now for me and Hodges."

Melinda lit up at the idea, "I love it! Will it be okay with Rudi, you think?"

"He likes you," Kraus said, "and you'll have the senior partner's vote."

"I really can't see you as the 'senior partner' of anything," Melinda said. "That will take some getting used to."

"Keep it up," Kraus said, "you'll find out how fun it is to make four Metro transfers a day from your place to Pasadena and back."

"The 'senior partner' thing will grow on me, I think," Melinda laughed.

"Good to hear it," Kraus said. "Got anything for me from last week?"

"Some mail I prioritized on your desk," she pointed towards his office door. "Also, this," Melinda opened a bottom desk drawer and took out a manila envelope.

"What's this?" Kraus asked. He turned it to see both sides. "Didn't come in the mail."

"Larry Butler, a cop from PAB, stopped by Friday afternoon. Said he'd just gotten back from a fishing trip and found the note you'd left him. Apparently, he knew Ollie pretty well and wanted to help anyway he could. He said everything Ollie asked him about is in there. He left his home number in the envelope also. Hinted it would be better to call him at home if you had questions."

"Great," Kraus said, tucking the envelope under his arm. "I'm following up on a couple of leads this morning." He told Melinda everything that he'd uncovered so far and about the electronic parts brokers he was going to visit after he left.

"Be careful, Gordy," Melinda said. "It sounds like you're getting closer, but you don't know what exactly you're getting closer to."

"I'll know it when I find it," Kraus said. "You coming to Louise's shower this afternoon? I'll tell you all about it then. We'll talk to Rudi about the office and your new position. Your long-lost friend, Margaret Woodward, will be there."

"Really? Part of the family now, is she?" Melinda said in a suspicious tone.

"You'd rather I set her loose and let her former associates take a stab at her? Literally?" Kraus asked.

"You've got a point," Melinda said.

"Ouch," Kraus said. "You usually leave the bad puns to me."

"I'm excited. Lost my head," Melinda said. "Okay. Sounds good," she said. "Just keep your eyes open and be cautious. I'm even more worried after Violet's attack on Sunday."

"Always am," Kraus said.

FORTY-FOUR

The first of the two schlockers Kraus planned to look over had warehouse space off San Pedro Street near the Flower District. Within spitting distance of the Arts District where Ollie was murdered. Pushed up next to Skid Row. The old wino told the cops he'd seen a car speeding west from the vicinity of Ollie's murder. The direction of the Flower District.

Kraus called a Central Division desk sergeant he knew to find out anything he could about the first broker. It seems that everyone called him "Dirty Neck John", but his real name was Jonathan Traina. The desk sergeant said Traina had called the division a number of occasions with complaints. Cars parked too close to his driveway. Graffiti on his walls. Things like that.

"He have any kind of sheet?" Kraus asked.

"Naw," the desk sergeant said. "Guys have been around there a couple of times. Reports back say he runs a pretty tight ship. Not what you'd expect from someone with the nickname 'Dirty Neck'." The sergeant laughed. "Good locks on the doors. Keeps his outside lights in working order. Clean place of business. Licenses current. No fire hazards."

"Okay," Kraus said. "Thanks for the info."

The broker's office looked very neat on the outside. Kraus backed his car into a space with "VISITOR" spray-painted in stencil letters on a concrete parking block. He took the electronic hearing aid prop from the seat and went through the warehouse office entry door.

A beefy man was hunched over a workbench tinkering with the interior of an open-faced metal box. The front plate of the box was leaning to one side. It was a meter of some sort with a large needle pointer and intricately marked meter face. A plastic selector dial was centered below the needle window.

The front of the warehouse space was used as part-office and part-workshop. A large cabinet set with small, pull-out bin drawers was against one wall. The balance of the open warehouse was separated by a metal security screen. Behind the mesh screen were shelves holding dozens of meter boxes like the one on the worktable. Clean. Everything very organized.

"What can I do for you," the husky man said. His hairline had receded to the point that his scalp was entirely bald with shaggy hair on the sides. Outcrops of beard stubble appeared in the folds of his jowls he'd missed while shaving. His neck hair was dark and thickly matted. A feral animal pelt that ran below his collar line. Kraus figured the hairy neck was the source of the "Dirty Neck John" sobriquet.

"I'm looking for John Traina," Kraus said. "'Parts Unlimited'?

"You found him," the man said. He eyeballed the box Kraus held in his left hand. "Need something tested or repaired?"

"No," Kraus said, "Milestone Electro Supply was out of these," Kraus touched his fingertip to one of the small parts on the Bakelite board of his prop. "They mentioned you might have some I could buy."

Traina took a penlight from his shirt pocket and directed the beam at the part Kraus had indicated. Porcine eyes squinted at the component. "Hundred-ohm, carbon films," Traina muttered. "If they're out of those, business must be very good or very bad."

"I think they're expecting a delivery this week," Kraus offered. "Maybe the product is hung up with the holiday shipping crush."

"Maybe," Traina mumbled. "I was an RTO stationed at Petaluma with Eddie Stone. He was a pretty good supply chief. Not like him to run out of top movers." He waved his penlight over the rest of the box Kraus held. "What you got here? Prototype? Looks like a lot of sockets. They must love you at Milestone."

"Yeah," Kraus said. "A new hearing aid design. Still in development."

"Hearing aid, huh?" Traina said. "Pretty burly potentiometer there for delicate work," he said. Skeptical. Suspicious.

Kraus knew zero about electronic design. He couldn't explain the criticism away and didn't try. No need to dig a deeper hole. "You know Eddie, huh?" he said. Changing subjects. "Just met him yesterday. Impressive guy."

"He can fill a bandwagon, alright," Traina conceded. "The resistors are in bin drawers over there," he pointed to the wall of small drawers. "They're all labeled. Pick out what you need while I finish up with this voltmeter."

Kraus stepped to the array of bins and ran his eyes over the labels. He had no idea what he was looking for but thought he could fake it for a minute. "You a Milestone customer?" he asked while scanning the drawer fronts.

"Yeah," I buy surplus meters and other electronics from manufacturing companies. I take broken equipment, too. Fix and refurbish all of them. Sell 'em for five or six times my cost. Most of the parts I need come from Milestone now."

"Sounds like a good business," Kraus said. Still floundering in front of the drawers.

"Keeps a roof over my head," Traina admitted. "I buy more parts than I need. Sell the excess parts on a onesie-twosie basis to hobbyists. Guys making ham radios. High fidelity phonograph systems. Even television sets. I'm pretty well known in those circles," he said. "You're looking at the half-watt row. You want the quarter-watt row above it."

"Oh," Kraus said with a dry chuckle. "I can never find the mustard in the fridge when I'm looking right at it either." He finally spotted the number, "100", followed by a Greek "Omega" symbol. *That must be for 'ohm',"* he thought. Kraus slid the little drawer out and pulled out six little bug-like parts with wires protruding from either end. "Got 'em," he declared.

"Decided to go with a one-percent tolerance, huh," Traina remarked when Kraus showed him the resistors he held in his palm. "Okay. That'll be three dollars."

Kraus went through the stalling motions of feeling for his wallet in several pockets. He noticed that the box Traina was working on rested on an open front-page section of the Herald-Express. Page two and three were face up. Kraus recognized that particular edition. It was from last Wednesday. A short article about Ollie's murder was buried on the third page. An odd coincidence in a series of bizarre coincidences. If it was a coincidence at all.

"Had some excitement just east of here a few days ago," Kraus said, pointing at the article. "Know what happened?"

"Huh?" Traina asked. "Oh, the paper. I lay these down to keep the mineral oils and wax from some of the capacitors leaking onto my workbench. Crap builds up and it can be a fire hazard." He glanced at the article. "I heard something about it. Goddamned Arts District is a magnet for every scumbag in town. Anything's liable to happen there."

"That so?" Kraus asked. He handed Traina three singles he'd finally found in a pocket.

"Ask me, the mayor should have a fleet of bulldozers go through the district. Push every stick into the riverbed. Raze the place to the ground and start over."

"Too late for that poor policeman, though," Kraus pushed it a little further.

"Don't know nothin' about that," Traina said as he turned his attention back to the meter he was working on. "But if the guy was in the Arts District at night, he was probably up to no good."

"You're probably right," Kraus said. "Well, thank you for saving me the wait on Milestone's delivery."

"What'd you say your name was?" Traina asked.

"Partlow. Mark Partlow," Kraus said. A frequent alias he used in situations like this.

"Well, Mark Partlow," Traina said. Doubtful tone. No sale on the alias. He stood up straight and looked Kraus in the eyes, "I don't know what you're up to, but I don't want to see you here again. You understand me?"

"You're absolutely right," Kraus said. He held Traina's stare for a couple of beats. "You *do not* want to see me here again. If I end up with a reason to return, it won't be nearly as friendly a visit." He poured the resistors from his palm onto the workbench. The tubular components rolled on the table's surface. Some tinkled to the concrete floor. "Keep the money. Put it towards a good haircut and a decent shave."

He turned and walked out the door. He was glad he was carrying his back-up Remington automatic in an ankle holster. The visit had turned ugly in a hurry.

The parts broker stood in the open doorway of his warehouse office, arms crossed over his gut, watching Kraus climb into his car and drive away.

FORTY-FIVE

Galani Surplus was the second broker on the list. Kraus made this one last for the sake of convenience. It was in Torrance, a town south of Redondo Beach. He'd go right from this visit to his mom's house for the party.

Torrance was incorporated in the early '20's. From the beginning, its coffers were stuffed full from the booming oil business there. The Torrance Police Department was founded almost on the first day of cityhood. It grew into a very insular organization.

Kraus had never been able to cultivate a source in the Torrance PD. No one to call for any advance research on Yiorgos Galani, the owner of Galani Surplus.

"Just as well," Kraus thought. *"Advance info didn't keep me from making a dog's breakfast of my first interview."*

The Galani office-warehouse space was a little east of Western Avenue, in one of the dozens of little industrial parks dotting the area. Many had sprung up in the 20's, after a major Pacific Electric Red Car hub was built there. It was a stop on the north-south route from Los Angeles to San Pedro. Easy way for hundreds of workers to get there and back each day for jobs in the workshops and oil fields.

Kraus reached the driveway leading to the office park where Galani Surplus rented space. A map showing the building layouts stood inside the lot entrance. Each building on the schematic was numbered. A numbered list of the tenants was below the map. Galani Surplus was number twenty-four, which was an end unit at the rear of the furthest row of one-story units.

He passed various tenants on the drive around to the rear of the complex. Naramore Welding, Granville Industries, South Bay Fashions, Natone Soaps. Kraus reached the end of the back row and saw "Galani Surplus" on a wooden sign mounted near the entry door. The lettering on the sign was done in cheap paint and badly faded. A small loading bay next to the entry door was closed. Weeds had pushed up through the asphalt at the corners of the bay door. The handles were pitted with rust.

Kraus backed his Lincoln into an open space next to an old '40's step van. He thought it must have originally been a small bakery van. The name, "Galani Surplus" was hand-painted on the door in crude letters. An even cruder Greek Flag had been painted below the name. The dark blue stripes had faded to a washed-out sky blue. The alternating white stripes and cross in the flag's canton were dingy and yellowed. The van could have used a good wash.

The door had a simple "Office" stenciled on it. Kraus turned the knob and walked in. No fluorescents. Soft lighting from several hanging pendant lamps. Two smeared and dusty Jalousie windows set at the top of an outside wall contributed some natural light. The room smelled of garlic, lemons and fresh oregano. A desk sat six feet or so inside, facing the door. A green shaded banker's lamp lit the surface.

A man wearing a rough cloth cap and tattered sweater vest over a gray turtleneck sat at the desk. His back to the door. He swiveled around in his chair at the sound of the door opening. An older man with graying sideburns and eyebrows like white caterpillars. He didn't wear a beard but a day or so of black and white speckled stubble covered his cheeks, chin and neck. He looked Kraus up and down and gave him a tentative smile.

"Good morning to you, my friend," the man said. "How can I be of help?"

"Yiorgos Galani?" Kraus asked.

"That is I," Galani answered. "What can I do for you?"

Not a lot of Greeks lived in Los Angeles. But Kraus often got take-out food from Papa Cristo's, a Greek deli near his house and often came in contact with the Greek transplants eating and working there. Yiorgos Galani spoke with the same halting, atonal accent he'd heard many times at Papa Cristo's.

"I'm looking for some quarter-watt, hundred-ohm carbon film resistors," Kraus said. Hoping to improve his earlier deception with more precise detail. "Milestone Electro Supply is temporarily out and suggested I try you."

"Is that so?" Galani asked. Suspicious tone. "It isn't like Eddie Stone to turn business away from his door."

"*Christ,*" Kraus thought, "*first that Dirty Neck John prick. Now this suspicious Greek. An undercover narcotics cop wouldn't get this much push-back making a buy during a sting operation.*"

"A guy in the back mentioned you might have some. Young blonde kid. Little goatee," Kraus said, making a pulling motion at his chin.

"Ah," Galina exclaimed. "Calvin. Yes. Very nice of him to remember me." His tone sounded as though he considered it anything but nice.

"Do you sell resistors?" Kraus asked.

"My friend, everything I have is for sale," Galina said. "For the right price," he added with a wink. Galina stood up from his chair. A short, well-fed man. The Greek shuffled a few feet further inside his warehouse. He dragged his left foot slightly. Galina edged up to an ancient refectory table that sat against the cage wall separating the office space from the formal warehouse portion. The trestle legs of the table were mottled with years of dust, oil and bright splashes of solder drippings. A worn pegboard hung from the cage wall behind the table. Ply layers of the fiberboard were separating and dogeared at the corners. Various hand tools dangled from crude hooks fashioned out of coat hanger wire.

The old man stood on tiptoes and peered over the edge of a small metal drum sitting on the table. Satisfied, he turned towards Kraus and reached out an arm. He held his hand palm down and made a scrunching motion with his fingers.

Kraus was reminded of a Movietone newsreel he'd seen as a boy. The short film was about the Greek sponge divers in Tarpon Springs, Florida. One sequence showed the market stalls along the Sponge Docks. Greek sponge mongers hawked their wares from little booths lining Dodecanese Boulevard. A seller would pull a soggy sponge out of a bucket, hold it away from his body, and gently squeeze the water out of it. Then the damp sponge was slapped on a cutting board where a sharp knife was used to trim off roots and excess tendrils.

"Come over," Galani said. He crumpled his fingers together again. "Let me show you something."

Kraus walked to the worktable and looked down into the small drum. Inside was a tangle of electronic parts. Resistors. Capacitors. Chokes. Other part types he recognized from the Allied Radio catalog. All of the components were clearly used. The leads were shorter from having been clipped from a machine at some point. Some parts had little globs of solder on the connector wires. It looked like an elephant's graveyard of electronic parts.

"You want me to fish my parts out of that keg?" Kraus asked with a comical tone. "Like rooting around in a scrap yard for parts to repair my car with?"

"No, my boy," the Greek laughed. "This is how my inventory starts out."

"Rough start," Kraus said.

"Cheap start," Galani corrected. "My father used to tell me when I was a boy, 'Yiorgos, an ambitious man can make a very good living buying things in big containers, then breaking those things down into smaller containers.'"

"Is that how he made a living?" Kraus asked.

"Oh, to be sure," Galani said. "He'd buy a few barrels of olive oil from a freighter coming from Crete. Pour the olive oil into little bottles. Stuff a handful of dried tomatoes in the bottles. Seal it with wax and glue on a cheap label with the Greek flag. Sell them as souvenirs to tourists in Athens."

"A lot of little bottles to sell for a living wage," Kraus said.

"Certainly. But it adds up," Galani said. "That was only one of his ventures. Buy a half-dozen tobacco bales coming from Crete before they reach the Athens Tobacco Exchange. A few village women roll cigarettes and cigars. Take them to Larissa to sell to the factory workers leaving their shift at the carpet and bicycle factories."

"Sounds like he was quite a hustler," Kraus said.

"The best," Galani proudly agreed. "I would have taken over his business. But the Second War. Then the civil war." The Greek looked sadly around his shop and shrugged. "So I am here. Electrical parts instead of olive oil and tobacco."

"So, you buy these salvaged parts. Then what?" Kraus asked.

"They are mostly free. Companies allow me to haul their broken and obsolete material away. I strip out the copper, the parts, the little knobs. Clean them up, test them and organize the products. Many, many people buy these resurrected parts from me."

"Big job," Kraus said, pointing to the metal pail.

"Yes," Galani chortled. "The cost comes from the effort. I have help, though. But enough of all that. You came for some hundred-ohm resistors, I believe. Quarter-watt, you say? How many?"

279

"Quarter-watt, yes," Kraus said. "Twenty should hold me until Milestone restocks."

"So you say, my friend," Galani laughed. "Wait until I give you the price. You'll return to Galani Surplus. I assure you." The Greek shambled through the gate that led to the main part of his warehouse.

Kraus took the time to scan around the office space. Looking for signs of the big henchman Wersky had described. Two other rolling desk chairs in sight. Both set to the same seat height as the one Galani used. All the tools on the pegboard were hung lower than normal. No boxes set on the top shelf of any storage bay.

A small room was situated across the office space from Galani's desk. Curtain drape instead of a door. The curtain was partially open, and Kraus saw the top half of a neatly made camp bed inside. The pillow indentation came from a smaller than average head. A door marked "Restroom" was next to the makeshift bedroom.

A narrow closet was near the office door. Another curtain instead of a door. The curtain hem hung a few inches above the floor. He saw the bristles of a broom and the sled rails of an Electrolux vacuum cleaner canister through the bottom gap.

"Here we are," Galani announced as he moved towards Kraus with his scuffing gait. "Twenty resistors," he rattled a little paper sack. "We package the pick-up orders like this." He pronounced "package" as "pack-as". His Greek accent made the hard "g" come out as a "z".

Kraus pulled open the bag. Twenty carbon film resistors. Shiny color-striped surfaces, like a colony of striped beetles. The axial leads were shorter, but long enough to thread into sockets.

"What do I owe you?" Kraus asked.

"Ahhhh," Galina exclaimed. "The sixty-four thousand drachma .. I mean dollar ... question, as that man says on television." He paused for dramatic effect. "Sixty cents. Three cents each," he said. "Each" was another casualty of his Greek accent, coming out as "eats". Accent or not, there was a tinge of pride in his voice.

"Wow," Kraus said while fishing some change out of his pocket. "You weren't kidding about returning for more." He handed Galina the money and shook his hand. "Mr. Galina, you have a new customer."

"Yiorgos, please," the Greek insisted. A little kitchen timer dinged. Galina limped to a sideboard where a kettle had been simmering on an old Edison hot plate. "I was steeping my tea," he said while snapping off a chocolate square from a partially wrapped Hershey's bar. "Would you care to join me?"

"Thank you, Yiorgos," Kraus said. "I have to get going."

"Very well," Galina said. He pushed the square into his mouth and sipped some tea. "I hope to see you again."

"Count on it," Kraus said.

The sky had clouded up since Kraus went into the Galina Surplus office. He was examining the darkening sky as he took a few steps towards his car. "*Maybe some rain coming,*" Kraus thought. He shifted his focus back to the pavement in time to see his shoes step into the looming shadow of a man. A big, long shadow.

FORTY-SIX

"Hey, buddy," Kraus called out while backstepping to avoid colliding with the approaching figure. "Watch yourself."

A short man with a stepladder in his hands was walking backwards towards the Galani Surplus van. A couple of towels were draped over the top rung of the ladder, which cast the shadow of a much larger man. A galvanized aluminum pail was hanging from the crook of his left elbow. He was tugging a rust-colored garden hose along the ground as he shuffled backwards. He abruptly stopped moving when he heard Kraus' warning.

"Oh, my Lord," the man said after turning half-around to see Kraus near his side. "I am so sorry, sir. I was concentrating too much on pulling this dang hose along without having it twist and kink up on me. Already had to put one splice in it."

Kraus surveyed the shorter man. Five-six or so. Medium build. Brown hair. Face shaped like the spade of a foxhole shovel, rectangular with a tapered jawline. A few blood-red threads of burst capillaries laced across a slightly upturned nose. The man had done some heavy drinking in his time. He wore a pair of shabby, khaki coveralls and work shoes.

"It looks like rain is coming, buddy," Kraus said. "You thinking about washing that van?"

"Oh, that's what George, uh, Mr. Galani was worried about" the man said. "My daddy used to tell me that a car will stay cleaner during the rain if it starts out clean. He was right, too."

"You work for Yiorgos?" Kraus asked. "Are you his only employee? I thought a really big guy worked for him. Ran deliveries. That sort of thing. Tall. Wild hair. Big square jaw. He anywhere around?"

"Big guy?" the man with the ladder mused. "No. I've been working for Mr. Galani … I can't say his first name very easy. Comes out like 'yogurt'. I've been working for him almost a year." He carefully leaned the stepladder against the van and set his pail on the ground. "My name's Mason Barlow." He held out his hand.

"Gordy Kraus," Kraus said, shaking Barlow's hand. "You were saying about a big guy?"

"Oh," Barlow said. "Oh yeah. No. No one else works for Mr. Galani but me. He's a real good boss. Found me down on my heels in a soup kitchen over on the Nickel," Barlow said. He pointed the nozzle of his hose in the direction of Skid Row, about twenty-five miles east of where they stood.

"Well, it looks like he found himself a good worker," Kraus said. "You both got lucky."

"Oh, Mr. Galani is the best boss there is," Barlow beamed. "He has me watch the shop at night." He lowered his voice to a theatrical whisper. "It's against the rules here, but I sleep in the shop. Mr. Galani set up a little room for me. Real comfortable."

"I saw it," Kraus said. "Looks pretty cozy. Hot plate for grub. Bathroom. You've got a great job here."

"Oh, you know it," Barlow said. "I keep the shop spic 'n' span. Sort out the parts all day. Clean the knobs and other accessories. Make 'em look like new."

"Sort out parts?" Kraus asked. "What do you mean?"

"You know," Barlow said. "We get bunches of them from companies don't want 'em anymore. But a lot of times they're all mixed up. The different values have to be separated. Bad boys rape our young girls, but Violet gives willingly."

"Huh?" Kraus said. He realized off the bat that Barlow was punchy from what was probably years on the sauce, but he didn't expect the man to start babbling nonsense.

"You know," Barlow snickered like a little boy caught saying a bad word. "How you remember the color code for resistors. Black. Brown. Red. Orange. Yellow. Green. Blue. Violet. Gray. White," he recited. "Let me see what you bought from Mr. Galani." He pointed at the little bag Kraus held.

"Take a look," Kraus said. Amused at Barlow's childish enthusiasm.

"Hmmm," Barlow murmured. "Not great light out here. Brown-black-brown-gold." The tip of his tongue darted out of his mouth while he thought about it. "One hundred ohm. Five percent tolerance," He proudly exclaimed.

"Looks like you broke the code," Kraus said. "You're learning a lot here."

"Oh, it's a great job, alright," Barlow said. He opened his mouth wide. A baby bird waiting to be fed. Several teeth sported the dull, gunmetal gray steel of dental work. "Mr. Galani took me to have my teeth fixed. I'd almost forgotten what it was like to chew stuff without feeling pain."

"You don't say," Kraus said. Impressed by Galani's generosity. "You've snagged a great spot here, Mason. Keep working hard. Stay off the sauce. Don't blow this one."

"You bet I will, mister," Barlow insisted. He crossed his heart.

"Well, I'll let you get back to your work," Kraus said. He drew his car keys from his pocket and stepped towards the Lincoln. Turned back three-quarters to the handyman. "No big guy, then?"

"No, sir," Barlow shook his head with certainty. "Never seen anyone like that."

"Okay, then," Kraus said, "I must have heard wrong. You keep up the good work. Like I said, do yourself a favor and stay straight and sober."

Barlow held his empty palms out, then pressed them together. He brought them together then lifted them to his face. A man offering thanks or a prayer. A miniature palm frond suddenly appeared from his fingertips. So firm and verdant it had to have been fake.

"Don't worry, Mister. I've turned over a new leaf," Barlow grinned from ear to ear.

FORTY-SEVEN

"So, what did you find out from the brokers you visited?" Anna asked as they drove back to Kraus' house after the baby shower.

The party for Rudi's wife, Louise, was a very nice gathering. Austie and Anna had teamed up to decorate the house to the nines. Little cherubs and storks with cloth bundles in their bills floated below the ceiling on strung fishing line. The food was delicious. Austie had organized some hilarious games. Kraus' favorite was one where everyone split into teams of two. The game was to see which team could remove and re-diaper a life-sized baby doll. One team member gave verbal instructions while the other attempted the feat wearing a blindfold. He and Anna joined forces. They came in last. Anna laughed so hard she lost her breath at one point. Kraus maintained he *was* first with the most times he pricked himself with a safety pin.

Anna and Melinda circled each other for a short while. Melinda was wary of an interloper in the group. Anna was wary of anyone she didn't know. Anna broke the ice when she warmly congratulated Melinda on her new job with the Kraus brothers. By the end of the evening, they were trading makeup tips.

"I'd like to say that I blew my cover with Dirty Neck John, but that would imply I'd sold it to begin with. He was on to me before I got both feet across the threshold."

"Do you think he's playing a part in the blackmail or theft?" Anna asked. "Sounds like he's in a good position to be a fence."

"I have a feeling he has some hand in the scheme. Nothing concrete. He served with Eddie Stone during the war. Now in the same business. Suspicious and very sharp. I'm going to watch him from a distance. See if I can spot what he's up to."

"Anything from the visit to Galani Surplus?"

"Older Greek guy. A hustler from a long line of hustlers. Nice enough. No sign he's hiding anything. Seems to have a good heart," Kraus said. He told her about Mason Barlow, the man-child he'd met in the parking lot.

"That sounds nice," Anna said. "At least they're not all stinkers."

"Never all one or the other," Kraus said.

"No sign of the big bruiser?" Anna asked.

"None that I could spot. I'm back on it tomorrow," Kraus said.

"Hey, can we stop at the drug store on Normandie?" Anna asked.

"Sure," Kraus said. "What do you need? I can pick it up for you tomorrow if you'd like."

"Something you'd be too embarrassed to take to the register," Anna laughed.

"There aren't many things that would embarrass me," Kraus said.

"These are girl things, buster," Anna chided. "Once a month girl things."

"Oh. Those. Okay," Kraus said. "First a baby shower, now this. Must be Female Mystery night," he added.

"Childbirth and monthlies are mysteries to you?" Anna laughed. "Some detective."

"Here we are," Kraus said. He steered his Lincoln into the drugstore parking lot. "I'll go in with you. I want to pick up the Herald-Express."

A dark, heavy sky had been building up all day. Before sunset, the clouds looked the color of fresh plumber's putty. A persistent wind had kicked up. The thermometer had dipped into the fifties. Kraus and Anna picked up their pace across the parking lot when they left the store. A damp chill was in the air. A rainstorm wasn't far off.

"I'm glad the rain is coming," Anna said. "It'll wash all the nasty smog away."

"You goddamn asshole!"

Both Kraus and Anna turned to see where the shout had come from and who screamed. Traffic noise on Normandie along with the steady breeze scrambled the direction of the voice. The front wall of the drug store was fixed with bright lights trained on the parking lot. The scattering of people in the lot between them and the store were backlit. They were little more than shadows.

When he first heard the shout, Kraus imagined it to be a couple of people arguing in the parking lot. Holiday season. Pressure to overspend. Fraying nerves. A quick scan of the area didn't show any people appearing to be squabbling. But there was something in the tone of the shout that was out of the ordinary.

"Bitch! You're in on this, too?"

The cursing was now closer, and Kraus could now hear the sound of feet in a rapid trot towards them. A man's silhouette appeared from where it had been merged with the shadow of a large station wagon. He was waving something in his left hand. His right hand was rising. Straight out. Chest level. It held a pistol.

"Try and pin this shit on me!"

It no longer mattered to Kraus who the running figure was. Or what he was yelling. The man held a gun and was leveling it at Anna and him. He wrapped his right arm around Anna's shoulders and pulled her to the ground, keeping his body between the gunman and her. He heard a gunshot as they began their tumble to the pavement.

"*Damn,*" Kraus thought. The round had hit his left arm. Training kicked in. Everything slowed down for Kraus. He didn't know how badly he'd been wounded, but his arm still moved. More importantly, his right arm was undamaged. He sprawled his body over Anna's. His chest covered her head. He bent his right leg and reached for the Remington 51 in his ankle holster.

Kraus thumbed the safety off while extending his right arm. The Constabulary training in Sonthofen included endless drills for every conceivable combat shooting situation. Their Bible was the handbook, "*Shooting to Live*", by Sykes and Fairbairn. It was the last word on one-handed pistolcraft. The manual touched upon the fundamentals of firing from a prone position, but his Constabulary shooting instructor didn't believe it was enough.

"You'll be in more dicey dustups in that bleedin' cesspool than you can imagine," the range chief, a pugnacious Irish-American from Boston, would preach. "You're going to learn how to shoot from the top of a moving car, through the spokes of a tinker's wagon, while you're takin' a shit in the fookin' crapper." Kraus instinctively assumed the rollover prone shooting position he'd practiced and put into use several times in Berlin.

He bent his left leg to hook his foot over the back of his right knee. At the same time, he moved his left hand to the pistol, enfolding it over his shooting hand. His wounded left arm screamed as he did this. He ignored the pain. His cheek was resting on his right bicep. Kraus aimed at the advancing shadow man. The figure was shorter than average, so he dropped the angle a fraction.

The shadow figure fired off a second shot. It fell short of Kraus and Anna. Asphalt fragments exploded from where the bullet punched into the blacktop. Grit peppered Kraus' forehead and hair. He had a firm grip on the Remington. His support hand was solidly planted on the deck to steady the aim.

Kraus fired and swore at himself. He'd rushed the shot. He knew from experience the pistol would be heeled over five degrees or so from vertical, but he still didn't compensate enough. His shot hit their assailant high up on his left arm. Almost into the shoulder.

The attacker cursed and twisted away for a moment. He swiveled back and leveled his weapon for a third shot at Kraus and Anna. On the ground, they were in near darkness. Kraus could smell the powdery vanilla scent of Anna's French milled soap. *"God, I don't want this to be the last time I smell that,"* Kraus thought.

He figured the muzzle flash from his own shot would have temporarily blinded the shooter. The silhouette man was still fifteen feet or so away. If he had time to get off another shot, he was apt to miss. Sure enough, the shadow figure's third shot went high, passed over Kraus and hit the rear quarter panel of the car behind him, making a deep, tuneless chiming sound.

Kraus braced himself for his own next shot. He took dead aim. The Remington's rear sight notch and front post were small for night work. But the flat top of the slide was cross-hatched and cut some of the glare from the drug store wall lamps. He put the center of the shadow man in his sights and squeezed off three shots. All three hit the gunman in a rough triangle pattern below the hollow of his neck.

The dark shape dropped his right arm to his side. Something fluttered out of his left hand. He groaned and wobbled for a moment before his knees gave way and slammed to the pavement. He made a gurgling noise. The figure rolled to the left like a sandbag tipping over. The head bounced once on the asphalt before settling into a quiet stillness.

Kraus kept his eyes on the fallen man while he lifted himself off of Anna's prone figure. "You okay, Anna?" Kraus asked.

"I think so," she said in a breathless tone as she scrambled up onto her hands and knees. She looked at Kraus. "Gordy, you're bleeding!"

"Yeah," Kraus said, "the first round hit my arm as we took cover. I think I'm okay."

"Is he dead?" Anna asked as she rose to her feet, brushing pebbles and dust from her palms and knees. Several drugstore patrons in the parking lot were screaming. A few had sprinted into the store when the gunfight began and were now peering out the store doors.

"I think so," Kraus said, "but stay right here. It's always the dead rhino that gores you."

"Huh?" Anna said.

"Never mind," Kraus said as he took a step towards the fallen man. "Just stay here."

When Kraus pulled Anna to the ground, he dropped his copy of the Herald. The wind had blown the newspaper apart. Several pages had tumbled across the lot and were pinned by the breeze against the fallen body. Dry leaves blown against a downed tree trunk. Kraus approached the prone figure slowly at an oblique angle, away from the barrel of the gun still clutched in the man's hand. He placed a foot on the gun and crouched to see if the man was alive. Dark slacks and shoes. Light wool navy cardigan.

The breeze had plastered a piece of the sports section across the man's face. A picture of Frank Robinson receiving the "Rookie of the Year" award looked up at him. Kraus pinched a corner of the page and moved it away from the assailant's face. Frank Robinson had been smiling. Underneath the page, Tommy Thorp's mouth was fixed in a fierce grimace.

Tommy Thorp. The golf pro. Eddie Stone's sometime golf partner and fellow gun range member. The man who'd been trying to swindle and bed Violet McBride. Kraus felt for a pulse. None. His attention was caught by a small puddle of blood forming next to his own shoe. Kraus felt a little dizzy and plopped to the pavement on the seat of his pants.

"Please call an ambulance," Anna shouted to the people huddled at the drugstore door. She bent down to pick up the bag she'd carried from the store and dropped during the confrontation. She chased down something else that had fallen to the ground and was blowing across the parking aisle. Anna tucked the second item into her little merchandise sack.

FORTY-EIGHT

"Gordy, I was there when the lab boys tossed his place. He'd been keeping a detailed timetable of Ollie's movements. I don't know all his motives yet, but Thorp was our shooter."

It was late Wednesday morning. Kraus was taken by ambulance to South Hoover Hospital from the drugstore lot Tuesday night. Anna had some scratches from the fall. Nothing serious, but she insisted on riding in the ambulance with Kraus. An ER team worked on him. Thorp's first shot had grazed Kraus' left triceps. The bullet carved a horizontal divot across his upper arm. The ER doctor talked to him while suturing his arm.

"You're lucky, Mr. Kraus," the young intern told him. A little higher and further in, it could have torn the lateral head muscle right off the humerus. You'd be wearing slip-on shoes the rest of your life." A nurse bandaged his arm and gave him a tetanus shot before he was released.

Next, a ride to the station where Kraus and Anna were kept for hours. Questioned separately. Given statements to sign. Taken back to Kraus' car. Anna drove them to the Harvard Heights house. Neither one of them had slept more than an hour or so before Laveroni showed up at their door.

"What about his alibi?" Kraus protested. "He told Anna he was in Oxnard that night. Slept over at his mom's house. She made special pancakes in the morning. Didn't get back to L.A. until the next morning. Ollie was killed the night before."

"I'm not going to land on you for running your own investigation on this. Not yet, anyhow. If Gowan wasn't at some boondoggle leadership seminar in Frisco right now, he'd want to put you back on ice," Laveroni said.

"It's not exactly like you and your leadership suck-up were looking at the guy," Kraus said. His left arm was throbbing, and he couldn't hold back the peevishness.

"Gordy, we've plowed that field. Let's not hash it over again," Laveroni sighed in exasperation. "Look, the eighth floor at the Glass Tower wants this one closed. No waves. No awkward questions. That's just the way it is."

"'The Glass Tower'," Kraus laughed. "Is that what it's being called now? Sounds like something out of a Disney cartoon."

"Hey," Laveroni barked, "Thorp used a thirty-two last night. Same caliber that killed Ollie. Guy had a couple of shooting range trophies, for Chrissake. He was runnin' a con on Violet. Either makin' time with Violet or close enough to get his tip wet." Laveroni looked up at Anna. "Sorry."

"Nothing I haven't heard before, Lieutenant," Anna smiled.

"Anyhow," Laveroni continued, "The mom isn't a reliable alibi. Oxnard to L.A. Make it a half hour to get in and out of the alley. Right back to Oxnard. Could've done it in four hours. Not a hard stretch."

"Lots of unanswered questions," Kraus pressed. "Who beat up Violet? Why kill Ollie?"

"I dunno, Gordy," Laveroni groaned. "Maybe him. Maybe the guy he was runnin' the swindle with. Maybe another accomplice. Thorp isn't in a position to be questioned, is he? That was a neat grouping you pumped into his chest. I was at the post before coming here. Could've covered all three holes with a prayer card."

"Still a lot of 'maybes'. I don't like it," Kraus said.

"Gordy, you aren't drawin' a city paycheck. You don't have to like it," Laveroni asserted. "But this case is officially closed. Signed, sealed, delivered. Listen up, boy. You're as clean as a whistle on this right now. Four independent witnesses back both your stories about the attack. No heartburn on the shoot. Just count your blessings. You lay off, or so help me, I'll pull you in for interference. Suspend your license. Don't make me do that, Gordy. Please."

"Okay, okay," Kraus said. "When do I get my Remington back now that the case is closed?"

"I'll rush the paperwork. Pick it up from me on Monday. Your back-up piece, right?"

"Yeah," Kraus admitted. "I've got my Colt."

"Probably a couple others, knowin' you," Laveroni said. He slapped his hands on his knees and stood up. "Okay, I've got some pencil-pushing to do. It's rainin' out there like a cow pissin' on a flat rock. Traffic back to PAB will be impossible. I'll be in touch."

"Thanks, Gino," Kraus said.

"Take it easy with that arm. And you," Laveroni said, turning to Anna. She had an alarmed look at the sudden attention, "thanks for takin' care of this dummkopf. I don't want to see any bulletins about you cross my desk, either."

"You won't, Lieutenant," Anna said.

"Call me Gino, please," Laveroni said. "You're part of the family now." He shrugged on his car coat and left through the front door, closing it behind him.

Anna reached into the pocket of her slacks. She pulled a card out and handed it to Kraus. "Gordy, take a look at this. I think it was something Tommy Thorp was holding and dropped when he fell."

Kraus bent forward and reached out to take it from Anna. He bumped his left elbow against his knee and drew in a sharp breath with a grimace.

"Your arm bothering you?" Anna asked. "You have those painkillers they sent with you."

"I don't want to take them unless it really gets bad," Kraus said. "Maybe when I go to bed."

"The ER doctor said they see flesh wounds all the time," Anna said. "Routine stuff."

"Yeah, routine doesn't mean painless," Kraus said, peering down at the card he'd taken from Anna, "there's a Mark Twain book on the shelf over there. '*Roughing It*'. Stories about Twain's time in the West. He commented how 'flesh wounds' are treated as minor scrapes in dime novels. All but ignored by gunslingers and lawmen. He wrote that in real life, 'flesh wounds hurt'."

"Okay," Anna said. "You've got Mark Twain on your side. Just do something for the pain."

"You picked this up in the parking lot?" Kraus asked. "Where have you been keeping it?"

"I tucked it inside my box of girl things," Anna giggled. "No cop was going to look in there."

"Good thinking," Kraus said. He held the card up to read its face. "Aleksander Hresko" was centered. "the investigator" was centered below the name in smaller letters. Kraus flipped the card over. Nothing on the back. Held it up to the light. Nothing. He handed it back to Anna.

"What do you make of it?" Kraus asked.

"Cheap card stock," Anna said, rubbing the card stock between her thumb and forefinger. A disapproving tailor. "The printing was definitely done by one of those one-color duplicator machines. Kind of schlocky job you get from those shady places you find next to pawn shops and bail bonds outfits."

She looked at the face of the card again. "the investigator", she read aloud. "Odd structure. It's a Slavic name. Still, why not just 'investigator'? Also, 'the' is a definite article. For this usage, 'investigator' would require an indefinite article, if it needed one at all. This wasn't made by an English-speaker."

Kraus gave Anna a quizzical look. "Definite and indefinite articles?"

"I spent four months fronting for a secretarial school scam in Jefferson City. Missouri," Anna said. "You need to know your way around a sentence diagram to work that con."

Kraus shook his head and laughed. "God, this whole thing is such a can of worms," Kraus moaned. "Plus, we haven't slept in twenty-four hours. Let's get some shut eye. Maybe it'll all make sense when we're fresh."

"Sounds great to me," Anna agreed.

Anna woke up first. She chose to sleep in the guest room to avoid accidentally bumping Kraus' wounded arm while he was trying to get some rest. She poured herself some orange juice from the fridge and began quietly cleaning up the kitchen.

Kraus shuffled into the living room a few minutes later. His hair was tangled and mashed flat on the side where his head had rested on his pillow. He took a seat on one of the kitchen island stools.

"Did I wake you up with my noise?" Anna asked.

"No," Kraus said. "Woke up naturally. How long were we asleep?"

"Over four hours," Anna said. "It's almost dark outside."

"God, I feel like Rip Van Winkle," Kraus said. He stretched, being very ginger with his wounded left arm. "I'm starving, though. How about you?"

"Me, too," Anna said. "Want me to cook something?"

"No," Kraus said. "I don't have much in the fridge and it's too late to defrost anything. I got a whiff of some Greek food yesterday. Jesus, just yesterday. Feels like it was a week ago. Anyhow, I'm in the mood for a gyro. I'm going to go to Papa Cristo's and pick us up some food."

"That restaurant-deli place on Pico?" Anna asked.

"Yeah," Kraus said. "It's about two minutes away. What would you like?"

"Greek food, hmmmm," Anna mused. "A large Greek salad. With lamb meatballs."

"Done," Kraus said. He walked back to his bedroom. Anna heard the sounds of him washing and dressing. In a few minutes he came back out in slacks and a sports shirt. He was holding his shoulder holster. "Help me on with this?" he asked.

"Think you'll need this?" Anna asked while working the harness buckle.

"Don't know what I'll need anymore," Kraus said. "I'm not sold on Thorp as Ollie's killer. If he was, he wasn't working alone. Now's not the time to go waltzing around unarmed. With my backup piece being held, I'll have to carry my Colt."

Kraus unlocked the bottom drawer of the corner secretary in his living room. He withdrew his .38 Colt Commander. He released the magazine, checked the load. Slammed it back home. Racked the slide and slipped it into the holster.

"While I'm at it," Kraus said. He lifted another automatic from the drawer. It was the Beretta 51 Brigadier Ollie had squirreled away in his Bean Slot locker. He showed it to Anna.

"What's this?" Anna asked.

"The gun Ollie kept hidden in his saloon locker. It was tucked in a folder, charged and ready to fire. He was being extra cautious. With good reason. Do you know how to use one of these?"

"I've fired a gun before," Anna said. "But it was a revolver. Out in the Arizona desert." "Okay," Kraus said. He pulled back the slide, chambered a round and let it snap back.

"So, there's a bullet in the chamber. I've set the safety. It can't accidentally go off." He showed her a button set just under the hammer. "You push this button to release the safety. Point. Squeeze the trigger. Don't jerk it. Eight nine-millimeter rounds. Plenty of stopping power."

Anna took the weapon from Kraus. "Jeeze, it's so little, but heavy."

"Over two pounds. Lets you know you're holding something. Easier to keep on target. A light one's too easy to wave around."

"I hope I don't have to find out," Anna said. "Who do you think we need protection against?"

"Thorp's confederates. People we're not even aware of," Kraus said. "Thorp knew enough to follow us from my mom's house. Maybe planned to shoot us from his car as we went into the house. Our drugstore stop made him change plans. Could've saved our lives."

"Okay," Anna said. "But I'm not going to carry this around like Ma Barker."

"Let's put it in the top drawer of the secretary," Kraus said. He slid it open, deposited the Beretta and closed it. "You hear anyone trying to get in, you'll be able to grab it in plenty of time. I'll be back in less than an hour anyhow."

"Just be careful," Anna urged.

"Always am," Kraus said. He put a hat on and left through the side door. He pulled out of his driveway and turned towards Pico. The night sky was cloudy, intensifying the darkness. Everything was wet from the earlier rain.

He didn't see the dark shape blended into the shadows of bougainvillea that bordered his yard on the opposite side of the house.

FORTY-NINE

Papa Cristo's was busy for a rainy Wednesday night. Lots of locals going in and out to buy groceries from the delicatessen. The dining area next to the deli was almost full. The air was an intoxicating mixture of stomach-growling scents. Olive oil. Braised lamb. Garlic. Fruity honey. Almondy crushed pistachios. The restaurant-deli opened right after the war and quickly grew into a popular neighborhood food shopping and eating spot.

Kraus ordered food for takeout and looked into the small dining area. It was noisy with the clatter of plateware and clanking of eating utensils. Groups of four or more were served family-style with large platters of food placed in the center of their tables. Families shouted at one another across the table as though they were at home. Truth be told, the Greek community was small. For many, this was their second home. He wouldn't have been surprised to discover Yiorgos Galani was a customer.

A television set had been mounted on one of the dining area walls since Kraus had been there last. "*Criminy,*" Kraus thought, "*you can't get away from those things anywhere.*" The picture was rolling a little, but he could see it was tuned into some program with the ridiculous title, "Circus Boy". A little boy with hair as blonde-white as Calvin Wersky's was riding an elephant with an ethnic-looking boy sitting behind him. The elephant was being led by an actor he'd seen in a lot of westerns. The unlikely trio was walking into the Hollywood version of a gypsy camp. Many diners looked up while eating, keeping their attention fixed to the screen.

Kraus shook his head and walked back into the deli part of the building. He looked out the window at the Saint Sophia Greek Orthodox Cathedral across the street. An impressive structure with its mix of Byzantine Revival and California Mission architecture. The land and building were funded by three brothers. Greek immigrants who arrived penniless at the turn of the century. All three made an improbable rise to the top of the Hollywood movie industry. The cathedral was the fulfillment of their vow to God that they would build the most magnificent church if granted success in show business.

"*Other studio bosses behaved like they'd made their deals with the Devil,*" Kraus thought. He considered Yiorgos Galina again. A hustler who seemed as though he'd fit right in at any studio. "*Maybe Jews didn't have a monopoly on the sharp-elbowed brashness required for studio bosses,*" he chuckled to himself. "*Dore Schary might be wise to keep a bottle of ouzo next to the Manischewitz.*"

Kraus' thoughts circled back to Tommy Thorp and the LAPD's quick embrace of him as Ollie's killer. He understood the brass wanting the whole thing closed and forgotten. But Kraus only cared about finding Ollie's murderer and he didn't think it was Thorp. He kept having a nagging feeling he'd missed something. Something right in front of him. Something key.

"Gordy," the girl at the deli-counter called out. Her name was Angeliki. She'd often waited on Kraus. Angeliki held her forefinger to her lips. A librarian shushing a noisy patron. Kraus knew it to be the Greek mannerism for summoning someone, like crooking a finger.

"Hi, Angeliki," Kraus said when he reached the counter.

"Hi, Gordy," Angeliki said. "Do you want the dressing to be poured over the salad, or in a container?"

"Good question," Kraus said. "Let's keep it on the side."

"Okay," Angeliki said. "Your order will be ready in one minute."

Kraus started to turn back to the window, then stopped. "*Goddamn it,*" he thought, "*that's it.*" He closed his eyes to hold onto the half-formed thoughts in his mind. Sifting memories.

"Gordy," Angeliki sang out, "it's ready."

"Great," Kraus said. He took some bills from his wallet and handed them to her. "Keep the change, Angeliki. One question about your menu, though."

Angeliki thanked Kraus for the tip and listened to his question. She answered. "Thanks," Kraus said. He caught hold of the sack and rushed out to his car.

FIFTY

Louis Applebaum crouched in the shadows of the bushes at the edge of the private eye's house. He was cold and wet. Getting angrier with every passing minute. He'd been waiting for an opportunity to snatch the brunette, Margaret-something, for over an hour.

He and Lester Fox got over three thousand bucks from the phony stick-up they'd set her up for. Lester figured she'd come running to them with her tale of woe. They'd force her to go to work on her back to quickly repay the loss. Rent a nice pad up in the hills. Start of a real *zunhhouse*, as his old man used to say. A *Hurenhaus,* as his mother would screech when the old man came home smelling of bootleg hooch and stale sex. Their place would be classy, though. Not some ramshackle blind pig in Detroit's Black Bottom.

Lester boasted they'd put the Margaret-whatsit on the Mexican Horse to keep her in line. She'd be the centerpiece of a stable of girls they planned to assemble and run. Louis had suspicions Lester actually planned to make the brunette his private squeeze. Maybe set her up in charge of the other women. But the bitch never showed back up. Lost their money and just took off. Nervy broad knowing she owed them money.

The three grand they netted on the fake hold-up was running dry. They'd made a few little scores, but they didn't come to Los Angeles to be *yutzes*. He and Lester were not about to get stalled out like they did in Denver. After a few weeks in L.A., the only person left who believed Lester's bullshit about being in the Purple Gang was Lester himself. They had to start building themselves a legitimate rep or their next stop would be running lightning rod sales scams in Omaha.

Lester pinned his hopes on running a successful, high-end call-girl racket. Applebaum would help with the muscle for the johns and discipline for the twists, but he had his own ambitions. He'd been a decent boxer in his teens and twenties, winning his share of bouts at Legion Halls and small auditoriums. For a time, he was Solly Krieger's sometime-sparring partner when Krieger fought as a heavyweight to close out his career. Krieger said Applebaum was the toughest check-hooker he'd ever faced.

Applebaum longed to get back in the fight game. This time as a manager. An owner and promoter. Parlay his bordello earnings into a string of decent boxers. Attend all the fights in a nice suit, smoking a Cuban cigar with a hot dame on his arm. Everyone seeing him and knowing he was a big shot. That would be the life. But they had to get something started right now.

It hadn't been easy finding where the brunette was holed up. He'd tried looking at all the likely apartments. Walked through neighborhoods where he thought she might be running solo rental scams. Checked around high-class beauty parlors where she'd get worked on. Nothing panned out. They'd finally spotted her going into the May Company on Wilshire the week before. Applebaum waited in a car they'd boosted while Lester ambushed her in the parking lot as she was leaving.

Everything was going fine until the keyhole peeper stepped in. Applebaum stayed in the car. Watched from a distance. He'd seen Lester work with a knife before. He was good and Applebaum figured he'd handle the guy with no problem. Instead, the buttinsky snatched it from Lester's hand like he was plucking a Chick-O-Stick out of a toddler's fist. The gumshoe took Lester down like a limp egg noodle. Over before it started. The brunette lammed it during the dust-up. They had to start all over.

A few nights later, Applebaum was tired of looking for the brunette all over hell's half-acre. He'd stopped into the Cockatoo for a drink and some cards. The front room bartender mentioned a private cop was asking questions about the girl who'd been with him and Lester a few weeks before. Took a little bit of digging, but he found out where the private dick lived.

Lester declined to come tonight. Said it would be less conspicuous if one guy grabbed the broad. Applebaum guessed that Lester was scared to face the guy again. The hankshaw handled Lester pretty slick, but Applebaum was sure he'd have no problem with him if it came down to it.

But the detective had driven away. The broad was there alone now. For how long? Better take her now without a fuss than deal with both of them later. Applebaum began to rise from his crouch. "*Fuck, what now?"* Applebaum thought to himself. *"My damn collar is hung up on this friggin' bush."* His collar felt snagged, then it was as though a hydrangea branch was tangled in his hair. Tugging his head back as he tried to rise. He began to utter a curse but couldn't seem to catch his breath.

FIFTY-ONE

Kraus placed the bag of takeaway food on his backseat. He opened his trunk and rummaged around. Clutching the material he wanted, he raced back into Papa Cristo's and took a small table near the corner of the deli counter waiting area.

Ollie's notebook was the first thing he opened. He riffled through the pages containing info on his final case. Kraus spotted the address entry he'd been looking for. It was a street address in Ollie's frenetic mixture of print and cursive writing style. He'd drawn a crude five-point star next to the notation. No names or comments. Kraus had skimmed over it during his first examination of Ollie's case records. He'd felt a vague familiarity about the address but couldn't put his finger on it at the time. A few minutes earlier he'd suddenly recalled why he knew the address. A memory from his final months of LAPD patrol duty.

Kraus pried open the manila envelope Larry Butler, one of Ollie's former LAPD colleagues, had left with Melanie. He wiggled two sheets of paper from the envelope and laid them out on the table. Ollie had evidently been asking about information on a Russian national living in Los Angeles. Kraus read over both pages.

"*Damn it*," Kraus cursed to himself. "*How could I be so blind?*"

Butler had written a note on the second page with his home phone number. He'd told Melinda that Kraus was to call him at home with any questions. Not at his office.

There was a phone booth near the restroom doors. Kraus fed a few coins into the slots and dialed.

"Hello," a man's voice answered.

"Larry Butler?" Kraus asked.

"Who's this?" came the cautious reply.

"Gordon Kraus," Kraus said.

"Kraus," the man said in a cheerful tone, "this is Larry Butler."

"Hi, Larry," Kraus said, "thanks for the paperwork you dropped at my office. I've been a little busy, but I've had the chance to read your info just now."

"I'll say you've been busy," Butler said, "Heard you plugged the guy who killed Ollie. Good job, buddy! Word is you took one in the leg. Almost lost it."

"He winged me," Kraus said, "nothing as serious as that." Department gossip was already blowing the story out of proportion. LAPD legends have short gestation periods.

"Glad to hear it," Butler said. "Good to know Ollie's killer was put down. McBride was the last of a breed. What can I do for you?"

"I'm trying to get my arms around Ollie's last few cases. Maybe wrap some up, get some extra money for Violet," Kraus said.

"How is she doing?" Butler asked. "Heard she was busted up pretty bad. Another reason I'm glad you punched that guy's ticket."

"Holding her own," Kraus said. "Larry, I read your note about Ollie looking at a Russian national. Kuznetsov. Is the consulate still up on Glendower? Last couple of months on patrol before I went into the Army, I worked crowd control there a few times. Swanky digs for Communists."

"Yeah, that's still the place. Kuznetsov works there. Bunks there, too," Butler said. "Ollie said he'd piled up a stack of markers at the Cockatoo. Moretti wanted the guy to make good on the debt and gave Ollie the collection job. Same fuckin' story with all these diplomats. Every last one is a mush artist. Leaves a trail of red paper all over town before buggin' out. Frogs are the worst," he added. "Anyhow, Ollie knew I was working the Russian desk in G-2."

"G-2" was Chief Parker's intelligence unit. It cast a far wider net than the "Red Squad" established by Jim "Two-Gun" Davis. Back then, the Red Squad mainly kept tabs on political agitators bent on stirring up trouble amongst students, farm workers and Negroes. Under Parker, G-2 investigators spied on a wide range of influential citizens, celebrities and organizations. Like J. Edgar Hoover, Parker gathered dirt on real and imagined political enemies. The LAPD chief used most of the intelligence for blackmail or trade-offs.

"What did he want to know about him?" Kraus asked.

"Well, I'm tellin' it backwards," Butler said. "Ollie didn't come to me with a name. He described the guy. Asked if anyone workin' out of the consulate fit the description. Had Kuznetsov down cold. Down to his miserable shoes. I gave him the name. Told him a little about the guy. What I knew about his habits and work activities."

"Your notes say he's some kind of engineer," Kraus prompted.

"Yeah," Butler confirmed. "Electronics expert. Word is he spends some time vetting the stuff their industrial espionage section winkles out of Lockheed, Hughes and Northrop. Most of his time is spent scrounging electronic parts to be spirited back to Moscow."

"Sounds like you've got someone inside," Kraus said.

"No comment," Butler said with a laugh. "G-2 is primarily focused on their attempts to stir up labor problems at the defense plants and studios. Stuff like that."

"Doesn't it bother you that this Kuznetsov appears to be sending U.S. electronics gear back to Moscow?" Kraus asked.

"No more than it would bother me to see a water buffalo buy a pair of ice skates to compete in the Olympics," Butler said. "The buffalo couldn't use 'em if it wanted to. That's Parker's take on it, anyhow. He gives the FBI what we have. Lets them deal with it."

"I didn't see a picture of Kuznetsov with your notes," Kraus hinted. It would help if he knew what this bird looked like.

"Don't have any pictures," Butler said. "Seen him myself a couple of times when I've been out in the field. He frequents that Russian joint, Bublichki, on Sunset. North edge of the Norma Triangle. Know the place?"

"I've passed by it," Kraus said. "Never been there."

"Well, your man holds court there one or two nights a week. Plays up the homegrown Soviet man with the émigrés and student crowd. Leads the folks in teary singalongs of the Kalinka. A real ham. Loves to perform. Performs all kinds of impressions with a dozen accents. Does fucking magic tricks for them."

"Magic tricks, huh," Kraus said. "Turning over a new leaf," he said under his breath.

"What's that, Kraus?" Butler asked.

"Nothing. Something I thought of. Larry, what does he look like?"

"Short guy. Five-five. Maybe five-six. Wavy brown hair. Eyes almost like a Chink. Not as odd as you'd think with the Russkies. Centuries of Mongolian bloodlines creeping in. Not a clothes horse, but nice threads. Must have brought the shoes with him from Moscow. You couldn't buy a pair that gruesome in all of L.A. Sharp facial features. The sketch artists at the station would call his face 'pentagonal'. What an umpire sees looking down at home plate. Square on top but straight slants at the bottom."

"Like the face of a foxhole shovel," Kraus said.

"Exactly," Butler agreed. "Kraus, if you're going to brace this character, better do it fast. Scuttlebutt at the consulate is that his operation is being shut down. All the shady procurement moving to the Frisco area. He's been ordered home before the end of the year. Probably explains why he was putting away so much Russkie potato juice last time I saw him. Looked like he could hold it, but he'd never get pulled over anyway with that license plate."

"License plate?" Kraus asked, his stomach lurched into a tub of ice water.

"Yeah," Butler said. "His car has the diplomatic plates California DMV issues. Left side reads, 'FOREIGN GOV'T' in big letters. Right side has just three numerals. Patrol guys never pull those over. No sense in it. Can't cite 'em. Might cause a stink downtown that finds its way into your jacket."

"Larry, you've been a big help," Kraus said. In a hurry now. "Thanks for the info."

"Not a problem," Butler said. "Hey, let me know if you collect on him. I'll add it to his file. Anonymous source, naturally."

"I'll collect. You can count on that," Kraus said. "Thanks again." He hung up and walked back out to his car. He slid in behind the wheel and fanned out the material on the passenger side of the seat. He picked up the "*Adventures in Electronics*" comic book Katz had given him to study.

Kraus thumbed to the last pages of the comic book. A section was titled, "*Electrons In Uniform*". Cartoon depictions of how electronic parts were being used to beef up radar system capabilities. Develop mortar location machines. Improve defense sonar applications.

In Milestone Electro Supply terms, these were probably called "military sockets". Kuznetsov was getting parts to fill "Red Sockets".

Kraus closed his eyes and tilted his head back. He shuffled through his thoughts.

A beaten-up Russian lieutenant slumped against a wall with his mouth hanging open. Angeliki, the Papa Cristo's counter girl, and what she told him about the menu.

"*The Russkies don't like loose ends,*" his sergeant had told him.

The combined significance of these thoughts shot a jolt of adrenaline through Kraus.

"Anna," he called out loud without even realizing it. His eyes popped open, and he sat straight up in his car seat. He started the car, threw it in gear and sped out of the parking lot.

FIFTY-TWO

Anna busied herself by folding and putting away some clean laundry that rested in a basket near the kitchen. She laughed when she opened a hall closet to stow away some clean towels. The clean bed sheets on the upper shelf were a mess. Anna thought men folded bed linen the way paratroopers are shown after landing in war movies. They wad up the parachute silk into a tight ball and bury the whole thing as quickly as they can. She felt another pang of regret at the thought of soon leaving Gordy's little world. She knew she would miss it.

Laundry chores finished, she settled into a chair by one of the living room windows and continued reading the novel she'd bought the week before at the May Company. The day she'd met Kraus. Only a week ago? It seemed like years. The closed-up house had gotten a little muggy and she'd opened the window a little bit to let in some rain-freshened air.

"*What was that*?" Anna thought. She had only read a few pages when a soft noise sounded at the side of the house. It was nearly drowned out by the melody of raindrops dripping from tree limbs and rainwater gurgling down gutter drainpipes.

There had been no preceding sound of Gordy's car. She didn't think he'd returned. It couldn't be Lester and Louis. They had no way of knowing where she was hiding out. Even if they had discovered her whereabouts, they weren't good enough to break into a house with only a barely audible noise.

Another faint noise. "*That's inside the house,*" Anna's mind insisted. She gauged the second noise to be just inside the third bedroom Kraus used as an office. "*Whoever it is will be in here in five or six seconds. He's still now, listening to see if anyone heard his entrance,*" she thought.

Anna looked around the room. The gun Kraus had deposited in the little secretary was too far. The intruder would hear the drawer open and be on her before she could get a bead on him. She silently slipped her shoes off while pushing the living room window up a few more inches. The startlement had made the back of her neck a little clammy. She lifted her hair for the briefest of moments. The cool breeze felt good on her skin.

The door to Gordy's bedroom office issued a thin rasp as the interloper eased it open. Anna knew this was her final chance to make a move. She didn't hesitate.

FIFTY-THREE

Kraus didn't take the time to pull into his driveway. He slid the Lincoln next to the curb in front of his house, braking so hard his tires made scuffing noises on the wet street surface. His home was centered on a wide lot and did not receive a lot of light from the neighboring houses on either side. He didn't spot the dark bulk against the shrubs until he was almost at the front steps. He veered towards the shape and kneeled down.

"Shit," Kraus murmured to himself.

He didn't recognize the man lying dead in his yard, but even in the weak illumination of the streetlight, he could see the man's throat had been cut from ear to ear. Dripping water from the hydrangea branches mingled with the pool of gore puddled around the man's throat, making it difficult to guess how long the body had been there. Kraus didn't really care. He was too concerned about what was happening in the house. He pulled the forty-five from his shoulder holster. He'd chambered a round before leaving the house, so he just thumbed off the safety as he strode up the front porch steps.

The front doorknob was locked. He took his keys out and stood with his back to the wall next to the door. His wounded left arm throbbed as he pushed the key backhanded into the lock and turned the knob. He pushed the door open with a fierce, backhanded shove of his left hand. The door bounced against the inside wall. No one behind it. Kraus remained still. Listening for movement or breathing. Nothing.

The living room lights were on. From the oblique angle Kraus had into the house, it looked as though the kitchen lights were on as well. He reached to his right and quietly removed a small cushion from the porch chair nearest to him. Kraus tossed the pillow through the door towards the left and waited a beat. Nothing. He slid his back across the right side of the door frame, pressing against the inside wall, slithering further into the room. Gun held in a two-handed grip, tracking the kitchen and living room areas from left to right. No sign of anyone.

He closed the front door and relocked the knob. An assailant could be hiding outside to pull a reverse ambush by following him into the house. He'd seen it happen before.

A living room window above one of the armchairs was open. The book Anna brought with her was on the small table next to the chair. Her Espadrille slippers were tucked under the chair. Some random mail and loose papers were skidding around the hardwood floor, propelled by the breeze coming in through the open window. No signs of any kind of struggle.

Kraus peered down the dark hallway. The floor runner was flat and undisturbed. Not a drop of blood anywhere in sight. He backed towards the center of the living room, gun in the ready position.

"Anna," he called out. Not shouting, but loud enough to be heard throughout the quiet house. Nothing. He could hear cars driving around the neighborhood through the open window, their tires producing a sizzling sound as they rolled over the wet blacktop.

Kraus stepped towards the little secretary in the corner of the living room. He wanted to check if the gun had been taken. Maybe Anna heard the struggle outside, took the pistol and escaped through the window. *"Would she have taken the time to close the drawer?"* he asked himself.

His right arm suddenly went numb. The automatic fell out of his hand and clattered on the floorboards.

"Kick the gun under the couch," a deep, Slavic-accented voice commanded. "Now."

Kraus smacked his fallen gun with the outside edge of his shoe. It made an abrasive rasp as it skidded under the couch. He rubbed his numb right arm with his wounded left while turning to see who had hit him. *"How the hell did he come up on me so fast?"* Kraus thought.

Standing before him was a large, tall man with deep-set, black eyes and a craggy face. Hair cut in the Russian *khokhol* fashion. Prison cut. Shaved sides and back with a thick patch of longer hair left on top. The longer top hair was parted in the middle. Stalin mustache. A Neanderthal auditioning for a barbershop quartet. Wide shoulders. Muscular. He smiled at Kraus, which only made him look more menacing.

The man was wearing a black, long-sleeved pullover and black pants. Black crepe-soled shoes. Rough hands the size of brake drums.

His right hand brandished a Great War-era trench knife. Double-edged blade. Razor sharp. Blood stained the blade's black oxide finish. Probably the remains from the earlier handy work in the front yard. The blackened handle was molded in the form of a set of brass knuckles, with sharp metal spikes extending from the bows of each finger hole. The takeaway move he used on Lester Fox would be useless here.

"Lift your trouser legs," the giant demanded. *Lift* came out as *leaf*. "Slowly." Checking for hideout pieces.

The numbness in Kraus' right arm was fading. He guessed the thug had slammed the pommel of the knife handle into his arm. It sported a conical nut and he'd heard it referred to as a "skull basher" during his time in Berlin. The strike was probably intended to break his arm, but only managed to hit a key nerve. Kraus gingerly pulled up his pants legs from the thighs, like he was preparing to walk through a deep puddle.

"Good," the man said. "Your woman is gone," he growled, jerking his square chin at the open window. "Barefoot. No money. Nowhere to go."

"First thing she'll do is call the cops," Kraus said. "You don't have a lot of time."

"Maybe," the man said. "I think she's not so comfortable with police. Maybe just hiding. After I'm done with you, maybe I find her. Treat her like our soldiers handled your little German *shlyukha* in Berlin after the war."

Kraus' eyes flared at the mention of Charlotte's ordeal.

"Oh, yes," the man smirked, "we have a file on you, Captain. I know all about your little crusade. Don't worry. After I play with this one, I'll kill her quick." He twirled the knife point in a tight circle. "Show her some mercy."

"I'll be a little harder to handle than a middle-aged woman or a scared teenager in a pool hall," Kraus said, hoping he was right. "Your time is running out."

"We'll see," the knife-wielder said.

Kraus undid his belt and held it apart with both hands, like he was stretching taffy. He was not going to let this goon get to Anna if she did return. The guy looked as strong as an ox, but Kraus figured he could get a belt loop around the wrist of the man's knife hand. Check his mobility for a few seconds. Keep him from doing lethal harm while he used his own fingers to gouge the man's eyes out.

It was a messy move. Discussed in theory but never practiced during Constabulary training. A last-ditch survival method. He was bound to sustain some knife wounds. He had a chance If he wasn't killed immediately. Anna had probably already called the police. Medics would not be that long in coming.

No matter what, the man would not be able to kill him before Kraus disabled him. Of this, Kraus was sure. He would not fail Anna like he did Charlotte.

The roughneck widened his stance a few inches and crouched a little, getting ready to spring at Kraus. The breeze pushed one of the loose papers on the floor between his feet.

Kraus widened his own stance and rocked on the balls of his feet. His opponent held the trench knife in a saber grip, thumb along the handle's top edge, pushed against the crossguard. Pointing up. Pro technique. Kraus moved his hands up and down, looking for the best angle to snare a wrist thrust. The bruiser feigned a move with his left foot, then quickly shifted his weight and shuffle-stepped towards him off his right.

"*Here it comes,*" Kraus thought. He readied his belt for a wraparound trapping move.

FIFTY-FOUR

Kraus planned to slip his attacker's first thrust by pivoting sideways and letting the thrust of the knife arm pass by him the way a bullfighter dances away from a bull charge. He'd then loop his belt around the gorilla's wrist from the side. Subdue the arm against a lateral swipe of the blade while blinding him with a stiff, two-fingered jab into his eyes.

His assailant hadn't even begun his lunge. Almost two full strides still separated the men. Kraus heard a whistling sound and the kind of hollow thump of a ripe melon splitting open. The man's eyes rolled back in his head. Kraus backpedaled a step to avoid the man's head as his limp body fell forward.

The assassin toppled face down onto the hardwood planks. Behind the sprawled figure was Anna. Barefoot. Bent forward. Hands on her knees. Breathing hard. Ollie's Monkey Paw dangled from her right hand. Behind her, the door of the secret Craftsman column cabinet was open. She must have hidden in there, then quietly emerged when she heard the standoff developing.

Anna had to have almost run towards the man's back, left her feet while swinging the weighted rope and connected a pound of lead shot square to his temple. The athletic agility she'd shown at the driving range on full display.

Kraus stepped beside the prone body and placed a knee on the right forearm. The man's fingers were still gripping the knuckle duster knife handle. He felt the body's neck for a pulse.

"Dead," Kraus said, looking up to meet Anna's eyes. "Good shot."

"Thanks," Anna gasped. Still winded. "I pretended he was my stepfather."

"Second time that thing has saved my bacon," Kraus said, pointing at the dangling Monkey Paw.

"If you hadn't noticed," Anna said as she knelt next to the other side of the body, "this thing didn't swing itself. I was on the other end of the tether."

"Thank you," Kraus conceded. "Although I don't know if I should kiss you or be angry at you for pulling that stunt. But I'm glad I hadn't found the time to put a safe in that cabinet yet."

"I was glad I knew it was there," Anna said. Anna snaked her hand into the dead man's back pocket and came out with a small leather wallet. She shuffled through the contents, pulled out a cheap business card and held it up for Kraus to see.

"Our friend, Aleksander Hresko. Dollars to donuts that isn't this monster's name, and poor grammar or not, he's no investigator. But now we know who got Tommy Thorp all stirred up," Kraus said. "The ploy with Tommy didn't go as planned, so he came here to finish the job himself. Instructed to come here, in all likelihood."

"Gordy, what is this all about?" Anna asked.

"In a minute," Kraus promised. "I'm starving and there's food in the car. Let's bring it in. But I have to show you something first." He groped under the couch and retrieved his Colt. Checked the safety and holstered it. "I'll grab a flashlight from the kitchen. Follow me."

The flashlight played against the ashen face of the corpse lying against the side lawn fence line. The broad, tell-tale scars below the eyebrows and a rubbery cauliflower ear were shiny in the beam of light. The bungalow courtyard owner described the man asking about Anna as having the face of a boxer.

"That's Louis Applebaum, Lester's partner," Anna said in a flat tone. No sympathy.

"I figured," Kraus said. "The stiff inside probably took him for a lookout. I wonder where Lester is?"

"Too afraid to face you again, knowing him. Sent Applebaum alone," Anna said.

"Doesn't mean he won't work up the courage when his buddy doesn't return," Kraus said. "We've seen more dead bodies in twenty-four hours than a lot of funeral directors. You still up for some food?"

"You bet," Anna said.

"Okay," Kraus said, "let's go inside and I'll bring you up to speed."

While they ate, Kraus told Anna about his Papa Cristo's epiphany and all the pieces he'd fitted together.

"What now?" Anna asked. "Are you going to call Laveroni?"

"No," Kraus said. "This is something I have to do alone. No police. For a lot of reasons. Not least of which are the dead bodies here, to name two."

"It's pretty clear the big guy there," Anna pointed her fork at the body of the knife artist in the living room, "cut Applebaum's throat before breaking in. I killed him in self-defense. I don't see the problem."

"I don't want to get bogged down with all the time the investigation and endless reports would take. I'm certain our short foreign guy is making a move tonight. I think he sent Tarzan," Kraus waved his gyros at the body, "as much to get him out of the way as to kill us."

"Okay," Anna said.

"Besides, self-defense wouldn't be as solid as you'd think. One of Abe Lincoln's biggest law cases was defending an Illinois man accused of murdering a man with a Monkey Paw. He discredited an eyewitness account using the Farmer's Almanac, of all things."

"Where did that come from?" Anna asked, almost choking on a lamb meatball.

"I had a sergeant who knew a lot about Abe Lincoln," Kraus said.

Kraus went over to the little secretary desk in the living room and took the automatic from the center drawer. He placed it on the counter next to Anna's salad bowl.

"New pepper grinder?" Anna asked.

"Remember how to use this?" Kraus asked.

"Of course," Anna said.

"Good," Kraus said. He dangled a key ring. "I took this from one of Mack the Knife's pockets. I'm going to look around for his car. It couldn't be parked too far away. I'll announce myself before I step back inside. If anyone appears who you don't know while I'm out there, shoot them."

Soon Anna heard a large car rumbling up the driveway. She placed the palm of her hand on the butt of the Beretta Kraus had left with her. The door leading in from the garage opened.

"It's me," Kraus called out. "He parked it a block over. You think Applebaum used a car to get here?"

"I doubt it," Anna said. "He would have taken a bus from wherever, transferred to the Adams route, gotten off at Western or Vermont. Walked the rest of the way. He probably planned to nab me and drive us in my car back to where he and Lester are holed up. And before you say it, I know it's not my car. Just a figure of speech."

"You think I'd say something like that in the same breath I'm asking you to help me get rid of two dead bodies?" Kraus asked. "But good, though. One less complication. Help me move this burly asshole out the door and into the trunk of his car."

Kraus and Anna took opposite ends of the strongarm man and hoisted him out the side door of the house. A large, black, late-model Chrysler Imperial sedan was backed into the driveway, its bumper nearly inside the open garage door. The trunk lid was open.

After stuffing the body in the cavernous trunk, Kraus led Anna around the front of the house. He carried an old painting tarp he'd taken from a shelf in the garage.

"We'll roll Applebaum's body in this, then put it in the trunk next to his killer," Kraus said.

"Aren't you afraid of the neighbors seeing any of this?" Anna asked while glancing around the street.

"No," Kraus said. "We lucked out. The family across the street went to Ohio for the holidays. Family visit. They asked me to keep an eye on their place while they're away. The neighbors on both sides look to be out for the evening. Christmas shopping. Dinner. Picking up a tree. Holiday stuff."

The dead man's jacket and pants were soddened from the rain and runoff from the hedge. Wrapping it in the tarp made lifting and carrying an easier job. They managed to get Applebaum wedged in the trunk next to his own murderer. Kraus closed the trunk lid and pointed his flashlight at the bumper.

"There's the license plate I kept hearing about," Kraus said.

Anna looked at the plate, which had the stacked words "FOREIGN" and "GOV'T" stamped into the left side of the plate.

"'Foreign Government'," Anna read aloud. "I don't think I've ever seen one."

"Not many around L.A. Probably why it didn't register with the witnesses," Kraus said.

"What's next?" Anna asked.

"Let's go back inside," Kraus motioned to the door. "You clean any fresh blood and tissue on the Monkey Paw knot. Pick up all the mail and paper scattered around and put them back on that little entry table, with the cosh as a paperweight. I'll check for any other evidence." He looked at his wristwatch. "Then it'll be time to make a phone call. It's going to be a long night for both of us."

FIFTY-FIVE

"**Does it bother you to** be driving around with two dead bodies in the trunk?" Anna asked.

"Not in this car," Kraus said. "I have it on good authority that the cops never pull over cars with Foreign Government plates. Pointless to write them a ticket and it could backfire on the patrolmen who made the stop."

"Good plates to have on a car when you're pulling a job," Anna mused.

"Don't get any ideas, miss," Kraus laughed. He turned off Pico north onto Main Street. "The Bean Slot isn't far from here."

"Why do I have to wait it out in some bar?" Anna asked. "Wouldn't it be better if you had some backup tonight?"

"Yeah," Kraus agreed, "but I don't want you to be part of what may happen. Also, if I lay an egg, I'll need you to take the whole story to Gino."

"Gordy, I'm worried you've pressed your luck too much in the last twenty-four hours," Anna said.

"I think I'll be okay. I've got the element of surprise working for me. I'm sure our man thinks his enforcer finished us off," Kraus said.

"How's your right arm where he struck it with the knife handle?" Anna asked.

"Probably has a bruise looking like a puddle of chocolate pudding. It hurts. But the good news is it's made me forget the pain of the gunshot wound in my left," Kraus explained.

"That's staying positive," Anna said, sounding anything but.

"You have to be in this racket," Kraus said. "Here we are."

The wet pavement outside the tavern reflected the twinkling Christmas lights showing through its high windows. It gave the Bean Slot a warm, festive appearance, more than just the promise of a cold beer and cool refuge from the normally dry, road-dust encrusted sidewalks.

Hayashigawa closed the joint early at nine o'clock every Wednesday. He'd been hosting a private poker party for his friends every Wednesday night since he opened the place.

"What's the significance of the name 'bean slot'?" Anna asked.

"It's that open space in the bars of a cell big enough to push a food tray through," Kraus answered. "You'll find out first-hand if you keep thinking about things like using diplomatic plates on a caper."

"Just fanciful speculation," Anna huffed.

"Come in, come in," Hayashigawa exclaimed when he answered the knock Kraus laid on the front door. "And this must be Anna," the barman said. The inside of the bar had undergone a holiday transformation since Kraus was there a few days before. Fake garland was strung on the walls and along the face of the bar. A Christmas tree stood in its fully-trimmed glory next to the jukebox. The tap handles were topped with little felt Santa hats.

"Anna Bjorkquist, Dave Hayashigawa," Kraus made the formal introduction. "You two have a lot in common. You've both hidden in cabinets."

"Hey," Hayashigawa protested. "Not in front of my pals, please. I've told you a dozen times before, I wasn't hiding. You came up on me when I was searching for the good silver."

There were five men sitting around one of the poker tables near the back of the room. All Japanese. They laughed and waved at Kraus and Anna. The room smelled like boiled hot dogs and grilled hamburger meat. Kraus had sat in on a few of Hayashigawa's poker parties. You may leave with empty pockets, but no one left with an empty stomach.

"Hi," Anna threw them a wave. "Sounds like a story's in there somewhere."

"Later, later," Hayashigawa said. "After this knucklehead gets going. You like to play cards, Anna?"

"I play a game or two every so often," Anna said. Teasingly modest.

"Hey, take it easy now," Kraus said.

"We'll go easy on her," Hayashigawa laughed.

"I was talking to her," Kraus chuckled.

"Oh, ho," Hayashigawa said. "We've got a live one, huh?" He reached over the hammered zinc bar top and brought back a filled ice pack. Beads of evaporation had formed in the pleats of the heavy cotton fabric. "What you asked for," he said, handing the frigid bag to Kraus.

"Thanks," Kraus said. "For my arm. Did you and your guys bring your gear?" Hayashigawa nodded. "Now, Dave, remember, no one you don't know gets in. We've had a rough twenty-four hours and we're not out of the woods yet."

"Gordy," Hayashigawa said, "we're all One-Puka-Puka's. She's safer than she'd be locked in Fort Knox. A Waffen-SS unit wouldn't get through the door."

Kraus smiled. One-Puka-Puka was the nickname for the 100th Battalion, the fiercest fighters in the 442nd Regiment. The most-decorated infantry group in military history. Hayashigawa and the other players were all from the same outfit. Even eleven years after VE-Day, you couldn't find an assembly of six more dangerous men anywhere.

"I'm serious, Dave. Any guy looking for her will be a trained killer. I want her to be safe."

"Gordy," Hayashigawa, taking a somber tone, "Seriously. No one is going to harm her. We'll protect her with our lives."

Kraus turned to Anna. "Okay, I'm taking off. Remember, if I'm not back by eight or so tomorrow morning, call Laveroni. Pour the whole thing in his lap. Dave's got his number."

"Gordy," Anna said, doing a poor job of holding back some tears, "please, please be careful. Trained killers. You said it yourself."

"I'm a trained killer, too," Kraus said. Anna threw her arms around his neck and burrowed her face in the crook of his neck. He kissed her. "See you in a few hours."

FIFTY-SIX

Even the least accomplished commercial burglars, the petty cash and stamps guys, will tell you an office complex at night has a discernible energy.

Kraus thought of what he'd been told by dozens of cracksmen of every stripe. *There's empty and there's empty.*

All the workers have clocked out, but is there a janitor or two hard at work, the lights only on in the spaces they're cleaning?

Is there a night watchman? Does he patrol on a predictable schedule? Is there a skeleton crew night shift? Is some Horatio Alger type pulling an unexpected all-nighter?

Countless pitfalls. Every single *yegg* said only a fool would forgo watching the target from a distance for fifteen minutes or so. Be still. Let your sixth sense pick up the vibration always radiating from a building at night. It wasn't foolproof. Everyone can have an off night. But the technique can increase the chances for a smooth, uneventful job.

Kraus reached the rows of office-warehouses, turned the car's headlamps off and parked in a dark corner of the side parking lot. He stayed in the car. Let his eyes adjust to the near darkness. No movement outside the buildings. No sign of office lights being on. No janitorial or maintenance vehicles parked near building entrances.

The earlier squall soaked the parking lot. Oil-filmed puddles of water dimpled the lot surface. Kraus smelled the mixed aromas of dust and gasoline a good rain kicks up off bare asphalt. He walked close to the front row of office spaces. In the shadows. No fiery showers of molten spatter showing through the windows of Naramore Welding. No whirring of sewing machines from South Bay Fashions. No signs of a night watchman patrol. Dead quiet.

Kraus took a less-direct course than the one he used to drive up to Galani Surplus the day before. This route would buttonhook around the end of the building, bringing him right up to Galani's door. He didn't want to expose himself during a walk along Galani's side of the complex.

He was under no illusion he had the element of surprise, despite the assurances he gave Anna. The killer who invaded his home probably had instructions to call the office when the job was done. A simple signal, like three rings and a hang-up would have worked fine. Unless Hell's waiting room had a phone booth, the Russian goon never made that call.

Kraus turned the final corner and stopped to survey the front of Galani Surplus. Silence. The garage door must have been opened and closed since he was there yesterday morning. The base of the door didn't quite meet the cement threshold strip. A faint glow of interior light showed through a quarter-inch gap.

The flashlight he'd been using earlier was in his coat pocket. He flicked it on and played the beam over the small van he'd seen the day before. It was cleaner than it had been. Mason Barlow had managed to wash it before the rain began. No one was visible in the cab or under the van. He switched the flashlight off.

He crept past the garage panel and stopped beside the front door. Faint light appeared through the high Jalousie windows. He tried the entry door. The knob turned and he could feel that the deadbolt was not engaged. A bad sign. Kraus couldn't imagine the man-child, Mason Barlow, going to bed without locking up. An unlocked door in the middle of the night did not bode well.

The front door pushed open without a squeak. Kraus slipped his automatic out of its holster, thumbed the safety off and held it at his side. The dim light in the office and warehouse areas came from the green shaded banker's desk lamp he'd seen yesterday. Kraus switched on his flashlight.

The office was a little different than it had been the morning before. A bowling ball bag was cached in the knee well of the office desk. The food and spice aromas had been replaced by exhaust fumes and a hot metal smell coming off a dark sedan backed into the warehouse area. It hadn't been there long. Kraus approached the sedan cautiously and ran his light over the interior and undercarriage. Empty. "FOREIGN GOV'T" stamped on the license plates.

Kraus carefully made his way to the bathroom in the far corner of the office. The door was slightly ajar. The interior was dark. He stood back from the closed door and pushed it open with the stick of a broom that was leaning against the wall. Empty.

Next, he made his way to the little curtained off space that served as Mason Barlow's bedroom. The curtains were drawn, but they didn't reach the ceiling or the floor. No light showed through the open spaces. Kraus positioned himself a couple of feet from the curtains and swept them open with the broomstick. Barlow was on the camp cot. Uncovered. Fully clothed. On his back. Arms neatly at his sides. Out cold.

Barlow was taking shallow breaths. His chest barely moved. Kraus pointed his flashlight beam underneath the cot and at both corners of the little, informal bedroom. Barlow was the only one there. Kraus stepped into the little sleeping area and pried open one of Barlow's eyelids. The pupil dilated.

"*Drugged with something,*" Kraus thought.

He waved his light at the small, curtain-faced closet near the office door. The toes and upper face of two extremely ugly black shoes were pointing forward, just visible between the curtain hem and the concrete floor. Kraus stood back and away from the center of the closet. He used the broom handle to swiftly draw aside the curtain while pointing his Colt automatic at the mouth of the little cupboard. The flashlight beam illuminated the closet. Mops, a vacuum cleaner and a high shelf holding cleaning supplies. The shoes were empty.

"Mr. Kraus don't turn around. Please drop the broom and kick it away. Then kindly walk into the closet and place your gun on the top shelf. Push it way to the back of the shelf, then slowly turn around with your hands plainly in sight."

FIFTY-SEVEN

Kraus followed the instructions issued by the voice behind him. He held his hands out from his sides. A signal of completion. Both arms ached.

"Very good," the voice said, "now, slowly turn to face me."

He turned to stare down the muzzle of a flat black Maxim suppressor pointed at his face. It looked like a cylindrical eggplant jammed onto the barrel of a small pistol. The man holding the weapon bore a strong resemblance to Mason Barlow, the former Skid Row dweller, now lying unconscious a few feet away. A more polished look, but the same short height. Same wavy brown hair. Same square face and tapered jawline. Same almond-shaped eyes. Same body frame.

Kraus looked his captor over. Light wool sweater over a checked sports shirt with a button-down collar. Neat khakis. Brown, lace-up, stitched leather deck shoes with rubber soles. Snazzy. Dressed for travel. The gunman smiled when he saw Kraus examining his shoes.

"Better looking shoes than your trademark brogans," Kraus said, dipping his shoulder back towards the decoy shoes in the little closet.

"Ah, yes," the man chuckled, "real clodhoppers, as you Americans say." He twitched the end of the silencer a fraction, gesturing towards the abandoned shoes. "They made for an effective misdirection, though. A magician's deception," he said with an apologetic shrug.

"So, it seems," Kraus said. "You've lost your Greek accent, Comrade Kuznetsov."

"Ah, yes" Kuznetsov said, "so, we each have knowledge of the other. Good. It eliminates the natural temptation to ask so many tedious questions." He glanced at a stainless steel Longines watch fastened on his wrist by a shiny brown, crocodile leather strap. "I'm on a bit of a tight schedule."

"*Russians and their wristwatches,*" Kraus thought sardonically. "Leaving town?" he said aloud.

"To be sure," Kuznetsov said. "I was expecting Balabanov to return here. Since you are the one who has arrived, I presume he came to a bad end."

"Balabanov. That was his real name? No. His plan didn't work out," Kraus said. "Much like your first try at killing me fizzled out."

"Yes," Kuznetsov said in a regretful way, "the unfortunate Mr. Thorp. Your Constabulary record did not overstate your skills, Mr. Kraus. Two attempts on your life and two failures. Although the third time may prove to be the charm, as they say," the Russian waggled the gun barrel.

"I have a hunch your knee breaker wasn't long for this world anyhow," Kraus said.

"Just so," Kuznetsov said. "I couldn't very well leave poor Balabanov behind to expose the little duplicity I've orchestrated. He was ignorant of my real game plan, but Moscow would undoubtedly have assigned more imaginative men to piece things together. Mr. Kraus, you saved me the trouble of dispatching him. Although, your presence here complicates the narrative I'm constructing."

"Sorry to be such a pest," Kraus said.

"Oh, I'll contrive something," Kuznetsov said. "Tell me, though. I know Balabanov would not betray me to you. How did you determine Yiorgos Galani was not what he seemed to be?"

"*That's why he hasn't killed me yet,*" Kraus thought. "*He wants to learn from his mistakes.*"

"I haven't figured it all out yet," Kraus said. "But I really don't care about the little fiddle you were running on your Soviet masters. They give you funds to buy electronic parts in the guise of a parts broker. You coerce people to just steal the product for you. You pocket the money. I see variations of that scheme every day in my business. I'm just after the man who killed my friend. That's you, Kuznetsov."

"How can you be so sure?" Kuznetsov asked. "I myself accused Balabanov of the deed."

"I'm sure you did," Kraus said. "Probably kept him in line, making him think he was under suspicion for breaking some sort of MVD protocol. But it was you, alright."

"Just tonight, I read in the Evening-Herald that the unfortunate Thomas Thorp has been tied to Mr. McBride's demise," Kuznetsov offered.

"Yeah. *Pravda* isn't the only newspaper that prints a lot of bullshit," Kraus said. "Ollie could sniff out a scam like a dowser stick. He looked into the blackmail stunt you pulled on that poor kid at Desilu and it probably took him less than a day to figure out what was going on. But he got greedy. Made him a little sloppy. Somehow you lured him into that alley. Probably with the promise of some sort of payoff. Your bad luck was that the killing got me looking into it."

"I'm not sure if it is I suffering bad luck at the moment," Kuznetsov said, jiggling his pistol. Reminding Kraus who held who at gunpoint. "Had your friend left information about me behind, the police or yourself would have come straight to me. He must have been more than a little circumspect with his records, because no one came to apprehend me. Until now."

"I didn't come to apprehend you, Comrade," Kraus said, letting that hang there for a moment. "Ollie was secretive. That was his way. It slowed me down. But I ultimately followed the trail to you."

"To Yiorgos Galani, you mean," Kuznetsov said. Prodding. Wanting to hear more about his missteps.

"Yeah," Kraus agreed. "You were good. Really good. I was completely fooled. Even thought you were a good egg because of what you'd done for poor Barlow over there."

"That was only yesterday morning," Kuznetsov observed. "What happened to change your mind?"

"You made several mistakes," Kraus said. "No shame in that. This kind of masquerade has a lot of moving parts. You've been in the States for a couple of years. I spent a lot of time with Russians in Berlin. You aren't the first Ivan I've known who went native after being seduced by the comforts and freedom of the West. You knew you'd eventually be ordered home, but you didn't want to leave. You started plotting. Funneling Kremlin money into your own pocket. A grouch bag for the day you'd make your getaway."

"You gleaned all this information from spending a few minutes with my Greek alter ego?" Kuznetsov demanded. Getting impatient.

"Not exactly," Kraus admitted. "LAPD intelligence told me you've been called back. Kruschev's name is on the door now, but nothing's changed since Stalin. You couldn't just go AWOL. Defect? Sneak off to another country? They tracked Trotsky to Mexico. Even American soil wouldn't be a safe refuge. They took out Walter Krivitsky in Washington, D.C. Less than a mile from FBI headquarters, for chrissakes."

"Russian intelligence is a very efficient organization," Kuznetsov said in a caustic tone.

"Yes, they are. But if they could be convinced there was no one to look for?" Kraus said, nodding his head at the little room where Barlow was lying. "I met your Doppelganger outside when I left here yesterday. He told me about the dental work you arranged for him. Opened his mouth to show me. I'd seen that kind of work before, but I didn't recall it until a few hours ago. Know where I first saw an example of it? The mouth of a Russian officer my sergeant had just beaten the shit out of. Collapsed against a wall with his jaw hanging open. A lot of dull, gray steel metal work. Just like the fillings Barlow has. You must have looked high and low to find an American dentist who did that kind of work. Everything here is silver amalgam."

"And how could this benefit me in any possible way, Mr. Kraus?" Kuznetsov asked. Worry lines forming on his forehead. Not so cocky now.

"You handpicked that poor schmuck in there to be your stand-in double for a faked death. Lets you disappear without anyone coming to look for you. The dentistry has me guessing a fire or car accident ending with an exploding tank. The real victim would need to have authentic Russian dental work to pass muster. A clever guy like you wouldn't have any problem swapping out your own dental records for Barlow's in the consulate files."

"Evidently I'm not the only clever one here," Kuznetsov said. "Was that my only sin?"

"Not hardly," Kraus chuckled. "Yesterday you invited me to have a cup of tea with you. I passed, but you started to sip yours as I was leaving. You put a Hershey's square in your mouth to sip the tea through. You know what? The best Greek eatery in L.A. doesn't even have tea on their menu. They only drink it for tummy aches and such. Coffee is their hot beverage of choice. And they sweeten it with sugar, not sucking it through a piece of chocolate. You know who drinks their tea that way? Russians. Saw Ivans do it many times in Berlin."

"Fascinating lesson in cultural comparisons, Mr. Kraus," Kuznetsov said. An air of conclusiveness.

Kraus saw the Russian had subtly tightened his grip on the pistol and squared his shoulders a fraction. "*Getting ready to put a bullet in my skull,*" Kraus thought.

"But the worst mistake you made," Kraus continued, "the one that triggered all the other realizations, was this ..." He saw Kuznetsov relax his stance. Postponing the execution. The Russian wanted to hear about his biggest gaffe.

During their back and forth, Kraus had rocked on his hips slightly, shifting his weight from one leg to the other. Showing discomfort in his wounded left arm. He wasn't pretending. Every time he performed this maneuver, he shuffled his feet a half-inch or so closer to Kuznetsov. He was now within two feet of the Soviet's weapon. Inside Kuznetsov's "Widow's Circle". Time for Kraus to orchestrate a little misdirection of his own.

"Go on," Kuznetsov urged, nervously licking his lips despite himself.

"When you were playing the Greek merchant yesterday, you motioned me over to you like this," Kraus extended his left arm and made the palm-down squeezing motion. The Russian was so intent on learning about his biggest error, he didn't take notice of how close Kraus had brought his hand to the silenced pistol.

"I'd seen that gesture made by Russian soldiers dozens of times in Berlin," Kraus said, shaking off the painful memory of the Soviet major requesting his papers while in Charlotte's miserable basement flat. "I didn't recognize it yesterday morning. Later in the day I was at a Greek deli and the counter girl motioned for my attention. Know what gesture a real Greek makes when they call you over to them?"

Not waiting for a response, Kraus slowly bent his right hand towards his face and moved the forefinger gently to his lips, like shushing a rambunctious child. He saw that for the moment, Kuznetsov was mesmerized by the motion, as though he wanted to memorize how he'd blundered. The Russian ignored Kraus' left arm despite it still being very close to the weapon being held on him.

Kraus snapped his body forward, thrusting his already extended left hand past the silencer to apply a vise grip over the top strap portion of the revolver's frame, clamping his fingers hard on the gun's cylinder.

FIFTY-EIGHT

His left arm felt as though a hot branding iron had been laid on it, but Kraus held fast. He'd known his luck was holding when he first saw the silenced pistol Kuznetsov was gripping.

Revolvers fitted with silencers are a Hollywood fantasy. Gas and noise escape from the cylinder gap when a revolver is fired. Too far away from the barrel exit to allow a silencer to do its job. Only one revolver model in the world was designed for a suppressor. The one Kuznetsov was pointing at Kraus.

Kuznetsov flourished a Nagant M1895 revolver with a silencer attached. Kraus saw many of them in post-war Berlin. The action of the gun pushes the cylinder forward to make a seal with a barrel fitting, preventing the release of gas and sound through the cylinder gap, sending all of it through the barrel for the suppressor to muffle.

It was the favored firearm of Soviet Army teams carrying out what the Germans called *"Nacht und Nebel Aktions"*. Night and Fog Actions. Clandestine missions beginning with the identification of high-value Germans and others living in Berlin sectors outside the Russian one. Once pinpointed, these targets were kidnapped or assassinated in bold, nighttime actions.

Kraus confiscated several Nagant M1895's during his time as a Constabulary police officer in Berlin. He was very familiar with the weapon.

Kuznetsov had a double-action model. Standard-issue for Soviet officers. The trigger was set farther forward in the trigger guard. Had it been a single-action model, the hammer would likely have been cocked and the cylinder already pushed into firing position. The grip Kraus had on the cylinder wouldn't matter. It would already have been primed to be fired. The Russian would have only had to wrench the barrel back towards Kraus and pull the trigger.

The double-action model Kuznetsov held could be fired by simply pulling the trigger, which would cock the hammer, push the cylinder forward and drop the hammer in one smooth sequence. However, if the cylinder was unable to move, the gun wouldn't fire. The entire action would be frozen. Kraus had immobilized the cylinder by clenching it and the gun frame. He swung his right fist at Kuznetsov's face, but the Russian had instantly realized there was no chance of firing the pistol. He'd immediately released the pistol grip and hopscotched backwards. Kraus only managed to land a feeble, glancing blow on the Russian's retreating shoulder.

Kraus was left with sole control of the revolver, but it was pointed backwards in his grip and the balance was awkward. He fumbled his hold while trying to reposition it in his hand. The front-weight of the suppressor caused it to pinwheel out of Kraus' hand and fall to the cement floor with a clatter. Kraus looked up to see Kuznetsov had recovered and was taking a long, aggressive stride back towards him. A hypodermic syringe was in his hand, thumb on the plunger. The Russian was bringing the syringe down at him in a hammer strike motion. Kraus figured the spike was loaded with a knockout drug. Most likely a Hank Williams Cocktail. A chloral hydrate and morphine mixture. Likely the same stuff that put Mason Barlow out on the army cot a few feet away.

Kraus knew he was done for if that needle squirted its payload into him. The drug might not immediately hit him full force, but he'd probably only have ten minutes or so to incapacitate Kuznetsov, get away and make himself safe. Not nearly enough time.

Kuznetsov came within an inch or so of hitting home with his first strike. Kraus intercepted the descending wrist with his left hand and gripped it harder than he'd held the Nagant's cylinder. He shuffled backwards, trying to move out of the arc of the Russian's hand. Kuznetsov pivoted inside the arc and drove his left fist into Kraus' ribs.

"*Christ, he's strong for a little man,*" Kraus thought while pressing his bent right elbow against his side to ward off a second rib shot from Kuznetsov. Instead, the Soviet tried to spin away and twist loose from Kraus' grip on the syringe hand. Kraus thought that to an onlooker it would have resembled an especially rough Apache dance. It was about to get rougher.

In turning away from Kraus, Kuznetsov's body became perpendicular to Kraus. Keeping his grip on the Russian's raised right wrist, Kraus pivoted, planted his right calf behind the Russian's right leg and pushed him over the leg to the ground. A standard judo *Waza* throw. Kuznetsov hit the concrete floor with a grunt as Kraus straddled the Russian's body.

Kraus still gripped the Russian's right wrist and now turned the direction of the needle towards Kuznetsov. He hurried before it occurred to Kuznetsov to empty the syringe. It looked to be a heavier-gauge needle and gave Kraus confidence in his next move. The Soviet's eyes widened as Kraus drove the needle through his clothing and into his left shoulder, close to the base of his neck. He used the flat of his hand to press the plunger all the way to the hilt of the syringe barrel.

"Got you now, Comrade," Kraus growled. He moved away from the prone Russian and kicked him square on the side of the head. "Stay down, Sleeping Beauty, while your poisoned apple takes effect." Kraus stepped over to the little closet and yanked the power cord out of the Electrolux canister. He rolled Kuznetsov over and used the electrical cord to bind his hands. Kraus then undid his belt and wound it tightly around the man's ankles, cinching the buckle with a savage tug.

Kraus looked around the office while he waited for Kuznetsov to pass out completely. Mason Barlow was still alive. He was dressed in quality clothing. Things that were recognizable as being part of Kuznetsov's wardrobe. He only wore socks. Kuznetsov had needed the homely shoes as lures before lacing them on Barlow's feet. The shoes would complete the ensemble and reinforce the conclusion that the dead Barlow was actually Kuznetsov.

He searched the office desk drawers one by one. The center drawer below the desk surface held what he was looking for. He took the items out and laid them on the desk.

Next, he slid the bowling ball bag out from the desk knee hole. It had some heft to it. Kraus hoisted it onto the desktop and adjusted the lamp for better light. It was made from heavy, tan-colored canvas. Looked almost like an old-time dewlap bag. He opened the bag to find it filled to the top with neatly bound stacks of U.S. currency. All fifty-dollar bills. One hundred bills per stack. Fifty stacks total.

Two hundred and fifty thousand bucks. Kraus let loose a long, low whistle and smiled. Ollie was never wrong about a swindle. He removed ten of the stacks and jammed them into one of the paper sacks Galani Surplus used to bag customer purchases. The bag went into the center drawer of the desk. Kraus wedged the items he'd first removed from the desk drawer into the bowling bag and zipped it closed. He stepped over to check on Kuznetsov. Out cold.

Kraus loped over to where he'd parked the Russian operative's car. He drove it to the Galani Surplus space and parked it next to the van. All the conflict Kraus had engaged in over the past twenty-four hours had taken its toll. His arms felt like cooked strands of Spaetzle noodles. He struggled to get the bodies of Applebaum and Balabanov out of the car trunk and into the Galani office. He looked at the sky. Still pitch black at one-thirty in the morning, but time was running short. Still no sign of anyone in the complex, but who knew how early some of these outfits got going?

All three of the prone figures were positioned side by side on the floor of the office. Kraus had to high-step over them to navigate the office. It was like an Army training obstacle course.

He picked up the Nagant M1895 and propped Balabanov's head steady. He aimed the silencer muzzle near the depression the Monkey Paw had left on the corpse's temple. He fired a round into Balabanov's skull. No exit wound. The suppressor did its job. The shot sounded no louder than a stapler toppling off the desktop onto the floor. The entry wound and powder burns masked the Monkey Paw's exterior damage. It wouldn't fool an LAPD coroner, but Kraus didn't think this body would end up on the slab of an L.A. morgue. From what he'd seen in Berlin, the Russians wouldn't be surprised by any degree of brutality if he was autopsied by his own people.

Kraus wiped the Nagant, held it with a rag and worked it into Applebaum's right hand, pressing the pad of the hood's index finger against the trigger face. He'd already put the trench knife in Balabanov's dead hand. Kraus knew he was leaving behind a tableau cluttered with confusing clues, but that would work in his favor. No logical thread to start pulling on. Now the car Kuznetsov had parked in the warehouse needed scrutiny. Kraus opened all the doors, the hood and trunk lid. Went over the car twice with his flashlight. Butler said Kuznetsov was some sort of engineer. A talented one based on what he saw in the sedan.

Kuznetsov had rigged up a very sophisticated explosive apparatus. A short-length timer controlled the trigger. Maybe five or six seconds. The accelerant looked to be several full vodka bottles. He imagined they were fortified with kerosene. Higher flashpoint than gasoline, but not as detectable. Kraus easily figured out the method to arm and set the firebomb.

Kraus didn't know where Kuznetsov planned to stage the accident, but he himself had the perfect place in mind. He hoisted Kuznetsov into the passenger seat of the car, leaving his hands and feet tied.

Now for Barlow. Kraus couldn't just leave Barlow to be found with a muddled head and wearing stolen clothes. If the cops kept control of the scene, Barlow would be the easy suspect. He'd be in prison faster than you could say "fall guy".

Barlow was from the streets. He wasn't so civilized by his time with Kuznetsov that he'd have forgotten how to survive. Kuznetsov probably forced Barlow at gunpoint to put the clothes on, then injected him with a Mickey Finn. He'd know the intention was to kill him. His instinct would be to run and stay quiet.

Kraus thought for a moment. He took a set of keys from a hook by the door. A little tag dangling from the top of one key read "Van". He pocketed the keys and started to put Barlow into a fireman's lift. He had a thought and paused. He grabbed the ugly shoes from the closet and tied the laces together. He hung the shoes around Barlow's neck. Before lifting him, Kraus pried two-dozen fifties from the bowling bag and stuffed them into the toe of one of the shoes.

Putting Barlow into the fireman's carry, he took him out to the Galani Surplus van, where he laid the would-be victim down on the floor of the cargo section. Barlow would wake up soon, find the money while putting on the shoes and make a beeline back to Skid Row. Hopefully even further.

Kraus wiped down the van, the car he'd driven to Galani Surplus, and the inside of the office and warehouse. He retrieved his automatic and tucked the bowling ball bag onto the rear seat of Kuznetsov's car. Kraus opened the bay door, drove the car out, closed and locked up. He took one last look and drove away into the darkness of the night and his own intentions.

FIFTY-NINE

Driving up Sunset towards Will Rogers State Park took Kraus back almost twenty-five years. Back then the property was still Will Rogers' private estate. His father had been contracted for some finish work on a remodel of part of the main house. The great humorist was so pleased with his craftsmanship, he invited Kraus' father to bring his family to a picnic and watch a polo match being held on an upcoming Sunday.

His father had casually mentioned Leslie Howard was going to be playing polo that day. Kraus and his brother, Rudi, were so excited. The siblings had convinced themselves Howard would be dressed as "The Scarlet Pimpernel" in all his swashbuckling glory. The big day arrived, and they were nearly inconsolable when they saw Leslie Howard dressed merely in traditional jockey garb, barely recognizable with his helmet on. Another dream crushed by the Hollywood threshing machine. At least the fried chicken was good.

His thoughts snapped back to the present as he made a quick U-turn into a turnout past a hairpin curve. The spot was just beyond the southern boundary of the park. Almost three in the morning and there was no traffic. He'd met only one car on the drive up Sunset. This part of the boulevard was on a steep rise. No headlamps showed in either direction.

Kraus pulled the still-unconscious Kuznetsov across the front bench seat of the KGB officer's car. He untied the Russian's hands and unspooled his belt from around his ankles. Kraus reached into the rear seat and removed the bowling ball bag, setting it near the edge of the road. He restarted the engine and stood next to the opened driver's door. Reflecting on the moment. The occasional croak of a Pacific chorus frog was the only break in an uneasy quiet.

What he was preparing to do seemed cold-blooded. But this man was just as ruthless. More so. Blackmail, threats, espionage, assaults and murder. Kraus believed justice was a balancing force. Idealists believe the courtroom, with its symbolic scale, is the best balancing tool. His years patrolling L.A. streets and bringing order to a war-torn Berlin taught him that was often untrue. Or feasible. Kuznetsov needed to answer for his crimes. If his life was spared, he'd never see the inside of an American courtroom.

The brief gut check confirmed his conviction that this was the just thing to do.

Kraus took a deep breath. He reached his foot into the driver's side footwell, depressed the clutch pedal and levered the shift arm into first. Balancing on his left foot, he bent over the unconscious Russian, armed the makeshift incendiary device and activated the timer. He slowly let out the clutch and hopped away from the car, slamming the door closed as it lurched forward. Kraus gave the rear end a final shove as the dark sedan careened off the edge of the sixty-foot embankment.

The nose of the sedan cleared the edge of the road. Momentum kept the car moving forward, its frame sliding on the dirt and gravel of the shoulder's edge. Then gravity took over. Kraus watched as the nose of the vehicle slammed down on the slight slope of the drop. The hood flew open while the force and weight of the rear put the car into an end-over summersault. The car then slewed into more of a horizontal position, rolling sideways to where the slope bottom met the little service road below. The sedan burst into flames a moment before it slammed into the ground. Kraus felt the slap of heat from the initial blast.

"Ollie," Kraus said, looking up into the dark sky, "whatever pub you're sitting in right now, I hope you saw that tumbril roll by just now."

He fished his pocketknife from a pants pocket, crossed the road, and cut a small branch off a eucalyptus tree bordering the inside lane. He used the leafy end to brush away all footprints he'd made while staging the accident. Kraus stepped back and quickly scanned the work with his flashlight. Good enough. The hairpin curve was still very wet from the rainfall. It wouldn't be difficult to believe a car ran off the side in the dark of night.

The car fire raged on. The tarry smell of burned tire rubber wafted up from the crash site. Kraus gazed down at the car. Kuznetsov had remained in the car during its descent. The impact did not eject his body. The car interior was an inferno. Angry flames from the blaze stabbed through the shattered glass, as though frantic to escape a destruction of their own making.

The plaintive coo of a mourning dove floated out of the nearby trees.

"*Fitting*," Kraus thought. Time to get moving. He tossed the tree branch over the side, grabbed the bowling ball bag and started his trek overland to a neighborhood a few miles south of the park.

"Heading back to the barn?" Kraus asked a milkman who was removing his carry racks from the back of his van. "I could use a lift."

Kraus had hiked from the crash site down to Rustic Creek and continued crossing overland to the edge of the tony neighborhood bordering the Riviera Country Club. He kept watch from a stand of trees near the end of a cul de sac. It was still an hour before daybreak, but a woodpecker in the little grove began pecking away as a Carnation milk van braked to a stop near his hiding spot.

The milkman looked up at the sound of Kraus' question.

"Mark Partlow," Kraus said, extending his hand in a greeting. He held a folded ten-dollar bill in his palm. Kraus could have taken a fifty from his bag, but he didn't want to leave that strong of an impression.

"I'm heading back in after getting these last houses done," the milkman said. "But it's against company policy," he continued, eyeing the ten-spot, "unless you sit in the back." He winked, taking the bill and pushing it into the breast pocket of his shirt.

The "barn" Kraus referred to was the big Carnation building on Wilshire, not far from his office. The residential delivery guys returned their vans to the lot, turned in their paperwork and headed home from there. Kraus cleared a comfortable spot to sit near the rear of the van, parked the bowling bag between his bent knees and waited. The delivery man trotted back, the empties he carried back tinkled in the metal carrier rack.

"Christ," the milkman said, "that last house?" He pointed to a large Tudor style home on the curve of the cul de sac. "They have a fucking cat. Name's Johan, of all things. Goddamned thing nips my ankle every time I drop an order off. Like he's mad I don't leave a bowl of fresh cream or somethin'." The Carnation man rubbed his ankle.

"Sounds like a character," Kraus said.

"That's one word for it," the milkman grumbled. "Fuckin' thing looks Satanic. It has different colored eyes."

"Heterochromia. Like Gracie Allen," Kraus laughed.

"Huh," the milkman said as he shut the van doors. "Thought she was Jewish. Hey, those two bottles of chocolate milk next to you were extras. Have one if you're thirsty."

"Thanks," Kraus said, realizing he was starving. He pried the foil cap off one of the bottles and took a few gulps.

"Early morning," the van driver said, "you get stranded out here?"

"Spending the night with a lady friend in that big Spanish Colonial nearer to the course," Kraus said. He didn't know the neighborhood, but there's always a big Spanish Colonial near a Los Angeles country club. "An actress. Her husband came home a day early."

"Ahh," the milkman crooned in an understanding tone. Man of the world. "Lots of Hollywood types out here. Anyone I would know?"

Kraus thought for a moment. "You know who Rhonda Fleming is?"

SIXTY

Full sunrise was a few minutes away by the time Kraus rolled up to the Bean Slot. The Christmas lights still twinkled through the windows. The streets and sidewalks had returned to their bone-dry condition. Earlier, he'd ridden the MCL bus from the Carnation building the seven blocks to Detroit Avenue. Near his office. A cab ride from there to his home. The taxi ride established a verifiable timeline alibi.

Hayashigawa's Wednesday night poker games were marathon affairs. The game didn't break up until dawn. The Bean Slot owner always cooked breakfast for the exhausted gamblers. Kraus knocked on the locked front door. The affable proprietor opened it himself.

"Gordy," Hayashigawa exclaimed, "you're among the living. Come in. Come in."

Tradition held firm. The tavern smelled like a pancake house. Bacon was sizzling on the griddle behind the bar. A large glass beaker, half-full of batter, sat next to a bottle of Log Cabin maple syrup near the fry top. The metallic snap of a popping toaster came from somewhere close. Five haggard-looking poker players sat at the rear tables, working on their breakfast plates. A fresh pot of coffee sat in the middle of each table. "*My Foolish Heart*" was playing on the jukebox. Billy Eckstine, not Gordon Jenkins.

"Any trouble last night?" Kraus asked.

"Only with the cards," Hayashigawa laughed.

Anna was seated at the bar wearing a baseball sweatshirt and jeans, nibbling on a corner of toast. She looked up to make eye contact with Kraus at the same moment he saw her.

"Gordy!" she cried out. She leapt from the stool and rushed towards Kraus. "Oh my God, you're okay. You're okay. Jesus, I was so worried."

They came together in the middle of the barroom floor and wrapped their arms around each other in a fierce embrace. Anna buried her face into the crook of Kraus' neck, hiding her tears. Kraus once read a Jake LaMotta interview. The champ said the reason two boxers hugged one another at the end of a bout wasn't about who won or lost. Both fighters were just so happy it was over. Kraus now fully understood what LaMotta meant as he hugged Anna tighter.

"Looks like you're an Angels fan now," Kraus said as they broke their hug, and he got a look at what Anna was wearing.

"Oh, yeah," Anna laughed. "Dave gave me this after I spilled mustard on my blouse."

Hayashigawa had dozens of souvenir pullovers and hats he'd bought at Wrigley Field. The Angels had a spectacular season. Their beer-swilling first baseman, Steve Bilko, won the Pacific Coast League Triple Crown. The team won the PCL pennant. Bean Slot patrons, intoxicated by the team's success as much as the booze, would buy team clothing to wear while the games blared from the Bean Slot radio set.

Kraus almost blurted out that they'd have to take in some games next season, but knew Anna might not be sticking around. He held his tongue. "Ready to get going?" Kraus asked.

"Yeah," Anna said. "Hey, thanks guys," she shouted to the men eating their breakfasts.

"Anna," Hayashigawa said, giving her a hug, "come back anytime. You're a Bean Slotter now."

"They just want a chance to win back some of their money," Anna teased.

"Dave, thank you," Kraus said while shaking Hayashigawa's hand.

"Don't mention it, Gordy," Hayashigawa said.

"Is everything really okay?" Anna asked as they drove away.

"Pretty much," Kraus said. He didn't elaborate. His grim tone said it all. Anna didn't press for details. "Lester Fox is still a wild card. For now. Which brings me to the next thing."

"Oh," Anna said. "Is he where we're headed?"

"No," Kraus said. "Austie left me a note at the house. Louise went into labor. Rudi's at the hospital and my mom is at their place. Bustling around. Nervous as a hen. Austie asked if you could come and stay over tonight. Everything that's happened has made her a little jumpy and she doesn't want to be alone."

"Gordy," Anna objected, "I don't need a babysitter. Lester Fox doesn't scare me."

"I know," Kraus said, "I saw you handle him the day we met. It's Fox who should be scared of you. It's my sister who needs a sitter. She needs some moral support and I have to tie up some loose ends. Okay?"

After dropping Anna off at his mom's place, Kraus drove home and caught a few hours of sleep. He woke up, showered, shaved and put on a fresh set of clothes. Both his arms hurt like the dickens, but a few aspirins made it bearable. He began his errands. The Desilu Studios guard recognized Kraus and waved him through the gate. The place boiled with activity. Every sound stage was in use. Barely two weeks left before the long Christmas weekend. Every production was hustling to get their holiday episodes in the can.

He found his way to the little office Delbert Blanchard occupied. The door was open, and the purchasing agent was hunched over his desk making ledger entries. Kraus lightly rapped his knuckles on the door.

"Mr. Kraus," Bowers said. Surprise turned to alarm. "Please come in."

Kraus walked into the office, closing the door behind him. He placed a manila envelope over the open ledger on Bowers' desk. "Here you go," he said.

Blanchard picked up the envelope like it was ticking. He finally pried open the flap and peered into it, leafing through the contents without removing them. "Is it over, then?" Bowers asked.

"This episode is," Kraus said. "The negatives are in a little white envelope at the bottom. Just don't get hamstrung again," he warned. "You might not be so lucky next time."

"There won't be a next time. Believe me," Blanchard said with a heavy sigh. "God, what a relief. Mr. Kraus, how much do I owe you?"

"Just stay out of trouble," Kraus said. "You know, when I was a kid, my mom used to drag us to church. Lutheran. Very German. I remember one sermon the minister delivered. He explained that the word, 'secret', had a pedigree linking it to the words, 'seduction' and 'excrement'. A powerful word. Entices people to look closer at something they'd rather not see. I've found this principle is a cornerstone of the investigation business."

"What are you trying to say, Mr. Kraus?" Bowers asked.

"Remember, that envelope gave the blackmailer power because there was a market for the secret. Secrets are irresistible commodities," Kraus answered. "You know what Oscar Wilde did whenever someone threatened to blackmail him with indiscreet letters he'd written?"

"No. What did he do?" Blanchard asked.

"He published them," Kraus said. "Stripped the power from the secret."

"Yeah," Blanchard said in a fatalistic tone, "and look how he ended up."

"*The kid had a point,*" Kraus thought as he left the studio.

———◆———

"I need to talk to Andy and Moretti," Kraus told the bartender. The Cockatoo looked like all the decorations for the Hollywood Santa Claus Lane Parade were being stored in the restaurant. Christmas adornments reigned supreme. Two Christmas trees sagging under the weight of glass ornaments. Miles of tinsel garland. Strings of bright Christmas lights. Lococo didn't do anything in half-measures.

Kraus was ushered through the side door into the gambling hall. Here the Christmas garnish was understated. Almost non-existent. Lococo watched Kraus looking around.

"Yeah," Lococo said, "don't want a lot of decorations back here. Makes the plungers guilty about risking their gift money." Moretti walked over from the other end of the bar and stood next to his boss.

"Good thinkin'," Kraus said. "*Always an angle with this guy,*" Kraus thought.

"What can we do for you, Gordy?" Lococo asked. "You had quite a time Tuesday night."

"That wasn't the half of it," Kraus said. "Which is why I dropped by." He withdrew a thick envelope from his inside pocket and handed it to Lococo.

"What's this?" Lococo asked.

"It's the dough Moretti said Ollie was in to you for," Kraus said. "He didn't get a chance to work it off, so I'm carrying his weight on it. There's the principle and the vig."

Lococo cocked his head in a *whaddya know* expression. He passed the envelope to Moretti, who opened it and thumbed through the bills. "Why?" Lococo asked.

"I don't want any of Ollie's debts to land back on Violet. She's getting out of the hospital next week and will have enough on her hands without that sort of thing."

"Fair enough," Lococo said. "But you know we wouldn't do that to her."

"I know," Kraus said, "but a little goodwill all around never hurts."

"There's three grand more than what's called for," Moretti said.

"Yeah," Kraus said. "I was getting to that. The guy you told me about the other day. Lester Fox. He's still around town and I'd appreciate it if someone with an air of authority told him L.A. isn't his kind of town. Maybe Frisco or Portland would be healthier for him."

"What about the mug he runs with?" Moretti asked.

"Fox is a lone wolf right now," Kraus said.

"Fox. Wolf. Good joke," Moretti laughed, then weighed Kraus' words. "I see," Moretti said. A tone of respect. He looked at his boss. Lococo bobbed his chin. "Done. Frankly, it'll be a pleasure. I didn't like the little shit."

Kraus had already phoned the other people Kuznetsov was blackmailing. Told them the heat was off. Christmas coming early.

He had one more stop to make on his way home.

Once home, Kraus sat on the couch drinking a cold Oly right from the bottle. He took a mental inventory of the last few days. Five people dead. One person hospitalized. No more blackmail threats, but the victims were still as vulnerable as they had been. Was it too little at too big of a price tag?

Last week, he'd seen justice as offering little more than a vague feeling of relief. He'd shifted his perspective. Ollie's murderer paid back. Anna was safe. Violet was on the mend.

Both could move on to better lives. While the blackmail victims were still easy targets, they were arguably wiser. Justice? No. Topsoil for the roots of justice? Maybe.

That was enough for Kraus.

EPILOGUE

"Ebeneezer Benny," a deep, sepulchral voice boomed. "Will you choose to devote your life spreading goodwill to man, spending your wealth helping others and honoring the Spirit of Christmas? Or would you rather hoard your money? Never put a farthing towards the benefit of others and dooming your soul to eternal damnation?"

A long pause. Titters of laughter from the radio speaker. "Ebeneezer Benny?" the voice prompted.

"I'm thinking. I'm thinking," Jack Benny cried out in the mulish whine he used when playing the skinflint. It was said he wasn't acting.

Gales of laughter through the radio now. Bob Crane, the hilarious new KNX morning radio host, had Jack Benny as his guest that morning. It was the Christmas season and the "Jack Benny as Scrooge" sketch was the best Kraus had heard yet.

Now, Jack Benny's Scrooge stammered a promise of a raise for Rochester, his clerk. Eddie "Rochester" Anderson, Benny's longtime sidekick, voicing the clerk role, could barely keep from laughing as the schtick continued. Kraus laughed out loud while he made his breakfast.

The doorbell rang. Kraus dried his hands on a dish towel while moving to the front door. "*What now*?" Kraus thought.

"Hello, Gordy," Gino Laveroni said, "what were you chortling at in there?"

"Radio show. New guy on KNX," Kraus said. "Funny as hell."

Laveroni didn't wait for an invitation to walk through the door.

"The LAPD three times in a week. Neighbors are going to start talking," Kraus said.

"The neighbors don't need cop visits to start talking about you, Gordy," Laveroni said. He sat down on the leather wingback chair in the living room. "You've had quite a few days."

"Is this going to be another one of them?" Kraus asked, taking a seat on his couch.

"Depends," Laveroni said. "Got called out on a strange one yesterday morning. Had an alert out on a mook. Louis Applebaum. Snatched an old lady's purse at Bullock's Wilshire couple of weeks ago. Broke her arm."

"You put out an alert on that? On pickpocket detail now, Gino?" Kraus asked.

"Victim was the maiden aunt of a commissioner," Laveroni explained, "went high-profile in a hurry. Pawnshop squad found where he'd hocked her gold compact. Got lucky. Pawnbroker was from Detroit. Remembered seeing the guy in some smokers. Legion Hall bouts. A stumblebum."

"So you got his name. Nabbed him yet?" Kraus asked.

"Good as. Got a call from a baffled Torrance desk sergeant. They'd gotten a disturbance report from one of those small industrial parks. Guy pounding on the locked doors. Yelling for the owner. Radio car checked it out."

"What was baffling?" Kraus asked.

"The scene," Laveroni said. "Cop arrives. No guy in sight. Gets the park manager to open the door. Had to cut the padlock on the bay door. Two stiffs inside. Both looked like ex-pugs. One took a bullet to the temple. Other one was Applebaum. Throat sliced."

"What happened?" Kraus asked.

"Don't know. Torrance P.D. wouldn't touch the scene. Car outside had diplomatic plates. They did run Applebaum's I.D., saw my alert and tossed the hot potato to me. Hell, I didn't want to touch it. But I had to confirm it was really Applebaum to close out the purse snatching beef."

"So, you're the hero," Kraus said.

"The commissioner's off our backs," Laveroni admitted. "Here's the thing, though. The bigger guy? The one with a slug in his brain? He's holding a wicked-looking trench knife. Applebaum? He's holding a silenced Russian pistol. Silenced. Russian," Laveroni emphasized. "Who did who first? Applebaum gets his throat cut, then puts one in the other guy's noggin? Or the opposite?"

"Chicken or the egg mystery," Kraus said. "Third person? Drug deal gone sideways?"

"Good enough explanation as any," Laveroni admitted. "Applebaum had a full artillery kit in his pocket. Hypes, a length of surgical tubing and a couple bindles of black dragon. Found twenty-grand in a desk drawer. Neat bundles of fifties."

"*Twenty grand,*" Kraus thought, "*pretty heavy street tax.*"

"State Department types took over the scene not long after I got there," Laveroni went on. "Word came down they turned it over to the Russian consulate. It was their car outside. We might get Applebaum's corpse someday. Might not. But you know what else I found?"

"What's that," Kraus said, hoping his sudden apprehension stayed in his stomach and off his face.

"Applebaum had this in his pocket," Laveroni held up a limp strip of cheap newsprint paper. Dampness had smeared it, but the printing was still legible. "Metro bus transfer. Wednesday's date. The Hollywood line to the Adams line, which runs a couple blocks from your front door."

"Runs a couple of blocks from lots of people's front doors," Kraus countered.

"Yeah," Laveroni said, "but not every person fits the description of the man who took a knife away from Applebaum's partner in the May Company parking lot. Coming to the rescue of a woman who fits Anna Bjorkquist's description."

"Like you always say," Kraus said, "it's a small town."

"Look, Gordy," Laveroni said, sounding annoyed, "I'm too tired to sit here and play pattycake with you. You have any ties to this Torrance thing? More payback for Ollie?"

"Don't know what you're talking about," Kraus said. "The brass closed Ollie's case already. Don't think it would be politic to try and reopen it. Just when you've won the gratitude of a police commissioner." "*And thirty-thousand more reasons,*" Kraus thought but didn't voice.

"Okay, smart guy," Laveroni said. "Gordy, you're my friend. I came here to see if there was anything you needed to tell me. Anything I could protect you from. But so help me, if you're hiding anything and it blows back on me, I'll hook you up myself."

"Nothing to hide, Gino," Kraus said, thinking about the bowling ball bag he'd stashed in the secret cabinet. "Get you anything to drink or eat?"

"No, thanks," Laveroni said. "I'm swimming in paperwork needs finishing before the weekend." He got up to leave and looked Kraus in the eyes. "Gordy, tread carefully." He balled up the little bus transfer slip between his thumb and index finger and let it drop to the coffee table.

"Thanks, Gino," Kraus said.

Kraus was putting a slice of bread in his toaster when he heard the familiar chug of his sister's car, then Austie shouting to her "Uncle Gino." Some laughter and unintelligible banter. The sound of both cars driving away.

"Hello, there," Anna chirped as she breezed in the door.

"Stork arrived yet?" Kraus asked.

"Still circling," Anna said. "Anytime now, according to your mom." She examined the bread slice that popped out of the toaster. "Is your power off?" she asked as she waved the alabaster white bread slice.

"Very funny," Kraus said while cracking eggs into a bowl. "I wrote Santa for a new one."

"What's on the agenda, today?" Anna asked, putting two slices of bread into the toaster.

"Eating a delicious breakfast and heading over to Manhattan Beach Motors," Kraus said.

"Oh," Anna said. Suddenly sad. Facing the inevitable. "I guess it's time for me to pack up and get going. I should have some money left after I pay what I owe them. Would you drop me at Union Station after we're done there?"

"Anna," Kraus said, taking a deep breath, "I don't want you to leave town. I want you to stay. Make a life here. I like the idea of you being around."

"Gordy," Anna said. "I like you. But I'm not interested in a fully committed relationship. With anyone. I have really loved this break you gave me. I'm going to quit the grift. I've spent so much time being someone else, I want to figure out who I am. On my own."

"I *was* talking about you, not us. I'm no more ready to commit to a relationship than you are. But you can go straight in L.A. just as easily as anywhere else," Kraus said.

"I've run too many scams in this town. One or the other is bound to catch up to me," Anna insisted.

"Well, if you're set on leaving town, okay. But you can drive to a new city in your Studebaker. We're going to Manhattan Beach Motors to sign the papers. Arranged it yesterday."

"Gordy!" Anna exclaimed. "One of your loose ends?"

"That's right. After that, we're going to drive around and pay restitution to each one of the would-be renters you bilked. Square all that away."

"What if one of them wants to turn me in?" Anna asked.

"We're going to the Redwood tonight. Retain a good attorney for you. Get everything put to bed."

"You've got it all figured out, don't you?" Anna said. "If I stay in L.A., what will I do for work? Where will I live?"

"Same decisions you'd face anywhere you went. I think the studios are always looking for people who know the difference between a definite and indefinite article," Kraus said. Anna giggled. "I know most of the studio people. I'll ask around."

"At the Redwood tonight, do we really swing a dead cat? Is that some sort of ritual, like Masons giving pennies to new members?" Anna teased.

"Don't be ridiculous," Kraus said. He held the mixing bowl in the crook of his arm, his fork making a wet, rattling noise as he whisked the eggs. "Just in case, though, keep your eyes peeled for roadkill while we're driving around today."

"Gordy, we're about to eat," Anna scolded. "Poor cats."

"Say," Kraus said, "Maybe you can get your old place back at that bungalow court."

"You'd like that, wouldn't you?" Anna smiled. "Me in one unit and that little strumpet in another. Your own little harem."

"I'm curious how her career is going," Kraus protested in a mock innocence.

"Which career?" Anna laughed.

"Hey, I'll give you my mattress as a housewarming gift," Kraus said while pouring his egg mixture into a skillet on the stove.

"That'd be a literal housewarming present. First thing I'd do is set it on fire," Anna tittered.

"I thought I'd already done that the other night," Kraus teased.

"This is what you did to that mattress, mister," Anna said, holding up the two warmish, light tan bread slices the toaster had served up.

"Room for improvement, you're saying," Kraus chuckled.

The two sat down to breakfast, laughing and teasing one another. Anna looked genuinely happy and hopeful. Relaxed. Secure in the knowledge she had friends whom she could trust. Maybe for the first time in her adult life.

That look was better than justice, Kraus thought.

ACKNOWLEDGEMENTS

It takes a village to write a novel. Particularly a historical whodunit. Historical fiction writers of every stripe stand on the shoulders of many others, past and present. I owe a debt of thanks to so many, it would take another book to adequately credit everyone. But there are certain people I do wish to single out and recognize for their particularly valuable contributions.

I wish to thank (in no particular order):

Joe Mayer, one of the twins who portrayed "Little Ricky" on "I Love Lucy". (Although Keith Thibodeaux eventually portrayed the older "Little Ricky" character, Joe and his twin brother, Michael, actually logged much more screen time than their successor.) Joe was generous enough to spend a hot July 4th afternoon with me. We sat in a cool tavern in Independence, Oregon while he shared many first-person accounts of the activities on the "I Love Lucy" sets. Many of his revelations were used in the depiction of Desilu Studios in *Red Sockets*.

Mollie Jensen, former Dallas, Texas and McMinnville, Oregon police officer, shared with me many insights and experiences from her life as a police officer. Her input on police procedure and the ways police officers see the world in their law enforcement role was - and will continue to be - invaluable source material for *Red Sockets* and future novels.

Jim Dye (deceased), one of the prominent electronic distribution pioneers in Southern California. I worked for Jim at the distributor he founded for several years and benefited from many of his first-hand accounts of the very early days of the electronics industry.

Frank Wyle (deceased), an iconic pioneer and one of the true visionaries of electronic distribution - and a real character. During the time I worked for Frank, he and several of the more-senior members of his executive staff added to my knowledge of the beginnings of the electronics industry. (The actor, Noah Wyle, is one of Frank's grandchildren. As it happens, producer-director Jon Avnet is the grandson of Avnet founder, Charles Avnet.)

Jack Berman (deceased), another true pioneer in the Southern California electronics distribution world. Jack was a talented and lively raconteur who - in addition to founding and operating a successful manufacturer's representative firm - taught a comprehensive sales training program for the electronics industry. Several of his stories found their way into *Red Sockets* with little alteration. Jack was a true philosopher. His teachings changed my life in many important ways.

Rhonda Fleming (deceased), arguably the queen of American *film noir*. She makes a cameo appearance in *Red Sockets*. Her husband, Dr. Lewis Morrill, delivered me, and - frankly - saved my eyesight, if not my life. How I came to enjoy a friendship with Rhonda Fleming throughout my adult life is a story that can be read on the Raw Noir website. (rawnoirpress.com) Her stories of 1940s and 1950s Hollywood - and the *film noir* genre in particular - became priceless memories that ended up serving as background material for *Red Sockets* and upcoming novels.

Sam Ross (deceased), whom this book is dedicated to. Sam was the single most influential person in my life as a writer. He was my instructor at UC Irvine for several years. Sam became my mentor and close friend. Among so many fine books, screenplays and television scripts, Sam wrote the novel, *He Ran All the Way*, a seminal work in the *noir* style. The novel was adapted by Dalton Trumbo (under a pseudonym) into a film of the same name, starring John Garfield (his final film) and Shelley Winters. The film is recognized as one of the finest examples of American *film noir*. Every page I write includes something Sam Ross taught me. I plan on writing much more about Sam Ross on the rawnoirpress.com website.

I was born in Los Angeles and grew up in Redondo Beach and Orange County, California. Although much of how I describe 1950's Los Angeles comes from my own memory, no one person can do complete justice to the city and the time period.

I am a history lover and had a lot of fun preparing for the creation of *Red Sockets*. Several books stand out as part of the research I conducted to capture the full flavor of 1940s and 1950s Los Angeles:

"*The Long Winding Road of Harry Raymond: A Detective's Journey Down the Mean Streets of Pre-War Los Angeles*", by Patrick Jennings, was a wonderful window into 1930s and 1940s Los Angeles in general and the LAPD of that time period specifically.

"*The Gangs of Los Angeles*" by William Dunn also provided a great deal of background on 1940s and 1950s Los Angeles along with a lot of detail about the criminal element in those times.

I had zero personal experience of post-war Berlin, but I did have a treasured source of first-hand information. Over the years, my Aunt Irm, a German who married my Uncle Clifford and came to the United States as a war bride, provided me with a treasure trove of information about wartime and post-war Germany as well as a lot of amusing anecdotes about the challenges of acclimating to her adopted United States. Her son and my cousin, Rudi, became the brother I always wished he was in *Red Sockets*. My family members will recognize the scene in *Red Sockets* in which Gordy's mother rants about the difficulties of learning English in 1930's Germany. This was an oft-told gripe of my Aunt Irm.

For more post-war Berlin research, I turned to Giles Macdonough's comprehensive work, *"After the Reich: The Brutal History of the Allied Occupation"*. It is a masterful overview of a difficult period in world history.

Facebook and YouTube are in many ways like time machines. I'd like to thank the creators of a few Facebook pages and YouTube channels for a continuous stream of photos, videos and snippets of obscure knowledge that provided me with a rich foundation of visual content and information that allowed me to build so much texture into the world of *Red Sockets*:

Alison Martino's *Vintage Los Angeles* Facebook pages are a continuously updated, living archive of Los Angeles' rich past. *Red Sockets* would have been so much harder to write without Alison's voluminous collection of 1940's and 1950's L.A. imagery and stories.

I owe many thanks to the creators of the *LostAngeles* and *Historic Los Angeles* Facebook pages for their tireless quest to find and post every image of Los Angeles' past.

Greg Kinman, the creator and host of the YouTube channel, *"Hickok45"*, was an irreplaceable source of information about the history, design, operation and sound of every firearm described in *Red Sockets*. I cannot overstate how helpful his segment on the Nagant 1895 was.

Stefanie Fontecha was a joy to work with in the creation of the *Red Sockets* book cover art. She used her incomparable talent to take my vision for the vibe of the story and metabolize that into a moody piece of artwork that fits the novel and time period like a custom Brauer Brothers shoulder holster. She is a marvelous graphic artist and has done an equally fine job with the cover art of Gordy Kraus' next adventure, *"Requiem for a Waterman"*.

Rachel Bostwick designed the book for Red Sockets. I don't know what was more difficult for her: creating the framework for the printing and digital renderings or dealing with my anxiety about taking the novel from my computer to a print and download-ready condition. She is an exceptionally talented person and deserves more thanks than I can bestow on her.

It's not only writers who suffer for their art. I came to the novel-writing party pretty late in life and am determined to leave at least a quintet of 1950s Los Angeles Mysteries as part of my legacy. My determination soaks up a lot of my time and focus. The creative process is rough on one's social life. My friends and family can attest to that. My partner, Debbie, suffers through the ups and downs of my writing more than I do, yet she is always my biggest cheerleader. She is a prominent artist in her own right and - lucky for me - understands the challenges of the creative process and how important a form of self-expression it represents. I owe her a debt of gratitude and can never fully repay her for her understanding and unflagging support. She is my sounding board and always gives me a king's ransom worth of advice about characters, dialog and plot structure.

Finally, thank you to the real Anna, whose courage, intelligence, determination and charisma supplied the inspiration for the "Anna" character in *Red Sockets*.

AUTHOR NOTES

I tried to stay as faithful to real-life Los Angeles as possible.

Like all *noir*-style novels set in 1950's Los Angeles, the city itself is a major character in *Red Sockets*. Los Angeles in 1956 was still on the crest of a post-war-boom wave; its growth and prominence was at a zenith. Its rich mélange of architecture and popular culture combined with a tapestry of Hollywood myths and unsolved mysteries resulting in a moody backdrop for any *noir*-themed work.

There were instances when I stretched the timelines a little to fit the story. Like Mark Twain told Rudyard Kipling in an 1899 interview, "I got all the facts first, then distorted them as I pleased."

Several of the geographic references in *Red Sockets* deserve mention:

The Russian consulate on Glendower Avenue really did exist. There are divided opinions as to when the Soviets exited the location. I was pushing the envelope a bit in depicting it as still in operation in 1956. Most believe the Russians left in '52 or '53. In the late '90's, the magnificent Tudor-style mansion became the home of world-famous singer, pianist and musical revivalist, Michael Feinstein. When he put the home on the market in 2019, he hosted a wonderful video tour of the mansion interior and grounds. I doubt Adolphe Menjou ever lived there, but if he didn't, he should have.

Andy Lococo did get the wish he made in *Red Sockets*. The Cockatoo burned down in 1957. He quickly rebuilt it into a Southern California landmark. I'm not certain what significance the Cockatoo played in Quentin Tarantino's mind when writing and directing "Jackie Brown". The place was clearly on its last legs in that film. In the 1950s through the mid-80's, the Cockatoo was a legendary place in the electronics industry. If you worked in electronics distribution during those times, taking lunch there was *de rigueur*. I worked with a guy who regaled anyone who would listen with breathless tales of seeing one gangster or another dining in a curtained-off booth at the back of the restaurant. I remember being so excited the first time I went there for lunch. It was like a rite of passage, and I cannot tell you exactly why. Perhaps because of its association with the L.A. mob scene, going there was like being a kid taking a dare to knock on the door of an old, haunted-looking house after dark.

The Redwood on 1st and Broadway was a real saloon and the watering hole for many of the top-tier L.A. defense attorneys. In fact, every defense attorney but one Gordy named off to Anna was a real lawyer. (The other name was fictional, but sharp-eyed modern crime fiction fans are apt to recognize it more readily than the real-life names.) The Redwood's 2nd Street iteration remains a gathering spot for Los Angeles defense attorneys.

Speaking of the mash-up of legendary real-life and fictional L.A. attorneys, the Angelus Hospital on Trinity was a real hospital. Built at the turn of the 20th Century, it was one of the most-advanced hospitals of its time in the nation. One of the hospital's biggest investors was L.A. defense attorney, Earl Rogers. Rogers contributed money and prestige to the ambitious project. After Angelus was built, he devoted much of his time delivering lectures to the Angelus Hospital College of Surgeons on subjects such as "The Legal Rights of Physicians". Rogers was also the model for Earle Stanley Gardner's immortal character, "Perry Mason". (In the HBO Season One production of "*Perry Mason*", there is a delicious art-imitating-life-imitating-art scene in which Hamilton Burger, played by Justin Kirk, mentions Roger's name to Perry Mason, played masterfully by Matthew Rhys.)

I was born at Angelus Hospital - delivered by Dr. Lewis Morrill. Dr. Morrill, like all his Angelus Hospital colleagues, was a leading physician in his field. I was born over two months premature, and he did not give my parents a lot of hope I would survive. He told them he had been reading studies about too much oxygen in incubation chambers causing blindness in infants, so he intended to alter the mixture in mine. Although he feared that the reduced oxygen content may have lessened my chances of survival, he felt it was the right course of action. (Composer Tom Sullivan, for one, born several years ahead of me in Boston, was left permanently blind by too much oxygen in the incubator.)

I was in the hospital incubation ward for several months and - being super-tiny - was evidently quite the attraction. My mom told me many of the hospital staff would visit the ward just to look at my doll-like body slumbering in the incubation chamber. Dr. Morrill's wife was one of the frequent visitors to the ward. She stopped coming to see me in June of that year, because she was shooting a film, "*Slightly Scarlet*", for RKO. Her name was Rhonda Fleming and we ended up becoming friends for over three decades, right up until her death in 2017.

I'm certain many readers who are *noir* aficionados will notice the sly world of *noir* references I wrote into the novel. There are many, many "Easter eggs" in *Red Sockets*. To paraphrase Dickens' "A Christmas Carol", hints from the ghost of "Hollywood Mysteries to Come".

I hope all of you enjoyed reading *Red Sockets* as much as I enjoyed writing it. Thank you.

ABOUT THE AUTHOR

Sam Seegmiller is a Los Angeles-born writer of 1950's *noir* fiction set in his home city. He holds degrees in accounting, multimedia and law and spent the bulk of his career as an electronics industry executive. He settled in Oregon twenty-plus years ago and now lives in the Yamhill County wine country, in a Craftsman-style home he largely built himself. *Red Sockets* is his first novel.

www.ingramcontent.com/pod-product-compliance
Lightning Source LLC
Chambersburg PA
CBHW070624260626
47161CB00007B/2569